William McIntyre is a partner in Scotland's oldest law firm Russel + Aitken, specialising in criminal defence. William has been instructed in many interesting and high-profile cases over the years and now turns fact into fiction with his string of legal thrillers, The Best Defence Series, featuring defence lawyer, Robbie Munro.

The books, which are stand alone or can be read in series, have been well received by many fellow professionals, on both sides of the Bar, due to their accuracy in law and procedure and Robbie's frank, if sardonic, view on the idiosyncrasies of the Scots criminal justice system.

William is married with four sons.

More in the Best Defence series:

Relatively Guilty

A Best Defence Mystery
First in the Best Defence Series

William McIntyre

To Gillian

Published by Best Defence Ltd
www.bestdefence.biz
wm@bestdefence.biz

A truth that's told with bad intent,
Beats any lie you can invent.

~ William Blake ~

CHAPTER 1

He'd been stabbed through the brain.

'Via the eye or the ear would have been the professional's choice,' said the man in green scrubs. 'This is clumsy work.'

Sometimes I suspected that much of Professor Edward Bradley's non-clinical research was Hollywood-based. I'd have thought that by now the aging pathologist would have come to realise there were very few professional hitmen around, certainly in Central Scotland. From my experience, most murders were not committed by highly-trained assassins, were not even premeditated, but were spur of the moment acts involving young men with too few functioning brain cells in their heads, the result of too many pints of beer in their stomachs.

'Yes, very clumsy.' The Professor, scratched the wiry grey hair under his scrub cap. 'But, I suppose, showing a certain degree of amateur enthusiasm.'

He tilted the dead man's head towards me. 'You'll notice that the wounds are all through the left sphenoid bone. That tends to suggest the deceased was lying on his right side. The close grouping indicates a rapid succession of blows. Takes a fair bit of force to do that.' He shoved a shiny metal probe through one of the holes. 'And, of course, a good quality screwdriver.'

My stomach heaved. It was too soon after lunch for a defence autopsy. I should have sent Andy. It was the sort of thing young legal trainees enjoyed.

I swallowed the wad of mucus that had gathered in my throat and was threatening to choke me. 'What makes you so sure it was a screwdriver?'

The Professor pointed a slimy, blue, latex finger at a patch of flesh, swollen and suffused with dark blood.

I couldn't see anything of note.

He lifted the flap of skin and cartilage that had once been the face of Police Constable Callum Galbraith to reveal the underside, a thin, creamy layer of adipose tissue and some puncture wounds, small but clearly visible. 'Your woman must have been running out of steam. Some of the blows haven't penetrated full-thickness.'

He was talking about my client, Isla Galbraith: a Highland lass, pretty, docile and prime suspect for the vicious, cold-blooded murder of her policeman husband.

Using the probe, the Professor indicated some more of the round marks under the skin. He was quite correct; a few of the blows hadn't penetrated far and one or two had left distinct cross patterns at the hair-line.

'A Phillips type,' he said. 'Small gauge, long-stemmed. The sort of screwdriver watch repairers use. Like so.' The Professor mimed a series of fast jabs.

'Painful.'

'No, not really. He wouldn't have known much about it. For all intents and purposes, he was a goner after what I presume was the initial blow, received to the back of his head.'

'Consistent with an axe?'

'Entirely.'

That more or less summed up the Crown's position. Callum Galbraith was in bed, sleeping, when he was clunked over the head with an axe. If you assembled all the items under Britain's beds, kept handy in case of that late-night intruder, you'd have an immense armoury of pokers, hammers, rolling pins and other deadly weapons. Callum Galbraith had kept a tomahawk; a souvenir from a trip to the States. I'd already examined it through the thick plastic of a Crown production bag and recalled a cheap replica with a brass axe-head and an eagle painted on the heavily-lacquered handle. Goodness knows how he'd got it through customs. The force of the blow must have broken it, as it was now in three pieces. A tomahawk; it was a strange choice. You'd have thought a cop would have kept a truncheon.

The consensus was that, after being knocked senseless, Galbraith's wife had finished him off with a series of frenzied and rather unnecessary blows with a screwdriver, smashing through what I'd have called the temple, but which Professor Bradley and the Crown post-mortem report referred to as the sphenoid bone of the skull. Both attacks had caused serious and irreparable damage to the brain.

'Anything else you can tell me?' I asked, hoping that, if there was, he could relay it quickly so I could get back out into the fresh air.

The Professor replaced the flaps of skin and shaved scalp that he'd peeled back from the top of the head. The brain was missing and in a glass jar or somewhere.

'I'd say we can draw two conclusions from this examination,' he said, scrunching up a few pages from a Daily Record and packing them into the head cavity before fitting the lid of the skull back into place. 'Firstly, he's definitely dead and, secondly, whoever did it to him was seriously pissed off about something.'

'And you're definitely ruling out suicide?'

Professor Bradley tore off his gloves, crossed the room and dropped them into a bucket. 'You're a funny man, Robbie. About as funny as your client's life sentence is going to be.'

'Unusual, though, don't you think?' I said, following him to the sink. 'A ferocious attack like that, by a woman?'

'It's certainly unladylike, if that's what you mean.'

'Unladylike? Is that the best you can give me?'

The Professor turned on a tap with an elbow and shoved his hands under the stream of water. 'What do you want me to give you? Your client is found covered in her dead husband's blood, clutching the weapon that killed him and

3

then she confesses everything to the police. I'm not a lawyer, but it sounds like guilty to me.'

The whole blood, murder-weapon, confession thing was a chain of evidence that hadn't escaped my finely-tuned legal brain, and yet from the look of my client I couldn't imagine her having a cross word with a fly far less harming one.

The Professor squeezed soap from a dispenser and began to lather his hands. 'So, if you're expecting me to come up with a crazy theory to provide you with the basis for some kind of a defence—'

'I'd be eternally grateful.'

'Sorry. No can do.' He rinsed his soapy hands and ripped a bunch of green paper towels from a box on the wall. 'I don't know about harming flies...' The Professor squashed the paper towels into a ball and missed the bucket by a mile. 'But your girl did a hell of a good job of swatting her husband.'

CHAPTER 2

A spider; I could see it from the doorway, crawling on my bedroom ceiling. It was all I needed after a Friday afternoon spent cutting up a dead bloke.

I let my jacket drop to the floor and ripped off my tie. The last day in June. Blue skies and soaring temperatures, sun shining like the West Indies and not West Lothian. It might have been a freak spell of weather or all down to global warming; whatever, it was decidedly un-Scottish.

Meanwhile, the spider continued its slow, relentless, upside-down march. I hated them. All those legs, eyes and fangs, webbing with the equivalent strength of hi-tensile steel – evolution or God – it seemed a lot of bother to go to, to catch a few flies. I removed a shoe. Exhausted and ready for a cold shower and an even colder beer, before I could relax I'd have to dispatch the beast. Eyes fixed on the ceiling, I jumped onto the bed and steadied myself. Careful; I might only get one shot at splatting it. What I didn't want to do was send it scurrying off into a dark corner, leaving me not knowing when or where it might reappear.

Deep breath. Arm coiled. I was about to let fly when the bed beneath my feet shifted. Losing balance, I fell and landed on a big lump snuggled under the duvet. I leapt backwards, granting the spider a stay of execution, my arm still raised, the shoe held aloft. With a snort and a grunt, the bump in my downy struggled to the surface.

'Robbie?' it croaked.

'Malky?'

'Sorry. I must have dozed off. Just got in a few hours ago. Still a bit jet-lagged.'

Last I'd heard my brother lived in London. It was a one-hour flight.

He yawned enormously and rubbed a tousled head of hair that, unlike my own, showed no trace of grey and was way too long for a man of his age. 'Dad gave me a key ages ago in case of emergencies. He said you wouldn't mind.'

'No, he didn't.'

'Okay, you got me there. But he did give me a key.'

'So why are you here? What's the big emergency?'

'Why am I here? That all you can say? No, how's it going Malcolm? What have you been up to these last two—?'

'Three.'

'Three years? Can't believe it's been that long.'

He swung his legs out of bed. An ugly scar ran down the front of his left knee, a lasting reminder of the injury that ended a short-lived but, according to experts like my dad, brilliant football career. He stood up. My big brother. Three inches taller and two years older. I couldn't help noticing the pair of baggy jockey shorts. 'Y-fronts? Get them from dad too?'

'Cat's idea,' he said, leaning over to pick his trousers off the floor. 'All to do with air circulation. Supposed to keep my… well they help me stay cool. Good for the wee fellas apparently. Makes for better swimmers or something. I've sort of got used to them.'

I'd first met Cat, or rather Dr Cathleen Doyle, raven-haired beauty of Northern Irish descent, when I'd worked in Glasgow with Caldwell & Craig: T-Rex in the world of legal dinosaurs. She'd had a spot of bother with a red light on her way to an emergency call-out and I'd talked the Fiscal into dropping the charges. It had been no big deal, but on the strength of that minor victory I'd asked her out and we'd dated for a while until it had seemed only natural to move in together. There had been a time when I thought of her as the future Mrs Robbie Munro. That is, until I came home one

6

evening to find her giving my big brother a thorough physical examination on our bed.

I picked up a paperback from the bedside table, gave it to Malky and pointed at the bug on the ceiling. 'Squash it.'

'Don't tell me you're still scared of spiders – at your age?'

'They give me the creeps.'

'There speaks the boy who used to have a pet rat.'

'Geordie was a gerbil.'

'Horrible scratchy feet. Bit me once. What's scary about a wee spider?'

'Arachnophobia. If it was a rational fear it wouldn't be a phobia.'

He took the book and stood on the bed. 'Your big brother still comes in handy for some things eh?'

'Just get rid of it.' I jumped down from the bed and went through to the bathroom to wash my face. When I returned, the spider was nowhere to be seen and Malky was pulling on his trousers, tightening his belt.

'And how is Cathleen?' Her name tasted like battery acid. 'Knocked her up yet? Or are the wee fellas insufficiently chilled?' I was on a roll. 'Come up to Scotland hoping for a cold snap, did you? Sorry, but, as you'll have gathered, we're in the middle of a heat-wave.'

I glanced down at the paperback, now returned to the bedside table, the cover suspiciously devoid of splattered spider. 'So, where is she? Is the delightful Dr Doyle not with you?'

Malky zipped-up his fly, sat down on the edge of the bed and started to put on his shoes.

'Cat's dead,' he said. 'I killed her.'

CHAPTER 3

Monday morning, I took my feet off the desk, tore June from the calendar and filed it in the bin. The first day of July and the sun was still shining. I went to the window and looked out at Linlithgow. Population 13,423. Birthplace of a Queen of Scots who got her head chopped off.

Grace-Mary walked into the room. Sometimes I wondered if the woman had been born in that green cardigan and tartan skirt, a pair of spectacles dangling on a gold chain about her neck. Congratulations, Mr and Mrs Gribbin, it's a legal secretary.

Grace-Mary looked down her nose at my big desk diary. She did not approve. Not after I'd made the mistake of sending her on a night school computing course, since when she'd never stopped harping on about networking and integrated diary systems. Me? When it came to the recording of important information, I still preferred the security blanket that was a piece of paper.

She lifted the diary with an air of faint disgust and flicked over a few pages. 'The Faculty Dinner. You going? I think there is a window in your hectic social calendar.'

I didn't answer, coming to grips, as I was, with an on-line legal aid form and realising that the problem with e-applications is that you can't write notes in the margin to explain that your client doesn't have an address, lives in any handily unlocked outbuilding and has an income derived from whatever he can thieve.

'You should go. All work and no play…'

I pressed the submit button and hoped for the best.

My secretary wasn't for giving up. 'You could take Zoë…'

Now that was a thought. Zoë was new. Zoë was gorgeous. Zoë was going to be my girlfriend - I just hadn't plucked up the courage to break the news to her yet. I wasn't sure if I ever would. Zoë had temped earlier in the year when Grace-Mary was on holiday and because business was picking up I'd offered her a job. Since Grace-Mary's return, Zoë had been put on reception duties. She was fun, fit and, if not the highly efficient secretarial machine that was Grace-Mary Gribbin, she was a trier. Even my secretary found it hard to find fault with the new receptionist, apart, that is, from her habit of wearing exceptionally tight satin blouses to work. I was not one to complain.

Grace-Mary's suggestion was nicely timed to coincide with the arrival, dead on nine o'clock, of my receptionist. Today's blouse was ruby red.

Sensing she might have struck a chord Grace-Mary pressed ahead. 'The girl's on the phone all day. It would be nice for her to meet some of the local lawyers. Put faces to voices.'

Tempting. I wondered. Would she go? Since Cathleen, my luck with the opposite sex mirrored the state of the FTSE one hundred, down and showing little sign of rallying. I had no time to ponder the subject because my diary was packed with appointments. Sometime after eleven, when I was between clients, Andy marched into the office in a hail-the-conquering-hero sort of a way. The eyes beneath the curly black hair and behind the dark frames of his specs were sparkling, his face flushed. I'd forgotten how even a trip to the Justice of the Peace Court could seem exciting to a newly-qualified solicitor.

'Another beautiful day,' my young assistant announced.

The clear sky and blazing sun corroborated his remark, but he wasn't looking so pleased with life simply because of the weather.

'I take it all went according to plan down at the Palais de Justice?'

My young assistant tossed the tatty, spare court-gown into a corner of the room and perched himself on the edge of my desk, partially demolishing a pile of files that Grace-Mary had stacked for my attention. 'As predicted, the P.F. forgot to serve the speed-camera calibration certificates and had to move to adjourn.'

'And?'

'I opposed the motion, the magistrate saw things my way, the case was deserted simpliciter, et voila: no totting-up disqualification for Mr Turpie.'

I was pleased to hear it. Jake Turpie was owner of the first floor flat which, with every expense spared, he'd converted into office space now home to the recently established law firm of Munro & Co., senior partner, only partner, yours truly: Robbie Munro.

Access to the premises was gained via a close off the High Street and up a flight of stairs to the front door: the only solid fitting in the building because I'd installed it myself on the recommendation of a dealer client who assured me that breaking in with a police battering ram would be like trying to crack open a coconut with a banana. Once inside the office, there was a central corridor. To the right: reception, the biggest room, where Zoë sat at the phones and Andy took up a desk by the window. Further down on the same side of the corridor was a small room occupied by Grace-Mary, when she wasn't marching about the place firing orders, and which doubled as the cashroom. The waiting room was situated at the end of the corridor while, coming back up the other side, there was a kitchen, toilet, broom cupboard and then, directly opposite reception, my room where Grace-Mary and I were now congratulating my assistant on his victory.

Grace-Mary finished giving Andy a small round of applause and turned to me. 'How much do you want to charge him, Robbie?'

There was little point in sending Jake Turpie a fee-note. My landlord was notoriously tight-fisted and requests for money were seldom well-received. I thought it best simply to deduct my fee from the rent; a cash payment that Jake demanded monthly and in advance and, occasionally, with menace.

'After today's display I reckon I'm ready for the Sheriff Court,' Andy said. 'What do you think, Robbie?'

I thought the prisons were sufficiently overcrowded as it was.

Andy removed a fifty-pound note from his top pocket and began to fan himself with it. 'Oh, and I nearly forgot. A small token of Mr Turpie's esteem.'

A bung? From Jake Turpie? Unheard of. He must have been well-chuffed. I snatched it from my assistant's fingers.

'Hey!'

'Hey, nothing. Whose idea was it to challenge the speed-camera calibration in the first place?'

'Andy's, as I recall,' Grace-Mary said, never one to take my side in any argument. 'You told Jake to blame whatshisface, that big numpty he hangs about with.'

She was referring to Deek Pudney, Jake Turpie's gormless but brutal minder.

'A perfectly sound defence,' I said. Or it had been until the speed-camera photos came in showing a clear picture of a small, bald headed man in oil-stained overalls, and not a six-foot six gorilla in a suit and turtle-neck.

'Yeah,' Andy said, uncertainly and looking to Grace-Mary for support. 'Challenging the calibration was my idea. Wasn't it?'

'Okay, okay,' I relented. 'We'll go halfers.' I slipped the fifty into the top pocket of my jacket that was hooked over the back of my chair. 'Grace-Mary, give him twenty quid out of petty cash.'

The two of them opened their mouths in unison. Anything they might have said was drowned out by a roar from reception.

'It's for you, Robbie!'

11

'Still hasn't quite mastered call transfers yet – they're quite tricky,' I felt compelled to say in mitigation of Zoë's telephonic failings.

'Who is it?' I yelled back.

'Your brother!'

'Tell him I'm busy!'

Grace-Mary didn't say anything. She just did that thing where she stiffened, pursed her lips and stared out of the window. I had come to recognise it as a sign of major disapproval.

Andy took a rolled-up newspaper from one of the side pockets of his suit jacket. 'Your brother being prosecuted?'

I shook my head. 'Doesn't look like it.'

'Lucky.'

'Lucky?' my secretary frowned. 'It was an accident. Could have happened to anyone.' Grace-Mary Gribbin for the defence. Not an everyday occurrence.

Andy inhaled deeply, blew out his cheeks and released. 'Not what's suggested here.' He turned to the middle pages of his red top.

'I don't think anyone is particularly interested in what that rag has to say on the subject,' my secretary said.

Andy ploughed on regardless. 'Someone was telling me at court that Robbie's brother was out cold when they cut him from the wreckage and by the time they got him to hospital he'd lost so much blood already that taking a sample seemed churlish.' Andy was in danger of getting on the wrong side of Grace-Mary, a place from where many a young lawyer never returned.

I took the newspaper from my assistant. Malky's crash had happened early Friday evening and had only now made it onto page fourteen.

'Unfounded rumours.' Grace-Mary elbowed Andy out of the way and began to re-organise the files on my desk into neat piles. 'Has he been convicted of anything? No,' she declared in answer to her own question. She cocked her head and glared at my assistant, daring him to come back at her. Then she looked at me. 'Are you going to just sit there and let him talk about your brother like that?'

That was the thing about Malky. People liked him; even battle-axes like Grace-Mary. When he'd gone off with Cathleen, somehow it had all been my fault.

Working all hours, never there for the girl when she needed you. A woman thrives on attention. No wonder she found comfort elsewhere.

Zoë came through with a smile that wafted over me like a warm summer breeze. 'Is Malcolm Munro really your brother, Robbie? Big Malky Munro the footballer? My sister used to have a huge crush on him. There was a ginormous big poster of him on her bedroom wall. Great hair. Don't you think shorts were a lot tighter back then?' Zoë stared into space, no doubt calling up the mental image of my brother in his restrictive playing kit.

'I play a bit of football,' Andy said. 'Five-a-sides, mainly. Got a hat-trick Sunday night.'

'Robbie used to play,' Grace-Mary piped up on my behalf. 'A lot of folk say he could have been just as good as his brother.'

'Is that right?' Andy asked, a hint of admiration in his voice.

'Oh, I don't know...,' I replied. 'I was young. Foolish. I should have stuck in at it instead of frittering away my time getting a law degree.'

Zoë wasn't listening. 'Mr Munro, that is, Malky,' she giggled, 'says you're always busy. I told him he was right about that. Anyway, you've to pick him up at your place, half twelve.' She wagged a finger at me. 'And no buts.'

A little box popped up on the monitor to say that the on-line legal aid application had been rejected and I was to contact the administrator; whoever that was. It had been my third attempt.

I banged the desk with my fist in frustration.

13

'Don't get angry with me,' Zoë said, slapping my hand as she flounced from the room. 'You're the boss, do what the hell you like. I'm only here to pass on the messages.

CHAPTER 4

Prestonfield Park, home of Linlithgow Rose FC, was situated behind a red brick wall across the road from the cemetery, not far from my old school. Linlithgow Academy: uniform colours black and blue. How fitting.

As we walked through the car park, a Club Official: grey slacks, white shirt and a wrinkly maroon blazer that matched his face, came out to meet us. He seized a grip of Malky's hand and the two of them embraced and slapped one another's backs for a while before we were shown through the main door.

Sauntering into the lounge bar with Malky Munro leading the way, was like being escorted into Sherwood Forest by Robin Hood. Malky had started off his career at 'The Rose' and, after being scouted in his late teens, had moved onto greater things with Glasgow Rangers, leaving his home town Club on a firm financial footing.

Soon we found ourselves at a table in the centre of the room, and, later, as I was presented with an excellent steak pie and chips, people were still coming over to shake Malky's hand and bask in the glow of his patented boyish grin.

'Dad not joining us?' I asked, once the tide of autograph hunters and well-wishers was on the ebb, along with my brother's practised smile.

He nicked one of my chips, sprinkled salt on it. 'I'll drop by to see him later.'

The old man would like that. He'd never admit to having a favourite, but he'd never asked me to go down the boozer with him so that he could show me off to his mates. Despite Grace-Mary's attempts to talk up my footballing skills for the benefit of the lovely Zoë, when it came to sports Malky had always been the gifted Munro boy. Malky was a natural.

He'd made his name at football but would have excelled at most sports. After his forced retirement from the game he'd taken up golf. I'd been playing for years and was still struggling to break ninety when I took him for a round to try out his new clubs and enlighten him on the etiquette of the game. He shot a scratch twelve over par and I'd wanted to brain him with my sand-wedge.

Malky leaned back in his chair to allow a beaming waitress, white blouse, maroon skirt, to set a smoked mackerel salad in front of him. It had been his favourite during his playing days and they'd prepared it especially.

'Enjoy, Malky,' she said, coyly, giving my brother's chin a little tug and winking at him. 'Let me know if there's anything else you'd like.'

'Don't worry…' Malky read the name badge, 'Veronica.' He patted her bottom. 'I will.'

It was sickening. The way he could carry on as though nothing had happened. As though Cat's death was only a minor pot-hole in the Malky Munro highway to happiness.

'The accident,' I said, once he'd quite finished accosting the serving staff, picked up his knife and fork and prodded his food once or twice. 'Do you want to talk about it?'

He leaned across the table towards me. 'Of course I do. Why do you think I've come back to this dump? Why do you think we're having lunch?'

That more or less ruled out any, I've-come-back-to-beg-your-forgiveness-for-stealing-your-girl-and-then-killing-her, theory I might have been formulating.

'I need your help,' Malky said. 'There are a few things I haven't told you.'

He'd already given me his account of Cat's death. That had been hard enough for me to hear. I started in on my steak pie. The soggy underside of the crust, the bit I liked the best, brought back images of a creamy layer of adipose tissue punctured here and there by the end of a Phillips screwdriver. I tried not to think about it and, fortified by a slug of house red, told Malky to start at the beginning.

He took my biggest chip, broke it in two, popped it all in his mouth and chewed slowly for a moment. 'You know how me and Cat moved down south a couple of years ago—?'

'Not that near the beginning. Fast-forward a bit.'

He reached for another of my chips, but I fended him off with a jab of my fork.

'The day of the accident we met in Brighton for lunch. I'd moved there from London after we separated.'

'Separated?'

'Aye, about six months ago. It started out as a trial separation and was a success - at least I thought so. Cat was busy all hours at the hospital and my job takes up a lot of my time. I'm a sports pundit on local radio. It's hard work but I quite enjoy it.'

Hard work? Talking rot on a football phone-in? That wasn't work. Work was engaging in bitter battle with Sheriffs like Albert Brechin who thought the presumption of innocence was a malicious rumour put about by defence agents.

'When we separated, I'd left a lot of loose ends; just moved out really and left it at that.' Sounded chaotic, irresponsible, very Malky. 'Cat was always going on about tying things up properly, kept phoning me. Last Friday, she insisted we meet up to finalise division of our joint finances over lunch.' Sounded sensible, civilised, very Cathleen. 'There wasn't that much to discuss. Once everything was agreed and I was about to leave, Cat got all upset. She'd had some wine and I didn't want to send her home by herself. I'd only had a couple of beers, so I offered to drive.' Malky flaked some mackerel with his fork and balanced a chunk on a piece of crusty bread.

'Go on,' I said, pleased to see he'd directed his attention back to his own plate and wondering when he'd come to the point.

17

'The weather had been fine all day, then we came out of the restaurant and it was total stair-rods. On the way back to her place, I took a corner and woke up in hospital. All I had was a bump on my head and a cut arm. There was a lot of blood, but, after the doctors had stitched me up, I was good as new and walked out of hospital the next day.' Malky set down his fork. 'Cat never regained consciousness.' He took a bite of bread and smoked fish. 'I have absolutely no memory of what happened – none at all,' he said with his mouth full. 'I don't know if it was my fault, if I was driving too fast…' He swallowed. 'Or,' he continued, 'could have been a blow-out, faulty brakes or something. The crash investigators haven't ruled out mechanical defect as a cause.'

Having experienced Malky's driving on many occasions, my money was on the driving too fast theory.

'And you never thought of letting me and Dad know?'

'I know, I know. I'm sorry. I never thought. Must have been the bump to the head. I got out of hospital Saturday afternoon and the doctors said I just needed to rest for a few days. It was only when the funny phone calls started that I put two and two together and knew I should come and see you - so here I am.' He stole another chip and dipped it into my steak pie.

'So why do you need my help?' I asked. 'I don't understand.'

'He wants me dead.'

'Who?'

Malky bit the gravy end off the chip. 'Dexy Doyle.'

'Stop exaggerating.'

'I'm not.'

'You are. Cathleen despised her father. They hardly spoke.'

'I've just told you – I've had phone calls. Threats.'

'Hoaxes.'

'Pretty convincing then.'

18

'It was an accident,' I reminded him. 'Dexy might be upset and looking for someone to blame; it's only natural, but that's a far cry from trying bump you off. He'll come to see reason. Time is the great healer.'

'Oh, please.' Malky slammed down his fork, banging the table and upsetting my bottle of brown sauce. A few people looked over, saw it was Malky and smiled. 'Robbie, the man's had folk knee-capped for spilling his Guinness,' he hissed. 'What do you think he'll do to the person who killed his daughter?'

My brother did have a point. Dexy Doyle had swapped West Belfast for the east end of Glasgow back in the eighties, and his empire of pubs and clubs had not been built on the basis of a benevolent disposition or forgiving nature. His actual Christian name was Dechlan. 'Dexy' was a nickname earned as leader of a gang that became known as the Midnight Runners because of the late-night raids that, in those early empire-building days, had encouraged rival publicans to sell up and run away while their kneecaps were still operational.

'You'll just have to lie low for a while. Let things cool down a bit,' I told him.

'Cool down? He isn't going to cool down. This is Dexy Doyle we're talking about.'

'It was an accident,' I reminded him yet again. 'He'll understand that - eventually. Until then, keep out of his way. It's not like you move in the same circles.' I forked in another mouthful of steak pie. 'When's the funeral?'

'Cat's is tomorrow; family only. I'm trying to delay mine.' He wiped his mouth with a paper napkin. He laughed: I didn't. 'Sorry, that wasn't funny. I just don't know what to do. You've got to help me, Robbie.'

He seemed so relaxed about Cathleen's death. I'd only lived with her a few weeks. Malky and Cathleen had spent over two years together. Then again, my brother's primary interest had always been for number one. Even coming to see

19

me for help; you'd think he'd be too embarrassed. Not Malky. It was so simple to him. He was in trouble and now I was expected to drop everything and come to the rescue. The thought that I might be annoyed with him, or even enjoying his paranoid ramblings after what he'd done to me, would have never entered his head. After all he was the great Malky Munro. Didn't everyone want what was best for him?

'What can I do?'

'Speak to Dexy. Tell him it wasn't my fault. That the car hit black ice or something.'

'In June? Why don't you just go back to Brighton and get lost for a while? You've managed to do that okay for the last three years.'

Malky stretched out a hand across the table, dipping a shirt sleeve in his cole-slaw. He grabbed one of my wrists; the one attached to the hand holding another forkful of steak pie. 'It's not that easy. I'm recognisable. People know me. Dexy's boys would find me in two seconds.'

I pulled my hand away, put the food in my mouth and chewed slowly. I was trying not to enjoy it; watching him squirm.

'Come on Robbie,' he said, reaching over the table again and taking a firm hold on both my wrists so that my fork and knife pointed upwards, unable to get at my plate. 'We're brothers. I know you took it hard when Cat left you,' (interesting choice of words) 'but this is my life we're talking about. Dexy likes you. He respects you. You got his brother off with that fraud charge. The Doyles owe you big time. If you could just speak to him, tell him my side of the story—'

'Make something up you mean?'

He let go of my wrists, deftly nicking one of my chips as his hands retreated across to his side of the table. 'Wouldn't be the first time.'

CHAPTER 5

Tuesday, and after a day in court spent banging my head against the brick wall of the criminal justice system, the last entry in my diary was a meeting with Isla Galbraith, whose husband I'd left lying on a mortuary slab the previous Friday afternoon. Isla was pretty and shy and her voice carried the sing-song lilt of the Western Isles. In physique she reminded me of Zoë, which is to say: five feet five and around the nine-stone mark. Unlike Zoë, her hair was long and blonde, held at the back in a clasp, and the two women obviously didn't share the same taste in clothes; my client eschewing sexy, satin blouses for handmade summer frocks or extreme knitwear. Other differences included the ring, still on the fourth finger of Isla's left hand, and the beautifully-crafted silver charm bracelet on her right wrist.

I tried not to get emotionally attached to my clients, especially those charged with murder - they often disappeared for long stretches - that said, I couldn't help liking Isla. Even though she wasn't a private fee-payer, which is what I tended to look for most in a client, I especially liked the reason she had chosen me to act in her defence.

'I spoke to some people from the Federation,' she'd told me at our initial interview at Cornton Vale women's prison, where she'd spent a seven-day-lie-down before being fully committed for trial and released on bail. 'They'd always helped out with legal matters in the past,' she'd said, rather sweetly surprised that the Scottish Police Federation hadn't wanted to finance the defence of the person charged with murdering one of its members. 'But they were horrible. Eventually I begged them just to give me the name of a good lawyer and I heard one of them say, 'anyone but Robbie bloody Munro.'

That advice had more or less clinched it for Isla and by instructing me she'd shown, I felt, a degree of faith that would be needed for the ordeal ahead.

'Do you think I should plead guilty?' she asked, the words almost whispered.

'Not to murder,' I told her for the umpteenth time. 'My job is to persuade the Crown to take a plea to culpable homicide.'

That would pose something of a problem initially, but I was sure the prosecution would see things my way, once I'd apprised them of all the facts. Isla's husband had been a violent man. She'd suffered frequently at his hands. On the night of his death, Callum Galbraith had come home late. They'd argued, he'd hit her and gone to bed. As regards what happened later, while her husband was asleep, Isla had been more than helpful with the police during a taped interview at which her then legal representative, a lawyer from the Public Defender Solicitors Office, had allowed her free rein to get it all off her chest. The brave new face of the Scottish legal system: accused persons investigated by the Government, prosecuted by the Government and defended by the Government; usually shortly before being locked up by the Government. To be fair, something I tried not to be where the numpties at the P.D.S.O. were concerned, even before Isla's confession there was already a wealth of other incriminatory evidence, ranging from blood-stained clothing to possession of the murder weapon, complete with finger-prints, to a distinct absence of any other suspects. When I took over the case I quickly realised self-defence was a non-starter and that the only route to take was one of damage limitation.

Isla wiped away a tear with a finger, erasing the thin smear of make-up she'd used to cover the fading bruise around her left eye; an injury I'd already had photographed from several different angles. A single teardrop fell onto my desk.

'Sorry,' she said, brushing it away with the back of her hand, silver bracelet clinking against wood. I pushed the box of tissues at her. Isla cried a lot during our meetings, which was why they tended to drag on. I sat back and let her sob. In fixed fee cases, delays caused by weeping clients were an unaffordable luxury; however, the Legal Aid Board permitted murder to be fee'd time and line. I wondered if paper hankies were a chargeable outlay.

Isla dabbed at her eyes. 'Are you going to say it was an accident?'

'That's one thing your husband's death wasn't,' I said. 'We have to persuade the Crown, or a jury, that at the time of… At the time of your husband's death—'

'You mean when I murdered him?'

I fought off the urge to face-palm and continued. 'On the night in question, you weren't thinking clearly. Your normal thought processes were short-circuited, your actions extreme due to emotional factors outwith your control.'

'Like I was crazy or temporarily insane or something?' she asked so innocently, so politely, that we could have been chatting about the cross-stitch embroidery she had been working on in my waiting room before our meeting.

'Diminished responsibility is what we lawyers call it.' If the Crown, or, if it came to it, the jury, accepted that, there would be no mandatory life sentence.

'Can you do that, Robbie?'

'Not without some pretty strong mitigation.'

'And how do we get that?'

'You've told me how violent Callum was. Now we need to back that up with hard evidence.'

'And if we do?'

We'd been through all this before in great detail. These meetings with Isla were like making sandcastles on the beach. Just when I thought I'd accomplished something I came back

23

the next day to find all my work washed away with the tide of her tears.

'Then we'll hit the Judge with a stonker of a plea in mitigation.'

'Will I go to prison?'

'If things go to plan they'll probably give you a medal.'

Isla smiled, and then started to cry again. I looked down at the pages of detailed notes I had taken on her background. Information from which I hoped to piece together a picture as to why a gentle young woman from the Long Islands would bludgeon her husband to death with a tomahawk and then stab holes in his head with a screw-driver. In my mind I had the pieces all laid out. I just needed to stick them together with some evidential glue.

My client's tear-ducts in full flow, I flicked to the beginning of my notes. Callum Galbraith and Isla Clegg, as she was then, had grown up on the Hebridean Islands of Lewis and Harris, respectively, and met in their late teens when Callum's brother, Fergus, brought the pretty blonde girl home from a craft show in Stornoway Town Hall. Isla and Fergus had dated for several months until, like so many young islanders, they had left for the mainland and from there each gone their separate way.

Years went by before Isla and Callum met again, both in their twenties and working in Aberdeen; Isla as a nurse at Forresterhill Hospital, Callum pounding the beat with Grampian Police. According to Isla, the two Galbraith brothers were physically alike: tall, ginger-headed and handsome, but very different in nature. Fergus, the older by less than two years, was witty, flirtatious and fun, always the life and soul of the party, while Callum was a quiet man, strong and good-natured. Though she had paid little heed to the younger Galbraith brother when a teenager, she had fallen in love with him on their very first date, something that came about unexpectedly when Callum was admitted to A&E after a roll around on Union Street with a bag-snatcher.

24

His wounds bandaged, they'd gone for coffee together. Looking back, it was a cappuccino they both would have done well to avoid. As it was, romance blossomed and months later, when Isla took up a post as staff nurse at the Southern General in Glasgow, Callum made the decision to follow her south, transferring to Strathclyde Police. Within a year they were married and trying to start a family. It was after Isla's second miscarriage that Callum had first raised his hands to her. From then on it had been a regular occurrence.

'My mum and dad are very religious,' she told me. 'They've never had a cross word and they loved Callum. I couldn't bring myself to say anything to them about what was going on. Deep down I think I hoped someone would notice the marks, the bumps and bruises, would see through all the lies, put two and two together. After all, how often does the average person walk into a wardrobe door? Or fall down the stairs?' She smiled through the tears. 'Or trip over a cat they don't have?'

I grinned at her brave attempt at humour.

'In the end,' she said, 'I just got used to it.'

I let my client prattle on in her gentle voice, weeping and using up my Kleenex supply, while I took notes and planned ahead. I needed to requisition around ten years' worth of medical records, obtain a statement from Isla's G.P. regarding any confidential conversations between them on the subject of domestic violence and then it would be time to go calling on the Crown. The more I thought about it the more certain I was the Lord Advocate would not want to run this to trial. Sure, it was an exceptionally violent death and the victim was a cop, but the accused was young, she was pretty, she was a nurse. For ten long years she had stood by her man, a brute who made her life a misery until, one night, traumatised by the pressure of that violent relationship, she had snapped. I was almost tempted to go to the jury with a defence of let's face it, folks, he deserved it.

Isla sniffed and tugged another tissue from the box.

I put down my pen. 'I think I have enough to be going on with.'

'Has the prosecution said anything?' she asked. 'You know, about dropping the charge to… what was it?'

'Culpable homicide. No, not yet. But they will.'

'And if they don't...?'

'Then there'll be a trial and it will be up to the jury. But I can't see it coming to that.' I set a mandate in front of her. 'Sign. It's your consent so that I can contact your G.P. for medical records.'

For once my client was way ahead of me. From the large bag that held her cross-stitch she produced a thin cardboard folder. It was orange, a bar-code sticker along the bottom and her name and date of birth on the top front cover. She was thirty-two: a couple of years older than Zoë.

'All my records are here,' she said. 'I think you'll find everything you need, Robbie.'

I scanned through them. Interspersed between the to–be-expected sore throats and tummy bugs were the tell-tale signs of domestic abuse: bruises to the throat, broken fingers, black-eyes. It was all good stuff. 'This is great,' I said. 'The more we can show what an animal Callum was the better. If you can think of anything else…'

Isla's bottom lip trembled. Her face crumpled like one of the paper hankies piled up on my desk and she began to sob uncontrollably. I buzzed Grace-Mary and asked her to bring through a glass of water. Isla wiped her eyes. What little mascara she had been wearing was now black blotches on white tissue.

'Sorry,' I said. 'That was thoughtless of me.'

Grace-Mary came in with the water and set it down on the desk. Isla looked at it but didn't take a drink. She ran a fingernail up the side of the glass, leaving a thin trail in the condensation.

'There's really no excuse for what I did,' she said with a tight little laugh. 'It's all my fault. I deserve whatever happens to me.'

I put a finger under her chin and lifted her head. 'Don't you ever say that again.'

CHAPTER 6

Wednesday, and like most mornings, I set off in search of my two best pals: Bei & Nannini.

The proprietor of Sandy's Café, or, rather, Bistro Alessandro as the High Street signage now proudly proclaimed, was a friend of mine from school days. Then the premises had been his dad's fish and chip shop, but upon his inheritance Sandy had converted the place into a café popular with legal aid lawyers and other court users in need of caffeine and cholesterol injections between trials.

Recently there had been further, more drastic changes made. The authentic cracked lino was no more, the floor now planks of reclaimed oak timber. Minimalist rubberwood furniture had replaced the plastic bucket seats and shoogly Formica tables of yore, and, pride of place, where the cigarette machine had once been, stood a revolving chrome and glass cake cabinet stocked with scones, French fancies, pastries and, on the bottom tray, some high-fibre brown muffins that looked good for what ailed you. Just about the only thing that hadn't changed was the old guy sitting on a high-stool near the door, watching the world through the big front window and groping the buttocks of unwary female customers. I didn't understand why Sandy put up with him, except that the old guy never seemed to be without a mug of milky tea and a Tunnocks teacake. I supposed every business needed its regular customers.

'Check the state of you,' Sandy said, already at the espresso machine.

I glanced at my reflection in the cake cabinet and winced.

'You're not getting any younger you know. What are you now? Forty?'

'Thirty-three.'

'Really?'

'Yeah. Which makes you thirty-two and a half.'

'Well you older boys can't expect to burn the candle at both ends. Leave that to us young guys. By the way how is the new girl?'

'Zoë?'

'Why you not ever send her down here for your coffee? Why you always send Andy?'

Sandy was as Scottish as a wet weekend in Wishaw but insisted, when he could remember, on lapsing into a faux Italian accent.

'You got something against Andy?'

'No. It's just… I just…'

'Fancy Zoë?'

Sandy smiled, 'I am only a man.'

'Me too,' I told him. 'A man that needs his caffeine level topped-up at regular intervals. I send Andy for my coffee because if I send Zoë, you chat her up and she comes back half an hour later with a cup of cold mud.'

'You sure that's the only reason? I mean, if you can't stand the competition…' Sandy tailed off with a shrug. 'Oh, and your dad was in earlier,' he said, still clattering and banging away at the espresso machine. 'He was looking for you.'

Earlier? It was only seven-thirty now – did the man never sleep? 'What did he want?'

'Didn't say.' I could hardly hear Sandy over the hiss of steam. 'He'd been phoning you but couldn't get an answer.'

I vaguely recalled a phone ringing in one of my dreams. I think it was the one where I was not on the couch but back in my own bed; my lovely, soft, double-bed. The one Malky had commandeered so that he could rest his injured arm and stretch the leg of his that had an alleged tendency to cramp.

Sandy placed a cardboard cup of coffee on the counter. 'You want a bran muffin with that?' He put a brown paper bag on the counter. 'Only kidding. White roll, crispy bacon, brown sauce.'

I held the cup to my nose and inhaled deeply. 'Bung this lot on my tab will you Sandy?' I put a lid on the coffee, the greasy bag in my jacket pocket and, with practised ease, performed a swift about turn as I headed for the door, the gap between my shoulder blades tensing to receive the verbal arrows.

'No problemo, Robbie. Arrivaderci.'

I stopped, turned around. 'No problemo? What do you mean *no problemo*? I've a slate you could use to roof Linlithgow Palace.'

'Not anymore.' Sandy drew a damp cloth over the counter and tossed it into the sink. 'Your old man - what a gent - settled your tab while he was here.'

I left the café and wasn't entirely surprised to happen upon former Police Sergeant, Alex Munro, a short distance away at Linlithgow Cross, down the cobbled brae from the Palace, sitting on his usual bench and taking up most of the space. As I approached, he looked over the top of his newspaper and stared at me, or, more precisely, at the cup I was carrying.

'You pay for that?' he asked through his bushy moustache.

I didn't answer. Took a sip of coffee.

'Bloody disgrace. That man's got a living to make.'

'Thanks, Dad - for settling my tab.'

'Twenty-seven quid. I'm a pensioner you know.'

Perfectly true, though, having been a cop for thirty years, they probably delivered his monthly payment by armoured car.

'I know, I know. I'll pay you back.'

'Forget it,' he said, which I'm sure he knew I'd do anyway. 'Just try and remember that I wasn't put on earth just so you could sail through life without troubling your wallet.' He folded his newspaper. 'Seen your brother lately?'

'Yes, you gave him the key to my flat – thanks for that.'

'You're not still angry with him, are you? Where's he staying? He was supposed to come and see me. Did he say how long he's going to be up here on business?'

So, Malky hadn't been back to visit my dad. Great. If the old man found out that Malky was staying with me, it would somehow be my fault. Like I was hogging Golden Boy all to myself.

'He's around somewhere. You know what Malky's like, he'd get a piece at anyone's door. I'm sure he'll be descending on you soon.'

My dad seemed happy at that. He moved his bulk over a fraction and patted the slats of the bench. I sat down, and he draped an arm around my shoulder. It was all a little worrying; first settling my debts, now signs of affection.

'I've a favour to ask you,' he said. I could sense his pain. The words struggled to come out. He cleared his throat. 'This woman. The teuchter. The one who killed her man... You know, the cop.'

'Isla Galbraith? What about her?'

A wee girl in a summer frock toddled past us and went over to the Cross Well: an intricate sculpture in the form of an octagonal Crown which, as any attentive Linlithgow school child knew, was carved by a one-armed stone mason in 1807 after the original well head had been destroyed by Cromwell's army back in the 17th Century. The girl dropped a few coppers into the water and closed her eyes to make a wish.

'She's guilty,' said my dad, masterfully stating the bleeding obvious.

'And?'

'I think it would be best if she pled guilty.'

'Dad, you're a cop. You think everyone should plead guilty.'

'She brained him and then stabbed him through the head while he was sleeping. Do you really need to run the thing to trial? I know you. You'll dig up dirt, throw mud, blacken the poor man's character, embarrass his family, his friends.'

Now we were coming to it.

'I don't know about his friends,' I said, 'but his family? He has no kids, his parents are dead and his wife killed him. As far as I know he's got a brother - that's his family.'

My dad wasn't listening. 'Everyone has their faults—'

'He used to hit her.'

'Perhaps he was a mite heavy-handed now and again.'

'She had injuries.'

'The door to the matrimonial home wasn't locked. She could have left him at any time.'

'He was a wife-beater.'

'And that gave her the right to scramble his brains with a screwdriver?' my dad roared.

The wee girl had returned from the well. Her big blue eyes were wide open now and staring at my old man. A woman steering a bag of messages in a pushchair came over, scowled at us and pulled the child away by the arm.

'Your buddies been giving you the low-down?' I asked, once I felt my dad's blood-pressure had reduced sufficiently and aware that the bacon roll was growing cold in my pocket.

But he was there to ask not answer. 'Come on, Robbie. You must know it's the right thing to do.'

How rich. An ex-cop telling my client to do the right thing and plead guilty. In my years at the criminal bar I'd seen a lot of police officers in the dock, acted for a few of them, but I'd never even heard of one pleading guilty to anything; not until they'd spent every last penny the Police Federation would fork out on legal fees, running the case into the ground, doing everything and anything to avoid one night in prison or, even worse, loss of pension rights.

'You know the score, Dad. No-one in their right mind pleads to murder. And as for Isla Galbraith? Wait until the Crown sees the medical records: the black-eyes, broken fingers, a history of unreported assaults – there's photos too.

The Lord Advocate will bite my hand off when I offer a plea to culp hom.'

That was the plan. It had worked before. Medical records, photos, perhaps a helpful psychology report. Combine that little lot with a tear-jerker of a plea in mitigation in front of the right judge, and, notwithstanding her husband's gruesome demise, P.C. Callum Galbraith's widow would be looking at eighteen months tops with an outside chance of probation.

My old man let rip a trademark snort that parted his moustache. I'd made my point. I didn't have to say any more, but I did. 'You do know what we defence agents call a woman with a violent partner?'

He didn't answer. So far as he was concerned the conversation was over. He stood, tucked his newspaper under his arm and started to pick his way across the cobbles to the High Street.

'Jane Bond,' I called after him. 'Double-o-seven. Licensed to kill.'

CHAPTER 7

'I've seen it all now,' Grace-Mary said, marching into my room waving a piece of paper.

I'd scoffed my bacon roll, drunk my coffee but was still feeling the effects of my night on the couch and more inclined towards a quick kip than a sift through the day's mail.

My secretary floated an official looking form down on to the desk in front of me. 'Can you believe it? Mags MacGillivray applying for widow's allowance and she wants you to countersign her application?'

Andy was at a loose end and couldn't resist sticking his nose in.

'Credit where credit's due,' he said. 'Kill your man and then claim the government for money because you're now a widow? Pure class.'

I signed the form and gave it to Grace-Mary. 'Send it back to her. It's worth a try.'

'You think so?' my secretary asked.

I did. I had a soft spot for the widow MacGillivray. Everyone likes a winner and Mags had hit the sentencing jackpot. She'd lived with Pete, her violent husband, for twenty extremely-long years during which time she'd had his tea on the table every night, put up with his drinking, his gambling and come to be on first name terms with personnel at the local A&E department.

One afternoon, Mags was in the kitchen cutting vegetables for broth when Pete came in after blowing the house-keeping on yet another sure-thing. He was drunk and aggressive, gave Mags a few practice slaps and crashed out in front of the fire. He never got up again. Mags came through from the kitchen with a chopping knife, stapled her slumbering husband to the laminate flooring and then called the police while she brought the soup to the boil.

She was charged with murder, of course, but, on the morning of the trial, after weeks of discussions, the Crown agreed to take a plea of guilty to culpable homicide and I'd wheeled-in the delightful and ever-dramatic Fiona Faye, the Faculty of Advocate's most recently appointed Q.C. Once the judge had heard Fiona's heart-rending plea in mitigation, perused Mags's medical records and read affidavits from friends testifying to the years of abuse she'd suffered at the hands of her husband, the result was a formal admonition and no further punishment. The decision was welcomed by various women's organisations and most of the dailies carried the story along with a rather good photo of me, senior counsel and my client outside the High Court looking pretty pleased with ourselves.

'What with Isla Galbraith on board, it looks like you've got the husband-killer market cornered,' Grace-Mary said. 'Or should I say mariticide-market?'

'No, that's killing your mother,' Andy said, trying to put my secretary right. Big mistake.

'No,' Grace-Mary said, patient but firm. 'You're thinking of matricide. I said mariticide.'

'She's right,' I said, as though my secretary could have been anything else. 'Mariticide is killing one's spouse and most commonly associated with the killing of a husband. I felt it an appropriate moment to dust down my Standard Grade Latin. After all, if you've got it... 'The killing of a wife by her husband is known as uxoricide and is statistically much more common.'

'Not for your clients it's not,' said Andy, tetchily.

'So, what are your plans for the rest of today,' I asked my assistant, ignoring his lack of respect and a classical education. 'You're not just going to stott about here are you? It's a lovely day, why don't you get out there and prec some witnesses, like I'm fed up asking you to do?'

Andy sighed hugely. 'Precognitions, precognitions. When do I get to go into court?'

'You do go to court,' Grace-Mary pointed out.

'Yeah - the J.P. Court,' Andy sulked. 'Whoopee.'

'You did really well the other day.'

'Because Robbie was busy at the Sheriff Court doing important stuff.'

'Nonsense, yours was an important case and you got the whole thing chucked out on a technicality.'

'And if I hadn't, my instructions were to have the trial adjourned so that Robbie could do it.'

'Jake Turpie is a special client,' I reminded Andy. 'Grace-Mary's right; you did well. Business is picking up. It's not easy for me to be in two places at the same time. Your chance for the Sheriff Court will come.'

'Speaking of which, are you watching the time, Robbie?' Grace-Mary asked. 'Remember, you've a trial at ten.'

I checked my watch. It was ten to the hour. 'Precognitions are an important part of trial preparation,' I lectured Andy, as I unhooked my gown from the back of the door.

'I'd rather go to court with you.'

Grace-Mary gave me an *aw, go on* look.

'All right,' I relented, 'but tomorrow I want you take that pile of witness lists from my in-tray and precognosce everything that moves.'

'Will do,' Andy said, beating me out of the door. 'I can't wait to see the master at work.'

CHAPTER 8

'Guilty.'

Scots law had generously provided three possible verdicts: guilty, not guilty and not proven. That was two verdicts too many, so far as Sheriff Albert Brechin was concerned. The trial had lasted all day. It had taken the Sheriff five seconds to reach a verdict. I wished, just once, the old fart would let me get my bum back down on the seat before convicting my client.

'Mr Munro,' he sighed, 'is there *anything* that can be said in mitigation?'

There was, but not enough to prevent Brechin launching my client on a nine-month sentence.

'Appeal it, Robbie!' were the prisoner's shouted instructions to me as he was led away. I knew that appealing the conviction would be a waste of time; the High Court never interfered with a Sheriff's take on the evidence. In a routine summary case there was no jury and it was for the Sheriff alone to decide upon those witnesses he believed and those he didn't. In over twenty years on the shrieval bench, I doubted if Albert Brechin had ever had a credible or reliable defence witness pass through his witness box.

So, with a disillusioned assistant in tow, I trudged downstairs from Court One to the Clerk's office where I drafted an appeal against sentence on the basis that nine moons was excessive for a relatively minor breach of the peace; an offence that prior to the recent change in sentencing powers would have carried a three-month maximum.

It was nearly five o'clock by the time the appeal was lodged and so I let Andy go home while I visited the cells to bid my client adieu. Criminal clients were, on the whole, a

37

stoical bunch and could forgive a lot of things, but not a lawyer who didn't take the trouble to say cheerio to them after they'd been sentenced. On the way back to the office I passed the Cross Well and recalled the earlier conversation with my dad. I rang Malky at the house using our pre-arranged system of three rings, hanging up and then ringing again.

'That you Robbie? Is everything okay?'

'Have you been to see Dad yet?'

'I don't want to be seen out and about. It's dangerous.'

'You went to the Rose Club with me, yesterday. It's a wonder he never got wind of that.'

'Come on, Robbie, I'm trying to keep my head down. You know what dad's like. If he finds out where I am I might as well take out an ad in the newspaper.'

'If he finds out you're staying at my bit and I haven't told him – I'll be in the newspaper: the obituaries.'

'Look Robbie. I'm going nowhere until you've sorted things out with Dexy Doyle. Simple as that.' The line went dead.

Back at the office, the only person around was Zoë.

'What are you doing still here?' I asked.

'Grace-Mary wanted me to wait behind and give you this.' She held out a yellow Post-it note on which a name was jotted down: Simon Hart. I'd never heard of him.

'I think he's going to call back later. Something urgent about your brother.'

I took the note and stuffed it into my pocket.

'I'll just tidy up a few things and then I'll be off,' Zoë said and busied herself, tidying up an already tidy reception desk, laying out the phone pad, squaring up the Rolodex and carrying out other such non-essential duties.

I was on my way through to my office to begin dictating some letters when Zoë shouted through to ask if I wanted her to make me a coffee, even though she must have known I wouldn't. Life was just too short for instant coffee. I wondered: Grace-Mary asked Zoë to stay behind and give me a message she could have stuck on my computer screen in time-honoured fashion?

I turned around in the doorway, smoothed my hair and took a deep breath. 'Tell you what,' I said, trying to keep it casual. 'Coffee - why don't we go down to Sandy's for one? You and me,' I added for the avoidance of doubt.

'Great.' Zoë sounded pleased. 'Just let me finish up here.' She arranged some pens in a jam jar.

The phone rang.

'Ready.' Zoë slinked around the reception counter, looking at me expectantly, apparently oblivious to the ringing phone.

I hesitated.

'Coming?'

'I think maybe I should just take that,' I said.

The smile fell from her face. 'Do you?'

I extracted the yellow-sticky she had given me moments before. 'Remember? The important call – about Malky?'

'Robbie Munro?' the voice on the phone was English, Midlands accent.

I heard the click of the front door as Zoë let herself out. 'Simon Hart?'

'Yeah, that's me. I'm phoning about Malky. Where is he?'

'How is it that you know my brother, Mr Hart?'

'Sorry, of course, can't be too careful eh? I thought maybe Malky might have mentioned me. I'm like his unofficial agent down here.'

'Really? For what?'

'Endorsements, stuff like that. Malky has made some good money on the after-dinner speaking circuit thanks to my contacts. I'm pretty well known hereabouts: played for the Seagulls - back in the seventies - when we had a team. Maybe you've heard of me?'

I hadn't.

'Anyway, he continued, 'the station has been pretty good about the accident, despite the rumours, but they're not very happy about your brother's sudden departure up to Jock-o-land. Tell him to get in touch pronto.'

If I got rid of him quickly, I could catch up with Zoë. 'Thanks for calling. I'll be sure and tell Malky. Good —'

'Well, actually, there's more to it than that. The real reason I'm phoning is because there has been a…an incident.'

'What kind of an incident?' I said wishing I hadn't. Would Zoë go to Sandy's? Would she wait for me there?

'Some idiot came into the station yesterday looking for Malky. He was asking lots of questions and generally causing trouble. In the end I had to have security throw him out. I didn't think much of it really, just assumed it was a stalker or something.'

'Oh, well, not to worry. I expect all you famous footballers have your share of nutters stalking you.' If I ran I reckoned I could make Sandy's in under a minute.

'It gets worse. This morning on her way to work the show's producer was attacked. We think it was the same guy. He had a knife. He slit one of her nostrils.'

'He did what?'

'Slit her nostril. He wanted to know where Malky had gone.'

Maybe Malky wasn't completely paranoid.

'And did she tell him?'

'Of course she told him. Are you listening to me? He slit one of her nostrils. That's why I'm calling. You've got to warn Malky.'

I said good-bye, promising to let my brother know what had happened and to pass on Hart's best wishes to him. From my window I could see a pink satin blouse further down the High Street, heading for Sandy's.

Go see Zoë or go see Dexy Doyle?

Zoë was beautiful, fun, I loved it when she was around. One day - who knew? But for now she was only my receptionist. Malky was a royal pain in the butt but he was, and would always be, my brother.

CHAPTER **9**

The bar stank of smoke and stale beer. Dexy Doyle sat alone at a corner table. Near the door a group of four men, white shirts, black-ties, had a bottle of Bushmills surrounded. One of them I recognised: Cathleen's Uncle Kieran, off-white sheep of the Doyle family. Kieran was a local councillor, pillar of the community. With the amount of money, he had to be making in kick-backs alone, he could surely have afforded a better toupee than the highly-unconvincing, shiny-black rug that looked like it had been dropped onto his head from a great height. He was smartly dressed and clearly uncomfortable and feeling out of place beside his brother's bunch of rag-tag cronies. He gave me a half-smile of acknowledgement as I entered the bar and then lit up a Capstan full-strength. The anti-smoking regulations hadn't quite made it to this part of Glasgow. They probably never would.

Behind the bar, a tall, lanky lad dressed in a Glasgow Celtic football top and black Kappa tracksuit bottoms, leaned against the counter, eyeing me suspiciously as he whistled an out of tune rendition of 'The Fields of Athenry' through the gap in his front teeth.

Other than those mentioned, the place was empty. None of the regulars, it seemed, was keen to encroach on Dexy's grief. I took a few paces forward. One or two of the men threw me a concerned, sideways look before turning their attention once more to the bottle of Irish whiskey. Kieran sucked on his cigarette and nodded to the boy in the hoops who, without missing a tuneless beat, led me across the vastness of the deserted bar to the dark corner where Dexy sat staring into a glass of milk.

I stood for a while at the side of the table, not sure what to say or do and was beginning to think that maybe I should call back later when my host lifted his chin from his chest and used it to point to the chair opposite.

Like his brother, Dexy had plenty of hair, though his was real. The untidy brown mop he'd had when I'd first met him during my time at Caldwell & Craig was now mostly grey, the fringe tinged nicotine-yellow, flopping down, partially obscuring the lenses of the sort of specs the NHS provided in the 1960's. I suspected he kept his hair long to help cover the right side of his face where the mottled red skin was stretched tight and shiny. He'd had the scars since he was a boy growing up in the Falls Road. It's what happened when you cut too short a rag for your petrol bomb.

I sat down. Cathleen had been buried earlier that day; the funeral strictly family. Dexy still wore a band of black crepe around his left bicep and a thin, black tie knotted tightly at the collar of his white shirt: pretty serious mourning for a man whose daughter had all but disowned him many years before.

He raised a pale hand, showing skin grafts, cratered and translucent, beckoning the lad in the hooped top. 'Get Mr Munro a drink.'

'What'll you have?' Hoops asked.

I knew my host's liver had waved the white-flag many years ago and he was now tee-total. Rumour was his daughter had been chauffeured to her death by a drink-driver. I didn't feel comfortable shouting up a cheeky wee Laphroaig.

'I'm fine,' I said. The boy shrugged and drifted away.

'Get the man a drink!' Dexy roared after him, sending the boy in the hoops ducking under the bar.

Dexy took off his glasses and began to polish them with the end of his tie. 'Bloody specs. So filthy you'd need good eyesight to see through them.' He put them back on his face and began to shove the glass of milk from side to side between his hands.

Mr Hoops returned with a shot of Bushmills and set it down in front of me.

'I was very sorry to hear about Cathleen,' I said, after what I thought was a suitably respectful interval.

'Why?' Dexy said. 'She dumped you for your brother. Got what she deserved. That's what you really think isn't it?'

'No,' I said. 'It's not.'

A quiff of yellowy hair fell across his face. He brushed it back. 'Why are you really here?'

'To express my sincere condolences.'

Dexy grunted.

'And I'm here to ask you not to do anything rash. Something that you might regret.'

The sound of Dexy's harsh laughter caused the men at the end of the bar to turn in our direction. The lad in the hooped top loped back over to our table, game as a pebble. Dexy waved him away again.

'Are you trying to threaten me,' he asked.

'What I'm trying to do is tell you that harming Malky isn't the answer.'

Dexy lifted the glass of milk to his lips. A thin dribble escaped the side of his mouth where his disfigured face seemed to run out of lips. 'Orange bastard,' he muttered.

If Malky held strong views on Roman Catholicism then he'd always kept them well hidden.

'There's no reason to bring religion into this,' I said.

'When I heard Cathleen had hooked up with your Hun of a brother it nearly killed me. But, I said, if he makes her happy that's all that's important. I set aside my own feelings, sent her mother money for them so they could put it down on a house, even bought him a car so he could keep up his image as the great football star. And for what? So he could murder her?'

'Cathleen's death was an accident.' Maybe Grace-Mary would have been more convincing. 'It could have happened to anyone.' Dexy stared at me. I'd seen that look before: in the eyes of Sheriff Brechin around about the time I'm asking for community service and just before he packs my client off to jail. I pressed on. 'What you're trying to do is not what Cathleen would have wanted.'

'We'll never know that because she's not here to tell us. Maybe, if you'd been more of a man, she'd still be alive.'

Great. Now I was getting the blame.

Dexy stood and swept his fringe from his face. He was in not bad shape for a man in his late fifties. Tall and lean, sharp-featured and yet - scars aside - he was nothing special to look at. Not someone you'd give a second glance if you met him in the street; all the same, if he had his way, there'd be football fans all over Glasgow chucking scarves on a make-shift shrine to the late, and nearly-great, Malky Munro.

'Was there something else?' he snarled at me.

I remained seated. 'I did a lot of work for you when I was working through here with Caldwell & Craig.' He looked away. 'Never too busy. Always ready to drop everything at a moment's notice, pull any stroke I could to spring your boys. Kieran couldn't have run for a bus far less the City Council if it wasn't for me.'

'And you were well paid.'

'I know that, Dexy, but what I'm trying to say is –'

He thumped the table with a fist. 'I know what you're trying to say. I'm just not listening.'

I looked up at him. 'Dexy, I want you to give me your word you'll leave Malky alone.'

'That it then?' he sneered. 'The bitch is dead, now the brothers can settle their differences.'

'It's not like that.'

'No?'

He delved into his pocket, took out a photograph and threw it down on the table: Cathleen, wearing a black gown, a red silk cape trimmed with white fur across her slender shoulders, in her hands the burgundy scroll that held her medical degree. She was smiling. She was very young and so very beautiful. I turned away. Dexy seized the collar of my jacket. 'You want me to forgive and forget?' He forced my head down, making me look at the photo. 'Then tell me you can do the same.'

I wrenched free of his grip, stood and picked up the glass of whiskey. 'To Cathleen,' I said and downed it in a oner.

'Didn't think so,' he said.

I straightened my jacket. 'Thanks for the drink.'

'Get out,' Dexy growled. 'And tell your brother he's a dead man.'

CHAPTER 10

Malky was lying on the couch when I returned home later that evening. 'Where have you been?' he asked from behind the sports pages.

'Glasgow.'

He discarded the newspaper. There was a mixture of fear and hope in his eyes. 'You spoke to Dexy?'

I nodded, pushed his legs to the side and sat down beside him, balancing my briefcase on the arm of the sofa.

'What did he say?'

I tried to sound upbeat. 'Could have been a lot worse.'

'What did he say – exactly?'

'He… he didn't promise anything.'

Malky slammed the palm of a hand hard against his forehead.

'I tried.'

'Yeah? Well thanks for nothing.'

'I can work on him some more. Give it time. The man's just buried his daughter.'

'I don't have time.' Malky got up and went through to the bedroom.

I followed and watched while he filled a holdall with the few clothes he'd brought with him. 'Going somewhere?'

'I can't stay here any longer.' He stuffed a shaving kit on top and zipped up the bag. 'Now Dexy knows I've been to you for help, this'll be the first place he sends the boys in the back-to-front balaclavas.'

'Where will you go?'

'Why should you care?'

'Because you're my brother.'

He snorted. 'You care more about your precious clients than you do about me, always have done.'

'You think so?' I left him, went through to the livingroom and returned with my briefcase from which I took out a sheet of printed-paper that I handed to him. 'Then sign this.'

'A contract?'

'My terms of engagement letter. I'm obliged by the Law Society to provide a copy to all my new clients. He stared at the document long and hard. 'Standard terms,' I said, pointing to the pencil line at the bottom of the page. 'Sign and I'll do everything I can on your behalf. You know I'd never let down a client.'

'Would you like it in blood?' he said, eventually, still staring at the sheet of paper.

'No,' I said, pushing a pen between his fingers. 'Ink will do just fine.'

CHAPTER **11**

First thing to do was find Malky a safe house. My dad had been sworn to secrecy, so when we arrived at his place shortly after five on Thursday afternoon, it was just him, half a dozen of his mates and a crate of Deuchars I.P.A.

In the midst of the party atmosphere, I took the old man aside while his pals swarmed over Malky and had him sign autographs, purportedly for grand-children with names like Archie and Big Dode and who, if they actually existed, would surely be too young to remember Malky's brief but golden era.

'No-one's to know he's here – okay? He's taking Cathleen's death very hard. He wants some peace and quiet, away from the media. You know how it is.' I found it difficult lying to my dad even though I'd had plenty of practice. Perhaps it was because I was beginning to have second thoughts about taking Malky there. After all, it wouldn't be much of a safe house if word filtered back to Dexy Doyle that his target was being baby-sat by a geriatric.

'Yes, yes.' My old man ushered me down the hallway. 'Have no fear, our lips are sealed. We're all ex-cops, well not wee Vince but he was in the Black Watch – you'd need to torture him for weeks to make him talk. That or buy him a few drams.'

'I mean it.'

He opened the front door. 'I know and it's good of you to be so concerned,' he lifted one bushy eyebrow. 'Considering.'

'He's my brother.'

'And don't you forget it.'

Malky came out of the kitchen. 'Dad, you got any more pint tumblers?'

'Bottom cupboard under the cutlery drawer.' My dad nudged me out of the door. 'Now away you go. We're going to watch some fitba' and I'm sure there are loads of criminals needing their hands held.'

Malky returned, bottle of beer in one hand, glass in the other. 'You know I might just get to like it here.'

I left him to it. A few days with my dad and his mates, endless video re-runs of past World Cup failures: death would come as a welcome relief.

I was halfway down the garden path when I realised my mobile phone was buzzing in my suit pocket. By the time I had fished it out I'd missed the call. I re-dialled and to my surprise Zoë answered.

'Robbie, thank goodness,' she said. 'I've gone and left my handbag at work.'

It was absolutely no trouble for me to nip back to the office, collect the handbag and personally deliver it to Zoë's place, a one bedroom flat in the residential development of what had once been St Magdalene's distillery on the banks of the Union Canal on the outskirts of town. Whisky had been distilled in the area for hundreds of years. By the early eighteenth century, and before his meeting with a certain Mr Hare, William Burke was one of the navvies who'd helped route the Union canal past the distillery to ship the casks of fine Lowland malt. When Malky and I were boys we'd spent many an evening fishing at the spot where the distillery's outlet poured into the canal in the hope that the warm water would attract 'Big Joe' a mythical giant pike, said to live in the canal and so enormous he had to swim further along the canal to the basin in order to turn around.

'I don't know what I'd have done,' Zoë said as I stood on her front doormat holding her handbag like an obedient stick-fetching puppy. 'I'll need to go to the supermarket, there's not a bite of food in the house. Not that I'd have starved to death.' She patted her flat stomach as though it were a paunch.

'Well, I'm not prepared to take that chance,' I told her as I handed over the bag. 'Can't have the staff dying of hunger. Not when business is picking up.'

She laughed.

'Sorry about the other night…' I said.

Blank stare.

'When we were supposed to go out for coffee…?'

'Oh that? Don't worry about it. Sandy kept me company.'

I thought I detected a mischievous glint in her eye. 'Anyway, I was thinking, seeing as how we're both, you know…?' A puddle of sweat formed in my lower back. What was I doing? Zoë was so pretty. Really pretty. Out of my league pretty. I stumbled on. 'And it's that time of …' I checked the wristwatch that I never wore. 'Maybe…' Zoë smiled encouragingly.

'Fancy a fish supper?' I asked.

She didn't.

The Champany Inn, a mile out of Linlithgow on the road to Blackness, is one of Scotland's finest eateries. As we discovered, bookings for the main restaurant were taken months in advance; however, if we were prepared to wait for a table, they could squeeze us into the less pricey Chop and Ale House. We sat at the bar where we eyed-up the menu and I carried out some mental arithmetic. I had a little money with me, but assuming marinated grilled herring for starters followed by steak and chips and a pudding of malted waffles and whipped cream; twice, by my calculations - if you added in the highly recommended soft, fruity Pinotage and coffee - I'd be at least thirty quid plus a tip short and that wasn't including a taxi. The realisation hit me like a crossbow bolt to my wallet. I was discreetly patting myself down for cash when I felt a reassuring crinkle in the top pocket of my jacket. Andy's fifty-quid bung. Never had I been so grateful to Jake Turpie. In fact, never had I been grateful to Munro & Co.'s landlord until that moment.

I burst the fifty on aperitifs.

'Here, try some of this,' Zoë said, after I'd finished my half of Rosebank, product of another former-distillery situated further west along the Union Canal at Falkirk. She lifted her tiny glass to my mouth. 'Arran Gold. It's like Bailey's but it isn't.'

I took a sip. Cream and whisky. It was just so wrong.

'Hmm, nice,' I said. Zoë giggled and with a finger wiped cream from my top lip.

Me and Zoë. An item? It could work. I was going to make it work.

'That's him over there.'

The loud voice jolted me from my reverie. I turned to see two black uniforms standing over me.

'Mr Munro?' said one of them.

Typical. That was life as a defence agent. I couldn't get away for a couple of hours without some zoomer getting lifted and needing me to tell them to say nothing to the cops.

'Who is it this time?' I asked the policeman with an air of resignation.

A hand clamped down on my shoulder. 'This time - Sir - it's you.'

CHAPTER 12

I'd been lying on the plastic mattress staring at the ceiling for what seemed like most of the night when I heard a key in the lock and the cell door swung open.

Andy walked in and looked around. 'Love what you've done with the place.'

'Get me out.'

'How do I do that? I don't even know why you're in. All they'd tell me was that it had something to do with counterfeit money.'

I pushed the cell door shut almost decapitating the custody sergeant. 'Think of something. After all you got me in here.'

'What do you mean? Wait a minute. 'It wasn't that fifty? The one Jake Turpie bunged me? You want me to tell the cops what happened?'

Not if it involved mention of Jake's name I didn't; I liked having fingernails. 'We'll discuss Jake later. For now, just engage your natural charm and concentrate on getting me out.' I banged on the cell door and eventually the custody sergeant returned with a rattle of keys. I put my hands on Andy's shoulders and pushed him forward. 'Mr Imray would like a word with the Inspector.'

'That wasn't much fun,' Andy advised me later when I joined him at the charge bar. 'I don't think they like you much here.'

Andy had yet to fully appreciate that if you were a defence agent and the cops liked you then you probably weren't doing your job properly.

The custody sergeant slapped a large plastic bag on the counter. He pinged off the red plastic security tag, drew back the zip and began to pull out my property, item by item.

D.I. Dougie Fleming hovered in the background, looking like he was enjoying every minute of my discomfort. Fleming had most of the attributes one would expect of a Detective Inspector: late forties, shabbily-dressed, a heavy drinker with a marriage on the rocks; the man was only an interesting car short of his own Sunday night TV series.

'One jacket. One belt. One pair of shoes. One pair of shoe laces. One tie – silk – very nice.' The custody sergeant shoved the clothes at me, then turned the bag upside down and emptied out the remaining contents. 'One wallet, containing three tens, two fivers…' he was about to count some loose change, but I swept the money off the counter and stuffed it into my jacket pocket.

'Let's go,' I said.

'I'll see you at the trial, Mr Munro,' Fleming called to me. 'Unless you'd care to agree my evidence. I'm only speaking to a few formalities.'

'There'll be no trial and I'll be agreeing bugger all,' was my response.

'Not even your reply?' he smirked.

'You made a reply?' asked Andy, incredulously.

When it came to police interviews, the Munro & Co. two-point plan was, one: say nothing and two: keep your mouth shut.

'Don't be stupid,' I told my assistant. 'Inspector, I'd like to see your notebook.'

Fleming grinned. 'All in good time. I'm sure you are aware of the Crown's disclosure policy. Wouldn't want to be getting away ahead of ourselves, would we?'

CHAPTER **13**

Linlithgow Sheriff Court, Friday, and I had to deal with a number of clients who, like me, had been released on police bail. Most were drink drivers from the previous weekend, looking to plead guilty and thus do me out of a trial fee. Each had some pathetic excuse from which I had to concoct a half-believable plea in mitigation. Presenting sheriffs like Albert Brechin with the plain truth: he got blootered and drove home – sorry 'bout that, just wouldn't do.

Shortly before noon, one of the resident band of court police officers began pacing the hall, shouting names and distributing summary complaints. Nestled among the section fives, was a summary complaint for me. I turned to the charge sheet. It alleged a contravention of section 15(1) (a) of the Forgery and Counterfeiting Act 1981.

'I don't know why you don't just march right in and tell the Sheriff exactly how you came by the forged fifty and let the cops take it from there,' Andy suggested for the umpteenth time that day.

'Because,' I said, 'Jake Turpie wouldn't approve and, unlike the Sheriff, his sentencing powers are not limited by the provisions of the Criminal Procedure Act.'

'But it's the truth.' Andy wasn't helping.

'Look,' I told him, 'it's not that bad. I don't know what Fleming's on about. Probably just trying to wind me up. I said zilch. He wouldn't dare verbal me. All the prosecution has got is me handing over a single fifty. The essence of the crime is tendering something which you know or believe to be a counterfeit bank-note. If I tell the court I got it somewhere else and was unaware it was a fake, who can say otherwise? It must have been a reasonably good forgery, because I never noticed and neither did you. There's no way they'll be able to prove beyond a reasonable doubt that I knew it was counterfeit. All I need to do is tell them I got it at the pub or something.'

'You're going to lie? Commit perjury?'

'But it's the truth. I didn't know it was a fake. The charge is uttering as genuine currency that I knew to be counterfeit. Where it came from is an irrelevant detail.'

'So, it's okay to lie about that part? No, I don't think so. Tell the truth, that's what I say. After all it's your career at stake. A conviction for uttering counterfeit money and you can kiss your practising certificate good-bye.'

'What about yours?'

'Mine?'

'If I tell the truth,' I reminded him, 'then all I can truthfully say is that you gave me the fifty. I don't know where you got it from.'

'I got it from Jake Turpie…'

'So you say. That's what's known in the trade as hearsay evidence.'

My assistant blanched.

'Court!' the Bar Officer called as the Sheriff came onto the bench and took her seat.

'Oh, just great,' Andy said.

'What's the matter?'

'The Sheriff. She used to be my Roman law tutor at Uni. I heard they'd made her a floater.'

'Foxy. I've been meaning to brush up on my Institutes of Justinian.'

'Don't expect me to introduce you then. We fell out quite badly over a late dissertation on Latin maxims.'

'Must have been pretty late.'

'Still is.'

'Oh, well,' I said. 'Dum spiro, spero.'

'What's that mean?' Andy asked.

I looked up and gave the Sheriff a smile. She responded with a curt little nod of the wig. I turned again to my assistant. 'If you'd only done your homework you wouldn't need to ask.'

'Robert Alexander Munro!' called the clerk once the end of the roll had been reached. I'd had a word with the clerk who'd agreed to call my case last so that there would be fewer people around. It was really up to the Procurator Fiscal, as master of the instance, to decide on the order of business, but if the clerk conveniently couldn't find the papers then there wasn't much the P.F. could do about it.

It was almost one o'clock when I removed my gown and took my place in the dock, pleased to see the court was clear of spectators and journalists and that, apart from one or two punters waiting to sign their bail papers, only officials remained in the courtroom.

If the Sheriff recognised her former student clad in a tatty black gown and rising unsteadily from his seat, then she never let on. Andy introduced himself and tendered my plea of not guilty. It couldn't have been easy for him; his first appearance in the Sheriff Court and he was defending his boss.

'It's a straightforward matter M'Lady,' said, Hugh Ogilvie, Procurator Fiscal. 'There is no reason why both parties can't be fully prepared in three weeks, so I suggest the clerk fix an intermediate diet in around two weeks' time and a trial the week after.'

It was an unexpected suggestion. The court diary normally worked on a minimum eight week turn around for summary trials. Either the P.F. couldn't wait to stick the boot into me or else he just fancied noising up my fledgling defence agent; probably the latter. I'd always figured Ogilvie for the kind of guy who'd enjoy drowning kittens in a bucket.

'M'Lady…' Andy stammered.

Personally, I hated it when I was addressing the court and a client shouted instructions to me from the dock; now I could understand the urge.

'No, I agree with the Crown,' said the Sheriff before I could attract Andy's attention. 'There is only the one charge and how many prosecution witnesses, Mr Fiscal?'

'Four,' the P.F. said.

I tried to work out who they'd be: the bar staff from the restaurant to identify me as the person handing over the fifty, D.I. Fleming who'd charged me and an expert from the Bank to verify the note was a fake.

'Then,' said the Sheriff, 'There's no need to delay matters.

'Sheriff Clerk, fix the trial for three weeks hence with an intermediate diet the week before - just in case there is to be a change of plea.'

CHAPTER 14

'I heard about you and the funny money.' My dad didn't look up from his newspaper crossword. He was sitting on his back step wearing a pair of brown leather sandals over black police socks and an enormous pair of light blue shorts. A tangle of grey chest hair spilled from the plunging neck-line of his white vest.

'A misunderstanding. I'll have it sorted out in a couple of days.' He grunted. I changed the subject. 'Callum Galbraith. The murdered cop…'

Now he looked up at me, a pen between the fingers of the hand that shielded his eyes from the early afternoon sun. 'What about him?'

'Did you know him?'

'Not really.' He put the newspaper down, the pen on top, stood, stretched and rubbed the small of his back. 'He was almost after my time. I may have heard his name mentioned once or twice, you know, during inter-Force relations, social events, that sort of thing.'

From the way my dad used to talk about the rivalry between east and west, I'd long ago formed the distinct impression that inter-Force relations between his former employer, Lothian & Borders, and Callum Galbraith's, Strathclyde Police, were about as frequent and friendly as inter-Force relations between the State of Israel and Hamas.

'Then why are you so concerned I might blacken his good name?'

'He was a cop. Okay he was with the Weegies - still a cop's a cop. And anyway, nobody who's had their head stoved in just for trying to get a bit of shut-eye should have their character slagged-off.'

I wasn't buying it. There was more to my dad's concerns than just the good name of a brother officer. 'And what do you know about his character that could be slagged?'

'If you don't know already, I'm saying nothing.'

'Out with it.'

'Leave it alone.'

'I'm your son.'

My dad sat down again and picked up the crossword and pen. 'And I'm your father and I said leave it.'

There was the sound of the loo flushing and then the shower being turned on. A few moments later the back door opened and Malky appeared, a towel tied around his waist. The wound on his arm was healing nicely.

'Oh, you're here,' he said when he saw me standing leaning against a clothes pole.

'That you just getting up? It's gone one. Some of us have done half a shift.'

'Some of us are available for work if their lawyers would do their jobs.'

'You trying to find Malky a job?' my dad asked.

'Something like that,' I said.

I saw the old man's quizzical look. He wasn't finished with me. 'Staying for lunch?'

'That was the general idea.'

'Good, you can make it. I'm struggling with the crossword and Malky is bound to be hungry.'

'Starving,' my brother confirmed. 'By the way, Dad, you're out of conditioner.'

My dad looked puzzled.

Malky clarified. 'You know, hair conditioner?'

'Ah.' My dad patted the grey stubble on the top of his head. 'Not much call for it these days.'

'Really? Then what do you use on that?' I gave his moustache a tug. 'It's so soft and silky.'

He pulled his head away and whacked my arm with the newspaper. 'Get in the kitchen, boy, and rustle up some scran.'

'I reached out to Malky and pinched an inch of flesh at his waist-line. 'You sure you need any lunch?'

He batted my hand away. 'You're one to talk. Laid down some lard recently haven't you?'

'What do you want to eat, Malky?' asked my dad, adopting a peace-keeping role.

'Not pancakes anyway. That's all Robbie ever made when I was staying at his place.'

Him and his big mouth.

'Oh, so that's where my girdle went to?' My dad's treasured pancake girdle had been bequeathed to him by my grandfather, a foundryman, who'd cast it himself. A circle of quarter-inch iron with a handle. It looked like a small frying pan with no sides and was never washed, only wiped with a dry cloth or occasionally boiled with potato peelings to give it what my dad called 'a skin'. It all sounded faintly disgusting. The plain fact was it produced the best pancakes bar none.

My dad filled in an answer on the crossword. 'Malky, you know your brother can only make three things and if we can't have pancakes and there's no time to make a pot of soup…'

'Roasted cheese it is,' I said.

I went into the kitchen. Malky followed, closing the door so that it was between us and my dad. I opened the fridge and found a small cube of orange rubber.

'Never mind cheese on toast,' Malky said. 'What are we going to do?'

'We? I'm going back to work in half an hour. I'd advise you to stay put.'

'I can't stay here forever.'

'Then go back to Brighton.'

Malky looked down at his hairy white feet. 'I feel safer up here. And I'd feel even safer if you could get Dexy Doyle off my back.'

'I've not forgotten about him.' I sat down at the table and lifted the lid off the bread bin. Two slices. Both heels. 'Be patient. I'm on the case.'

The door opened and my dad came in. He tossed the newspaper on the table. 'I'll need to come back to the crossword. Only two clues left and I'm stuck.'

'Give us a swatch,' I said.

He snatched the paper out of my reach. 'No thanks, I'll manage - once I've got some food inside me. Need a hand?'

'What I need is a miracle. Jesus had five loaves and two fishes, or was it the other way around? Whatever it was, it was a start.'

'Don't talk rot.' My old man yanked open the fridge door. 'There's eggs and cheese...'

'I meant to say,' Malky said. 'Got a bit peckish last night and made myself a wee omelette. Oh, and some toast.' He cleared his throat. 'I'll away and have my shower.' He backed out of the door.

My dad watched him go. 'It's nice having your brother around, but he's eating me out of house and home.'

I stood up. 'Put the kettle on. I'll nip down to the shop.' I was about to leave when I found the old man blocking my path.

'What were you two talking about just now?'

'Nothing much.'

'What's all this about him being your client?'

'A joke.'

My dad put out a hand and held the door shut. He loomed over me, face close to mine, like he was back in the good old days, interrogating a suspect in a time before inconvenient advances in audio-video technology had limited the opportunities for some of the more physical interviewing techniques. 'Do you really think I believe all that rot about Malky staying here for some peace and quiet? Your brother's in hiding. He never goes out anywhere. Is he in some kind of bother? I knew it,' he said, apparently reading my face, though I hadn't so much as twitched a muscle. 'Out with it. What's going on?'

'Calm down. Remember your blood-pressure.' I pushed him away. 'Finish your crossword. I'll get some food in.'

The old boy's moustache bristled with displeasure. 'Tell me, Robbie. I'm your father.'

'Sorry, Dad. I've already tried the blood is thicker than water routine. Remember? About Callum Galbraith?'

I opened the door an inch, but he leaned against it so that it closed again. 'You tell me yours and I'll tell you mine.'

I thought about it. He'd find out soon enough, Malky wasn't famed for his discretion. 'Okay.' I took a seat at the table. 'You go first.'

He sat down opposite me.

'Well, go on,' I said.

He released an enormous sigh. 'It's like this. You know how me and Vince are friends of St Michael?'

I nodded. 'He does all your underwear doesn't he?'

'The hospital!'

He was talking about the local hospice that provided care to elderly cancer patients. My dad and his pal, Vince, organised fund-raising events, most of which seemed to involve a good deal of drinking: race nights, quizzes, snooker evenings, in fact any type of event that could be easily accommodated within licensed premises.

'What about it?'

'There's a new consultant up at St Michael's. Dr Prentice. She knew Callum Galbraith from her last job at the Beatson in Glasgow. Apparently, he was a great guy. Their top fund-raiser. Been up and down the West Highland Way like a yo-yo and brought in thousands. Lost their best charity-worker the day your client killed him.'

'The West Highland Way? I did that once,' I said, recalling a painful, mud-splattered trek one Saturday afternoon several years previously from which I'd returned all chapped lips and blisters.

'No, son,' he said. 'You walked one section of the Way: Tyndrum to Bridge of Orchy. Seven miles of the flattest terrain in the Highlands. I should really organise another trip. We made a right few quid on that walk. Sponsors like to know you're suffering to earn their hard-earned. 'Course I couldn't go. Not with my gout.'

'Never mind that,' I said. 'What about Callum Galbraith?'

'Well, Diane… that is, Dr Prentice,' he said, quickly, 'was having coffee with me the other day and happened to say she wouldn't like to see Galbraith's character blackened, not after all his good works.'

'Oh, wouldn't she?' Now I was getting nearer the truth.

'So, I told her I'd have a word with you.'

I thought I detected a hint of a blush on my old man's face. 'Well, tell Diane, I mean, Dr Prentice, she can dream on. I don't care if Callum Galbraith could fill a sponsor sheet. Now dish the dirt on him. I've got to be somewhere else in twenty minutes.'

My dad scowled. 'A few years ago there was this lad – a vandal - doing graffiti.'

'Go on.'

'Well, Callum Galbraith arrested him and in the process there was a struggle. The boy's arm was broken. Turned out he was only twelve or thirteen. Galbraith was charged with assault, though it was later dropped. He was disciplined, suspended without pay. Strathclyde had to fork out compensation to the boy.'

'And?'

'And what?'

'And what else?'

'That's it. That's all I know.'

'That's it? That's what I'm supposed to blacken his character with? Let me get this straight. Super Callum, the charity-worker, catches some wee ned writing "Chungy ya bass" on a wall and twists his arm? Oh yes, that's really going to upset the jury – no wonder his wife clubbed him to death.'

'It shows he had a bit of a temper,' my dad said, defensively. 'But if it's of no use to you, then good.'

I took a grip of the door handle.

'Where do you think you're going?' he demanded.

'No time for lunch now. I'm going back to work. We're not all retired.'

'Not so fast,' he said. 'I want to know what's going on between you and Malky.'

'Sorry,' I said. 'I'd need something much more character-blackening on Callum Galbraith before I could even contemplate divulging confidential information on one of my clients.'

'That's not fair.'

I pinched his grizzly cheek. 'As you never stopped telling me when I was a boy: life seldom is.

CHAPTER 15

After my non-lunch I decided it was time to launch the mission to abort my prosecution. Step one was to seek out Maurice McNaughton, a disillusioned, middle-aged Fiscal-depute who should have listened to his mother and been an accountant. Mo was a diamond. Old school, polite, highly reasonable and without a vindictive bone in his body. He'd been in the Fiscal service forever, never been promoted and, unless he stopped accepting outrageously soft pleas and succumbing to reasonable doubts, never would.

'He's dead.' Hugh Ogilvie, Procurator Fiscal, stood behind the reception counter signing off on a stack of summary complaints and giving me his extremely divided attention.

'Since when?'

'Since about two months ago. Very sudden. His heart or a stroke or something.'

It was true; I hadn't seen so much of Mo in court lately, but I'd just assumed they'd put him on office duties out of the way.

'Why did you want to see him? As if I can't guess.'

'Hugh, this Monopoly money case —'

'Save your breath. It's going to trial,' he said, not looking at me, eyes fixed on his paperwork.

'Big deal. I may have accidentally presented a dodgy note.'

'No may have about it.'

'I could have picked it up anywhere.'

'Sorry,' he said, unconvincingly, 'no can do.'

'How about brushing it under the table with a wee warning letter? *We take a dim view, but in all the circumstances…blah, blah, blah.* You know the sort of thing. Just to mark my card. Remind me to be more careful in the future?'

'No, and if you don't mind, I've papers to mark.'

'A Fiscal fine, then? I pay a fixed-penalty. but it doesn't go down on my record as a conviction – everyone's a winner.'

Ogilvie shook his head. He still hadn't made eye contact.

'Tell you what, Hugh. You drop the charge against me and the very next case I get I'll plead it out. Even if the accused says he's innocent, I'll talk him into a plea. Don't care what it is, who it is – it will be guilty as libelled, M'Lord. You'd like that wouldn't you?'

The P.F. threw his papers onto the countertop. 'Will you just stop it? It's not funny… passing counterfeit money, currency of the realm... It's serious. It's… it's... disrespectful to the Queen.'

I tapped a finger against the bullet proof glass that separated us. 'Come on Shug. If you don't tell Her Majesty, I promise I'll not say a word.'

'Get out.'

'Not until you chuck the case.'

Ogilvie glared at me through the glass. 'You must know you're wasting your time. There's nothing I can do even if I wanted to. The whole thing – it's out of my hands.'

'What do you mean? You're the District P.F. Who have you got to clear it with? Your mum?'

Ogilvie tidied his papers into a neat pile and tucked them under an arm. 'As you very well know, or should do, any proposed prosecution of a solicitor has to be run past the boys and girls at Crown Office. Can't have Jock Public thinking that it's an old boys' network and we're ditching a case just because the accused is a fellow lawyer.'

Fat chance of that.

He sighed. 'Time to call in all those favours I'm sure you've dished out to the prosecution over the years.'

None sprang immediately to mind.

Ogilvie smirked. 'A man of your wide experience must have contacts at Crown Office - friends in high places.'

Me attempt to talk someone at Castle Grey Skull into dropping a prosecution in which I, a defence agent, was the accused? It was an option that I mulled over for about as long as it took me to turn around and head for the door.

CHAPTER **16**

Another Monday morning. I was in my office, reading through Isla Galbraith's file and finding it impossible to believe that my timid client could have so ferociously attacked and killed her husband. Even with the history of domestic violence, a culpable homicide deal was by no means a certainty. There was much work to be done. Andy entered showing signs of clinical depression, a concerned Grace-Mary close behind. She put a woolly-cardiganed arm around his shoulders.

Andy shrugged her off, pulled over a chair and dropped onto it like a sack of spuds.

'Who died?' I asked

Grace-Mary set down a sheaf of papers. It was only a few pages thick and stapled in one corner. On the front was a standard covering letter bearing the heading: P.F. Linlithgow –v- Robert Munro.

Already? I'd never had disclosure that fast before. It was usually hurled across the table at me by a PF depute on the morning of the intermediate diet.

'I met Agnes from the PF's office at Sainsbury's Friday night,' Grace-Mary advised me. 'She did me a favour and put the stuff on a pen-drive first thing. I had Andy nip along and pick it up and printed the statements off for you.' She patted me on the shoulder. 'I've sent Zoë down to Sandy's for coffees. She'll not be long.'

I wasn't so sure about that. I picked up the papers and scanned them, mentally summarising the case against me. I order drinks, pay with a fifty-pound note, the bar staff run it under the U.V. light and the police are called. Down at the police station I'm interviewed by D.I. Dougie Fleming who takes down my reply – reply? I'd said nothing. Under Scots law the right to remain silent was still sacrosanct. None of the: *you do not have to say anything, but it may harm your defence if you do not mention when questioned something which you may later rely on in Court,* nonsense, that they had in England. Keep schtum in Scotland and no negative inference could be drawn from your refusal to speak.

'You've read them?' I asked Andy. My assistant slumped further in the chair. It was obvious he had and that the significance of the words that appeared in the disclosure statements under the sub-header: *Reply to Caution and Charge,* had not escaped him.

'I wonder where Zoë's got to. Maybe I should just put the kettle on and make you a cuppa myself,' Grace-Mary said to Andy. Clearly, in moments of despair, hot drinks were the answer.

She left the room and I read again my alleged reply to caution and charge: *I'm sorry. I don't know where I got the money from.* It seemed innocuous enough to the untrained eye, the sort of thing somebody might say, but that was because in the black art of verballing suspects, I was dealing with a grand master in the shape of D.I. Dougie Fleming. I never thought he'd have the nerve to try it on me.

Right up until that moment, I hadn't been hugely concerned about my prosecution. It hadn't been pleasant rotting in the police cells for a few hours or sitting in the dock of the Sheriff Court; nonetheless, I knew that to secure a conviction on a counterfeit charge wasn't all that easy, and nigh impossible where a single banknote was involved - unless, perhaps, it was one of extremely poor quality. The crime couldn't be committed accidentally; there had to be criminal intent, and how did the Crown go about proving that an accused knew a note was a fake when it was uttered? The accused could just as easily have been duped when he or she received it. That's why, to convict me, the Crown needed something more than merely my possession. Unfortunately, it didn't need much more; just an adminicle of evidence from which it could be inferred that I was at it. Now into the mix could be added the entry in D.I. Fleming's notebook. Most Sheriffs, especially convicters like Bert Brechin, would raise an eyebrow at such a comment straightaway. People lucky enough to have a fifty-pound note in their pocket know how they came by it, especially a defence agent working for legal aid rates. If I gave evidence at my trial, I'd be cross-examined at length on that point and the Sheriff invited to infer that by my alleged ignorance of where the money came from I was in fact concealing the truth and therefore must have possessed the necessary criminal intent to utter forged currency. Even if, as Andy so naively suggested, I told the truth, the whole truth and nothing but the truth about where the note came from, it would still sound like I was changing my story and seem even more likely I was lying and therefore guilty.

'What are you going to do?' Andy asked. 'If you're struck off we're all out of a job. Do you know how hard it is to find a traineeship? How many interviews I went to?'

However, many, he must have crashed and burned at a good few of them if he'd had to settle for the newly-formed Munro & Co.

'Who's going to take me on now?' Andy pretended to read an imaginary C.V. in a posh voice. *'Oh, I see your last employer was struck off for dealing in counterfeit cash.'*

'I appreciate your concern,' I told him.

Grace-Mary had returned. 'Andy doesn't mean it like that, Robbie. He's worried. We all are.' She patted my assistant on the head. 'Kettle's on,' she assured him.

I put the statements to the side. 'This is a load of mince and if you don't trust me to sort it out then you don't know who you're working for.' Andy got up and slouched to the door, but I wasn't finished with him. 'And please remember that you are still working for me. Here.' I tossed Isla Galbraith's file through the air. He turned and caught it.

'What's this?' he asked with faint interest, his glum expression slowly lifting. 'The murder?' He thumbed the pages eagerly. A murder Petition was a big step up from a J.P. Court speeding complaint. It was what every young criminal lawyer longed for. No lawyer wanted anyone murdered, but, if it happened, it was nice to be in on the action.

'I've got a job for you,' I said. What I had planned might or might not assist Isla Galbraith's case, but it would keep Andy out of my hair for a while.

'Go on,' he said.

'I need you to do some private detective work. The P.F. has released Callum Galbraith's body. The funeral will be on Thursday, maybe Friday. It wouldn't look good if I went along, but no one's going to recognise you. Keep your eyes and ears open. A lot of the people who attend these type of affairs, fellow officers and the like, are only doing it out of a sense of duty or the chance to skive off work for a couple of hours and tuck into a purvey at a nice hotel. There's usually loads of gossip. Go along. Mingle. Listen to what people have to say about Galbraith. Was he well-liked? Was he ever in bother? Were there rumours of domestic abuse? Did anyone witness it? Anything you can dig up I want to know about. Got it?'

'You're looking to throw some mud?'

'Like a tractor in a slurry pit.'

'Just like Mags MacGillivray's case?'

'That's the plan.'

'All right!' exclaimed Andy. 'This is more like it.'

'Wait a minute,' Grace-Mary said, a confused look on her face. 'Am I missing something here? You're sending the boy to a funeral to try and cheer him up?'

Andy looked at her and cracked a smile. 'Has that kettle not boiled yet?'

72

CHAPTER 17

We needed senior counsel for Isla Galbraith's case and I'd decided that the very man for the job was Ranald Kincaid Q.C.

'I can't say I'm happy about taking it on,' he said as, late Tuesday afternoon, we paced beneath the dramatic hammerbeam ceiling of Parliament Hall, the leather soles of his shiny black shoes squeaking in time with the rubbery squidge of my Hush Puppies on the wooden floor. 'Not really my thing – crime.' He spoke the word as though he could taste the filth of it in his mouth.

Kincaid wouldn't have been everyone's choice for a murder, and I knew that he'd have been better pleased if I'd come to the Advocates Library bearing the brief for an agricultural holdings dispute. The Silk's experience of criminal work was minimal, the Criminal Procedure (Scotland) Act 1995 as amended or, indeed, in original form, was pretty much a closed book to him and he had the unfortunate civil lawyer's tendency of referring to Isla Galbraith as, 'the defender' instead of 'the accused' or 'the pannel', and to Callum Galbraith as 'the decedent' instead of 'the dead guy'; nevertheless, he did have the one qualification I was looking for most: he was Dean of the Faculty of Advocates. If, as I sincerely hoped, I managed to have the charge against Isla reduced to culpable homicide; thereafter, everything would rest on the plea in mitigation. Whatever his short-comings on the criminal side of things, as Dean, anything Kincaid had to say would have the ear of the judge and I was going to see to it that he gave the judge a right good earful.

'Nothing to worry about,' I assured him. 'I'll provide the ammo and you can blast away 'til your heart's content.'

'Quite,' he said, head held high, his eyes fixed on the painted glass of the great south window through which flooded streams of sunlight, dappling our path with colour.

Members of the Faculty of Advocates were supposed to be like cab-drivers waiting at the rank, ready to take on any client who happened along. Try finding a civil advocate, far less the Dean, to take on a murder case - a legal aid murder case at that - and normally you wouldn't see anything but exhaust fumes, as the civil taxis raced for the hills. The only reason I was even in with a chance of instructing Kincaid was down to a chat I'd had with his clerk when I'd been sounding her out on available seniors. In the course of our conversation she'd happened to mention that Kincaid was having difficulties finding a speaker for a sportsman's dinner the Faculty was hosting in aid of some charity or other. According to his clerk, sport, unless it was deer-stalking or salmon fishing, wasn't really the Dean's 'thing' and there being a shortage of fly-fishermen on my very short list of sporting clients, and only the wrong kind of stalkers, I'd offered Malky's services. Any initial reluctance was overcome when I'd explained there would be no fee in the circumstances.

'What circumstances are those?' the clerk had enquired.

'That the Dean will represent Isla Galbraith,' I replied.

We'd consulted by telephone the next day and Kincaid had agreed to take the case on. What really swung it was when I told him that Isla had been born and bred on the Isle of Harris and was a member of the Free Church of Scotland. That was hardcore religion by anyone's standards and commended her to Kincaid who was Wee Free right down to the tweed in his underpants and the orange juice in his crystal decanter.

'It's such a shame when a marriage doesn't work out,' he said, as, at the end of the Hall, we turned and started to pace slowly back the way we'd come. It was just the sort of under-statement I'd be looking for when it came time to explain to the judge why Callum Galbraith had a head like a colander.

'A woman pushed beyond her limits by a violent husband,' I said.

'It's what comes of mixed marriages.' By which Kincaid was referring to Isla's Free Presbyterian upbringing and her late husband's allegiance to the Church of Rome or, as Kincaid probably preferred, the Whore of Babylon.

I handed him the provisional brief. It was in two parts: the first part, or 'bundle', as counsel liked to call anything comprising more than one sheet of paper, contained the Petition, or charge sheet, along with my client's precognition, her medical records, the defence autopsy report and copy police statements. The second bundle, all printed on pink paper, held copies of the Crown documentary productions: death certificate, arrest forms and the transcript of Isla's taped interview with the police.

Legal briefs came in all shapes and sizes: in ring-binders, cardboard folders, even held together by rubber-bands - not so from Munro & Company. Grace-Mary Gribbin was a legal secretary from a time before word processors and spell-checks; the days when you typed an eighty-page lease and there couldn't be any mistakes unless you wanted to do the whole thing again. Ask Grace-Mary to make up a brief and she did it the old way, the proper way. Ranald Kincaid examined the spines, neatly stitched with pink thread, the two bundles tied with red legal tape. He emitted a small grunt of satisfaction and smiled for the first time.

'Thank goodness for small mercies,' he said. 'Got a brief last week in a dispute over a long prescriptive servitude right of way. It came inside a yellow plastic envelope complete with a sunglass-wearing cartoon sun on the front and Have a Nice Day, underneath. I sent it back. The Lands Tribunal wasn't established so that people could, *have a nice day*.'

We reached the other end of the hall, about-turned and walked back in silence, past Ravaillac's marble statue of Lord President Forbes of Culloden, until we were half-way down and adjacent to the great fireplace where the statue of Walter Scott sat by the entrance to the Advocates Library.

We shook hands.

'This dinner of mine…' Kincaid said, an anxious expression on his face. 'Your brother, you say he has some experience?'

'Bags.'

'It's only that I haven't heard the name before.'

At last; someone who'd never heard of Malky Munro.

'I can assure you, you've absolutely nothing to worry about. His is a weel kent name in the world of sport. Works a lot down south in the Home Counties. In constant demand for these types of occasions. You're lucky to get him.'

Kincaid relaxed a little. 'In that case,' he held up the two bundles in one hand and waggled them, like I expected he waggled his big black Bible at Sabbath-breakers, 'I'll read these and then I think we should consult with the client.'

I parted company with the Dean feeling pretty pleased with myself; so far so good. I had the big gun. All I needed now were the bullets. Isla Galbraith's medical records were a start but there had to be other skeletons in her late husband's cupboard. I'd go hunting and when I found so much as a bone I'd see that it received a very public airing.

CHAPTER **18**

For the Munro boys there was no such thing as too long a movie, only too few snacks. We were ten minutes in and already knee-deep in fake blood, latex innards and screaming teens when Malky returned from the foyer laden with munchies. 'What a size of a queue,' he said as he handed me a small paper cup of coffee.

'That it?'

'It's a large. Should have got one of these.' He held up a bucket of cola. 'This is a small.'

On the screen one of the living dead was having its head caved in by a crowbar, skull and brains squelching like an over-ripe melon. I had a sudden mental image of Callum Galbraith, sprawled across his bed and Isla, his tomahawk-wielding wife, standing over him in a blood-soaked nightie.

'And this is a regular-size.' Malky sat down beside me and dropped a paper sack overflowing with popcorn in my lap.

I settled back. It was like old times: Malky and me out for a night at the flicks. Of course, back then we'd have dates with us and by the end of the first reel Malky would be snogging the pretty one and I'd still be plucking up courage to feign a yawn and put my arm around her pal.

'Will you two shut it!' some guy shouted from a couple of rows behind us. We both turned around.

'Malky? Malky Munro! It is, isn't it?' exclaimed the voice in the dark. 'Sorry mate. Didn't realise that was you there. No offence.' The owner of the voice leaned across the row of seats that separated us, in doing so spilling a handful of peanut M&M's down the neck of the person in front. He reached out and shook Malky's hand. 'Tell your mate to keep the noise down, will you?'

Unlike the bag of popcorn, the movie had an end. Even then Malky wouldn't budge. Apparently, there was an extra bit after the titles. He'd heard the girls at the sweetie counter talking about how everyone always missed it. Ten minutes later the titles were still rolling. Everyone who'd made so much as a cup of tea during production was receiving a mention. We waited. And waited. The screen went blank. The lights came on. Some people in red and white uniforms entered and climbed the aisle towards us, collecting empty soft drink containers in black bin-bags and giving us funny looks.

'Must have been talking about another film,' Malky said as we walked through the lobby and outside to the car park. It was chilly now because, just as it had been another clear cloudless day, it was now a clear cloudless night.

I looked at my watch. It was after eleven. 'Dad will be wondering where you are.'

'Don't I know it? He's driving me crazy, him and his pals. All they think about is football. If I see Archie Gemmill's goal against Holland one more time I'm going to scream. A night at the pictures was a great idea.'

I accepted his thanks. Though I was quite partial to the occasional celluloid gore-fest myself, Malky was something of an aficionado, so a George A. Romero re-make was the ideal way to soften him up before raising the subject of Ranald Kincaid's sportsman's dinner. Malky might have acquired some after-dinner experience south of the border, but the Signet Library in Parliament House would have to be approached somewhat differently than, say, the Brighton & Hove Albion player of the year awards.

As I drove along the High Street on the way back to my dad's we passed my flat and I thought I could make out a figure lurking in the shadows outside. I slowed down. Malky had noticed it too. 'What are you doing?' he yelled at me. 'Drive on.'

I stopped the car, disentangled myself from the seat belt and jumped out. Malky, who was tugging at my sleeve, tried to haul me back in but I wriggled free. Not sure what to expect and with thoughts of Dexy Doyle on my mind, I walked towards my building. As I approached, a puff of smoke wafted from the mouth of the close and I heard the faint sound of someone whistling.

'Who's there?' I said.

Kieran Doyle stepped out of the gloom, a flat cap covering his nylon hair, a cigarette stuck in the corner of his mouth. Beside him, still wearing the green and white football top and whistling through his teeth, was the young man from Dexy Doyle's bar.

'Robbie!' Malky came running over.

'This has nothing to do with you,' Kieran snapped at him. Malky looked surprised.

'You deaf?' said the boy in the hoops. 'He twisted a knife in front of his face, leering at Malky.

Kieran slapped the hand holding the knife. 'Eejit. Put that thing away and go wait in the car.'

The boy in the hoops did what he was told, walking backwards, eyes fixed on Malky.

'What's this all about, Kieran?' I asked.

'Angie.'

It took me a moment or two to remember that, like his brother, Kieran Doyle also had a daughter; his being very much alive.

'What about her?'

'She was visiting her gran in Belfast. The police stopped her on the way home. She had guns in her luggage.'

'Handguns?'

'Aye. She's been lifted. He was too.' He jerked a thumb in the direction of Mr Hoops who by now was sitting in the passenger seat of a racing green Jag parked nearby. 'He's one of Dechlan's boys. They had to let him go – nothing on him.'

I'd never met Angie Doyle, but she sounded like a chip off the old Doyle block. Gun running had been one of her Uncle Dexy's favourite past-times. Back then it was from Scotland to Ulster but, in these enlightened times, with the paramilitaries supposedly decommissioning their weapons, what was the point of beating some perfectly good hardware into ploughshares when it could be sold back across the water?

'Angie's off the rails,' Kieran said. He shook his head, drew deeply on his cigarette and blew smoke heavenwards. 'She's always been a handful, but it would kill her mother if she went to prison. I'd have to resign from the Council.' He groaned. 'You know, I love her to bits but sometimes I wonder how I ended up with Angie and Dechlan with Cathleen.'

'Where is she?' I asked.

'Ayr police station. I've only just found out. She's appearing in court tomorrow afternoon and her mother's sick with worry. You've got to get her out.'

Bail on firearms charges? Handguns? Had the man never heard of Dunblane?

Kieran read my mind. 'I know it won't be easy. I've spoken to the lawyers.'

I'd foolishly assumed that, on matters criminal, I was the Doyle family's lawyer.

'Caldwell & Craig won't touch it,' he told me. 'Don't do crime any more. Not good for their corporate image. I didn't know you'd left there otherwise I'd have come straight here.'

I adopted a pained expression and rubbed the back of my neck. 'I don't know. I'm kind of busy…'

'Please, Robbie.'

Okay, that was enough playing hard to get. A reasonably-sized brown envelope, and I'd be there with bells on. I was preparing to reluctantly agree and start talking money when

Kieran came closer and put his face up to mine. I could smell the tobacco on his breath.

'I know Dechlan is behind it,' he said, 'and I know you and him are not exactly on the best of terms at the minute because of yer man there.' He took a final drag and pinged the stub of his cigarette on the ground at Malky's feet. 'But Dechlan's not me. Me and you, we're solid. Do this for Angie and I'll not forget it. I'll sort something out for your brother.'

'Then I'll see what I can do,' I said.

He lit another cigarette with a series of rapid puffs. 'Good. I'll pick you up the morn at noon.'

CHAPTER 19

We arrived in the 'Honest Toon', Wednesday, at the back of one. Kieran Doyle parked his Jag outside the Sheriff Court, not far from the sea front, and I went for a walk, glad to be away from his chain-smoking and Mr Hoop's incessant whistling. Angie's case wasn't due to call until two and I needed peace for creative thought so that I could conjure up some faintly plausible grounds in favour of bail.

The problem with bail was that it was one big buck-passing exercise. Although granted more or less automatically when the prosecution didn't object, the Crown hated the bad publicity that followed when persons accused of serious offences were released, or, worse still, offended while on bail. Accordingly, P.F.'s preferred to oppose bail, thus placing the onus and potential wrath of the newspapers squarely with the Court. Which, in turn, was why we defence agents had to be ready to step in and hit the Sheriff with tales of sick grannies, pregnant burds and exciting job opportunities that would all suffer terribly were the accused to be remanded in custody.

In Angie Doyle's case I had my work well and truly cut out for me. Where firearms were concerned, almost any Sheriff would err on the side of cowardice, refuse bail and let the accused take their chances with an appeal to the High Court. The boys at Parliament House earned the big bucks; if the accused was to be released, they might as well risk the tabloid flack. Although her clean record meant the odds-on Angie being granted High Court bail were fairly good, she would have to spend a week in custody awaiting her appeal and that wouldn't go down at all well with her parents. It was perfectly clear that my best line of attack was to soft-soap the P.F. into agreeing bail. Easier said than done. Or so I thought, until, through a coffee shop window, I spied a familiar face which at that precise moment was being crammed with a fudge doughnut.

The face and doughnut, it was hard to tell where one ended and the other began, belonged to Leonard Brophy. A former procurator fiscal-depute, Leonard had resigned on grounds of ill-health, joined the Scottish Executive and done the same thing there. No-one could ever accuse the civil service of scrimping when it came to paid sick-leave.

'Robbie. Long time no see.' Leonard pushed a plate of cakes out of my reach. One thing for sure, a life time of being proper poorly hadn't ruined his appetite.

How's it going?' I asked, once I'd waved the waitress over and ordered a coffee that I hoped she might add to Leonard's bill.

'As a matter of fact, I think I'm coming down with the 'flu or something.'

'So, what are you doing these days?' I asked, fingers crossed that he'd come back with the answer I was looking for.

'I was called to the Bar. Did you not know?'

I didn't, but wasn't entirely surprised. The Faculty of Advocates was made up of lawyers who were either very gifted or extremely unemployable. The former were snowed-under with work. I suspected Leonard rarely saw a sharp frost.

'At the Bar? You'll be raking it in then,' I said, keeping a straight face. At that moment the only thing Leonard was raking in was a fondant fancy. If my hunch was correct, the reason he was fighting off a sniffle down in deepest, darkest Ayrshire was to keep the wolf from the door by temp-fiscalling. Self-employment: the cure for most workplace ailments.

'Can't complain,' he said, popping a chocolate truffle into his mouth and pouring the loose hundreds-and-thousands in after it. He crumpled the paper cake-case in his hand. 'My clerk's got me some work as an ad hoc.'

With P.F. deputes forever going off on holidays, sick-leave, to have babies or find proper jobs, the Procurator Fiscal Service was constantly under-staffed and turned to the Faculty of Advocates for assistance. Regular Fiscal-deputes hated ad hocs for two main reasons; firstly, they were paid a lot more, though they generally knew a lot less, and, secondly, because they were only temping and not trying to make a career of it, they could actually exercise discretion in the cases they prosecuted since they didn't have to go back to the office and face some fire-breathing senior-depute ranting on about Crown Office guidelines.

'What brings you here?' Leonard asked.

'A Petition,' I said. 'Something to do with guns.'

'Guns?'

I suspected that, true to form, Leonard hadn't bothered to glance at the papers yet.

'Yes,' I said. 'The accused's just a wee girl, from a decent family. It's all some kind of a terrible misunderstanding.'

'Guns? As in firearms?' He frowned deeply over an iced gingerbread square. 'Not handguns?'

'Just a few. I was wondering… I don't suppose you'll be opposing bail in the circumstances.'

The waitress returned with my coffee and set down a saucer with a piece of paper on it weighted down by a pandrop.

Leonard picked up the bill, brows furrowed, deep in thought, some chocolate sprinkles still stuck to his lips.

'Here, let me get that,' I said tugging the bill from between his fingers.

'Bail? For handguns? I don't know about that.'

This was going to prove more difficult than I'd first thought. I smiled up at the waitress. 'Bring us a couple of those strawberry shortcakes will you pet?'

CHAPTER **20**

The accused came up the stairs from the cells handcuffed to a custody officer and stood in the dock. Petition cases called in private, so her father had been told to wait outside.

Angie Doyle had been in custody for more than thirty-six hours. By law accused persons were brought to court on the first lawful day after arrest, but since she'd been lifted just after midnight, Monday into Tuesday, the next lawful day was Wednesday and by the time the Fiscal had prepared the paperwork and the Sheriff Clerk had it linked into the court system, it was well into the afternoon before her case called.

'Are you Angela Bernadette Doyle?' asked the clerk. The accused curled a lip in confirmation.

'For the tape please,' the clerk said.

The prisoner tutted. 'Yes.'

The contempt in my client's reply would not have been lost on the Sheriff, but he chose to let it go without comment. 'Sit down,' he said, scanning the charge on the Petition which libelled a contravention of the Firearms Act and concerned the discovery of six handguns in my client's luggage after her car had attracted the interest of the police. Maybe it had been some kind of routine check due to the lateness of the hour, or perhaps the car registration showed up as suspicious on the PNC; whatever, the vehicle had been well away from the ferry port at Stranraer and into Ayrshire before it came to the attention of the police. The legality of that stop and search might have been the basis of a defence but, that aside, I had a sneaking suspicion we were dealing with a classic 'Romeo and Juliet' set-up, once an extremely popular smuggling method and which, like old pop-singers, foot and mouth and economic recession, was prone to making comebacks.

As far as I could recall the procedure went something like this: Mr Big hires two mules: Juliet, who is given a rucksack full of contraband, in this case shooters, and Romeo who is given an identical rucksack full of women's clothing. They travel alone. If Juliet is unlucky enough to be stopped and searched, she feigns ignorance and puts the whole thing down to a mix-up over luggage during a brief encounter with a young man she met on the crossing. The police then check the passenger list, pay Romeo a visit and lo and behold he does indeed have a rucksack full of women's undies. Hey presto, ladies and gentlemen of the jury, reasonable doubt. As for Romeo, he's also in the clear. He denies any knowledge of guns or a mix-up. He hasn't been found in possession of anything criminal and what a man chooses to carry in his luggage is his own business. It's an Exocet missile of a defence; the Crown can see it coming a mile off, but there's nothing they can do about it.

Yes, a classic Romeo and Juliet, that's how it looked to me. The Prosecution would have felt obliged to charge someone, and it was Angie who'd been found with the guns in her possession. Still, unless someone had been careless with fingerprints or their DNA, once I had the girl kitted out in a pretty frock and in front of a jury, I could see little prospect of a conviction. I climbed to my feet.

'Miss Doyle makes no plea or declaration M'Lord,' I said after I'd introduced myself to the Sheriff and handed the clerk a bail application form that I'd completed earlier, 'and I seek her liberation on bail.'

'What's the Crown's attitude?' asked the Sheriff.

Leonard Brophy shook his head. 'Not opposed.'

The Sheriff glanced down at the Petition. 'What did you say the Crown's position was, Mr Fiscal?'

The P.F. swallowed hard as though a chunk of strawberry shortcake had stuck in his throat. 'No opposition, M'Lord.'

'Very well,' said the Sheriff. 'If the Crown is content, who am I to disagree? Bail standard conditions.'

The clerk confirmed the grant of bail and continued the case for further enquiry. The Crown now had eleven months to decide whether or not to serve an indictment. With a cheery wave to the P.F., I followed Angie down to the cells where we sat at a small, bolted to the floor table, waiting for the clerk to print off the bail papers.

'Get your money easy, don't you?' my young client sneered.

It was hard to believe this was Cat's cousin. She was pretty all right, and there was a vague family resemblance, but take away the coloured contacts, dyed hair, the peaches and cream make-up and you could have sparked matches off her.

'What did you tell them?' I asked.

'The police? I said it was all a big mistake. I must have picked up the wrong bag.'

'Then it wouldn't be a good idea for you and Romeo to be seen together. Not until after the trial.'

She didn't say anything at first. Romeo and Juliet? Maybe it was called something else these days. She narrowed the blue eyes that peered out from beneath the fringe of her blonde bob. 'Thanks for the advice but I'm a big girl, I'll do what I like – okay?'

The bail papers arrived. 'Did my Uncle Dexy send you?' Angie asked, signing in triplicate whilst a female Reliance officer went to fetch her belongings.

'No, it was your dad.'

The first sign of emotion. 'He's not here is he?'

'Outside.'

She sucked in air through her teeth. 'Tell him I'll make my own way back to Glasgow.'

I stood up. 'You're a big girl. Tell him yourself.'

I left my client to collect her belongings and went out to find Kieran Doyle pacing up and down in front of the building, smoking furiously like an expectant father, which, I suppose, he was. The young guy in the hooped top, Romeo to

Angie Doyle's Juliet, was sitting on the stone steps that led down to the pavement. When Kieran saw me, he threw his cigarette away.

'She'll be out in a minute,' I told him.

He fell back against one of the Ionic columns that supported the façade of the building, exhaled in relief and put another cigarette in his mouth.

'I'll not forget this,' he said.

I wasn't intending to give him the chance.

The front door to the Sheriff Court opened and Angie Doyle walked out. Her dad spat out the un-lit cigarette, rushed over and hugged her. Then he held her at arm's length. 'What have I told you?'

'It's all right, Dad.'

'No, it's not all right. Guns? This is down to your Uncle Dexy, isn't it?'

Romeo looked anxious, but Angie just answered her father's question with a shrug. She was no grass.

I tapped Kieran on the shoulder. 'She's out. Now I'd like you to take me back to my office and I'd like to get paid. Though not necessarily in that order.'

'You'll get your money.'

People who said, 'you'll get your money,' worried me, mainly because it was something I said quite a lot myself, usually when I didn't have any.

'You've not got it? You didn't bring any cash?'

Kieran's face flushed. Atop his head a tendril of nylon hair broke free from the rest of the gang and waved gently in the light summer breeze blowing in off the Irish Sea. I walked down the steps. He came after me. 'I told you – you'll get paid.'

'And Malky? What about him and Dexy?'

Kieran winced. 'That's going to be trickier.'

At the pavement I turned to face him again. 'Tell you what then - don't bother.'

'About what?'

'The money,' I heard myself say. 'Keep it and I'll do Angie's trial for free.'

'What is this? What are you saying?'

'I'm saying, I got your precious daughter out of custody and I'm ready to make sure she doesn't get convicted of possession of handguns, which as you know carries a minimum five-year sentence.'

'And you don't want paid?'

'No, I would like to be paid, but I'd like it even more if your big brother would leave my big brother alone.'

Kiernan shook his head. 'I know I said I'd try and help, but the thing with Malky... Well, it's Dechlan's business. We're talking about the death of his daughter.'

'And I'm talking about the liberty of yours.' Kieran walked over to the car. I went after him. 'You promised if I helped Angie you'd do something to help Malky.'

'I said I'd try and I will but it's not that easy. Dechlan and me are having some problems right now. I'm not sure if he'll listen to me. And now there's this thing with Angie. I'm not happy. I know he's behind it. That one there...' he nodded over to the car where Romeo was already in the front passenger seat. 'He doesn't take a dump unless Dechlan gives him the bog roll.'

He walked to the car. I followed. 'Kieran, you didn't say anything about *trying*, you said you'd sort something out. That's the reason I came down here. You said—'

Kieran banged the bonnet with his fist. 'Okay, okay.' He composed himself after his momentary outburst. Squared up his hair. 'I'll do what I can - all right?'

Father and daughter were dropped off in a leafy avenue on the south side of Glasgow. Kieran had phoned home shortly after we left Ayr and was met by his wife who looked as though she had been standing in the street waiting ever since he'd made the call. As soon as Angie was out of the car her mum was all over her. The girl wriggled free and ran into the house. Kieran hugged and kissed his wife and they went in after her. A few minutes later, Kieran returned to the car. He tapped on the window. I rolled it down.

'Thanks again, Robbie' he said, slipping me an envelope. 'The boy will take you back to Linlithgow.' He walked away.

'Kieran,' I called after him. 'If Dexy won't listen to you who will he listen to?' He kept walking. 'I said, who will Dexy listen to?'

He stopped, turned and walked slowly back to the car. From his jacket he took out his wallet and removed a business card.

'I'll tell him to expect you,' he said and threw it at me through the open window.

CHAPTER 21

The University of Edinburgh's Old College on Chambers Street, next door to the Royal Museum of Scotland, was where I'd studied back in the day. Then, the prospect of a career in criminal law seemed so exciting, so glamorous. Fast forward ten years or so to a Thursday afternoon to find me directly across the street in a Crown Office elevator, juddering my way to the third floor.

I closed my eyes. I'd never been all that keen on lifts. Dangling above certain death in a box on a string always made me contemplate my mortality rather more than was healthy for a man of my relatively tender years. As soon as I entered the wood-panelled interior and watched the door slide shut, I felt uneasy. The compartment was so small and cramped it felt like being trapped inside a fat person's coffin; a thought made all the more disconcerting by the fact I had brought with me my very own fat person in the corpulent and heavily-perspiring shape of Leonard Brophy, who at that moment seemed to be sucking in far more than his fair share of the limited oxygen supply.

Junior counsel's presence on this occasion stemmed directly from my excursion to Ayr the previous day. A strawberry shortcake had not been enough to persuade the plump advocate, in his capacity as ad-hoc P.F., that Kieran Doyle's gun-running daughter was a candidate for bail and in desperation I'd offered him the chance of junioring to Ranald Kincaid Q.C. in Isla's murder case. It was the sort of opportunity that would seldom come Leonard's way and, not surprisingly, he'd jumped at it, meaning I was stuck with him for the time being.

Leonard's first engagement as Junior counsel for the defence in Her Majesty's Advocate against Isla Galbraith was to accompany me to Crown Office, where I had arranged a meeting with Crown counsel to discuss a possible resolution. The Lord Advocate's Deputes could be a bit touchy and preferred not to discuss a case with the defence solicitor unless their opposite number from the Faculty of Advocates was also present, so I'd asked Leonard along. There was nothing your average junior liked better than a consultation fee, except, perhaps, in Leonard's case at any rate, cakes.

Eventually, the ping of a bell announced our arrival on the third floor and the door slid open to reveal a woman, hair tied back in a bun and wearing a pencil skirt and twin-set. I suddenly remembered a library book I hadn't returned. She introduced herself as Lucy Meadows. She was young and very nervous. A sheen of perspiration glistened on her brow and the thin hands that held the file of papers were trembling a little. I knew that all junior counsel were expected to do a three-year stint prosecuting. The money was relatively rubbish but certain duties were incumbent upon those who aspired to a silk gown. Still, there was junior counsel and then there was *junior* counsel. Were murders so commonplace these days that Crown Office let the kids deal with them? I shook one of her limp, slightly damp hands. It felt like putty in mine.

You say you'll drop the murder to culpable homicide, my dear? How about a breach of the peace?

Leonard unwedged himself from the elevator doors and joined me in the corridor. 'I was seconded here for a while when I was a P.F.' he said. 'Do they still send out at coffee break for millionaire's shortbread from that place around the corner?'

Young Miss Meadows ignored the question and showed us to a small room with a coombed ceiling and painted wood-chip on the walls. We sat down, defence on one side of the table, prosecution on the other. 'I've asked Mr Crowe to join us,' she said and, as though he'd been waiting to be announced, the door creaked open and in strolled Cameron Crowe. Nosferatu in pin-stripes.

My heart sank. Cameron Crowe, a former colleague of mine, had been a know-it-all senior court assistant when I'd trained at Caldwell & Craig. Not long after I'd qualified as a solicitor, he'd left the Firm, moved to the dark side and joined the Fiscal Service. Things between us had never been particularly cosy but plunged sub-zero on the night of a Glasgow Bar Association dinner approximately three years previously. It was shortly after Cathleen Doyle had surgically removed my heart and around the time I had set out on a one-man campaign to prevent further distillery closures. My own recollection of events was impaired by drink and the passage of time, but witnesses to the incident had testified to Crowe's date for the evening, my favourite advocate, not yet Q.C., Fiona Faye, entwined with me in passionate embrace on the floor of the ladies cloakroom. Perhaps Malky and I weren't so different. Except it had been heat of the moment for me when I'd snogged Crowe's girlfriend; Malky had stolen mine in cold blood.

Crowe had since called at the Bar and was now a full-time advocate-depute, one of the Lord Advocate's representatives on earth and renowned for the ferocity of his prosecutions. Over the years we'd had numerous acrimonious encounters in various jurisdictions. Crowe wasn't a man to bear a grudge lightly. I felt sure that the only person in the world he liked less than me was Fiona. Now I had to try and talk him into dropping a murder charge. My turn to sweat a little.

Crowe took his seat opposite. Tall and slim, dark hair slicked back, the tailored suit that hung on his angular frame was a perfect fit. He contorted his features and manoeuvred his thin lips into the rictus of a moisturised cadaver.

Leonard struggled out of his jacket and hung it on the back of his seat revealing dark rings of sweat around each oxter. The small room filled with his smell.

'Now then, Mr Brophy,' Crowe said, apparently oblivious to my presence. 'Let's make a start, shall we?' He pulled his colleague's file of papers in front of him and extracted the murder Petition. 'So, what have we got?' He took a pair of specs from his top pocket and put them on. 'Ah, yes. Mrs Galbraith, in the bedroom, with the hatchet.'

'And the screwdriver,' Meadows chipped in.

'Lucy's our new girl,' said Crowe, his smile never reaching his eyes. 'She's cutting her teeth on this case. I'll be leading her, so when she told me you were coming in for a chat I thought it might be an idea if I tagged along.' He locked eyes with me for a moment. My card was marked. He turned his stare to Leonard again, laid the Petition on the table and smoothed it flat with the back of a hand.

I took a deep breath. I'd have to play this extremely canny. There would be no bulldozing Cameron Crowe into a soft plea.

'Callum Galbraith was a brute,' Leonard let fly. He spread out the photos of Isla Galbraith's black-eye on the table. 'He deserved all he got and we're not leaving here until you agree to culpable homicide.'

Crowe's left eyelid lowered dangerously.

'I wonder,' I said, 'if you'd excuse us for a moment?' A puzzled expression formed on Leonard's fat face. It was still there after I'd dragged him bodily through the door and into the corridor. 'What do you think you're doing?' I demanded to know.

'I'm negotiating a plea.'

'No, you're not. You're being a prat. Stay here, go around the corner for some millionaire's shortbread, but do not go back into that room.'

'Hey,' he whined. 'You can't talk to me like that. I'm learned bloody counsel.'

But I could talk to him any way I wanted, and he knew it. I held the legal aid purse strings and junior counsel were two-a-penny.

'Should we wait for Mr Brophy?' Crowe asked when I returned and took my seat at the table.

'Let's not,' I said.

I could tell from young Meadow's face that she was unhappy about defence counsel's absence from discussions.

'Lucy,' I said. 'What are the chances of a coffee?'

Frowning, her face bright red, she looked to her senior for support.

Crowe fixed me with a stare and held it until it began to hurt. 'That would be great,' he said. 'White for me.'

'Black. Three sugar,' I said.

Meadow's pushed back her chair noisily, got to her feet and left the room, closing the door firmly behind her. Very firmly behind her.

'Leonard Brophy?' Crowe smirked.

'Long story.'

'I don't want to hear it. In any case I expect you've come to tell me a different sorry tale.'

'Isla Galbraith was a battered wife. I've seen her medical records. Callum Galbraith was a violent man. You must know he had a police disciplinary record.'

Crowe sighed. 'He had a fight with a fellow officer during a football match,' that came as news to me, 'and a minor incident with a juvenile offender,' Crowe continued. 'So what?'

'It was more than a minor incident. He injured a twelve-year-old boy. Strathclyde Police paid compensation.'

The man across the table from me blinked. He knew the significance of that settlement. Unlike the rest of us mere mortals the Police were immune from compensation claims purely by reason of negligence. There had to be evidence of ill-will or mal fides, as we lawyers liked to say when the Latin was upon us. If Strathclyde shelled out damages it would only have done so if there was good reason to believe the boy's injury was down to more than accident or over-exuberance on the part of Callum Galbraith in the exercise of his duties.

I forged ahead. 'If we keep looking, how many more examples will we find of an officer prone to outbursts of temper?' I collected the photos that were scattered across the table and shuffled them to a close-up of Isla's bruised eye. 'A man who could assault a colleague, injure a young boy and do this to a defenceless woman.' I held the photo up in front of Crowe's face. 'Of course, we'll have to query police recruitment practices. Psychological profiling. Training. Vetting policies. In the event of a trial, that is.'

'Don't try the smoke and mirrors routine on me,' Crowe said. 'The fact remains that your client murdered her husband.'

'No – not murdered – killed. And she confessed to it. If we go to trial, what are you going to do? Spend a couple of days flashing post-mortem photos in the hope there'll be enough on the jury sufficiently horrified to come back with a murder conviction? Puh-lease. Come the defence case, we'll take a couple of weeks and ask why a police officer with documented anger management issues and a tendency to violence was allowed to continue in his post. Who else knew he was a wife-beater? His colleagues? His superiors? Did someone turn a blind eye? And why are there so few high-ranking female officers, except on the telly? Institutional misogyny - makes quite a good sound-bite don't you think? We'll ask the jury to accept that Isla Galbraith's actions were a clear case of diminished responsibility and in the meantime the name of Callum Galbraith and Strathclyde Police will be going down the shunky faster than last night's curry. We might even get a public enquiry out of it. I know how much the Justice Minister enjoys those.'

'That's quite a speech.' Crowe pinched the bridge of his glasses, taking them off and folding them in his hand. 'But you're forgetting one thing. She plunged him through the head a dozen times with a screwdriver!' He emphasised the point with a few rapid stabbing motions of his specs. 'The woman is a murderer!'

Crowe's raised voice was a good sign. I was beginning to get to him. 'A thirty-something nurse turned psycho? Doesn't that sound to you like a woman who's snapped? A woman whose ability to control her conduct was substantially impaired by reason of mental abnormality?'

'*Substantially impaired by reason of mental abnormality*?' he laughed. 'When did you start reading law books?'

I carried on regardless. 'A normal woman. A gentle woman. Someone who's devoted her life to caring for others just doesn't do that sort of thing – not unless driven to it.'

'Tell me. Who's your senior?' Crowe asked. 'No, let me guess, Princess Fifi? Or have they withdrawn her equity card? If the woman were any more of a ham she'd be honey-glazed.'

He was referring, of course, to Fiona Faye. I knew he still refused to speak to her, except when professionally necessary during the course of courtroom hostilities. Who'd have thought a drunken snog three years ago would have evoked such antipathy. It was crazy. They were both so able. While Crowe's cold, clinical, logical approach could be relied on to drive out the most stubborn of reasonable doubts; jurors loved Fiona's melodramatic, emotional performances. If I'd been looking to persuade a jury, then Fiona would have been a great choice as counsel for Isla Galbraith, but I wasn't. I needed someone to persuade a High Court Judge that a woman who had killed her husband didn't deserve to go to jail; that her particular circumstances mitigated in favour of clemency. Fiona was good but the gravitas of Ranald Kincaid Q.C., already on the inside track to the judiciary, made him the ideal candidate.

'I've instructed the Dean on this one,' I said matter-of-factly.

The actual process for the appointment of a Queen's Counsel is shrouded in mystery, but so far as I could glean, the Dean of the Faculty of Advocates had a big say in the matter, drawing up a short-list to put before a panel of Court of Session judges, the winners going forward to the Lord President and onward for rubber-stamping by the First Minister of Scotland. Ranald Kincaid Q.C. was the Dean, on whose recommendation hung the destiny of many a silk robe. The fact he still languished in the junior ranks while big, blonde and blousy Fiona Faye had recently taken silk must really have been eating at Crowe. This was his chance to do his career a favour and show the top brass that he wasn't the rabid prosecutor that everyone thought he was, but, rather, possessed those qualities: rationality, discernment and compassion that the Queen looked for in her Counsellors.

Cameron Crowe was many things, but he wasn't stupid. He replaced his specs into his top pocket, pushed his chair back and smiled like a snake. He stood, went to the door and opened it. Young Meadows arrived awkwardly carrying three mugs of coffee as we were walking out. Crowe escorted me to where Leonard was waiting by the lift doors. 'Show me something to back these up…' He gave the photographs back to me, simultaneously slamming the lift button with the flat of his hand. 'And,' he choked up the words, 'I'll think about a culp hom.'

CHAPTER 22

'Get a move on!' I yelled to Malky who was lagging way behind me, reading out loud lines from the piece of paper in his hand. Friday night and we were late. We had already missed our intended train from Linlithgow because on the way to the station my brother kept stopping to make amendments to his script. Now, in Edinburgh and halfway up the High Street he paused again, chuckled and jotted something else down. 'Hurry up,' I called to him. This time he seemed to hear me and stuffed the scrap of paper inside his jacket or rather my jacket. In Malky's haste to journey north he'd left his evening wear behind in Brighton. He was dead against hiring a suit, something to do with other people's skin flakes and fungal infections, and fortunately – for him – my dinner suit was more or less a perfect fit; if he let the trousers ride down on his hips to give them a little more length and tightened the elastic adjustables on the waist.

The ornate crowned-spire atop St Giles Cathedral loomed ahead as I quickened my westwards march along the Royal Mile. Malky broke into a trot, gaining on me, catching up as I veered left, side-stepping the globs of spit I couldn't see in the twilight of the Old Town, but knew to be always present on the Heart of Mid-Lothian, site of the former Tollbooth, which, as the name implied, was where the Town Council had collected tolls. In days of old the building had also served as a prison and a site for hangings, the heads of the more notorious victims displayed on spikes. Though the Tollbooth had been demolished nearly two hundred years ago, it was still the tradition to spit on the heart-shaped design set into the cobbles that marked the spot; whether as a sign of disrespect to the present Town Council or those long-departed criminals, I was never quite sure.

'All set?' I asked Malky.

He tapped his breast pocket and pointed across the cobbled courtyard to the bright lights of the Signet Library. 'Let's rock.'

'Robbie Munro and Malcolm Munro - guest speaker,' I advised the doorman.

The doorman touched the rim of his grey top hat. 'Saw you play, sir,' he told Malky, dipping in a shallow bow as he allowed us through the door and into the grand entrance hall. 'We're upstairs tonight,' he said, still addressing Malky, one white-gloved hand extended in the direction of the magnificent staircase that linked the Lower and Upper libraries. It was truly a splendid interior.

Malky looked awe-struck. 'This Signet thing: nothing to do with swans then? Just that I had quite a good joke about two nuns and a duck.'

'Nothing at all,' I replied, not bothering to explain that the Signet was the private seal of the early Scottish Kings, and the Writers to the Signet were those authorised to supervise its use and, later, to act as clerks to the Courts. These days, the WS Society was a professional body for lawyers, membership of which cost a few hundred a year and granted access to an excellent library. I suspected most in the Society already had enough law books and paid the subs so they could slap an extra couple of letters after their name: W.S.

Malky stood gazing about him. He took the piece of paper from his pocket and scored a line through part of it.

The doorman cleared his throat gently. 'I don't think they've sat down to table yet.'

We took the hint and set off up the stairs, rushing past several handsome portraits, including two Raeburns, not that I fully appreciated the works of art at the time, being more interested in getting to our seats before the seared scallops and coral sauce arrived. Upon reaching the top landing we were met by Ranald Kincaid Q.C., dressed in dinner suit and gripping the stem of a wine glass full of freshly squeezed orange juice.

'Where have you been?' he asked impatiently, eyeing up my dad's ancient but recently aired and ironed evening wear; not a bad fit on me, only let down slightly by a pale blue shirt with a frill down the front.

Without waiting to hear the excuse I'd been working on, Kincaid led Malky along the corridor to a pair of enormous wooden doors at the end. He opened one of them. The sound of chattering and laughing leaked out. In the soft glow of candlelight I glimpsed two rows of diners, men and women, either side of a long table on which crystal and bright silverware twinkled and glinted. That was about all I managed to see before Ranald Kincaid ushered Malky though the gap between the doors and it closed behind them.

I stood staring at the rich dark wood and was wondering if I should go in or knock first when one of the doors opened a crack and Kincaid stuck his face out at me. 'Carriages at midnight.' He shut the door again.

I began my descent of the staircase, looking over my shoulder lest there had been some mistake, the doors would open and I be summoned to the table.

'Splendid isn't it?' An old man in tartan trews and dinner jacket tottered up the stairs towards me. He had a florid face that I found vaguely familiar. In one liver-spotted hand he clutched a very full glass of something darkly amber. We met on the mezzanine landing where he paused, leaned his back against the banister and tilted his tumbler at a portrait in oils that hung on the wall above us.

'Lord President Hope,' he said, in a phlegmy voice. 'Everyone oohs and aahs at the Raeburns, but for me no one can render acute observant character like good old Sir John Watson Gordon, wouldn't you agree?'

He was asking the wrong person. The only Lord Hope I knew had a portrait in the consulting rooms further down the Royal Mile. A painting that suggested he was not a man to let the whimsies of fashion dictate his choice of spectacles. After what most would agree was too short a spell as Lord President he'd taken his big, round, tortoiseshell-rimmed glasses and shuffled off down to the House of Lords.

Not Hope of Craighead,' I was corrected, when I expressed my confusion. 'The first Lord President Hope. Wonderful judge. You'll recall his remarks in Auld v. Hall & Co. on the transfer of moveable property by constructive delivery?'

I must have missed that lecture at Uni; lucky escape by the sounds of it.

'Yes,' sighed the man in the tartan trousers,' eighteen-eleven and obiter dictum, yet it's still the law to this very day.'

'Give it a rest will you, Eric?' Fiona Faye didn't often manage to sneak up on anyone, but she suddenly appeared by my side wearing an off-the-shoulder number in cream silk, a flimsy lace stole around her shoulders. A single red rose corsage was tied about her wrist on a white ribbon. 'Good evening … lover-boy,' she stage-whispered in my ear. Fiona was happily married. In fact, she was on her third happy marriage. Her night out with Cameron Crowe, three years before, had taken place somewhere between husbands two and three but Fiona loved to kid me on about our cloakroom experience. 'I'm trying to keep an eye on this old rogue - keeps sneaking off – I think he's got a woman stashed away somewhere.' The old man chortled and took a sip from his glass. Fiona turned to her elderly male companion. 'Eric Ballantyne…' and then to me, 'Robbie Munro.'

Ballantyne was the name of the judge who'd admonished Mags MacGillivray after she'd run her husband through with a kitchen knife. Bereft of the judicial gear he looked completely different: just a wee old man. Of course, the whole purpose of the pomp and ceremony of the courtroom: the high ceilings, coats of arms and frock-coated personnel carrying the mace of office, was to put the accused at his unease, make him feel small, powerless and, above all, not think too much about what was really happening, i.e. some old bloke in fancy dress getting set to throw away the key. Start thinking along those lines and some people might decide they weren't going to let themselves be locked up. Too many people take that view and we were in trouble. The only difference between our present society and anarchy was that the guardians of our present society had a bigger gang and more weapons.

'Lord Ballantyne?' I said. 'Sorry, I didn't recognise you…'

'Without the wig and red silk dressing gown? Bloody hot this time of year, let me tell you.' He held his glass up to the light and admired it. 'I love coming here. You wouldn't believe some of the whiskies they have stored in the basement. The stuff's practically running out of the taps.'

I knew that the Faculty of Advocates held a number of whisky casks that were bottled from time to time and distributed to valued instructing solicitors, mainly at Christmas. I'd been presented with one or two bottles over the years I'd worked with Caldwell & Craig, but it was the first I'd heard of the W.S. Society having its own secret supply.

'Robbie's something of a whisky buff,' Fiona said.

'Really?' The old judge held out his glass to me. 'What's your verdict on this?'

I sniffed. No detectable peat or oil; not an Islay then. I held up the glass to the light. 'May I?'

'By all means,' said the judge.

I sipped the delicate, biscuity-sweet taste of a Lowland malt, fresh and dry. It was unusually dark for a Lowland malt, and yet, if it was old and had spent some time in amontillado sherry casks... 'Glenkinchie,' I pronounced confidently, not exactly sticking my neck out, given that the

Glenkinchie distillery, at the foot of the Lammermuir Hills was only about fifteen miles from where we were standing.

'I concur,' said the judge, taking the glass and imbibing deeply. He smacked his lips in appreciation. 'So, how's she doing, your client…? What was her name?'

'Mags MacGillivray?'

'Ah yes, the widow MacGillivray. Thought Fiona did a wonderful job on that one – didn't you? Talk about a tear-jerker of a plea in mitigation? I was expecting a gypsy violinist to stroll into court at any minute.'

'Yes, come along, Eric,' Fiona said, taking the whisky glass from the judge and using it carrot/donkey style to urge him on up the stairs towards the dining room. He took the first step from the landing, missed his footing and would have fallen had he not been able grab hold of Fiona's arm, accidentally ripping the corsage from her wrist in the process. The whisky tumbler fell from her hand and I reached out and caught it scarcely spilling a drop of the precious liquid.

'Nice catch,' Fiona said, politely ignoring the judge's profuse, if slightly slurred, apologies. I held out the tumbler to her. She didn't take it.

'I think you better look after that,' she said, trying unsuccessfully to tie the corsage onto her wrist and gently but firmly led his lordship back to the dining room.

I had plenty of time to kill and so was still hanging around on the landing, staring up at Lord Hope senior and trying my best to discern the artist's acute observant character, when Fiona returned minus one slightly tipsy High Court judge.

'They say there's no glass ceiling but when one of the old farts goes AWOL it's always a female member of Faculty who's sent out to round him up and bring him home. So anyway, how's tricks? Haven't exactly been killed by an avalanche of briefs from you recently.'

'Not much High Court work coming in at the moment,' I said avoiding mention of Isla Galbraith's case and hoping she hadn't heard that I'd by-passed her in favour of the Dean. For sure Ranald Kincaid wouldn't be broadcasting his foray into the world of crime. 'Linlithgow's not exactly a hotbed of serious criminal activity and with the Sheriff Court able to deal out five-year sentences, nowadays it's pretty much got to be rape or murder to get the length of the boys in the red jerseys.'

'Which will come as a relief to you,' Fiona said, a cheeky smile on her face. 'Eric might be an old sweetie with a whisky in his mitt but a lawyer spending counterfeit money? He wouldn't like it.'

'You heard?'

'Gossip – every girl needs a hobby. You worried?'

'It'll never prove. Just the local Fiscal on the wind-up. I'm expecting Crown Office to tell him to ditch it.' I noticed how difficult it was to sound confident about the outcome of proceedings when you were the accused.

'Don't be so sure about that,' Fiona said. 'Not now that a certain mutual friend of ours has taken a special interest.'

'Cameron Crowe?'

She raised her eyebrows in confirmation. The corsage fell off her wrist again and I bent, picked it up and handed it to her.

'I was speaking to him yesterday,' I'd said before I'd realised. I didn't want Fiona enquiring into the reason for my talks with Crowe. 'Didn't say anything to me.'

'Too sleekit for that. But, believe me, the man's got it in for you big time. Cameron Crowe holds a grudge like my Beamer's Pirelli's hold the road. My advice? You need to patch things up with him… you know… about—'

'Us? Why, have you?'

'No…' Fiona admitted. 'But then my career's not at stake.'

'Would you – if it was?'

Fiona smiled thinly and crushed the corsage like it was Cameron Crowe's nuts. She made to walk away, expecting me to follow. When I didn't she turned and looked over her shoulder. 'You not coming?'

'Not invited. I'm just waiting on my brother.'

'Of course,' she put on a deep voice, 'big Malky Munro. Some of the chaps in my stable have been quite excited at meeting him. Others, it has to be said, don't appear quite so enamoured. You know Mike Mulholland? Wouldn't come. Point of principle he said. Can I take it Big Malky doesn't kick with his left foot?'

Good old Scotland. Even such an august body as the Faculty of Advocates had a blue/green divide.

CHAPTER 23

A sunny Saturday afternoon. My dad and his wee pal, Vince, were sitting on the back green in deckchairs, Malky pacing up and down in front of them, swigging from a bottle of beer and cracking jokes.

Vince chuckled away merrily, big thick glasses bouncing up and down on a cherry tomato nose, tears rolling down his cheeks. 'Stop. I'm in pain.'

'I'm here all week,' Malky said, taking a bow.

I walked up the path towards them, picking my way through the minefield of empty beer bottles that littered what my dad laughingly referred to as the lawn. There were more divot holes in it from him practising chip shots than clumps of grass.

'Oh, it's yourself, Robbie,' Vince said, wiping the corners of his eyes with the end of his shirt. 'Your brother's been giving us a replay of his act. Tells us he knocked them dead last night.'

'Apparently so.' It was hard to believe but Malky had gone down a storm. I knew from bitter experience just how tough an audience Judges could be. I'd made some laugh before but usually when asking for a not guilty verdict.

'It's good to be back,' my brother said, beaming a big beery smile.

I should have been pleased. The sports dinner a success, Ranald Kincaid would be happy, and yet it irked. Cathleen had only been buried a few days ago and here was my brother, her former partner, her killer, doing what he did best: showing off, as though nothing had happened. Hypocritical of me given that I'd set up the gig, all the same I found it hard to even look at him.

'And it's good to be making a few quid again,' he said. 'Hopefully my agent will get me more bookings like last night's. Isn't that right Robbie?' I hadn't mentioned money to Malky because there was none to mention. 'How much did we charge them? Whatever it was you should double it.'

I made my way to the back door. Out of the corner of my eye I could see my dad's facial expression change and the ends of his moustache turn down. I was leaning over the kitchen table, reading Friday's newspaper when he walked in.

'Malky's in fine form,' he said. 'It's good what you've done for him. A man needs gainful employment, even if it is cracking a few jokes for some big wigs – get it? Big wigs?'

'I'll inform the London Palladium of your immediate availability.'

'I'm just pleased for him.' My dad was serious now. 'Glad that your brother's getting back on his feet. I know what it's like to lose someone. When your mother died I had the two of you to bring up. That helped to keep me going. Malky's got no-one. Only us.'

'He seems to be coming through the grieving process unscathed,' I said and turned the page. There were a number of 'Phew What a Scorcher' type articles in it with pictures of babes in bikinis and children eating ice-cream on Portobello beach.

'You two are getting on all right, aren't you?' my dad enquired.

I flipped the newspaper over to the back page. The crossword was only partially completed. 'You ever finish one of these?'

'Look, here.' My dad came over to me and laid a hand on my shoulder. 'I know you've a right to be unhappy. That business between you and your brother was... was unfortunate, but it's not like you were married to the girl. Malky's back home now. Can you not let it be like old times?'

I laughed. 'Get a grip, will you? The man ran off with my fiancée and then killed her with his crazy driving and you want me to pretend nothing happened?' I turned a few more pages in rapid succession, not reading the content.

He squeezed my shoulder. 'Robbie, the girl's dead. Malky's your own flesh and blood. We're family. Everyone else out there is just a stranger. Malky knows that and that's why he's come home. He must have known how difficult it would be to see you again. At least he's trying to build bridges. Can you not meet him half way?'

I didn't answer.

'Anyway,' my dad continued, 'things can't be that bad between the two of you if you're finding him work.'

'He's not getting paid for last night. It was a favour for someone.'

'A favour for you?'

'I think he's due me one.'

'Does he know? About this favour? Did you tell him?'

'Not yet.'

'So, you've screwed him out of a fee? He put in a lot of work for that performance last night.'

'I'll take it into account when I send him my bill,' I said, and walked to the door.

A hand slammed against the door preventing me from opening it. My old man had abandoned the softly, softly approach. 'Don't you dare turn your back on me!' He was red in the face. A blue worm writhed down the centre of his forehead. 'You're my son and you'll tell me right now what's going on.'

I turned and leaned against the door. 'Okay. You want to know what's happening? Why the prodigal has really returned? It's because his crazy, pseudo-father-in-law, Dexy Doyle is all set to give him a one-way hurl to a landfill and he thought his wee brother might be able to talk Dexy out of it.'

'Dexy who? What are you talking about?'

109

'Cathleen's father. You know who he is, right?' He didn't. 'Dechlan Doyle. Of the Falls Road Doyles?'

'Never heard of him.'

I eased him aside and opened the door. 'Then ask your pals in Strathclyde Polis about him. The ones you have all those inter-force relations with. They'll soon fill you in.' I made to leave but stopped in the doorway. 'And while you're at it, see what more dirt you can find out about Callum Galbraith. I'm going to need it.'

CHAPTER **24**

'You still here?' Grace-Mary asked. 'Court started five minutes ago.' The week had flown by in a flurry of trials, awkward clients and mountains of legal aid forms. It was Thursday already; remand court day. The day the convicted learned of their fate after the preparation of social enquiry reports and community service assessments. It was a slow process. Lots of lengthy pleas in mitigation, as defence agents tried to save their jail-bound clients, meant the court normally dragged on until well into the afternoon. I was in no particular hurry.

Grace-Mary set down, front and centre on my desk, a stack of mail that she had opened and date-stamped.

'What is this doing here?' I asked.

'What is what doing where?' she replied.

I picked out the offending item. 'This ticket to the Faculty Dinner - I told you I wasn't going.'

'As I recall, you never actually came to a decision.'

'And so you went ahead and bought me a ticket anyway?'

'No. As a matter of fact I ordered one for Andy. Just because you're a social Sahara doesn't mean everyone else has to be. Still, it's not too late to go. Could be your last chance,' my secretary added, under her breath.

'What was that?' I asked, pretending not to have heard.

'It would be a good excuse for you and Zoë to go out for an evening together. With a bit of luck you might make it to the soup course without being carted off by the fuzz.'

A night out with Zoë was certainly an attractive proposition; however, I didn't think dinner with a bunch of lawyers would be my receptionist's idea of a fun Friday night. It certainly wasn't mine.

'There's a disco this year,' enthused Grace-Mary, only making the event seem less appealing, were that possible.

I played with the ticket while I thought it over.

'And speeches, of course,' Grace-Mary continued her marketing campaign on behalf of the local Faculty.

I glanced down at the square of embossed cardboard in my hand. Speaker: Cameron Crowe, advocate. They had to be joking. The man was haunting me. I wasn't big on formal occasions involving other lawyers, and the local Faculty dinner was the annual opportunity to dine with those other solicitors I'd spent the last year trying to avoid. A dull meal followed by even duller speeches. The presence of Cameron Crowe at such a function would normally have put a clincher on my decision to stay home, and yet maybe this was a chance for me to meet with Crowe and finally patch up our differences. After all, what had happened had happened. The cloakroom affair might have ended his relationship with Fiona Faye, but it hadn't been much of a relationship anyway. Only his pride had been hurt.

'Zoë!' I yelled though to reception. In a moment she had crossed the corridor and into my room. I ushered Grace-Mary out, came around the desk and pulled up a chair for Zoë to sit down on. 'You doing anything Friday night?'

'As in tomorrow?'

I nodded.

Zoë thought for a moment. 'I've nothing special planned. Why?'

I slid a ticket across the desk to her.

'The Faculty dinner?' she said.

'It's a function for local solicitors.'

'And…?'

'And I wondered if you'd like to go.'

'With you?'

'Yes. With me.'

112

She lifted the ticket and looked at it and then gave me a smile and an encouraging bat of her eyelashes. 'Just me and you?'

'And a hundred or so lawyers.'

Zoë laughed.

'Andy will be going too,' I said and wished I hadn't.

The smile faded fast. 'So, it's more of an office outing?'

'Sort of but—'

Zoë let the ticket drop onto the desk. She stood. 'I'll think about it.'

She left the room and met Grace-Mary on the way in, bringing with her my files for the day.

'How'd it go?' my secretary asked.

'She's thinking about it.'

'You're hopeless. Am I ordering more tickets or not?'

'Get another two. Just in case.'

'You sure? They are forty-five pounds each and it's not like you'll be able to sell them on eBay if you decide not to go.'

'What is this? You've been trying to get me to go and now, when I say okay, you're arguing about it.'

'Oh dear, you have got it bad,' Grace-Mary said stuffing the files into my briefcase and holding it out to me.

I took it, collected my gown and threw it over my shoulder. 'Just get me the tickets.'

'I really, really appreciate this,' Malky said as, early Friday morning, I checked in for the Belfast flight. He'd been thanking me every few minutes since we'd left on the fifteen-minute drive to Edinburgh airport. Fifteen minutes with Malky at the wheel. Twenty-five for anyone else.

'You don't have to keep saying that,' I told him. 'Firstly, I haven't done anything yet and, secondly, I'm treating this purely as a business trip.'

I handed over my passport and booking print-out to a girl wearing a ridiculous amount of make-up and a rather strange hat.

'Any luggage?' asked the girl in the hat, trying hard, but failing to look excited about meeting another member of cattle-class.

I had no luggage, only a book to read on the journey. I took my boarding pass and set off for the departure lounge. Malky fell in beside me, acknowledging the occasional nod or uncertain smile that came his way from those old enough to remember his playing days. When he stopped to sign an autograph, I thought I'd managed to lose him, but he caught up again as I waited in line at the security check point.

'Robbie,' he said. 'About Cat…'

My brother could certainly pick his moments for a heart to heart. The guard waved me forward. 'Get this straight, Malky. I'll do my best because you're my client. So far as I'm concerned, this trip is about my protecting a business asset, nothing more.'

He cupped my chin with his hand. 'It makes me go all warm inside when you say things like that.'

I am not what you'd call an enthusiastic air traveller. Maybe it's the control freak in me, but there always comes a moment, usually somewhere around thirty thousand feet and over water, when it hits home that I am floating through the air in a metal tube with no say in what is going to happen next and with nothing to cling onto except the hope that the laws of aerodynamics have not been repealed and that the boys from Al Qaeda are taking the day off. A safe landing always comes as a pleasant surprise and it was no different on this occasion when we touched down at Aldergrove from where I embarked on the next stage of my journey, destination Stormont, home of the Northern Irish Assembly; a twenty-mile taxi-ride that cost more than my return air-fare.

After I'd been dropped off at the front of the Parliament Building, I took from my top pocket the business card given to me by wig-wearing, chain-smoking Kieran Doyle. Below the name Raymond McMenamin in the centre of the card were the words: Political Adviser – Sinn Fein and a telephone number. I pressed the numbers and had scarcely lifted the phone to my ear when the call was answered.

'Mr Munro,' said a high-pitched, cheery voice, 'you're early. Stay where you are. I'll be right with you.'

Before I could say anything, the line went dead. How the voice would know where to find me I couldn't say, but, doing as I'd been told, I sat down on one of the wooden benches that were situated at regular intervals either side of the wide central driveway. I must have brought the good weather with me from Scotland for it was a warm and sunny day and as I waited I admired the architecture of the great white building. With its ornate façade and six Ionic columns, it looked like the love-child of the Whitehouse and Ayr Sheriff Court.

'Mr Munro?'

From nowhere appeared a wee old man in a shabby tweed suit and behind him a large young man in a dark suit with creases like scalpel blades. I stood up. The wee man thrust a hand at me. He looked like a friendly old uncle who was liable to break out the toffees at any moment, but anyone who out-ranked Dexy Doyle knew more about Semtex than sweeties. 'Ray McMenamin,' he said, and we shook hands. 'One moment…' He stepped back to let the big man step forward. 'I hope you don't mind.'

The big man produced a black wand from inside his jacket and waved it at me. 'Turn around.' I did as asked and after he'd finished his wand waving, turned back again. When he tried to pat me down, McMenamin put a hand on his arm. 'That's all right Brendan.' The big man backed off. McMenamin cupped a hand to his mouth and whispered, 'the big lad's worse than me mother. Let's walk,' and, with that, he set off at a brisk pace. 'I had a call from Kieran Doyle,' he said, once I'd caught up with him.

'Then you'll know I'm here on behalf of my client, Malcolm Munro.'

'Client?' he laughed. 'Is that what he is? And here's me thinking the two of you were related.'

'Yes, Malky's my brother but I also act as his business agent and unlike Elvis Presley he won't make any money dead.'

'Are you really trying to tell me this is business and not personal?'

We walked past the statue of Edward Carson, staunch Unionist, founding member of the Ulster Volunteer Force and the man who cross-examined Oscar Wilde in his unsuccessful libel action against the 9th Marquess of Queensbury. He was frozen in time, standing, mid-oration, right arm outstretched in an almost Leninesque pose. In the background, atop Parliament Building, a light wind fluttered the Union Flags on the poles either side of Britannia and her lions.

Without breaking stride, McMenamin cleared his throat and spat on the plinth where the name, CARSON, was carved into the stone.

116

'Do pardon,' he said. 'Old habits.' He glanced at his watch. 'Mr Munro, it's a fine afternoon for a stroll in the sunshine but I'm a busy man so let me tell you where I stand.' He stopped suddenly and looked up at me. 'Kieran Doyle thinks very highly of you. Tells me you helped his daughter out of a scrape the other day.'

'Doing my job,' I said.

'And you did it well, by all accounts.' He pressed his forehead with thumb and forefinger. 'I'd like to help, for Kieran's sake if no-one else's. He's a good lad. One for the future. He's making a name for himself politically and it's good to have friends in high places… only it's handy to have them in low places too. Kieran's not happy with Dechlan.' I wondered who he was talking about for a minute before I remembered it was Dexy's Sunday name. 'I know all about that, he continued, 'in fact, sometimes I think he'd like him out of the way completely and I can understand that too. It's the new versus the old. Kieran's the future. Dechlan's old school, old brigade. The thing is, you see, Dechlan and me, we go way back. He was a good soldier. The very man to have with you in a tight spot. A man who knows the business, who can take an order, and, yet, this difficulty over his daughter…'

'Cathleen.'

'Yes, Cathleen, of course, terrible, terrible.' He blessed himself with one twitch of his hand. 'It's a very sensitive issue. You see, what I'm saying is, Cathleen's death, and what Dechlan may intend to do about it, it may be business to you but it isn't business to him - it's personal. If it was business, I would talk to him and I would expect him to listen. But what a man does in his own personal life… well… it is no concern of mine.'

He glanced at his watch again, a clear signal that my audience with him was nearing its end.

'There's got to be something you can do. A man of your undoubted influence.'

117

He gave me another one of his crinkly smiles, indulging my attempt at flattery.

'I've thought long and hard,' he said, 'and here's what I'm going to do - absolutely nothing.'

'That's it?'

'It's best for all. If Dechlan Doyle wants to avenge his murdered daughter how can I say no? I'd feel the same myself if it was one of mine.'

'Cathleen Doyle wasn't murdered,' I said. 'It was an accident.'

The man in the tweed suit stared at his ox-blood brogues. 'It was nice meeting you Mr Munro.' He turned to leave. I dragged him back by the shoulder. The big man in the dark suit was at his side in an instant.

I took my hand away. 'She wasn't just Dexy Doyle's daughter. She was Malky's partner. He killed her, yes, but it was an accident. Don't you think he's suffered enough?'

'I can see why Kieran rates you so highly,' McMenamin said.

'Kieran said you would help me, but it looks like I've been wasting my time.'

'I don't think you've understood me, Mr Munro. I can promise you what I said earlier is true. What Dechlan is doing is personal. It's no business of mine. I'll put the word about. Make it clear that he's on his own with this one. He'll get no help from me or from anyone else here.' He took my hand and gave it a squeeze. 'Dechlan Doyle isn't as young as he used to be.' He laughed. 'Who of us is? Your brother, sorry, your *client*, is a big lad. He could dish it out on the park. You'll just have to hope he can look after himself off it.'

CHAPTER **26**

The flight home was delayed. For the inconvenience of an extra two hours spent rotting at Aldergrove airport the airline had presented we passengers with a free miniature of Bowmore, one of my eight favourite Islay malts. By the time the wheels had touched down at Turnhouse my compensation package was long gone accompanied by a couple of its in-flight companions.

'Oh, fantastic,' Malky said as he drove me back from the airport. His earlier expressions of gratitude had retreated somewhat since I'd brought him the news from across the water. 'I've been given carte blanche to fight Dexy Doyle in a duel to the death – hang on I'll just unpack my AK forty-seven.'

I hadn't expected Malky to take it well, even though I had told him not to build his hopes up on my Belfast trip.

'It's definite progress,' I said. 'Once Dexy knows that he's got no back up he'll see reason. After all, there was never any major problem between the two of you was there? While Cathleen was—'

'Alive? Before I killed her? That what you mean?'

I checked the speedo. We were doing ninety-five. My mobile came to the rescue, vibrating madly. The office. At seven o'clock on a Friday night? I answered and got Andy. 'You still at the ranch?'

You told me to call if anything happened with Isla Galbraith's case. Well, the indictment was served this morning and the preliminary hearing is in two weeks' time.'

I hadn't expected the prosecution to move so quickly with a case where the accused was on bail; then again, HMA

119

versus Galbraith would be child's play to prosecute. How had Cameron Crowe decided to proceed?

'Murder or culp hom?' I asked.

'Doesn't say anything on it about culpable homicide.'

'It never does – read it out.'

'Isla Jane Galbraith you are indicted at the instance of Her Majesty's Advocate –'

'Cut to it will you?'

'All right, all right. Let me see. You did on—'

'Just the charge, please.'

'Assault Callum Galbraith, and did strike him on the head with—'

'You do know you're calling a mobile from the office phone don't you? Does it say murder or kill?'

That was the difference between the wording of a murder and a culpable homicide charge; one word that meant the difference between life imprisonment and the chance of a sentence far less severe for my client.

'Murder,' Andy said. 'And did murder him.'

'Stay there. I want a word. I'll be two minutes. We're turning off the M90 right now.'

I hung up.

'You can't go to the office,' Malky said. 'We need to talk about Dexy.'

'And we will,' I said. 'Later. Right now I've got a murder indictment burning a hole in my desk.'

It wasn't until I saw Andy in his suit, white shirt and black tie that I remembered he'd been at Callum Galbraith's funeral.

'How was it?' I asked.

'Mobbed. I'll tell you one thing: the cops know how to give a right good send off. It was standing room only in the Church and they could have sold tickets for the graveside.'

'What did you dig up?' Perhaps not a great choice of words.

120

'Nothing very helpful. No-one had a bad thing to say.'

I hadn't expected there to be anyone bad-mouthing the deceased at his funeral but there had always been the chance of a few minor indiscretions 'I take it no-one knew who you were?'

'I got a few sideways looks, that's all.'

'Find out anything?'

'He was very into sport. Highly competitive. I heard a couple of cops talking about a fight he once had with another cop, playing football or rugby or something.'

'Go on.'

'He got into trouble over it. The cops who were reminiscing thought it was great, him going radge. But, basically, they all seemed to think he was a good guy and the sort of bloke you'd rather have on your team than play against.'

I remembered Crowe's mention of a fight at a football match. It wasn't much, but it was more evidence of Callum Galbraith's temper.

'Oh, and wait until you hear this,' Andy said. 'The night he was murdered, Callum Galbraith shouldn't even have been at home. He was supposed to be on a boys' weekend away. Apparently, every year him and some mates, who passed out of Tulliallan together, used to meet up for a weekend golf-outing, slash, bevy-session. Eight of them booked in at the Lundin Links Hotel the night he died. They played a round of golf Friday afternoon, had dinner and a few scoops, then suddenly Callum said he was going home. His pals didn't want him to drive because he'd been drinking, but unfortunately there was no stopping him and off he went. If he'd stayed with the lads he'd have had a sore head in the morning, but it wouldn't have been full of holes. Talk about lucky white heather?'

'Anything said about him injuring a boy? An assault or something?'

'One of his police pals did mention it. Said it was a disgrace that he'd been disciplined for it.'

'Don't suppose you got a name?'

'Jamie Frickleton.'

'You missed your vocation. You should have been a P.I.'

'Wasn't that hard,' said Andy, modestly. 'Apparently this Frickleton guy's a right wee ned. Legal Aid gold mine. Quite a few of the cops there seemed to know him. One of them said Galbraith should have been given a commendation not a suspension.'

'Any family members there?'

'None that I could see. The front row was strictly scrambled egg, deputy Chief Constable and other top brass.'

'What about his brother?'

'Didn't trap. A few people mentioned it. The brother's a bit strange according to what I could make out. A recluse. Lives up in the wilds on the west coast. Still you'd have thought he would have come.'

'And the widow?'

'Came to the Church with her parents. Arrived after the coffin and sat at the back. She had a policewoman with her and left during the last hymn.'

It was all very interesting but not a great deal of help to Isla's defence. Still, Andy had obviously tried his best and I told him so. 'On Monday morning I want a detailed file note from you about the funeral, with times and mileage. Set it out in such a way that we might actually get SLAB to pay for it.' The Scottish Legal Aid Board was unlikely to stump up for Andy attending a funeral without some fancy wording on the account. 'Call it a fact-finding mission or something. So,' I clapped my hands together, 'where's the indictment?'

Andy left the room and came back with a sheaf of papers. I removed the thick rubber band that was holding them together. The indictment with the murder charge, lists of witnesses and productions was on top, then there were copies of the witness statements taken by the police, most of which I'd seen already. Also, there were four A5 books of photos, bound in bright blue covers with black plastic spiral binders. The first contained views of the Galbraith's house, inside and out. The second showed the bedroom from a number of different angles with the dead body lying on the bed, the head and face horribly mutilated, blood everywhere. The third book contained pics of Callum Galbraith's broken tomahawk and a long, thin, blood-stained screw driver with a measuring tape alongside each of them to give an idea of scale. The photos in number four, the thickest of the four books, had been taken at the Crown's post-mortem examination. Most of those showed the deceased's naked body lying face up on the dissecting slab during various stages of the autopsy. There was nothing like a few messy post-mortem snaps to get the jury on the side of the prosecution.

I thumbed through until I came to the head shots. There was a shaved area on the scalp approximately ten centimetres square, showing the horrific wound. Elsewhere the ginger hair was caked with blood, black and thick as tar in patches. I stopped at a close-up of the deceased's face. I had only seen it after the flesh had been peeled back from the bone. The pre-dissection photograph showed the facial features hideously deformed and lop-sided, the right side swollen and a deep-purple colour due to haemostasis, the eyelid hugely fat. On the left side there was a concentrated mass of dark-blue puncture holes from the top of the cheek bone to the hair-line.

I put the photos to one side. 'Any more pinks?' I asked.

Andy pointed to a ring binder that contained additional documentary productions from the Crown. I opened it and took a glance at the contents which included Callum Galbraith's hospital records along with the final versions of the Crown autopsy and toxicology reports. I'd have to check them thoroughly later, but I didn't expect any of the findings to be inconsistent with those of Professor Bradley. I turned to the part of the autopsy report headed: Time of Death. Based on body temperature, rigor and livor mortis, it was stated as sometime between 22:00 hours and 01:00; earlier than I had expected, given that Isla hadn't dialled 999 until after six in the morning; however, there was no evidence of the body having been moved. A horrible picture came to mind of Isla sitting by her murdered husband's side, shocked and traumatised and unable to comprehend the terrible thing she had done.

I went straight to the meat of the report. Under the heading, Blunt Force Injuries to head, it read:

The scalp is shaved post-mortem for visualization. On the left posterior parietal region there is a straight lesion six centimetres in length, which has sharp regular borders and shows full depth penetration into the scalp with associated deep scalp haemorrhage. The apex of the wound penetrates the skull, fracturing the bone and extends deeply into the brain tissue. When the skin of the calvarium was removed, fractures of the bones on the vault of the skull were found. The fragments extended deep in the brain cavity. Clearly the wounds were inflicted by an axe or similar instrument... blah, blah, blah. *Opinion: This is a perimortem, potentially fatal injury.*

Part two went on in similar detail to set out the screwdriver inflicted wounds in a fashion identical to that given to me by Professor Bradley, with mention of damage to the brain and the left sphenoid bone, which, anywhere other than in an autopsy report would have been called the left temple. It concluded that these wounds could have been peri or post mortem but if the former, were, unsurprisingly, potentially fatal injuries.

I flicked through the toxicology report. The results of the tests on body fluids were unremarkable. Although there were some traces of prescribed medication in the blood the findings were negative for ethanol or any of the usual recreational drugs: cannabinoids, cocaine, opiates, amphetamine or barbiturates.

I was about to close the binder when something caught my eye. It was a copy of Isla Galbraith's medical records.

124

What were they doing there? Why would the Crown want to lodge those? Had Cameron Crowe taken on board what I'd said about the records as proof of Callum Galbraith's violent behaviour towards his wife? Was he opening the door to the compromise of a culpable homicide plea? Was the lure of a silk gown proving too much for him?

I pushed the bundle of papers to one side and stuck a yellow-sticky on top with a message to Grace-Mary, asking her to prepare an updated brief and arrange a consultation with senior counsel for the following Tuesday. That would be exactly two weeks before Isla Galbraith's preliminary hearing and also, as it happened, exactly two weeks before my trial.

'Oh, and this boy, Frickleton,' I said to Andy. 'Find out where he lives if you can. He could be useful. Put your newly found private detective skills into operation. Fish around some more and see if you can track him down.'

Andy flashed me a smile. 'Polmont Young Offenders.' He breathed on his finger nails and polished them on his shirt front. 'Anyway. Enough shop talk…' He gave his hair a few run-throughs with his fingers. It was different, I noticed: shorter, neater than usual. 'What do you think?'

'Haircut?'

'Yeah. I gave my usual guy a miss.'

'Very nice.'

'Should be for twenty-five quid. Hope it's worth it. I want to look my best tonight.'

The Faculty dinner. I'd almost forgotten. In fact, no almost about it. 'Where's Zoë?'

'Here's Zoë,' my receptionist said walking into the room. She looked totally stunning in an electric blue satin dress that hugged every inch of her figure.

'You look—'

'Never mind how I look. The taxi's outside and you two aren't ready.'

I stared down at my crumpled suit. Andy whipped off his black funeral tie and quickly replaced it with a silk number; all swirls and splashes of colour.

'Ready,' he announced, slipping on his jacket.

'My flight was delayed,' I said, lamely. 'I'll need to go home. Won't be long. It's eight for eight thirty isn't it?'

'No,' Zoë said. 'It isn't.' She turned on a four-inch stiletto and walked out of the door.

Andy was about to follow until I grabbed him by the arm and pulled him back. 'I'll be as quick as I can but do me a favour. When you get there, see if you can get chatting to Cameron Crowe.'

'Who?'

'He's the guest speaker. You can't miss him. If he was chocolate he'd eat himself.'

'And?'

'He works at Crown Office. He's dealing with Isla Galbraith's prosecution, but he's also taken a special interest in my case and I want to try and talk him into dropping it.'

The taxi tooted its horn.

'Why's he going to listen to me?'

'Just soften him up until I arrive. Buy him a drink. Make sure he gets the last after-dinner mint—'

'Dark chocolate gives me the skits.'

'That's right. Dazzle him with your scintillating conversation, and should my name arise in conversation, as you will make sure it does, tell him what a really great guy I am and how much of an injustice it would be if my prosecution were to go any further.'

'He'll know I'm up to something.'

'No, he won't. He doesn't know I know he's taken a special interest in my case. When I turn up I'll take over. Me and him will have a few drinks and leave the best of pals.'

'I'm not sure…' Andy said. 'Obviously I want to help. I just don't want to mess things up.'

'You won't.'

'Yes, I will. I'm no good at that sort of thing.'

'When did I last review your salary?'

'You've never reviewed my salary,' Andy replied as he reversed back into the room.

The taxi tooted again.

'I was thinking three percent.'

'Ten.'

'This is for your benefit too,' I told him. 'Your traineeship is on the line along with my practising certificate.'

Deadpan, he stared at me through the lenses of his black-framed specs. 'Seven and a half.'

Andy held out a hand.

'Five percent,' I said, and shook his hand before he could pull it away.

CHAPTER 27

I could tell something was wrong the moment I arrived home. The kitchen window was wide open and next-door's cat was asleep on the table. I ran through to the livingroom. Everything seemed fine. My bedroom looked the same untidy mess as usual; no sign of a break-in.

Puzzled, but satisfied that nothing was missing, I had commenced my search for a less wrinkled suit when, in the wardrobe mirror, a glimpse of bright blue caught my eye; a piece of cloth rolled up and lying on my bed. I partially unfolded it. A Glasgow Rangers' jersey. One from years ago. An old sponsor's logo on the front. Different beer: same toxic fizz-water. It was the type of strip Malky used to play in during his short spell at the club, before his injury. I picked it up. Let it unfurl. A bullet fell onto the bed.

Dexy Doyle. It had to be.

My first thought was to phone the police, but what would they do? Make me miss the Faculty dinner for a kick-off. Then they'd dust the cartridge for prints and, unless I was very surprised, find nothing and go away again with warnings to be vigilant. After that they'd probably want to take a statement from Malky, which would only serve to fuel his anxiety and make him even more paranoid, but, worse, it would involve my dad whose blood-pressure couldn't take that kind of excitement.

No need for the police. Despite my lack of success in Belfast, I was still of the opinion that the solution to the problem was to approach Dexy via his brother. Kieran was the sensible one. He owed me. If I piled on the pressure, using his gun-running daughter as a lever, he'd surely talk his brother around.

After half an hour, phoning various contacts, I managed to acquire Kieran Doyle's mobile number. I caught him as he was leaving a planning sub-committee meeting. It was the back of nine on a Friday night. He was on his way home and sounded irritable.

'I've been in meetings all day, I'm tired, I'm hungry and I'm not talking about this now and certainly not on the phone,' he said.

'I'll come and see you then.'

'Waste of time. There's nothing more I can do.'

He hung up. I called again - answering service. I didn't leave a message, just kept phoning until he took the call.

'I don't know who you are or what you're talking about,' he said, 'now, stop phoning me or I'll call the police.'

'Maybe that's what I should do,' I said. 'Call the police and tell them how your crazy brother broke into my house and left a live round on my bed.'

'I'm sure Dechlan can account for his movements today.' I had little doubt on that score. Dexy Doyle had people to do his dirty work for him. 'However, if you feel that a crime has been committed, Mr Munro, then I would strongly recommend that you report it to the proper authorities.'

A man in Kieran Doyle's position couldn't be too careful about what he said on the phone, and yet I thought I deserved better than his patronising remarks and curt, 'good-bye.'

I went back through to my bedroom divesting myself of my clothes as I went. A quick shower, jump into a fresh or, at least, a fresher suit, and I might make the biscuits and cheese at the faculty dinner.

I sat down on the bed and pulled off my shoes and socks. It had been a long day. I lay back on the bed and rubbed my stubbly jaw. My early start meant it had been a while since my last shave. I thought of Zoë in that dress, closed my eyes for a moment and woke up two hours later.

CHAPTER **28**

'Where have you been?' Andy asked, when I pulled up a seat beside him at one of several large round tables that had been relocated to the edges of the function suite to reveal an area of polished wood floor. It was the end of the night and the DJ was playing a series of romantic numbers for couples slow-dancing. 'I thought you were only changing your suit?'

'Fell asleep. Don't tell Zoë.' I snagged a passing waiter and ordered an Ardbeg for me and another bottle of designer lager for Andy. 'Where is the object of my affection?'

'Here she is,' said a voice behind me in an unaffectionate sort of a way. I stood to give my receptionist a seat. She remained standing, hands on hips, creasing the smooth outline of her blue satin cocktail dress. 'So, just to recap - while I'm trapped at a table with a bunch of conveyancers, chuntering on about standardised missives, whatever they might be, you're at home sound asleep?'

I apologised. 'It's been a long day. Let me buy you a drink.' Without waiting for an answer, I drifted over to the bar and returned a few minutes later with a glass of champagne, but there was no sign of Zoë.

'Moon-dancing,' Andy said. I didn't think anyone still called it that. When had I last moon-danced? It was with Cat at a friend's wedding. At the time we'd joked, half-seriously, about what song we'd dance to for our first waltz. It made me feel sick to think about it.

My assistant nodded his head in the direction of the dance floor where Zoë, in the arms of a dinner-suited gent, was swaying gently to a Commodores track. Whoever he was, he was tall. With his back to me all I could see of Zoë were her hands resting on each of his shoulders, her head bobbing into sight now and again and the occasional glimpse of blue satin. The couple turned around in time to the music. Cameron Crowe. He was staring right at me over the top of Zoë's head.

'Seems quite smitten by Zoë,' Andy said. 'That's the third time he's asked her up to dance. Better dancer than after-dinner speaker, though. Forty-five minutes, no jokes. I've still got the marks on my wrists where I tried to saw them with a teaspoon.'

His eyes still fixed on me, Crowe grinned and lowered his hands so that they rested on my receptionist's buttocks. Zoë wriggled and reached back to slap them off. I set the flute glass on the table. My assistant must have sensed my intentions. He grabbed the sleeve of my jacket. I wrenched free and strode across the polished floor.

'Mind if I cut in?' I asked.

'Yes,' said Crowe, answering what he must have known was a rhetorical question. He spun Zoë around and manoeuvred her away from me towards the centre of the small dance floor. I followed, aware that my actions were attracting attention. I gently lifted one of Zoë's hands and rapped my knuckles on the shoulder of Crowe's dinner jacket. 'I'm cutting in,' I said.

He twisted his head to the side. 'Piss off.'

Zoë tried to peel away, but Crowe caught her around the waist and pulled her tight against him.

'Robbie…' Zoë said through gritted teeth. 'Go away.'

I couldn't have heard her correctly. Even if I had, it was too late for I'd already seized hold of Crowe's trapezium in the sort of grip used to great effect by Mr Spock in some of the earlier Star Trek episodes. He released Zoë and spun around to face me, knocking my hand away, at the same time catching hold of my shirt front, yanking me forward. Crowe was a tall man; two or three inches taller than me. His nose presented a perfect target for my forehead. One or two more Islay malts and I might have been facing an assault charge as well as a counterfeiting rap. By this time the music had stopped and the lights were raised. People were gathering around about us. I tried to step away but couldn't because Crowe still had a bunch of my shirt in his clenched fist.

'Don't ever—' he started, but before he could say anymore, Zoë was between us, pushing us apart. Shirt buttons spilled across the wooden floor.

'Stop it!' she yelled. I raised my hands in mock surrender and took a couple of paces back. 'You - go and sit down,' Zoë ordered me and glared around at the crowd of onlookers until it gradually began to disperse. The lights dimmed and Lionel Ritchie started to sing again. Crowe watched my retreat, flashing two rows of perfectly straight white teeth in a sickening smile of victory. Zoë waited until I had left the dance floor and made my way over to where Andy was standing apparently frozen, his bottle of lager poised at his lips.

I wasn't sure if Zoë would resume her dance. I hoped not. Crowe apparently assumed that she would. Still grinning at me, he tugged her to him by the sleeve of her dress and roughly clamped her against himself, hands restored to my receptionist's buttocks. Zoë lowered her hands to the hem-line of her dress and hitched it higher. I was surprised, but not as surprised as Cameron Crowe was when she rammed a knee in his chuckies.

'You're once… twice… three times… a lady,' Lionel crooned.

Zoë planted her four-inch spikes and with an almighty shove sent Crowe sprawling across the dance floor, scattering moon-dancers.

Andy tilted the beer bottle, downed the contents and set it on the table in front of me. He wiped his mouth with the back of a hand.

'Right,' he said, slapping a hand on my shoulder. 'I'll get the jackets.'

CHAPTER **29**

'You can't still be hung-over from Friday night.'

Grace-Mary's remarks were directed at Andy who, Monday morning, was sitting, head in his hands, studying the wood-effect surface of his self-assembled desk. 'Don't,' he muttered, 'Just don't.'

I'd already tipped-off my secretary that the Faculty dinner had not been an unalloyed success, but she wanted the full SP. We adjourned to my room, with Andy tagging along.

'Well, let's have it,' Grace-Mary said. 'It can't have been that bad.'

Zoë joined us on the pretext of doing a spot of filing. She was carrying a wire tray full of letters and wearing an ultra-tight black satin blouse.

'I'm really sorry about Friday night,' I said to her. 'If I'd been there earlier maybe things wouldn't have become quite so… complicated.'

The phone rang in reception. Zoë laid the wire-basket on top of the filing cabinet and left my room to answer it.

'Is someone going to tell me what happened?' Grace-Mary, demanded. 'The Faculty Dinner, how did it go?'

'Let me see,' Andy said, looking up at the ceiling, tapping his chin with a finger. 'On a scale of one to ten where ten is Robbie continuing to practice law and one is me stacking shelves at Tesco, I'd say Friday night's efforts come in at around a big fat zero.'

Grace-Mary cocked her head at him. 'What are you on about?'

'I'm on about that pair!' Andy exploded. 'Robbie and Zoë.'

'Oh, no you don't,' Zoë said, returning sooner than expected. 'Don't try and pin the blame on me. Have you told Grace-Mary about your great idea? About your cunning plan that I should chat up that Cameron Crowe person and see if he'd drop the case against Robbie?'

Sounded like Andy had been doing a spot of delegating.

'Oh, yes,' Zoë said, wrenching open a drawer in the filing cabinet and removing some folders. 'Don't know why I agreed. It was such a stupid idea, but...' she sighed like a martyr, 'I let that horrible man buy me a drink—'

'I bought him one too,' Andy interjected. 'I've got the receipt for that, by the way, Robbie.'

Zoë continued. 'Then after the meal we talked, danced, I told him all about you, how you were a super boss and a generally great guy and how unfair it would be if you got done...' She stopped for a breath and plonked a stack of files on top of my desk. 'I'm not sure if I was getting through to him but we'll never know because that's when you arrived, Robbie, and, as we know, the rest is history.' She studied the fingers on one hand. 'I broke one of my best nails.'

'Well...' I wasn't really sure what to say. 'Thanks for trying.'

But Zoë hadn't quite finished with Andy. 'So, if anyone's to blame it's you.' She jabbed a finger at him. 'Don't know why I listened to you. We all want Robbie to get off, but asking me to throw myself at that man... Only an idiot would think up something like that.'

I wasn't greatly amused about Andy propelling Zoë into the moon-dancing clutches of Cameron Crowe, but I couldn't help thinking my assistant had shown some initiative and, after all, he might have been thinking about me and not just his traineeship. I thought I'd spare him further grief. While Zoë was taking a breath, I shoved the stack of files on my desk in his direction.

'Andy,' I said. 'Take a look at these will you? I'd like you to nip along to the Court this afternoon and cover for me. I've got to be somewhere else.'

He took the files and glanced at them suspiciously. 'These are for the Sheriff Court. Me? Really? The Sheriff Court?'

I had never intended to let my assistant loose in the Sheriff Court this early in his career. Still, it was only a few DTTO reviews, and since the hearings for drug treatment and testing orders were held in private and the clients usually out of their faces on methadone, hopefully, no-one who mattered would know if Andy made a hash of things.

'So, what are you going to do about your case?' Grace-Mary enquired of me. 'Unless of course Andy has a plan B.'

Andy wasn't listening. He was eagerly flicking through the DTTO files.

'There's only one thing for it,' I told my secretary. 'I think I may have to tell the truth. But before I do there's someone I have to speak to.'

CHAPTER **30**

The home of Turpie (International) Salvage Ltd was a vast lunar landscape covered in heaps of rusting motor cars and heavy plant machinery. Jake's operation was spread across a hundred square acres of prime West Lothian scrub-land and the office, or administration centre, as his headed notepaper referred to it as, was a dilapidated prefabricated cabin served by a set of rickety wooden steps and guarded by an irritable mutt of indeterminate pedigree.

Jake was busy doing something behind a curtain that partitioned the cabin. He shouted through to me to wait, so I sat down on the orange-upholstered window seat at the far end of the cabin and picked up a recent edition of the Linlithghowshire Journal & Gazette: a big name for a small local newspaper. There was an old picture of Malky on the front page. He was squatting next to a football and wearing a pair of the tight shorts so admired by Zoë's sister. The article was headed: *Footballer Survives Death Crash* and went on in some detail about Malky's career with only a brief reference to the *accident* that had led to the death of *a friend*. The nearest it came to apportioning blame was to mention that, *no other vehicle was involved*.

After I'd read the article I got up to find out what was keeping Jake.

'I'll be right with you,' he said, noticing my head poking around the curtain, but not taking his gaze from the man seated across from him at a shoogly Formica table in what served as the kitchen. Two mugs, a milk carton, a burst bag of sugar and some plastic teaspoons had been pushed aside to make room for the man's left arm. The sleeve of his shirt was rolled up to mid-forearm, revealing a number of homemade

136

India-ink tattoos, his wrist pinned to the table by Jake's not so charming assistant, Big Deek Pudney. Before I could say or do anything to intervene, Jake brought a two-pound ball-hammer down with impressive accuracy on the man's ring finger. He'd obviously practised on the man's pinky because it too was a bloody pulp. The man screamed but little sound escaped the yellow tennis ball stuffed in his mouth.

Once the man had stopped shaking, Jake grabbed him by the hair and wrenched his head back. 'Any questions or have I made myself clear?

The man's frantic nods indicated that matters were crystalline. Jake held the hammer up to the man's frightened face. 'I can explain in more detail if you like. You have got eight more fingers after all.' The man's eyes were wide and showing mostly white. His head thrashed wildly from side to side. A spray of sweat and snotters landed on the table, dissolving granules of spilled sugar.

'Good,' Jake said. 'Then we've made some produce today.'

I supposed he meant progress; whatever, the man with mush for fingers seemed to understand well enough.

Deek yanked the man to his feet.

'You can go now,' Jake said to him, wiping the blood off his hammer with a grubby J-Cloth and putting it back in the drawer of a filing cabinet that so far as I could see held no files, only a selection of tools.

The man was frozen to the spot, too scared to move. 'On you go,' Jake said, reassuringly. The man tottered to the door, keeping a wary eye on Jake, not wanting to turn his back on the evil wee sod in the oil-stained overalls. He reached the door. The dog at the bottom of the stairs growled a warning. The man hesitated.

Jake walked over to him. The man cowered, his injured hand hanging limply at his side, the other raised to protect his face. Jake swatted the hand away, seized the tennis ball and wrenched it out of the man's mouth, trailing strings of

137

saliva. 'Where d'ye you think you're going with the dug's baw?' He pushed the man in the back sending him head first down the wooden steps and then turned to me. 'What brings you here?'

I folded the newspaper. 'I'm here about you and Andy.'

Still holding the door open Jake watched as his victim staggered off. 'Who?'

'Andy Imray. He works for me. Got you off that speeder the other week there.'

'Aye, that's right. Good lad. Knows his stuff.'

'You bunged him fifty quid.'

'I'm a generous man.'

Jake put his fingers to his lips and blasted a whistle. In response the mutt came up the stairs and into the cabin. It sniffed about warily. Jake tapped the wobbly table with his hand.

'It was a snider. And not a very good one,' I said.

'Tell me about it.' Jake went to an overhead cupboard, lifted the door and took down a shoe-box. He removed the lid to show me bundles of fifties. He tossed one to me. I riffled through the notes. Each had the same serial number. The paper also felt slightly strange, not bad, just not quite right. I'd been too busy trying to impress Zoë to notice.

'What am I supposed to do with this crap?' Jake asked me. He returned the bundle to the shoe-box and put it back in the cupboard. 'I've just been explaining to my supplier that quality is going to have to improve.'

'The problem is, Jake,' I cleared my throat. 'I spent the fifty and now I've been charged.'

He laughed, finding a funny side that, hitherto, I hadn't known existed. He shrugged. 'That's too bad but I'm not sure what I can do about it. You're the lawyer. I'm just a scrappy.' You wouldn't be thinking of doing anything stupid, Robbie? You know how me, and the police haven't always seen eye to eye in the past.'

He glanced over at the filing cabinet where he'd put the hammer.

I thought I'd let the topic drop for the moment.

The dog put its forelegs on the shoogly table and started to clean the surface with its tongue, licking off a mixture of body fluids and sugar.

Jake picked up the newspaper. 'See your brother's in the news again. What a boy.' Jake had come over all starry-eyed. 'And what a player. D'ye mind his goal in the cup final?' He stuck his shiny bald head forward, miming a header. 'Pure genius.' I'd never before heard Jake say anything nice about anyone.

The dog stopped licking the table and began sniffing at the bag of sugar. Jake tossed the damp tennis ball in his hand. 'Used to use a light bulb,' he reminisced. 'Must be getting soft.' He threw it out of the door and the mutt ran off after it. 'Now - unless there was something else - I've work to do.'

CHAPTER 31

The consulting rooms at Polmont Y.O.I. were all taken, so, rather than wait for one to become free, I'd volunteered to see the prisoner in the main recreation area as it would be empty for another hour until the start of open visits.

'They said this was an agent's visit but you're not my lawyer.'

'Quite correct, Jamie,' I said, as the young offender dropped into the seat opposite me. They'd removed the old round wooden tables which had been wide and set at an uncomfortably low height to help make any unauthorised transfer of material between visitor and prisoner more noticeable to the screws. We sat down at one of the new, much smaller, rectangular tables that was covered in a shiny grey laminate. 'I'm someone else's lawyer and I've come here to ask you a few questions that might help their case.'

He sat back and sniffed.

'Callum Galbraith.'

'That your client?'

'No, that's who I want to speak to you about: police constable Callum Galbraith. He broke your arm a few years back.'

'Him? I've news for you - he's dead. His missus plunged him. It was in the paper.'

'I'm acting for his missus.'

'What's that got to do with me?'

'I'm looking for information on him.'

'Like what?'

'Like how he came to break your arm.'

He glanced around, bored, looking to see who else was in, but the place was deserted apart from a passman emptying bins and sweeping up in between the ranks of tables, and a couple of screws standing chatting over at the door to the closed visit rooms.

'Your arm,' I said, bringing his attention back to me.

He sniffed and ran a hand across his throat. 'Hot in here init? I'm dead thirsty.'

I took the hint. 'Where did it happen?' I asked upon my return from the vending machine.

He opened the plastic bottle, drank most of the contents in one go and burped. 'The SPAR at my place.'

'Spray-painting it, were you?'

He shrugged and sniffed simultaneously.

'Anything profound?'

'Eh?'

'What were you writing?'

'Just tagging it.'

'The shopkeeper - Asian?'

'We called him Bin Laden.' He finished the bottle with another long swig, tried to burp again but managed only a squeak.

'So, what happened? What did Galbraith do to you?'

He screwed the top back on the bottle, laid it on the table and gave it a spin. 'One minute my mates are all there, next thing they've bolted. I look up and it's the polis. One of them grabs me by the arm, I pull away. He caws the legs from under me, I fall over and pop.'

The bottle slowed and came to a stop. He went to give it another spin, but I pulled it away and stood it upright out of his reach.

'Pop?'

'Aye. My shoulder. Kept coming out after that. Just needed to roll over in bed the wrong way. Had to get an operation and everything.' He pulled an arm out of a sleeve and lifted his orange polo-shirt up to reveal the clean arc of a surgical scar above his left shoulder.

'How old were you?'

'Thirteen. But I'm seventeen now and out of here the day before my eighteenth. Ya beauty!' He punched the air. One of the screws glanced over and shouted at him to behave.

'That it? Did he do anything else? Hit you a couple of digs, maybe?' I asked, perhaps over optimistically.

'Naw, he was brand new. Got Bin Laden to give me a fag and everything to keep me calm 'til the ambulance came.'

'How much money did you get for it?'

'Supposed to be two and a half but it was one of them no win no fee lot. By the time they'd taken their cut it was fifteen hundred I got, well ma maw got.'

Two thousand five hundred. The classic nuisance value settlement. Made with no admission of liability and probably just before Christmas. His mum would have jumped at it.

'What are you in for?' I asked.

'Fire-raising.'

'How long did you get?'

'Two year.'

With remission he'd do one. No doubt he'd have been out sooner if his mum had let him go home on a tag. She was probably enjoying the break.

'Only two month to go,' he called over to the screws. 'I've spent longer in the shower.'

'Wouldn't be saying that if this was still the Borstal,' one of the screws called back at him. 'No Playstation or Sky TV back then, son. A short sharp shock. That would have sorted you.'

The Thatcherite in the navy-blue uniform returned to the conversation with his colleague.

I stood.

The prisoner sniffed a long snottery one and swallowed. 'You going to need me for a witness or something? I wouldn't mind a day out of this place.'

I couldn't dislodge the notion that a jury would take one look at the ned in the orange polo shirt and wish Callum Galbraith had dislocated more than just his shoulder.

142

'I don't think so.'

''fore you go, gonnae get us a Mars Bar?'

Prices weren't any cheaper in the nick. The chocolate fell with a thud into the tray of the vending machine. I threw it over to the prisoner and he caught it in both hands.

'Cheers,' he said. 'Mr Galbraith brung a whole pack of these when he came to see me in hospital. Brand new so he was.'

CHAPTER **32**

The Faculty of Advocates had excellent consulting rooms on the Royal Mile at One Hundred and Forty-Two the High Street. They were part of a modern, purpose-built facility, centrally located and in regular use. So why was it, I wondered, that instead of meeting there, Ranald Kincaid Q.C. was leading Isla Galbraith and me down a narrow, winding and seemingly endless staircase into the uttermost bowels of Parliament House? Could it be so that fewer people would see him dirtying his civil hands with a criminal client and her nasty Legal Aid lawyer? I couldn't help but notice that the Q.C. was without his brief and hoped we weren't in for one of those consultations where counsel shook hands with the client, charged a whopping fee and then suggested another consultation, as well as another fee, in a week's time. Kincaid could screw the Legal Aid Board if he liked, but I couldn't afford to traipse in and out to Edinburgh on Legal Aid rates. Kincaid would be easily tucking away ten times what I was getting paid.

'All went well, Saturday night,' I said, by way of small talk, once we had reached the lowest level.

'I suppose you could say it was a success,' said the Q.C. He flicked at his nose with a crisply-laundered handkerchief before folding it carefully and returning it to his jacket pocket. 'Personally, I'd describe the whole thing as lurid and not befitting senior members of the Faculty or the Judiciary. I told Lord Dornion so on the night. The man was laughing so much I thought he was going to injure himself.'

Lord Dornion laughing? No matter how I tried, I just couldn't imagine the Lord Justice Clerk laughing at anything, except, perhaps, dishing out back to back life sentences to a bunch of peace-protesters. Truly, Malky must have gone down a storm.

We walked for a distance along a narrow corridor before squeezing into a tiny windowless room, the only contents of which, apart from a tatty-old rug, were three hard chairs and a 1960's oval-shaped coffee table that had some pieces of blank A4 paper lying on it weighted down by a huge glass ash-tray. I took a seat beside my client and laid my set of papers on the table. Kincaid remained standing holding the door open.

'I wonder, Mr Munro,' he said, 'if I might have a word.'

I stepped into the corridor with him.

'I'm extremely concerned about this case,' he said, closing the door after us. 'The Crown, I'm led to believe, is not to be swayed and intent on taking this matter to trial. Which leads me—'

'Don't worry. It's all brinkmanship.'

'Which leads me to believe,' continued Kincaid, ignoring my interruption, 'that I may not be best suited to your plans.'

He was trying to bail out on me. I couldn't let that happen. My visit to Crown Office had been only a minor sortie with the enemy; a softening up exercise. Soon it would be time to send in the shock troops. Kincaid dreaded Isla Galbraith's case going to trial, Cameron Crowe, as lead for the prosecution, had it in his power to do him a favour and see that it didn't; something that would do Crowe's career opportunities absolutely no harm at all. It was a match made in heaven with Robbie Munro playing the part of cupid. Once I'd primed Kincaid and fired him in Crowe's direction, I was confident any hurdles on the way to a plea of culpable homicide would quickly tumble.

'This case isn't going anywhere near a trial,' I told him. 'The A.D. hasn't ruled out culpable homicide and if I can set up a meeting between the two of you…' Kincaid looked as though he were going to protest. 'Armed with the necessary mitigatory information,' I assured him, 'the Crown will come around to our way of thinking.'

I could tell he wasn't happy, but, crisis averted for the moment, we returned to the small room and sat down. I edged my chair round so I was sitting beside him and laid out my updated set of papers on the table between us.

'We can share my set,' I said.

'No need,' Kincaid said. 'My junior should be here any minute.'

'Leonard Brophy's coming?' I hadn't told Leonard about this consultation because I didn't want him breezing in and chuntering on about almond slices or something.

'Yes, the new boy,' Kincaid said, 'the tubby one,' he added by way of clarification.

At that moment the door opened and junior counsel shoe-horned his way into the room. The small V's of toffee icing at each corner of his mouth screamed fudge doughnut. He looked in vain for a seat, put his senior's sewn-up bundle of papers on the table and left, returning a short time later with a high-backed dining room chair that he'd found goodness knows where and which was probably a rare antique. After a struggle and much chipped paint from the door frame, he managed to manoeuvre it into place between the Q.C. and me.

'Sorry, I'm late,' he said. 'Thought we'd be meeting down the road at one-four-two.'

Kincaid had spotted the toffee icing. He took the handkerchief from his pocket and mimed wiping his own mouth while staring meaningfully at his junior. Leonard took the hint and drew a sleeve across his lips, then he pushed his set of papers across to senior counsel, pulled my papers over to himself and began to thumb through them.

Kincaid crossed his legs, clasped his hands and looked over the top of his glasses at the client. 'Mrs Galbraith, the charge against you is a most serious one.'

146

Talk about stating the obvious? Leonard glanced up at me and rolled his eyes, then quickly, like a naughty schoolboy, returned his gaze to the new brief which Grace-Mary had put together for me using the latest batch of papers to come in from the Crown.

'Mr Munro has put together a fine brief. I can assure you that no stone has been left unturned.' The Q.C. gave me a tight little smile; it was convention for counsel to big-up the instructing solicitor in front of the client, but usually only when there was some bad news in the offing. Senior counsel sighed heavily. 'I know Mr Munro is of the opinion that the Crown will eventually accede to his request for a reduction of the charge, but, sadly, I do not share his optimism and time is fast running out, what with your preliminary hearing in only two weeks' time. Your husband was a police officer. According to the pathologists it looks very much as though he was asleep when you struck him on the head with a…' he looked down at his papers, 'with a tomahawk, and then repeatedly stabbed him through the temple with a screwdriver. Unless you are clinically insane, in which case you can expect to be sent to the State Hospital, I would strongly recommend you plead guilty at the earliest opportunity.'

Isla Galbraith blanched. Her bottom lip trembled. She turned and stared at me. Tears welled in her eyes. 'You said I wasn't to plead guilty to murder, Robbie. You said it would be that culpable thing.'

'And that's still the plan,' I assured her.

'Well it wouldn't be my plan,' Kincaid said. 'Plead guilty. Yes you'll receive a life sentence, but the punishment element will be discounted because of your early plea and you'll be eligible for parole all the sooner.'

Isla started to cry. I was out of tissues and Kincaid showed no sign of offering her his snowy-white handkerchief. I watched as my client rained tears onto the teak coffee table. I didn't care what senior counsel advised. No client of mine pled guilty to murder.

'The indictment has only just been served,' I told Kincaid, as politely as possible in the circumstances. 'Like you say, the preliminary diet is two weeks away and that means there's at least four weeks until the trial; plenty of time to turn the Crown around to our way of thinking. Take these.' I pulled the Crown's copies of Isla Galbraith's medical records from under Leonard's nose and waved them at Kincaid, who seemed more intent on studying a crack in the ceiling than looking at me. 'You're the Dean. Tell Cameron Crowe that if he knows what's good for his career and the reputation of Strathclyde Police he'll take a culp hom and like it.'

Kincaid took a deep breath and exhaled loudly. 'Mr Munro, I refuse to comport myself as though I were some kind of horse trader.'

Isla, head bowed, found a screwed-up tissue in her pocket and blew her nose.

I felt Leonard extract the copy medical records from my grip.

'Awooga, awooga,' he said.

Kincaid looked at him as though he were mad. 'I beg your pardon?'

Leonard took one of the sewn-up bundles from Kincaid's pile of papers and turned to Isla Galbraith's medical records: the original set she had given to me at our earlier meeting. He laid them alongside the copy of Isla's records sent to me by the Crown, and which now formed part of the updated brief. He slid both sets across the table.

Kincaid raised the specs from his nose and balanced them on top of his head like a pair of sunglasses. He lifted the documents, one set in each hand, and studied them closely. Gradually, his face darkened and the hands holding the copy medical records began to shake, at first slowly and then more violently.

148

'Thank-you, Mr Brophy,' Kincaid's voice was trembling with anger, 'for bringing this to my attention.'

'What is it?' I asked. 'Something wrong?'

Kincaid took a few deep breaths. He laid the two sets of papers down, one on top of the other and squared them up neatly on the table before him. He replaced his spectacles and looked me in the eye.

'Yes, Mr Munro, something is wrong - very wrong - and as such I am giving you immediate notice of my intention to withdraw from acting.'

I might have known. He had never wanted this case and now that his precious sports dinner was past he'd found some spurious reason for backing out. I had a good mind to report him to the Dean. It was just a pity he was the Dean. Without further ado the Q.C. rose, bumping a shin on the coffee table, and, bidding good day to junior counsel, but not to me or the client, he walked out.

'What was all that about?' I asked Leonard, as Kincaid's footsteps echoed down the corridor.

'The client's medical records,' he said. A smug smile had replaced the toffee icing at the corners of his mouth. I really wanted to give him a slap.

'What about them?'

I looked at Isla Galbraith. She had stopped crying and was holding her head in her hands and swaying gently, backwards and forwards.

'This set…' Leonard picked up the records Isla had given me at our earlier meeting, 'are different…' he picked up the records I'd been sent by the Crown and handed them to me, 'from this set.'

'In what way?' I asked.

'In many and important ways,' said Leonard. 'I'm afraid there's no doubt about it. Your client's copy of the medical records has been... doctored.'

After senior counsel's dramatic exit from the case, junior counsel felt the remaining contingent of Isla Galbraith's defence team needed to regroup, discuss strategy, have a scone on jam. And when it came to the search for the perfect scone, the quest began and ended in the Lower Aisle café in the basement of St Giles Cathedral, handily situated on the other side from us of the rapidly emptying Parliament House car park.

'Mind your feet,' Leonard said to Isla, pointing to a pinkish-brown slab about ten inches square in the middle of parking bay 44. 'John Knox,' he said. She stepped over it. I wasn't sure why. If the dead Calvinist could put up with a judge's car parked on top of him most of the day, what harm could come from one of my client's size fives momentarily stepping on his grave marker?

We entered through a side door of the cathedral and down a short flight of steps into the café. Once inside, Leonard made straight for a large plate piled high with fruit scones. Next to it was a glass bowl full of blackcurrant jam. It was late afternoon and the possibility that the day's scone supply might be long scoffed must have been a real concern to him. He grabbed a tray, laid a couple of well-fired scones on a side plate and slapped a great dod of jam alongside.

I wasn't being paid enough to sit watching junior counsel slobber over a couple of jammy scones and Isla was already in a state of some distress.

'On second thoughts,' I told Leonard, 'I think we'll go for a walk.' Leaving junior counsel to his snack, Isla and I set off down the Royal Mile, skirting a wide ring of spectators who were watching a juggler in true Edinburgh fashion: close enough to view the entertainment, far enough so as to disperse before he came round with his hat. *You'll have had your whip-round.*

'You must think I'm really stupid,' Isla said.

'Yes,' I said. 'I do.'

'You kept saying you wanted bad things to say about Callum and I thought how easy it would be to copy my records and add a few notes.'

'Did he ever hit you?'

'Never.'

'Not even the occasional slap?'

'No.'

The Clock on the spire of the Tron Kirk showed four-thirty.

'I'll walk you to the station,' I said, and we crossed the road and turned down Cockburn Street. We were at the top step of Fleshmarket Close when Isla broke the silence.

'Should I be looking for a new solicitor?'

'Let's not be hasty,' I said.

'But… Mr Kincaid…?'

'Counsel can be overly precious at times. Especially when they're being paid legal aid rates.'

'But, I lied to you,' she said.

I couldn't deny it, but a criminal defence agent refusing to take on clients because they were dishonest would be like a doctor turning away patients because they looked a little peaky.

'True,' I said, 'but at least you showed some initiative.'

Halfway down the steps we came to The Jinglin' Geordie, a pub named after George Heriot, the seventeenth century goldsmith much patronised by Queen Anne. He it was who founded the school that still bore his name, originally intended for orphans and the fatherless poor children of Edinburgh. Nowadays the school preferred children with living parents, rich ones who could afford the fees. At my suggestion we went in for a drink and after a glass of house

151

red Isla relaxed and wanted to know more about the benefits of an early guilty plea.

'Mr Kincaid was quite correct,' I told her. 'If you plead guilty to murder, avoid all the unpleasantness of a trial, you can't escape a life sentence, but the judge can seriously restrict the amount of time you require to spend in jail before becoming eligible for parole.'

'How long?' Isla asked, swirling the last drop of wine in her glass.

'I'd say you'd still be well into double figures for the punishment element of your sentence, so I'm not recommending you plead. I'll have another dash at the Crown, but I can't go empty-handed. I'm only glad I hadn't actually lodged your medical records in court or I might have ended up in the dock beside you on an attempt to pervert the course of justice charge.'

She knocked back her drink and held her hand out for my empty whisky glass.

'What would you like?'

'Same again,' I said, 'and an explanation would also be nice. 'A reason why you killed Callum. If he wasn't knocking you about, had he been unfaithful? Did he have a gambling problem? Drink too much? Were you sleep-walking when you did it? Give me something. Anything.'

Without a word, Isla took our glasses to the bar and came back a few minutes later with refills. 'Callum only ever drank wine with a meal and he hated whisky. He never really drank much at all. Just a glass of beer once in a while, if he was out with his pals or we were on holiday, but generally he liked to keep his wits about him. Didn't want alcohol clouding his judgement.'

He sounded like a real party animal.

'I know he injured a ned who was spraying graffiti,' I said.

'An accident.'

'More than that, I think.'

'He was just doing his job. I know he could have a temper at times, but he never took it out on me.'

Not what I'd hoped to hear. I wanted to give her a shake. There had to be a dark side to her dead husband. 'Any other accidents during his career that you know of? Was he ever disciplined for misconduct, anything like that? Do you know of any colleagues who might be able to dish some dirt?'

Isla shook her head and took a glug of wine. 'He fell out with a couple of the lads over a football match once. There was a punch-up on the pitch, he broke someone's nose and got suspended from duties for a fortnight. It was all brushed under the carpet. He never played again but I don't think he cared. Callum didn't socialise much with other police officers. He preferred his own company, and mine. We did a lot of hill walking together. I suppose it was our Highland upbringing.'

'What about his family?'

'There's only his brother.'

'Oh, yes, you mentioned him before. What's his name again?'

'Fergus.'

I sensed a note of hesitation in her voice. 'I'm told he wasn't at the funeral.'

Isla didn't reply.

'Don't you find that a little strange?'

'No,' she said curtly. 'They didn't get on.'

'Why not?'

Isla didn't answer.

'There had to be a reason.'

Isla finished her drink and got to her feet.

'It must have been something pretty important to stop him going to his brother's funeral.'

'No not really.'

'Then what's the big secret? Tell me. What did they fall out about?'

She stood beside me, gazing down at her empty glass. 'About me.'

A flicker of light at the end of the tunnel? With any luck a miner coming out of the pit carrying a big bag of filthy coal.

'Tell me more.'

'No. It's ancient history. Don't ask me again.'

She reached out to take my glass, but I pulled it away.

'Where is he – Fergus?'

She didn't answer. Just stood there.

'Isla,' I said, 'are you keeping something else from me? Is there something important I should know?'

She started to cry. I knew there was a lot for her to be worried about but her continual weeping was really starting to bug me.

'I'm sorry,' she said, eventually, wiping the tears away. 'I think I should go and freshen myself up. She handed me the wine glass, picked up her handbag and headed for the Ladies.

I went to the bar and ordered another glass of wine for her. After twenty minutes, when she still hadn't returned to our table, I realised I was going to have to drink it myself.

CHAPTER **34**

My ears popped as the train rattled west-bound and into the tunnel at Winchburgh Junction. What could possibly be so important about Fergus that the mere mention of his name had caused Isla to run out on me? And what was I going to do about the dodgy medical records that were now wasting valuable space in the briefcase resting on my lap? Emerging from the tunnel, my phone picked up a signal again and began to vibrate in the top pocket of my jacket. I checked the screen: my dad's number. No doubt Malky wanting to know how my discussions with Dexy Doyle were coming along. I bumped the call, but knew I'd have to try and resurrect negotiations with Cat's father sooner rather than later.

The train rolled on, hurtling by Turpie (International) Salvage Ltd, speed blurring the awkward shapes of former showroom specials, now crumpled and smashed and piled high, reminding me that my life had its own complications. How could I have been so stupid as to have spent a fifty-pound note that came from Jake Turpie? I should have known that if he was giving money away there had to be a catch. And why did it have to be a fake fifty? Why not a ten or a twenty? Nobody checked them. Fifties were such a scunner. Shopkeepers never had enough change; some places just wouldn't take them. If it had been a forged twenty, no-one would have noticed, but a fifty? People were always going to make sure it was genuine – everyone, that is, except me.

Having alighted from the train, I walked down Station Brae and trudged homeward along Linlithgow High Street, deep in thought about a forged fifty, a homicidal Irishman and a murder defence that had dissolved before my eyes. As I opened the front door of my flat, walked down the hall and into the kitchen, I was cursing my luck and thinking things couldn't get much worse, until I switched on the light and realised how wrong I was. Things could get a lot worse.

'What kept you?'

I jumped in fright. Sitting in a chair, picking at his nails with the tip of a knife was Angie Doyle's Romeo. He'd exchanged the green hoops for a darker strip, the sponsor's name printed diagonally across the chest, the shamrock on the left breast standing out brightly.

'What do you want?' I asked, rather lamely. What did you say in that type of situation?

Romeo swung back on the chair, his eyes on the knife as he dragged the point of it along the inside of his thumb nail. 'Dexy's not happy. He says you've been speaking to people across the water. He says you're a grass.'

'You're one to talk,' I said. 'Letting Angie take the blame for those guns. I thought she was your girlfriend.'

'She is whatever Dexy tells me she is.'

'And the shooters? They Dexy's idea too?'

The young man swung forward so that all four chair legs were in contact with the floor, at the same time sticking the point of the knife into the kitchen table so that it stood upright. 'I'm asking the questions. Where's your brother?'

'And if I tell you, you'll go?'

'Yeah. And if you're lying I'll come back.'

'And if I don't?'

'Dexy says I've to find out where he is...' he pulled the knife free of the table. 'Any way I can.'

'Okay,' I said. 'Let's negotiate.'

He stared at me all slitty-eyed. 'Dexy said nothing about negotiating.'

'Believe me son. There's always room for negotiation. Tell you what. Why don't I bung you a few quid and you can go back to Dexy and tell him I stayed out all night. How's that sound?'

'He said I was to wait until you showed.'

'Five hundred.'

He didn't reply. I moved closer to him and put my briefcase on the table.

'How about it?' I said. 'Five hundred cash.'

'You've not got it.'

I sprung the clips on the briefcase. The young man's hand tightened on the knife handle.

'Take a look in there.'

He stabbed the knife into the table again, pulled the briefcase onto his lap and swung back on his chair. It was now or never. I kicked the rear legs, the young man toppled, dropping the case, putting a hand down on the floor to steady himself.

By the time he had regained his balance and was leaping to his feet, I had seized my dad's pancake girdle from the cooker hob and brought it down to meet the top of his head. I raised the girdle again but there was no need. The young man dropped onto his knees then pitched forward, his forehead making a hollow sound as it cracked off the tiled floor. For a moment I was worried I might have killed him until he began to grunt and whimper softly. In his trouser pocket I found a mobile phone and, on the recent calls list, the letter 'D'. I pressed re-dial. The call was answered immediately. It was Dexy Doyle.

'Come and get your boy,' I said, and rang off.

I stuffed the phone back in the unconscious man's trouser pocket, took a hold of one of his ankles and was dragging him towards the front door when I noticed I was trailing blood across the kitchen floor. A carrier bag over his split-head stopped any further mess and actually made it easier to pull him along, his plastic-covered head gliding across the tiles and then over the wooden floor of the hallway.

At the front door, I ripped off the bag and the young man started to come to, groaning and moving about like he was in the throes of a nightmare. Taking him under the arms, I heaved him through the door and onto the pavement. On the street, double-parked, engine running, an emerald green Jag was waiting.

The Doyle brothers were dissimilar in many ways but clearly they had the same taste in motors. Dexy jumped out of the car, took one glance at his fallen comrade and came running towards me, his face a mask of fury.

I flipped him the prongs, turned around, walked into my flat and closed the door.

CHAPTER 35

Tuesday morning, I was mopping Romeo's blood off the kitchen floor when Malky rang.

'What are you doing?' he asked.

'Housework.'

'No,' he laughed. 'Really. What are you doing? You busy?'

'Oh, you know, I thought I might go into the office. Perhaps drop into court. Get some baddies off. Make money. Survive.'

'Okay, okay, listen, we need to talk. Dad keeps harping on at me. Don't get me wrong, he's a diamond but he thinks there's something up.'

'There is something up,' I said, in case he'd forgotten. 'Someone is trying to kill you.'

'Yeah, but you're sorting that out, aren't you? Look, I can't stay here any longer. Dad's doing my head in and he's started to ask questions. He definitely knows something.'

Typical. I'd told my dad to keep quiet about Dexy Doyle and already he'd commenced his enquiries. He'd probably opened a case file.

'How about I come back and stay with you again?'

That was a non-starter, especially now that Dexy Doyle was very much on my brother's trail. I hadn't mentioned the bullet on my bed and decided not to say anything about last night's visitor; not now that Malky was at last beginning to show signs of a return to normality.

'It would only be for a wee while,' he said. 'Just until you find me some more work, anything that turns over a few quid. One or two more after-dinners and I could rent a place of my own.'

'No way. You'll just need to stay where you are and be patient.'

'What am I supposed to do for money? Can't you find me some more work? And by the way, when am I going to see my end for that judges' gig?'

'Sit tight for the time being,' I told him. 'I'll see what I can do.'

I put the phone down. Who did you call if you wanted to find work for a clapped-out footballer?

The doorbell rang. Considering what had happened the night before I should have peeked through the spy-hole, but it was half eight in the morning, the sun was shining and I had an appointment with a bacon roll and a caffé Americano down at Sandy's.

'You owe her boyfriend an apology.' It was Dexy Doyle. He pushed past me into the hallway with Angie in tow and closed the door behind them. 'Four stitches and a lump on his head like Kilimanjaro.'

'What do you want?'

He turned to his niece. 'Tell the man.'

'You're sacked,' she said.

'Well, then, if that's all…' I gestured to the door.

'No, it's not all,' Dexy said. 'I don't want you speaking to Kieran about any of this, not about her…' he cocked his head in the direction of Angie, 'not about your brother. Understand?'

I did. Perfectly. Dexy had found himself a surrogate daughter; one that was actually prepared to pass the time of day with him. Kieran wouldn't like it, but that was something that needed sorted out between brothers and I couldn't care less about Angie and her rucksack full of shooters. The phone rang. It was my dad.

'Malky says he's going back to stay with you?' he said, accusingly.

'Can't speak just now, Dad,' I told him. 'Busy. Call you later.' I waved the receiver in Dexy's face. 'They have telephones in the east end of Glasgow. You didn't come all this way just to let me know I was no longer acting for young Juliet here.' He tried to speak but I wasn't finished. I wasn't really a morning person. Combine that with the memory of my late-night altercation with Romeo and the effects of caffeine deprivation and it could be said I was a mite tetchy. 'And if you've come to tell me not to smack your hired-help around, then don't have them break into my house in the middle of the night and threaten me with chibs. And you,' I turned on Angie, 'if you had half a brain you'd keep away from him,' I said, jabbing a finger at Dexy. 'Oh, and as for your boyfriend, I never hit him hard enough.'

Perhaps that was a bit insensitive. Angie seemed to think so at any rate. She flew at me. In a flash, her fingers were in my hair, twisting, pulling. It hurt. Those who hadn't been trained in the art of self-defence by their policeman father from the age of five might have instinctively pulled away; which would have worked but only as a means of losing a fistful of hair and allowing my attacker the chance to take a free swipe at me as I backed off. I did the opposite, lunging forward, colliding with Angie, knocking her off balance and causing her to fall backwards. She had to let go of my hair so that she could use her hands to break her fall. We ended up on the floor; well Angie did. I was on top of her. She landed heavily, winded, no longer a problem. Dexy was another matter altogether. I scrambled to my feet expecting him to come at me. He didn't. He backed off. 'Easy,' he said, bending down to help Angie to her feet. In panic, she fought him off, desperately gasping for breath.

'Stick her head between her legs,' I said, when satisfied the hostilities were over.

Dexy pressed his niece's head down and forward. Once doubled over she sucked in a great lungful of air.

'Just tell me where your brother is, and I'll leave,' Dexy said, still holding Angie's head down with one hand, the other rubbing the small of her back.

161

The adrenalin was pumping. I was ready to explode. He took his hands off the girl and held them up defensively.

'Easy,' he said. 'It's okay. I've been thinking - and you're right.'

'I am? About what?'

'About your brother. Is he here?'

'No,' I said. 'He isn't.'

'Then when you see him you can tell him I'm prepared to do a deal.'

I didn't believe him. 'And that would be?'

'I'll tell him face to face.'

'Tell me. I'm his lawyer.'

Recovering, but in no fit state to try and get frisky again, Angie shot daggers at me. Dexy told her to go wait in the car.

'I want blood money,' he said, once she'd left.

Dexy Doyle accept money for the death of his daughter? What would he spend it on? He owned enough pubs already and could only drive one emerald green Jag at a time. How could he enjoy anything that to his warped mind was paid for by the murder of his daughter? I played along. 'How much?'

'The flat in London for starters. It's was in joint names and the insurance will have cleared the mortgage on Cathleen's death. I want it signed over to me and a hundred grand cash on top.'

'I'll take instructions,' I said.

'Well make it quick. And tell your brother that once it's over I don't ever want to see his face this side of the border, understood?

CHAPTER 36

Paul Sharp was a man born a couple of decades too late, not that he was going to let that stop him. From the narrow lapels on his high-buttoned jacket, down sharply-creased drain pipe trousers, all the way to the tip of a pair of patent-leather winkle-pickers, he was a walking, talking advert for the swinging sixties. I didn't know where he got half his stuff. Finding suppliers of bri-nylon shirts, shoe-string ties and Safari-suits must have taken a lot more time and effort than reaching for an off-the-peg number like the rest of us, and his dedication didn't end there; he was also the proud owner of an ancient, but well-maintained Triumph Spitfire. He even sported a Sixties hairstyle, though, coming from Bathgate, the hair was easier to explain.

Seeing Paul just-a-walking-down-the-street and you might have dismissed him as another dedicated follower of fashion, or a nutter, but he was a good friend of mine and a fine criminal defence lawyer. I wanted him to conduct my defence if things ever went that far.

'Me?' Paul tapped a Woodbine on the flat of his silver cigarette case. We were standing on the steps outside Court 2 at the far side of Linlithgow Sheriff Court. The intermediate diets had finished and we lawyers were heading off in search of nourishment before the custody court started at two.

'They'll kill you,' I told him.

'So it says in very large black letters on the packet.' Paul put the cigarette in his mouth, swiftly dragged his Zippo down the sleeve of his jacket to flick open the lid, then back the way to strike a light. After he'd lit up he snapped the lighter shut and dropped it into his top pocket from where half an inch of square white hanky was showing. He blew smoke out the side of his mouth. 'Do you actually have a defence?'

I had a defence all right, but it involved my impeachment of Jake Turpie and, I supposed, my assistant. There were two main difficulties with that line of defence; firstly, because of the 'reply' in Dougie Fleming's notebook it was unlikely to be believed, and, if it was believed, two minutes after my acquittal the cops would either be off to charge Andy or kicking down Jake Turpie's Portakabin door in a search for counterfeit money. Even if they found nothing, it was the type of occurrence that Jake would not appreciate, and he was a man to express his dissatisfaction with events in a highly tangible manner usually involving industrial hand tools. I couldn't see any upside to the situation.

'I've got a defence - I've got the truth, but I need something better,' I told Paul.

'Better than the truth? Don't think my Gran would agree.' Paul dropped his cigarette. There was still most of it left. His smoking was more of a fashion statement than a habit. He trod on it with a pointy toe. 'Tell the truth and shame the Devil – that's what she'd say.'

'Well, let me know when she passes the Bar exams. Until then my defence is work in progress.'

Paul shrugged. 'Okay, sort it and I'll do it. Give me a call later. Not Thursday.' In answer to my unasked question he took off the court gown that was folded and draped over his shoulder. Holding it in both hands he mimed a golf shot. 'Blagged myself a ticket to the Pro-Celebrity. The boss was going and now he can't because he's got some big property transaction completing. I was knocking his door down as soon as I heard. The tickets are two fifty a skull. The only snag is I've got to meet up with this estate agent guy at the nineteenth and try and talk him into firing some conveyancing our way.'

My phone rang. It was Grace-Mary. 'Your dad's at the office,' she said. 'I think you'd better get here - fast.'

CHAPTER 37

'A gangster! A bloody murderer!'

It wasn't the welcome I'd expected when I got back to the office. Andy was eating a Pot Noodle and reading the sports pages, Zoë had gone for lunch and Grace-Mary had taken her place at the reception desk; not that I could actually see my secretary because she was obscured by the combined bulk of Malky and my dad.

'Right there on my doorstep! A terrorist!' my dad continued to bellow. Since I'd last spoken to him he'd obviously familiarised himself with Dechlan 'Dexy' Doyle's C.V.

'Dad,' I said. 'I've told you before about coming here and disturbing the staff. People are trying to work.'

Andy sucked his fork and flipped the paper over to the front page.

Malky butted in. 'It was Dexy. I don't know how he found me. He said he'd spoken to you this morning and that you were going to speak to me. He wants an answer - unfortunately Dad chased him before I could find out the question.'

'Can I get you something to drink, Malky?' Grace-Mary enquired as though suddenly I was running a cocktail bar. She had a stupid smile on her face. I knew the signs. Grace-Mary was as tough as they came. She treated me like an errant child, sales reps quaked at the thought of meeting her and she could frog-march an obstreperous client off the premises in a time that would astound the average nightclub bouncer, and yet in the presence of my big brother she metamorphosed into a giggly school girl.

'No thanks,' Malky said. 'I'd like to talk to Robbie.' He took me by the upper arm and pulled me aside. 'In private.'

We left my dad to fume.

'When were you going to tell me?' Malky demanded to know once we'd crossed the corridor, gone into my room and closed the door.

'Give me a chance,' I said. 'Dexy only came to see me this morning. I had to go straight to court. This is me just back.'

'Is it good or bad?'

I was still wondering that myself.

'On the face of it, it's good. He says he'll leave you alone if you transfer your share of the London flat to him and bung him a hundred thou.'

'That's blackmail!'

Extortion was the correct legal term, but Malky was on the right track. I couldn't understand why he sounded so surprised about it.

'The man was going to kill you and you more or less took it for granted. Now he wants money and you're outraged.'

'You think it's true?'

'Doubt it.'

'Why would he bother putting it to you if he didn't mean it?'

'I can think of only two possibilities. One, he wants to lull you into a false sense of security…'

Malky frowned at that suggestion. 'Or?'

'It's just possible, though highly unlikely, that with the lack of support from across the water, this could be his way of saving face.'

Malky seemed to like option two. He grabbed me by the ears and planted a smacker on the top of my head. 'Robbie, this is great. I think you've done it. I think Dexy is finally off my case.'

'Even if it's true, you'll lose the house,' I reminded him.

'I don't care. It was Cat who paid the mortgage on the place. I'd already agreed to transfer it to her. It was why we were meeting the day of the accident.'

'And the hundred grand?'

'I've a bit put away, not enough, not nearly enough, but hopefully he'll not want it all in one go.'

I couldn't see Dexy Doyle offering an easy payment plan for his blood money. 'And if he does?'

'That's where you come to the rescue again.'

'Eh?'

'You're my agent, stall him. Use your contacts. Get me onto the after-dinner circuit or set up an advertising deal and I'll have Dexy paid off in no time.'

CHAPTER **38**

The gown room at Glasgow High Court was hidden away at the top of a winding staircase accessed by a security keypad, the code for which was a rather unimaginative 1-2-3-4, and it was where, ten to ten Wednesday morning, I found Fiona Faye Q.C. buttoning up a voluminous white blouse over her impressive bosom.

'Ah, the lovely Robbie Munro,' she said. 'What have you brought me?' She stood to attention while, on tip-toe, the gown-room assistant reached up and wrapped a silk fall about her neck and fastened it under her chin with a single pearl stud.

The Q.C. reached out, took the lapel of my jacket between two fingers and rubbed the material. 'Legal Aid cuts beginning to bite?'

'It's a murder.'

'Excellent. Anyone we know?' She put her arms into a steel-grey, lace waistcoat and let the female robing room assistant button it up. 'Gown,' she said, like a surgeon ordering a fresh set of scrubs from a theatre nurse.

The assistant opened one of the metal lockers that lined two of the walls and removed a black silk gown in pristine condition.

'Whose rag is that?' Fiona demanded, eyeing it suspiciously. 'That's not mine.'

'No, ma'am,' said the assistant. 'Your junior, Mr Hetherington, sent yours away to be let out.' Fiona glowered down at the woman. 'I mean, altered,' she said hurriedly. 'Should have it back next week. Mrs Simpson has kindly said that you can use hers while she's on holiday.'

'Holiday,' Fiona snorted. She took the gown from the assistant and held it up for inspection. For a moment or two she studied the neatness of the crisply-ironed folds in the capacious sleeves and then put it on and admired herself in a full-length mirror, sideways and from the front. 'Too short, too wide, but I suppose it'll have to do.' She removed a dainty horse-hair wig from a black enamel tin box that had her name written in gold lacquer on the lid and balanced it carefully on the top of her coiffure. Fully dressed and ready for battle, she turned to me. 'I'm late. We'll need to talk on the hoof.'

I followed her at a pace out of the robing room, as always, amazed at how she could cover the ground so quickly.

'What are you doing a week on Tuesday?' I asked when we reached the bottom of the stairs and she stopped to allow me to open the door for her.

'What I'm doing right now I expect. Sitting, bored rigid, in a VAT fraud.'

She walked on and I trotted after her. We didn't pause until we were on the marble chessboard floor of the lobby outside the North and South Courts.

'Can you get away for an hour and do a plea?'

She looked me in the eyes. 'Plead guilty? To murder?' She gripped my upper arms and shook me. 'Who are you and what have you done with the real Robbie Munro?'

'Not to murder,' I said. 'I thought maybe, before that, you could come with me and have a word with the A.D.'

'Whose case is it?'

'Junior counsel is some girl Meadows.'

'And senior. . . ?'

'Cameron...'

Fiona raised one sculpted eyebrow.

'Crowe,' I finished.

Fiona held her hands aloft. 'Hold it right there, Tiger. Is this the policeman's wife?' She was onto me. 'The one the Dean dropped like a hot Catholic?'

The swing doors to the North Court parted slightly and a young man in a shiny-white wig peeked out. 'Miss Faye, the macer has gone for the judge.'

Fiona patted him on his horse-hair hat. 'Be right there, my dear.' She turned to me. 'What have you got? Apart, that is from some D.I.Y. medical records.'

She'd heard.

'I've got a young woman who's bashed her husband's head in with an axe while he was sleeping.'

'Yup, sounds like murder.'

'And then ventilated his skull with a screwdriver.'

Fiona shook her head. 'Where do you find them?'

'She's got no previous. Used to teach Sunday school.'

I flashed one of the photos of Isla Galbraith's black-eye that I had kept handy.

'No.'

'Oh, come on. What do you care if the Dean chickened out? It's not like taking it on might ruin your career ambitions. The day they make you a judge I'll be Law Society President.'

'It's not that.' She put a hand on the door, ready to push it open.

'What then?'

She pouted. 'Why didn't you come to me before now? I don't appreciate being second choice.'

My initial thoughts had been to instruct Fiona, but when the chance to instruct the Dean of the Faculty arose I'd felt sure he'd have the clout required to see everything end happily-ever-after for Isla Galbraith.

'Second choice? Never. You're the best. I know that, everyone knows that.' She absorbed my flattery effortlessly. 'It's just that you've been too busy. It's easier getting an audience with the Queen than arranging a consultation with you. And you're a bully. All your clerks are terrified to put anything in your diary until they've checked it three times to make absolutely sure you're not off on the ran-dan somewhere.'

Fiona loved it when she was ticked off for being a scoundrel. She took the photo from me, gave it a quick shufty. 'If you expect me to squeeze any juice out of the Prince of Darkness, then I'm going to need a sight more than your client's rendition of Jesus Loves Me and a dodgy mascara job.' She handed me back the photo. 'See what you can do.'

CHAPTER **39**

Wahid Sattar threw open the door. 'I'm not worthy. The great Robbie Munro.' He dipped in an extravagant bow. 'Please, come enter my humble abode.'

I wished I could have afforded so humble an abode as my former colleague. Kingsborough Gardens in Glasgow's west end, a townhouse in a terrace designed by Alexander 'Greek' Thompson or some other equally famous Victorian architect; even with the crunchiest of credit-crunches it had to be worth seven figures and the price had probably increased in the time it took me to walk from pavement to front door. I wiped my feet on an expanse of coconut matting and went inside.

'So, what brings you?' he asked, closing the front door and padding past me in threadbare tartan slippers and a maroon dressing gown with gold embroidery on the sleeves.

'I just happened to be in the area and thought I'd drop in to see how you are.'

'No, you didn't. You want something. It was the same when we worked at Caldwell & Craig. I'd not see you for ages and then you'd come into my room on the pretence of a chat and end up picking my brains about some crazy defence or other.'

He showed me through to a large sun-lit room where two small children, a boy and a girl, crawled about the floor, sucking soft toys, dribbling on the furniture and leaving indelible stains on the Axminster. I found an armchair under a pile of soft toys and sat down.

That it should come to this: Wahid Sattar watching the weans. No more for him the donning of the old tin helmet, fixing bayonet and going over the top into the bomb-cratered battlefield of civil litigation. Not that, with his steel trap of a legal mind, he'd ever needed to be good on his feet; such were his other attributes, his meticulous written pleadings and encyclopaedic knowledge of the law, the opposition had usually capitulated long before they reached the steps of the court.

'How's life at the Bar?' I asked.

'Are you kidding?' he laughed. 'With this pair to look after? I've forgotten what the inside of Parliament House looks like.' A toddler clambered up onto a small pile of buff files that were stacked against the far wall. 'In between nappies and din-dins it's all I can do to write the occasional opinion. Keeps my brain from stagnating, I suppose, but Debs brings in the real money.'

It was a sin; Wahid sitting at home writing notes for other lawyers when he should have been wowing them up at the Court of Session. It was like sub-contracting Michelangelo to Artex the ceiling.

'How is Deeba?'

'She's fine. Get down Fara! Still with Dickson Nimmo & Wright and biggest of the big in the A and M department.'

'Shouldn't worry, it's probably hormonal – after having the kids.'

'Acquisitions and mergers,' he said before realising it was an attempt at humour on my part. He gave me a wry smile as he pulled the female child over and poked a spoonful of gloop at her.

'Careful, 'I said. 'Some of that's going in her mouth.'

After a few unsuccessful tries to feed his daughter, Wahid let go of the child and she crawled off to wreak havoc elsewhere.

'Yes,' Wahid said with a sigh, 'Debs is off closing some deal or other. In London, no, wait, it's Wednesday, could be New York. Meanwhile I'm stuck here with the sprogs.'

'You seem to be coping all right, though. Twins can't be easy. After them a single kid will be a dawdle.'

'No fear. Two's enough. I've taken care of that.' He made scissors out of his fingers in case there was any need for clarification.

'Ouch.'

'You'd think so, but, not really. Bit of a disappointment actually. I mean, I was dreading going for it, but, I suppose, deep down, every man is sort of hoping the surgeon will take a look at his tackle and order in a squad of workies and some scaffolding. Instead all you get is a couple of toe-curling injections and ten minutes later you're a jaffa, waddling home to a salt bath.'

The toddler who wasn't Fara came over and rubbed his sticky face on one of my legs. I picked him up, not entirely sure what to do next. I smiled. He smiled. Then his features gradually puffed out until they fixed into a rigid expression of supreme concentration. The hue of his chubby little cheeks deepened and a powerfully wicked odour filled the room. I put him down and he toddled off.

Wahid laid the jar and spoon on the arm of a chair. 'I heard about Cathleen Doyle. Tragic. Must have been strange for you. Don't suppose you were too cut up about it, though.' Wahid caught the smelly child and toppled him onto a plastic mat on the floor. 'Sorry, that was uncalled for.'

'It's probably what most people think.'

'I also hear you've gone out on your own.'

'Over a year now.'

'Couldn't believe it when someone told me. I thought you were in with the bricks at C & C. Youngest partner in a hundred years.'

'They stopped doing legal aid work.'

'How noble of you.'

'Not really. Justice may be blind, but the other partners weren't, not for the bottom line. I was given a choice: turn my back on a life of crime or take up my green forms and walk. I walked. It was for the best. It's been slow, still, things are beginning to pick up. I've an assistant – Andy Imray. I've got high hopes for him. He has a good grasp of the law and he's young and hungry. Like you were before…'

'Before Deeba?'

Much to my dismay, Wahid whipped the nappy off the child on the mat.

'Lie still, Latif,' he said, raising the baby's legs and setting about its hindquarters with a handful of wet-wipes. He looked up at me. 'What it is to be young and hungry.'

I averted my eyes, no longer wishing to discuss hunger or anything at all associated with food. I had hoped to broach my difficulties in a more roundabout manner, but at that precise moment my driving ambition was to get out of that room and to breathe in some fresh air.

'Cameron Crowe,' I said after Wahid had slapped on some cream and parcelled-up the baby's now spotless behind in a disposable nappy that had little teddy bears printed along the waist band.

'What about him?'

'He's a shit.'

'You came here to tell me something of which I am already well aware?'

'Do you ever see him?'

'Not if I can help it.'

'How well do the two of you get along?'

'There are no hard feelings that I know of – then again, I never tried to wheech the knickers of his fiancée while he was collecting her coat.'

'We kissed, *and* it was only their second date.'

Wahid laughed. 'Are you looking for some kind of favour?' He laughed again. 'Of course you are, or why else would you be here? I very much suspect that unlike me,' he glanced down at the soiled nappy, 'you have a life – and a career.'

'The career part is a bit up in the air at the moment. That's why I'm here.' I told him about the fake fifty and Crowe's special interest in the matter of my prosecution.

'And you think I can talk him into dropping the charges?'

'You've things in common. You worked together at Caldwell & Craig. You're both at the Bar - you being senior to him...'

'That's it, isn't it? You think because we're both members of Faculty, I've got some kind of leverage.'

'Well don't you?'

'There's no secret handshake, if that's what you mean. Speak to him yourself.'

'I think I may have burnt that particular boat.'

'How badly?'

'Viking funeral badly. That's why I thought you might... you know, have a word.'

Wahid rolled the nappy into a ball and plopped it into an orange, scented disposal bag that had its work cut out. 'You know I'd like to help, Robbie, but this is your problem, you've got to face it like a man. Sit down with Crowe. Hammer out your differences over a drink.'

'Which blood-type does he prefer?'

'It's the only way.'

'What could I say that would do any good?'

'You could always try apologising. He'd probably respect you for that. Much better than me trying out the old boy routine on him.'

'What you actually mean is that you're scared of him.'

Wahid tied the handles of the nappy bag in a knot and lobbed it into a wicker basket by the side of the door. 'Petrified.'

CHAPTER 40

The golf ball soared into the afternoon sky like a little white dove with a rocket strapped to its tail feathers, eliciting a ripple of applause from the few spectators who, with apparently nothing better to do that sunny Thursday, had chosen to follow our group, or, rather, Malky.

My brother replaced the furry head cover and dropped the driver into his golf bag, like he was slotting a sword back into its scabbard after despatching a villain.

'Good shot,' said Steve, the young SPGA pro' who made up our three-ball. 'Better hope no-one on the handicap committee saw that one.'

Tuesday lunch-time, as soon as I'd evicted Malky and my dad from the office, I'd had Grace-Mary phone around and locate the organiser of the Pro-Celebrity golf tournament. As I suspected there had been some call-offs and has-been footballers were always in demand for such events. At first Malky hadn't been too keen but the mention of appearance money helped change his mind, as did realisation that the alternative was another day cooped up with my dad and his cronies, watching football DVD's and re-living his famous cup-winning goal.

'It was fourteen years ago. I'm beginning to wish I'd put it over the bar,' he told me as we searched for my ball in the rough. 'I never realised how skilful I was. I always thought the ball got fired into the box and I stuck my head in the way. It seems there was a lot more to it than that and wee Vince can prove it in super-slo-mo and from various angles.'

We reached the approximate area where my drive had buried itself in the long grass. I stamped around and eventually stood on something round and hard. I picked it up. It looked like my golf ball, but then there wasn't much to distinguish one from another. I tossed it onto the fairway and continued my slow progress to the green.

Malky missed a four-footer for a par. Steve sank his from double the distance. I slapped him on the back. 'That's why you're the pro. Malky, put me down for a six will you?'

'Why? Are you only counting your putts?' he asked. When it came to sporting activities my big brother was always a stickler for the rules. What was the big deal? It was a game. In my line of work laws were there for the bending, how much bending generally depended on the size of the fee. Malky put a ten on my card and marched off to the next tee.

The par three seventeenth at Linlithgow was a short dunt with a pitching wedge or, if you were me, a whack with a seven iron that scuttled along the ground, down the hill, across the green and into the canal at the back. The other two were still laughing about it as they holed-out at the last. Thanks to my performance we were out of the prizes. I put my lack of form down to the fact I'd had a lot on my mind lately. That and a paper-cut on my right index finger sustained on the edge of a particularly sharp legal aid certificate.

'You know, I feel like a weight has been lifted from my shoulders,' Malky said, as we were changing our shoes in the car park. He was really sold on the Dexy Doyle blood-money scenario. Call me cynical, but I couldn't help keeping a weather-eye out for snipers in the bushes. I had felt more at ease before Dexy had come over all conciliatory.

'Malky,' I said, 'I don't think we should completely-write off Dexy's previous threats. After all, nothing's really changed.' By which I suppose I meant that Cathleen was still dead and Malky the reason.

He chucked our clubs into the boot of my car. 'Calm down. Dexy Doyle's not going to try anything - not in broad daylight - and I've been thinking: first and foremost, Dexy's a businessman. When was the last time he was in any bother? Taking money off me is much more his scene these days.'

It was true. The small matter of half a dozen handguns aside, Dexy had kept a very low criminal-profile recently, and certainly his chain of drinking dens gave the impression of being legit. Perhaps Malky was right. Dexy had made his money, bought his pubs and, just maybe, he liked things the way they were. The older a man gets, the less appealing a prison sentence. Could be that my brother was entitled to feel relieved. I might have too if it wasn't for the fact that I could still remember the times I'd acted for Dexy and his associates. Some of the Crown photographs were still branded on my memory. Photos that showed or alleged to show – for it was never proven - what happened to people who displeased Mr Doyle.

I climbed into the car. Malky walked away.

'Where do you think you're going?' I called after him.

'If they're paying for the pleasure of my company, the least I can do is mingle. How much was my fee?' he asked when I caught up with him at the club house door. 'Five hundred?'

'Three. Well, two fifty-five - after my commission.'

'Not exactly the Nike deal is it?' he grumped as we squeezed our way into a main bar area that was heaving with golfers interspersed by the occasional D list celeb. In the middle of the room was a table stacked high with prizes. We were hardly in the place when Malky was dragged away by a couple of soap actors who were probably household names in some very sad households.

'Hey, baw heid!'

I recognised Jake Turpie's voice over the hubbub. Obviously, he'd had plenty of practice yelling orders over the sound of heavy plant machinery at his scrapyard. The stocky wee psychopath was sitting on a stool at the corner of the bar, his minder, Deek Pudney, beside him, sipping a lager tops and keeping an exclusion zone around his boss.

179

'Didn't know you were a golfer, Jake,' I said, once I'd managed to push my way through the throng. 'Should you not be at the yard crushing something?' Like cars – or fingers.

'Golf? That'll be right,' said Jake. 'Naw, I'm a sponsor. The thirteenth. Par three, whatever that is. Did you not see my sign?'

I hadn't.

'Oh yeah,' I said. 'Very nice.'

'I'm dissecting – into car sales.' He meant diversifying. I didn't put him right. He wouldn't have appreciated it. 'I'm having my whole yard done up and thought I should be doing more to provoke the new business.'

'You mean promote?' I blurted by mistake, still getting to grips with the idea that someone had actually managed to talk Jake into parting with cash for something as ephemeral as his name on a golf hole.

'Yeah, that's right.' He glared at me. 'Promote.'

A roar of laughter from Malky's group helped ease the tension.

'So,' I said, 'what's the beer like here?'

Jake pointed to the shot glass on the counter in front of him. 'Peppermint. My guts are killing me this weather.'

'Not easy to get served, is it?' I hinted.

Jake glanced in the direction of the barman who immediately shunned the hordes pressing in on the bar and came over.

'That dodgy note of yours…' I said casually, after I'd sipped the head off a pint of heavy. 'The one you bunged my assistant.'

Jake's face solidified.

'It did cross my mind,' I said, 'that someone might come forward and say they'd given the money to me and that it was all a terrible mistake. You could add any fine onto next month's rent.'

Jake snorted. 'I've not had this month's rent yet. And, anyway, I can't go getting done for stuff. I've just applied for my second-hand car dealer's licence.'

'What about Deek?' I suggested. 'It's not like he's going to notice another conviction.'

'Deek's busy that day,' Jake said. 'I think he's washing his hair.'

The big man grinned like a neep lantern and rubbed a calloused hand over his buzz-cut, pretty much exhausting that particular line of defence.

'So,' I said, 'how is the new arm of your business?'

'Early days.'

Which I was sure was his way of saying diabolical. Hardly surprising. Forget the dire economic climate; who in their right mind would buy a second-hand car from Jake Turpie?

'Like you say - you need to promote the business more. Get some publicity. Have you thought about having someone endorse it?' I said to a vacant stare. 'You know - someone help to advertise it.'

'Like a celebrity?'

'What about that wee bird that does the weather?' suggested Deek. 'She's here. I saw her.'

'Are you kidding?' I asked.

Jake winced and pressed a hand against his stomach. 'Like an acid pit.' He took a sip of peppermint cordial. 'The weathergirl. What's wrong with her?'

'We...ll, I suppose she's quite well known, but she's not from Linlithgow. You want someone the people around here can identify with. A local boy done good.

'You?' Jake asked, with what I thought was an excessive air of incredulity.

'Someone,' I went on, 'that people like and admire.'

'Not you then.' He took another drink of peppermint cordial. Cue hoots of laughter from Malky's group. Jake swivelled on his stool and looked over, his beady eyes zeroing in to fix on everyone's favourite ex-footballer. He jumped down from his stool. I put the flat of my hand on his chest. He stared down at it and then up into my face. 'Careful.'

'You want to speak to Malky?' I said. 'Then you do it through his agent.'

CHAPTER 41

The amount of dirt I had on my dead cop, Callum Galbraith, I could have put under a contact lens without making my eye water. If even the redoubtable Fiona Faye Q.C. wouldn't take on Isla's case it was clear I had a lot of work to do. That's why I couldn't get out of my head the guarded, yet highly intriguing, comments of my client during our drink together in the Jinglin' Geordie. With no other obvious line of enquiry, I decided that if I wanted to rake up some muck on the deceased his estranged brother would be as good a source as any.

According to information gathered by Andy at the funeral, Callum Galbraith's brother, Fergus, had a farm or steading somewhere along the way between Fort William and Mallaig, a forty-five mile stretch of the most beautiful countryside anywhere in the world and better known to all as 'The Road to the Isles'. I could have asked Isla Galbraith for directions but hadn't dared in case she instructed me not to go. She'd made it very plain that on the subject of her brother-in-law she had nothing to say, and, yet, it was her reluctance to speak of him, combined with his absence from Callum's funeral, that made me think there might be a rich seam of dirt there ready to be mined by yours truly.

So I decided to look north, though not alone. If, as I hoped, I elicited some helpful information from Fergus Galbraith, I needed a witness to it. I didn't want him going back on anything in court or saying that I'd pressurised him in some way. Zoë, I decided, would be the perfect travelling companion; she hailed from Oban and would have a better idea than me of the local geography. That was my story and I was sticking to it. Grace-Mary had given me a knowing wink when I'd made the announcement and Andy, at first slightly miffed, was placated by the fact he'd be given free rein on my court work while I was away.

The back of noon on that glorious Friday, we had rounded the top of Loch Linhe, climbed past Glenfinnan and were heading for Druimindarroch when I felt compelled to stop the car. 'How about that for a view?' I asked Zoë as she joined me to sit on a large roadside boulder, and together we gazed out at what seemed liked the whole of the Western seaboard opened before us, from the white sands of Arisaig and Morar, across the water to the dusky Isles of Rhum and Eigg and, beyond, the deep indigo of the Cuillin mountains. There was an old saying, that if you couldn't see the Cuillins for cloud you knew it was raining on Skye, and if you could then you know it was going to rain. But on this fine day there wasn't even the rumour of cloud or mist. The sea was a sheet of blue and a gentle, warm off-shore breeze brought with it the sweet smell of heather from the hills. I sat there enjoying being with Zoë, savouring the surroundings, basking in the sun and trying not to think of what might be happening at Linlithgow Sheriff Court. Andy, left in charge with all the court business, would either be in his element or flapping like a seagull in a force nine gale. I should have cared. I didn't. Not at all. Why did I bother? Toiling away in the industrial central belt of Scotland seemed a waste of precious time when a landscape of such breath-taking splendour was scarcely a hundred miles to the north.

'God's own country,' I said.

'Yes,' Zoë was prepared to concede. 'It's lovely when the sun shines, but take it from me, the rest of the time it's a rainy, midgie-infested wilderness with nowhere to go and nobody doing anything except making whisky or drinking it.' She said it like it was a bad thing.

All too soon it was time to cram myself behind the wheel again and set off once more on the quest. We had to be getting close. Along the route we'd stopped off at various outposts of civilization to ask the way to Fergus Galbraith's place and had been told to look for a farm called Ardfern, supposedly situated at the foot of the hills to the east of Arisaig. Nearing the village, we passed by one or two tracks leading off the main road and I was tempted to check them out until Zoë saw a sign for a hotel up ahead and suggested we make for there and continue our explorations after lunch.

The lounge bar of the Acarsaid Inn was a cosy pine-clad room with a couple of sofas either side of a fireplace in which there were no logs but an arrangement of dried wild flowers and grasses. There were some tables at a far window and, on the right as we came in the main door, a high counter behind which a barman was palely loitering, not to say swaying slightly. The window tables were taken so we sat up on bar stools. I fancied a pint. I asked for fizzy water. Perhaps I was thinking about Malky and Cathleen's fateful lunch. Zoë ordered a glass of Chardonnay.

'That's the white one, isn't it,' said the barman studying a set of optics that held a choice of two different coloured wines. His every action seemed to be carried out in slow motion, every movement an effort.

When at last we'd been served our drinks, a large friendly woman with a matt black beehive hair-do came over. She introduced herself as Netta and handed us a couple of laminated menus. 'I'll be your waitress today,' she said cheerily, before, in an instant, her happy expression changed to one of contempt. 'In fact, I'll do bloody everything,' she called over her shoulder at the barman, 'because someone got pissed last night and couldnae bite his fingers today.' She turned again to us, the smile restored to her plump, powdered face. 'See anything nice on the menu?'

We both saw a lot nice on the menu and agreed that so close to the port of Mallaig it would be madness to order anything other than fish. As, with some anticipation, we awaited the arrival of lunch, the door opened and a large man came in, breathing hard, sweat dripping down his tanned brow. He stood for a moment catching his breath. A Border collie threaded between the thick, hairy legs that exited from a pair of khaki knee-length shorts and descended into knitted socks and scuffed hiking boots. The man sat down beside us, ordered a pint of heavy and downed it in two goes while his collie-dog wandered about, sniffing inquisitively with, as Zoë soon discovered, an extremely cold and wet nose.

'Sorry about that, love,' said the sweaty man, clicking his fingers and bringing the dog to heel. Without being asked, the barman placed another pint on the counter and the man rubbed a hand up the condensation on the glass and wiped it across his forehead. 'He's young and I'm old and knackered trying to keep up with him.' He took a long pull from his drink. 'On holiday? Picked a good time. Best spell of weather we've had in ages. Should have seen it a couple of weeks ago - pissing like a brewer's mare it was.'

'Language, Norrie,' said the waitress emerging from behind the bar and setting knives and forks wrapped in red napkins on the counter in front of Zoë and me. As she did I noticed a bracelet on her right wrist. It was silver with charms of little fish and tiny filigree nets alternating around it. It looked familiar, though at the time I couldn't think why.

'As I was saying,' said the big man after the waitress had disappeared again, 'it's been hotter than hell this past week or so.' He took another mouthful of beer. 'Needed that.' He wiped froth from his top lip. 'Been sweating like a boxer's bawbag.'

'Norrie!' The waitress bellowed from out of sight.

'Tell me, what brings you up to the Back of Keppoch?' asked the man in the khaki shorts, unperturbed, his question directed at Zoë, eyes fixed on her sky-blue satin blouse. 'Business or pleasure?'

'Oh, just passing by and thought we'd look up an old friend,' I butted in.

He didn't look at me but gave Zoë a playful nudge with his elbow, 'as the gynaecologist said to the actress, eh?'

'Norrie!' barked the waitress returning with two plates of fish and chips that would have fed a coach party.

'Oh, wheesht woman. My mother's dead, who gave you her job?'

Cocking an accusing eye at the man in the khaki shorts, the waitress beckoned to Zoë and me and led us from the bar over to one of the sofas by the fireplace.

'You're better over here out of the way,' she said loudly, so that the man in the shorts could hear. She pulled over a nest of tables. 'Norrie's an acquired taste that most of the women around here have been fortunate enough never to acquire.' She placed a small table in front of each of us and set out the knives, forks and napkins again.

Norrie scooped the last of his pint. 'I'm a local character, that's what I am.' He rattled the base of his tumbler on the bar. 'And a thirsty one.'

'I'd bar him,' said the waitress, paying him no heed. 'If in a moment of weakness, I hadn't been stupid enough to go and marry him.'

When we were leaving after lunch and on the way back to my car, we met the man in the khaki shorts again. He was standing beside a battered and dusty Jeep that looked as though it might have seen some action in Korea.

'We're looking for directions,' I called to him.

'To your friend's place?'

'Yeah. His name's Fergus Galbraith. Owns a farm around here somewhere. I think it's called Ardfern.'

The big man laughed. 'A farm? Is that what he told you? Ardfern's a croft and you're a deal wide of the mark if you've travelled this far north.' He came over, turned Zoë around by her shoulders, stood closely behind her and pointed back the way we'd come. 'Go south five or six miles, take a left before the old kirk and it's another mile and a half after the road ends.'

He whistled. The dog stopped sniffing the grass at the edge of the car park and was by his side in an instant. 'That yours?' The man came over and cast a critical eye at my hatchback with its sagging suspension and low-slung exhaust. He kicked the tyres and shook his head. 'You'd better come with me.' He went over to the jeep, opened the passenger door and leaned the front seat forward.

'Come on. Get in,' he said.

'Are we under arrest?' Zoë joked.

'What d'you mean?'

She pointed through the rear window at a policeman's hat on the back, parcel-shelf. 'The hat. Are you the law around these here parts?'

He laughed. 'Oh. Aye. That's me. Norrie Baxter. The only law west of Fort William.' I was practically shoved into the rear seat, the collie jumping in after me. The big man climbed in behind the wheel and turned the key in the ignition. 'I'm retired. I keep the hat on the back ledge for when I go to town,' he shouted over the roar of the engine. 'Helps with the parking. The only policing I do nowadays is checking on the wildlife, making sure no-one's nicking sea-eagle eggs, that kind of thing. Keeps me busy and stops the wife from having to kill me.' He looked out at Zoë. 'Don't be shy.' He patted the seat next to him. Zoë gave me a slightly worried look, climbed aboard and we were off.

After a mile or so I thought I'd see what more information I could extract. 'If you know Fergus Galbraith, you might have known his brother, Callum,' I put to my guide.

Norrie, as he insisted we call him, shook his head and mopped his brow with a rag from under the dashboard. 'Can't say I do.'

'He's a cop. Or was a cop. He's dead now.'

'Sorry to hear it. Don't think Fergus ever mentioned him. 'Course he's a new boy in town. Hasn't been here more than five years. Gets about a bit, though.' He gave Zoë a sideways glance and a nudge of the elbow. 'Quite a lad for the ladies. Fond of a drink an' all.'

From which remark I couldn't help but recall the three pints our driver had recently poured down his throat and hoped that we wouldn't be waking up in hospital or, like Cathleen, not waking up at all.

'Aye,' Norrie said, accidentally groping Zoë's knee for the umpteenth time as he clunked down a gear and threw the car into a hard left-turn, 'let me tell you, there's not a single malt with which our Fergus is not intimately acquainted. The wife's aye trying to catch him out with drams from all over, but so far without success. She'll never do it now, of course. Not with him on the wagon.'

There was a dip in the road a mile or two after the Triagh golf course. At the bottom we took another sharp left onto a side road which quickly became a rough, pot-hole littered track.

'Got a bit of a problem with the falling down water has our Fergus?' I asked.

'I wouldn't like to say anything untoward about the lad. Him being your pal and all.' Norrie glanced at me out of the corner of his eye. He reminded me of my dad. His in-built police antenna might be rusty, but it was still functioning.

'I've not seen him for a while,' I said. 'Still, half the battle's recognising you've got a problem in the first place.'

'Ain't that the truth,' Norrie said. 'And a fine lad is Fergus. If he puts his mind to something you know he'll see it through to the finish.' Norrie spun the wheel and we lurched around another corner. 'Take the wife's bracelet.'

Of course. The charm bracelet. Now I remembered. I'd seen something very like it on Isla Galbraith's wrist.

'Don't know if you saw it.' Norrie laughed and nudged Zoë again. 'Fergus made that and what a palaver it was let me tell you. The fish weren't a problem; it was all those tiny wee nets. Intricate work. Took him ages. But she wanted nets for Netta, and you know what you women are like when you get your heart set on something.' He nudged Zoë once more and she just about managed a smile through tight lips. 'Aye, Fergus promised he'd do them and was as good as his word.'

'Is that what he does away up here – makes jewellery?'

Norrie gave me another suspicious glance, via the rear-view mirror. 'Aye, that's right. Does all sorts of stuff to order. Very popular. And not cheap either. Last I heard he was looking to buy a place abroad. Going to make his stuff here in the winter and sell it over there in the sunshine. Could be that's where he is now. Might explain why I haven't seen him for a while.'

We hit a bump. Any suspension the old jeep might once have had was completely shot and I felt like I'd been kicked up the back-side by one of Norrie's hiking boots.

'Feel that one, did you?' he laughed. 'I've been telling Fergus for long enough to chuck down a lorry load of hard core.' The Jeep careered on. I raised myself off the seat, bracing myself with rigid arms for the next jolt. Apart from our driver the only one who seemed to be enjoying the trip was the collie-dog, leaning across me, over the front seat, muzzle resting on Zoë's shoulder, tongue lolling out of a wide grin.

We climbed a short but steep incline and rounded a tight bend in the track. I hoped we were nearing our destination. The combination of a deep-fried lunch followed by a roller-coaster ride, not to mention frequent whiffs of dog-breath, was making me feel queasy. Another plummeting dip, a hairpin bend, the jeep skidded, spitting stones and came to a halt.

'What's this?' Norrie sounded surprised. The dog pushed its muzzle further over Zoë's shoulder, rubbing its wet nose along the side of her neck, all in the effort, or so it seemed, for a better look at the For Sale sign that was nailed to a locked five-bar gate.

190

CHAPTER **42**

According to the For Sale sign, Fergus Galbraith's croft was being marketed by a solicitor's firm in Inverness, and so, armed with a hazy knowledge of Highland geography and some general directions from Norrie, we set off from Arisaig thinking Inverness to be a short jaunt to the east. One hundred bladder-bursting country miles and two and a half hours later we'd learned that just because a village is officially within the boundaries of Inverness-shire doesn't mean it lies anywhere near the Capital of the Highlands.

It was dead on five o'clock by the time I parked the car and located the offices of Armstrong Liddell & Co. in a lane just off the main drag. There were four properties on display in the front window, three of which were ex-local authority houses in less salubrious parts of the city. Ardfern was advertised as a working croft, extending to 7.2 hectares on the Attadale Estate. The croft house, *'would benefit from modernisation'*, and garden were *decrofted*, whatever that meant, and it was offered for sale together with the outbuildings, *'in need of refurbishment'*, and the crofting lease of the surrounding fields.

We went in and were met by a woman in a hurry to be on her way out.

'The schedules are still at the printers,' she said, in answer to my initial enquiry, simultaneously looking over my shoulder at the clock on the wall that confirmed she was now officially working unpaid overtime. 'Should have them by Wednesday. Can I give you a call when they're ready?'

'I was actually interested in speaking to the owner direct,' I told her.

'Sorry,' she said. 'That won't be possible.'

191

Holding an arm out to her side, she walked forward in an attempt to shepherd me out of the door. I stayed put.

'I'm sorry too,' I said. 'You see I'm a solicitor. My assistant and I, we've come a long way and would really like to speak to your boss.'

'I'm the property manager.'

'I can see that,' I said, gazing down at the plastic plaque on her desk that gave her name and job description, just in case she forgot either one. Beside the plaque was a bundle of title deeds held together by a rubber band into which was stuck a scrap of paper with the word 'Ardfern' scribbled. 'And I'm sure you manage them very well.' All four of them, I nearly said, but I didn't think it would have helped any. 'Still, we have come a very long way—'

'So you've said already.' The receptionist took a set of keys from her pocket and jangled them meaningfully.

'Nancy!' a disembodied voice shouted from somewhere nearby. 'You still there?'

The receptionist breathed in through gritted teeth.

'Bring me those titles for that croft, will you?' The voice came, from an upstairs room.

The receptionist held the keys up in front of my face and gave them another little shake. 'Now, if you don't mind—'

'And could I have a cup of tea before you go?' yelled the voice. Nancy looked again to the clock. 'You still there Nancy?'

Zoë, who'd been standing behind me, stepped forward with a smile. 'Men, eh?' She tapped an imaginary wristwatch. 'I'll tell him you've left,' she whispered conspiratorially.

The property manager hesitated for a moment and then grabbed her handbag off the desk. 'First floor, on the left,' she said, and we'd only taken a few steps on the wrought-iron staircases when I heard the front door close quietly.

On the top landing there were doors to my left and right and one, promisingly marked W.C., straight ahead.

'That you Nancy?' Sure enough, the voice came from our left. We followed it to its source, a room located on the corner of the building with a view up the hill to the Castle from one window and across the River Ness out of the other. The office was small, the floor space mostly taken up by ancient filing cabinets and cheap MDF bookcases. It wasn't too dissimilar to my own. In the centre of the room sat a man with a bald patch right on the top of his head. It was slightly weird. He had a good head of hair except for right on the crown where there was nothing but pink shiny scalp, like a monk. I got a good look at it as I walked in for he was bent over, studying a photocopy map made up of several A4 size pieces of paper all stuck together by sticky-tape and spread over the entire surface of his desk.

I cleared my throat. The man looked up and when he saw me standing there he sat back, startled. 'Who are you?'

I went over to him, hand outstretched, ready to shake his. 'Robbie Munro. I'm a solicitor – from Linlithgow. That's near Edinburgh,' I said in reply to his blank stare. 'This is my P.A., Miss Reynolds, and you must be Mr Armstrong.'

'Liddell,' he said, emphasising the second syllable of his name. He raised himself a few inches off his chair and took my proffered hand in a firm grip. Formalities over, I gave him the bundle of title deeds. He took them, grunted and sat down again.

'Fine view you have,' I said.

He snorted. 'More than makes up for having to sit here all day buying Council houses at three hundred quid a pop.' Liddell was clearly a, the glass is half empty and there's floaters in the other half, kind of a guy. 'Know anything about crofting law?' he asked.

'Not as much as you do I'm sure.'

'I know almost bugger all.'

'Like I said…'

He folded the map. It wouldn't lie flat so he weighted it down with the titles deeds. 'Crofts. I could see them far enough. One wrong move and some poor hayseed can't graze his sheep and I'm being summoned to Drumsheugh Gardens to get strips torn off me by the Law Society Gestapo. And as for the professional indemnity premiums...' He stopped mid-flow and nodded towards the titles. 'The croft. That why you're here? Got a buyer interested in the place? Bloody quick. I'm still checking the title. It's hardly been in the window. Why don't you leave me your details and I'll sort you out with a set of particulars next week? Well, not me.' He smiled. 'I'll be away. But my property manager will do the needful.'

'Going on holiday?'

'Wimbledon.'

'Lucky you,' I said.

'Not really.' Liddell had managed to locate a lead-lining in his silver cloud. 'Should have had tickets yonks ago. My tennis club raffles a pair every year. The Williams girls were embryos when I first put my name in the hat and this is the first time I've been pulled out.'

'What's it like - the croft?' I asked, steering him around to the purpose of my visit. 'We went for a look, but it was boarded-up.'

'Never been down there myself,' he said. 'Probably a dump. According to Nancy it's in need of,' he coughed, *modernisation*. Estate agent speak. Probably means the place was raided by the Redcoats during the Forty-five and nobody's bothered to tidy-up yet.' He leaned back in his chair, yawned and stretched. 'You should have called ahead; we could have had a viewing arranged with one of the local boys.'

'The owner. Fergus Galbraith. What do you know about him?'

'Nice enough lad, I suppose. Friend of my son's otherwise I wouldn't touch a crofting conveyance. I haven't seen him in years. We've been doing everything by phone.'

'Good of him to give you the business.'

'Suppose. Although he'll be expecting me to sharpen my pencil when it comes to the fee, I've no doubt.'

'Does he keep in touch with your son much?'

'Don't think so. They were at Uni together. Fergus did some kind of Mickey Mouse course, logic and metaphysics or something like that. You know the sort of thing: two lectures a week for three years and at the end you get a degree you can hang in the loo if you run out of bog paper.'

Zoë tugged at my arm. 'Talking of which… it was quite a long drive from Arisaig.'

Liddell took the hint. 'Out the door and left.'

I smiled apologetically. Liddell sighed. 'Follow her. The gents' is just along a bit.

When I returned, Liddell was thumbing through the Scottish Solicitors Law Directory. I sat down opposite him. He looked up.

'Munro, you said?'

I nodded.

'And you say you're a solicitor? Strange because I can't find any mention of you in the White Book.'

'Your copy's three years old,' I said. 'Try Glasgow, under Caldwell & Craig.'

'C & C?' He whistled softly. 'Playing with the big boys were you? How come you can't tell me how to sell a croft? I thought that lot were always buying and selling estates for the landed gentry.' He leafed through the Directory again. 'Ah, here you are. You've moved. What's the state of the housing market like in Lesmahagow?'

'Linlithgow. And it's booming, I expect. Usually is. Even with the credit crunch.'

He stared hard at me. 'You expect?' He closed the book and laid it to one side. 'You're not really here about the croft, are you? You're not even a conveyancer.'

He said it as though he'd unmasked one not of the brotherhood.

195

'I didn't say I was. I'm a defence lawyer and I'm looking for information on Fergus Galbraith.'

'And why might that be?'

'His brother was murdered and I want to ask him some questions.'

'Is he a suspect?'

'No, and I'm not the police. I only want to meet him and get some background information that might give me a better understanding of what is a very strange case.'

'Sorry. Can't help you.'

'Do you have an address for him?'

'I do.'

'Can I have it?'

'No, you can't.'

He stood up: I didn't.

'It's really extremely important,' I said.

'I'd like to help,' he said unconvincingly, 'however, I'm sure you'll understand, there are certain professional ethics.'

'All I want is a forwarding address.'

'Which, I'm afraid, I'm not at liberty to divulge.'

He put his hand on the back of my chair. I remained seated.

'Mr Liddell,' I spoke his name as one syllable, 'are you refusing to disclose important information in a murder case?'

'Patently.'

'I can put you on a witness list.'

'Stop,' he scoffed, 'you're scaring me.'

'How about I cite you to attend court and give a precognition on oath before a Sheriff?'

'Feel free,' he said. 'Me and the wife would enjoy a wee jaunt down south. You'll have to meet the expenses of course. Train fare, hotel...' He smiled. 'Legal Aid is it? Good luck with that.' He stood and ushered me to the landing where we met Zoë on her way back from the loo. 'Allow me to show you out. Wouldn't want the door to skelp your arse on the way out.'

He led us downstairs, unsnibbed the front door and held it open. 'Oh, and if you do want a look at the croft give me a call next week. No. Not me - Nancy.' He mimed a graceful backhand drive. 'I'll be busy.'

At the door, I turned and shook his hand again. 'Be seeing you, Mr Liddell.'

'The pleasure will be all mine.'

I ignored his sarcasm. 'Yes, all going well, I'll have a citation served tomorrow and see you in court, say, middle of next week. How's Wednesday sound? Oh, wait a minute, that's women's semi-finals day. Never mind,' I called to him as Zoë and I walked out to find my car and set off on the long drive back to civilization, 'there's a telly in the witness room. You can watch the tennis on that.'

CHAPTER 43

Monday morning's mail was piled on top of Friday's mail and Thursday's was in turn supported by Wednesday's, Tuesday's and the previous Monday's and even some stragglers from the week before. It all needed serious and urgent attention. From the middle of the stack I extracted a new sheaf of papers to do with Isla Galbraith's case. In the covering letter from the P.F. it stated that this additional material was being supplied in compliance with the disclosure protocol. Following a ruling by the former judicial committee of the Privy Council, now the Supreme Court, the Crown had a duty to disclose all evidential material to the defence to ensure an equality of arms before the trial. Failure to do so could amount to a miscarriage of justice. The downside to that most welcome decision had been the Crown's tendency to err on the side of caution, or maybe it was just sheer bloody-mindedness, and bombard the defence with a lot of irrelevant bumph.

The latest disclosure papers amounted to a full compendium of Callum Galbraith's medical records dating back to his booster-jabs as a child. I had already seen the important medical information and was satisfied beyond any doubt that the cause of his sudden death was a compressed fracture of the skull in combination with a series of brain-puncturing stab wounds. I really didn't need to know that he'd had glue ear when he was four and his tonsils out aged twelve.

I was about to shove the copy medical records to the further-most outreaches of my desk when I suddenly wondered why it was they made up such a thick bundle. I'd always understood Callum Galbraith to have been a healthy, active, indeed, athletic individual, and my mental image was of a ginger-headed highlander striding through the heather on his latest sponsored walk. A brief perusal of the newly-disclosed medical records suggested otherwise and, upon closer examination, I discovered that a good portion of the records related to treatment at the Beatson Oncology Unit. Intrigued, I read on to learn that some years previously Callum Galbraith had undergone treatment for skin cancer. A suspicious-looking mole on the side of his head had been excised and a biopsy confirmed the presence of pre-cancerous cells. He'd been referred to the Beatson for post-surgery treatment, but his oncologist, Dr Diane Prentice, my old man's coffee-mate I noticed, not satisfied that the original excision had removed a border of healthy skin tissue from all around the affected area, sent him back to the originating hospital for more surgery. That was done, though some minor skin-grafting was required as a result. Subsequent follow-up treatment at the Beatson had been a complete success. Another example of the man's bad luck; beating cancer only to be beaten to death by his wife.

There were a lot more records: charts, graphs, diagrams and squiggly hand-writing, but I couldn't see any link to the matter that most concerned me: not if, but why Callum Galbraith's wife had murdered him.

'Robbie!' yelled Zoë.

I went through to reception.

'Guess who?' she said, handing over the receiver. It was Liddell. I looked at the clock. Nine fifteen. I had expected him to call earlier.

One minute later the solicitor from Inverness had salvaged his dreams of strawberries and cream on centre court and I had what I wanted: an address for Fergus Galbraith. Fat lot of good it was to me.

I returned to my room and pressed the yellow-sticky on which I had scribbled Fergus Galbraith's forwarding address against the screen of my computer. Interesting - if highly inconvenient. Fergus Galbraith had sold up, shipped out and berthed in sunnier climes: The Vendée. If my geographical knowledge of the North of Scotland was hazy, that of mid-west France was a good deal poorer.

Grace-Mary came in and switched on my PC. 'It works better like that,' she said, tapping the top of the screen with the court diary. 'And it has a facility for virtual Post-it notes. You could have little electronic yellow-stickies all over the screen if you wanted.'

What was the point when I had the real thing? But I wasn't getting into that argument again.

'So,' my secretary said, 'the big date, I mean, trip up north. How did it go?'

'It was strictly work.'

'Did you find what you were looking for?'

'Sadly not.' I removed the Post-it note from the monitor. The Vendée. Might as well be Venus. I stuck the note to the back of my hand.

Grace-Mary opened the diary. 'While you were off gallivanting,' she turned to the previous Friday's page in the diary and pointed to an entry, 'Andy had a run in with the Sheriff. From what I can gather things got a bit hairy and you'll need to lodge an appeal.' She went over to the cabinet to fetch the file. 'Honestly, I don't know what you were thinking, leaving the lad to do his first Sheriff Court trial while you're away off on a wild goose chase.'

'Everyone's got to learn,' I said. 'Sometimes in at the deep end is the best way to gain experience.'

'The deep end would have been fine,' Grace-Mary scolded me, 'but do a trial with Sheriff Brechin sitting? That's more like swimming with the sharks.'

Andy came rushing in, obviously trying to head Grace-Mary off at the pass. 'You heard?'

'You lost?'

'Shocking decision,' he said, taking the file from my secretary. 'Absolute disgrace. Brechin didn't believe a word of the post-drinking driving defence.'

Grace-Mary gave me a disapproving look. I should never have left Andy to deal with my cases when I was away. It hadn't been fair on him or the clients.

'What about the defence forensics?' I asked.

Andy handed me the file and I searched for Prof. Bradley's report. I'd had him do a back-calculation based on the accused's alcohol consumption after he'd driven. His findings clearly showed that my client's alcohol level at the actual time of driving would have been well below the prescribed limit. I found the report and pulled it out of the file.

'Flawed,' Andy said.

'Prof Bradley - flawed?'

'Not his fault. According to the Sheriff, Prof. Bradley had to use unreliable information provided by the accused and his lying witnesses. Drawing from a poisoned well was how he put it.'

Sounded like Brechin. Always ready to find ways to body-swerve a reasonable doubt. I found the court minutes. 'Three months? His reading was only fifty-eight and he got three moons?'

'The reading was eighty-five,' Andy said, tersely. 'More than double the limit. You'll get him out on interim lib, won't you?'

'You mean you haven't already?'

'It was last thing Friday. The clerks were out of their blocks before I had the chance and Brechin would just have knocked it back anyway.'

It was a strange system that allowed the sentencing Sheriff to decide if an accused should be released on bail pending an appeal against the very sentence he'd just imposed.

201

'The good news is that Brechin's on holiday now,' Andy said. 'Gone bird-watching on Arran. You'll have a much better chance in front of Sheriff Dalrymple or a floater.'

So, Bert Brechin was on holiday? Suddenly my own chances of an acquittal had increased significantly.

Grace-Mary took the file back again and placed it on a to-do pile that was threatening to avalanche. She unpeeled the yellow-sticky from the back of my hand and read again the forwarding address I'd been given for Fergus Galbraith's details.

'You want him to dish out the dirt on his brother?' she said. 'What do you expect him to tell you? If he hadn't spoken to his brother for years how can he help the case? He'll either hate him so much that he'll be hugely biased and therefore unbelievable, or he won't have anything bad to say at all because he won't have seen his brother in years.'

'Ever thought of taking a degree in logic?' I asked.

'No,' Grace-Mary answered. 'But I could give lectures on it.'

'How about metaphysics?'

'Metaphysics?'

'You know,' I said. 'Like how can Andy be here and down at Sandy's getting me a coffee at the same time?'

'Don't be stupid,' Grace-Mary said. 'He can't.'

Andy rolled his eyes. 'On my way.'

'Robbie!' Zoë called to me from across the corridor.

'What colour is the blouse today?' I whispered to Grace-Mary.

'White,' she whispered back.

'Who is it?' I yelled through to reception.

'The hospital!' Zoë yelled back. 'And it's not white – it's ivory!'

My dad's blood-pressure. Malky's kneecaps. I rushed through to reception and snatched the receiver from Zoë.

'Robbie Munro?' said a polite female voice on the other end.

'Speaking.'

'The police thought I should let you know.' My insides tightened. 'Your client, Isla Galbraith. She was admitted last night. Attempted suicide.'

CHAPTER **44**

'How is she?' I asked the nurse who let me into the psychiatric ward; a new brick-built structure with a high-pitched roof set in the grounds of Stirling Royal Infirmary.

'Stable. She's in the day-room. We've had her sectioned for seventy-two hours and the consultant is going to review things later today.'

There were only twenty-four beds in the ward and always enough patients with acute mental health problems to fill them. If Isla's suicide bid was merely a cry for help she'd be prescribed some anti-depressants, a follow-up session with a shrink and shown the door in short order.

The nurse took me into a brightly lit atrium where some patients padded about in dressing gowns and slippers. 'We like to get the para-suicides out of bed and moving around as quickly as possible. It helps if we can find them something to take their mind off things.'

I poked my head around the corner to see my client sitting in a large glass-walled room. She was working away at the cross-stitch tapestry stretched over a wooden frame on her lap. Her parents were in the room too. I recognised them from the second of her two brief court appearances and knew they'd been staying with their daughter since her release on bail. Mr Clegg was a likeable man, stout and cheery. He sat next to his daughter, head bowed, eyes closed. His wife, a small woman with a prune of a face, was on her feet. Though the room was sound-proofed, I could clearly see she was going her dinger.

'Mum and Dad are with Isla just now.' The nurse pointed to some chunky fabric-covered foam chairs. 'Take a seat and I'll let you know when she's ready to see you.'

'And you're sure she's going to be okay?' I asked as the nurse made to walk away.

'Looks like it. She took Disulfiram – a strange choice but enough of them would have done the trick if she hadn't been caught in time. Thankfully it's not paracetamol-based so we don't expect any long-term liver damage.'

I sat and waited. Five minutes later Isla's mother came through the swing doors.

'Hello Mr Munro,' she said, in a voice uncannily like that of her daughter. 'It was good of you to come.'

'How is she?' I already had the official version from the nurse, but I felt it only polite to ask. 'Isla's due in court a week today and I was wondering...'

Mrs Clegg pulled a small embroidered handkerchief from her sleeve and gave her nose a gentle blow.

'I'm sorry,' I said. 'This must be a terrible time for you.'

Mrs Clegg tucked the hanky away and laid a hand on my arm. She gave me a tight little smile. 'Sometimes,' she said, 'things seem better after a cup of tea.'

Despite my vague mutterings about the need to stay and talk to my client, Mrs Clegg assured me there was nothing I could do for the moment and in doing so gave me the clear impression she was a woman not used to having her commands questioned. 'Her father is praying over her. It's all best left in God's hands,' she said, leading me across the hospital grounds to a café in the main building. She sat me down at a table and came back with two Styrofoam cups of tea and a packet of shortbread fingers. 'All things work together for good for those who love the Lord,' she said, and wet her lips from the foam cup.

'Any sugar?' I asked.

Mrs Clegg looked me up and down. 'Better off without it don't you think?' She opened the packet of shortbread. I took a finger and bit into it. A piece went in my mouth, a piece stayed in my hand and another piece fell into my cup splashing tea across the table.

205

A young waitress came over and mopped up the spillage with the wipe of a damp cloth. Mrs Clegg pressed some loose change into the girl's wet hand.

'God bless you, my dear,' she said.

Looking slightly embarrassed the waitress pocketed the coins and retreated.

'You believe that, don't you Mr Munro?' Mrs Clegg asked. 'That God's in control.'

I smiled and munched shortbread. My opinion on most matters depended on who was paying my fee. I strongly suspected God could afford a better advocate than me; moreover, I had no children, far less a daughter up for murdering her husband and now lying in hospital after trying to kill herself. If faith that God would make everything all right kept Mrs Clegg from going under, my opinion counted for very little.

'The nurse told me Isla should pull through without any lasting ill-effects,' I said.

'And the court case? Will she pull through that? Don't tell me,' she said, before I had the chance to reply. 'It's confidential. That's all I ever get out of Isla. She can't talk about it because her lawyer won't let her.'

I fished out what I could of the soggy shortbread.

'Isla is facing a murder charge,' I reminded Isla's mum. 'Anything she says about the case to anyone other than her legal counsel is evidence and could be used against her. For that reason, it is best if she doesn't talk to anyone, not even her parents.'

'I understand your concerns,' Mrs Clegg said, 'but surely so long as she speaks the truth, what harm can there be?'

In response to her question I drank a mouthful of lumpy tea.

'In some ways I'd rather she was in jail than in that place.' The old woman gestured at the window through which the peaked roof of the psychiatric ward could be seen in the mid-distance. 'I'd understand it better. We've all a temper, Mr

Munro. Any one of us could react badly, violently, if sufficiently provoked – even you.'

'If you say so,' I said, popping the last piece of shortbread into my mouth and wondering if the butter in it would melt.

'But to deliberately attempt to take one's own God-given life… it's…'

'Unforgivable?'

Mrs Clegg lowered her brows at me. 'No, Mr Munro. To the Lord, nothing is that.'

She sat back and drank her tea. Occasionally she would nibble at a finger of shortbread. For a while there was little said between us.

'You've been trying to contact Callum's brother,' Mrs Clegg said, when the conversation had gone from a trickle to a drought. Have you found him?'

'Not exactly.'

'Then give up your search, Mr Munro. Anything that drunkard had to say would be of no interest to anyone. Trust me.'

'Perhaps. Still, I would like to talk to him all the same.'

The old woman sniffed dryly and looked away. 'You do know that Isla doesn't want you to?'

'Isla doesn't need to know.'

She pointed, her wizened face at me accusingly. 'But she does know. She knows you've been making enquiries about Fergus behind her back.'

Behind her back? True I'd been circumspect, but what did she expect? That I should sit around and do nothing? It was bad enough that Isla's case was dissolving faster than the shortbread in my tea without her getting fussy about what methods I employed to save her from a life sentence.

'I'm trying to do what's best for Isla,' I said. 'And if inconveniencing her brother-in-law helps save her from a life behind bars then I think it's worthwhile even if she is a little upset about it.'

'I don't think you understand.' Mrs Clegg finished her tea and laid down the foam cup. 'Isla is more than a little upset. She tried to take her life *because* you tried to contact Fergus.'

I couldn't believe it.

'It's true,' said Mrs Clegg. 'It's about all we've managed to get out of her.'

I was at a loss for words.

Mrs Clegg's facial features softened. She reached out and took one of my hands. 'I can tell you're a good person, Mr Munro. Deep down,' she added, I thought, unnecessarily. 'And, as you've just finished telling me, you want what's best for Isla.'

'I do. And it's still my professional opinion that Fergus Galbraith might have some useful information.'

Mrs Clegg gave her head a little shake. I could understand her exasperation even if she was politely trying to keep it under wraps. Isla's mother knew nothing of the evidence against her daughter. She was a seeker after the truth. I preferred to inject a little uncertainty into the proceedings. So far as Mrs Clegg was concerned, Fergus Galbraith was an irrelevance to the defence. To me he was my only hope to dilute what was a seriously strong Crown case.

Mrs Clegg removed her empty cup and, holding it under the edge of the table, swept shortbread crumbs into it using the side of her hand.

'You may be a professional, Mr Munro, but you're only human and what you think best and what is God's will are not necessarily one and the same thing.'

'Then you'll agree that the same applies to what you think is best?'

'I've prayed about it. A lot. Ever since the police phoned that night to say my daughter was in custody charged with murder.' Her wrinkly mouth trembled a little at the memory.

'Then if you've prayed for Isla's liberty,' I said, daring to dip my toe into spiritual waters and already way out of my depth, 'have you ever considered I could be the answer to those prayers?'

By the look on her face she hadn't and never would.

'Mr Munro, all I have prayed for is justice.'

'Even if it means life in prison for your daughter?'

'Justice.'

That was me told.

'Mrs Clegg,' I said, 'I only want Fergus to give me some background on his brother. An insight into how things could have ended up the way they did. I want to know what Callum was really like, and why this horrible incident might have happened.'

'No! For the last time. Callum Galbraith was a fine upstanding young man. If you want the truth about him, you can ask me or you can ask Isla. Fergus Galbraith is an embarrassment, nothing more.'

Embarrassment? I liked the sound of that.

'Let that be an end of it,' Mrs Clegg said sharply. 'There are matters in the past that should stay there. You've got your instructions. Neither Isla nor I want you to bring Fergus into this.'

The chances of me speaking to Fergus now that he'd left for the continent were remote, but I was fired up and not about to have a couple of teuchters tell me how to run a criminal defence. 'Then you're both being very foolish,' I said.

Mrs Clegg's face flushed, her eyes narrowed, the wrinkles in her face deepened. She'd told the truth earlier. She knew about people with tempers all right. She saw one every day when she looked in the mirror and right now she was fighting back the urge to stand up and scream at me. I didn't give her the chance. 'Your daughter is heading down a one-way street at the end of which is a life sentence. There are no sunny day-rooms in Cornton Vale and the only cross-stitching that gets done is on mail sacks or by the prison doctor. Now, as I've already said, the preliminary diet is less than a week away and I feel it my professional duty to explore every possible avenue of defence or mitigation even if it does offend Isla's sensibilities – or yours.'

Mrs Clegg took several deep breaths. Her lips formed themselves into a grim little smile. 'Very well,' she said, in a voice a pitch higher than normal. 'I'll give you all the information you need. I'll give you an insight into Fergus Galbraith's background with my daughter. Are you familiar with the seventh commandment Mr Munro?'

I knew there were ten and that I had previous convictions for most if not all of them. 'Remind me.'

Her eyes burned into mine as she reached into her handbag and produced a brown padded envelope from which she emptied onto the table between us the bracelet that I had last seen on Isla Galbraith's wrist. I counted. There were ten charms on it, each attached by a silver link. One for each commandment. One for every year of Isla's marriage to Callum. Mrs Clegg thumped a hand on the table scattering any crumbs that she'd missed and making the bracelet jump. A few heads turned in our direction. 'Thou shalt not commit adultery.'

CHAPTER 45

Sandy's café was like a steam room and the smell of roasted coffee beans had reached an almost spiritual plane.

Junior counsel cast a worried eye over the little glass cabinet inside which a wasp was merrily buzzing around the remains of Thursday's cake supplies. 'That it?' he said. 'Two doughnuts and a fly-cemetery?'

I would have been well shot of Leonard Brophy by now if it hadn't been all over Parliament House that the Dean had resigned from Isla Galbraith's defence and no-one with any common sense or hopes of furthering their career was prepared to take up the poisoned chalice. At that precise moment in time, the only thing in wig and gown without either common sense or ambition and sufficiently desperate for work, was Leonard. So, I'd invited him through for a consultation in order that I could butter him up and have him provide me with a Note for Legal Aid purposes.

The way it worked with the Scottish Legal Aid Board was that if a solicitor wanted to incur unusual expenditure then a formal sanction request had to be made in writing, giving reasons why the additional work was necessary. If I sent in a sanction request stating that I wanted legal aid funding to cover the costs of me travelling to France to interview a witness, it would come bouncing back stained with tears of laughter; however, if I sent in a sanction request accompanied by a supporting Note from counsel, the assessors at SLAB would, hopefully, tug their forelocks and bow to the considered opinion of learned counsel. The fact that I'd forgotten more criminal law than Leonard would ever know was irrelevant. What a difference a wig made.

Sandy filled two paper cups with coffee and placed them on the countertop. 'It's been all go today. You're lucky there's anything left. I had a bunch of Fiscals in here this morning after court. Nearly cleaned me out. Must be hungry work all that persecuting.'

'I suppose these'll have to do,' Leonard said, waving a podgy hand at the cakes. 'Put them in a bag, will you?' He turned to me. 'You didn't want anything did you?'

'Coffee's fine,' I said.

We left the café and walked up to the Cross Well, past the Burgh Halls and into the rose garden at the rear of St Michael's church. The good weather refused to relent. Three solid weeks of clear skies and sunshine. The world had gone mad.

By the time we'd sat down on a bench Leonard had scoffed the doughnuts and was scraping the icing off the top of the fly-cemetery with his teeth.

'So,' he said, seconds later, as he licked the last sugary raisin from his finger. 'How goes the Isla Galbraith case? Still in the nut-house, is she?' An expression of concern flitted across his fat features for a second. 'I'll still get paid for this consultation?' he said. 'I mean, even if the client isn't present?'

I reassured him on that point and cut to the chase.

'The case is going to bed in a bucket,' I said. 'I'm clutching at straws and I want to precognosce Callum Galbraith's brother.'

'Then why don't you?'

'Because he's living in France.'

'What's so important about him?'

'Isla and Fergus Galbraith went out together when they were younger,' I said. 'He gave her a silver bracelet as a wedding gift. According to her mother, every year he sends her another charm for it. It's become something of a tradition.'

'Nice of him. Either that or a bit creepy.'

'It gets worse. Five years ago, Callum was diagnosed with skin cancer. He was hospitalised for a while. Fergus came down to lend support and ended up jumping into bed with Isla.'

Leonard smiled in admiration. 'She shagged her brother-in-law? While hubby was in hospital? The little minx.' It wasn't quite how Mrs Clegg had explained it to me but learned counsel had indeed grasped the nub of the matter. 'Interesting if true, interesting even if not true,' Leonard said, quoting Twain or it might have been Wilde; for classy quips it was usually one or t'other. 'Who'd have thought it? Wee Free Isla part of a love triangle - the newspapers will devour it.'

'Precisely,' I said. 'And that's why Isla's mum doesn't want word of it getting out. So far as she's concerned, it's ancient history and any blame lies squarely with Fergus who, in her eyes, is nothing but a seducer, an adulterer and not half the man his brother was.'

'You raise an interesting legal point,' Leonard said, making a tent of his fingers and tapping his pursed lips. 'He may have seduced Island Isla, but surely adultery is restricted to married persons.'

'Whatever,' I said. 'The important thing is—'

'For instance, I am single.' Something that had never totally surprised me. 'If I were to have sex with a married woman she would be committing adultery, but would I?'

'No, Leonard,' I said. 'You would be dreaming. Now belt up and try to keep on track, will you?'

I opened my briefcase and took out a typewritten sheet and a pen. I wanted Leonard to tell the Legal Aid Board that my French trip was necessary to protect the interests of justice and had taken the liberty of writing his opinion for him.

'Sign at the bottom,' I said, but he was determined to read it first like a real lawyer.

He scanned the page. 'Still can't see what the big deal is with this guy.'

'Can't you?' I said. 'Up until I spoke with Isla's mum, I saw Fergus purely as a potential source of mud for slinging purposes. Now I think there may be more to it and, even if there's not, with a bit of work and some nudge, nudge, wink, wink, we could even have the makings of a reasonable doubt.'

'You mean, plead not guilty?'

'Possibly. For one thing I'd like to know where exactly Fergus Galbraith was on the night of the murder.'

'If he was in France – that's a pretty good alibi.'

'I'm not so sure that he was. He seems to have left the country at pretty short notice. The slightest uncertainty about his whereabouts and we could impeach him.'

Leonard's eyes lit up. In the distance I'm sure he could hear the cha-ching of a cash register. 'The trial could last weeks. Think of the publicity.'

I had. 'That's why I have to go see Fergus Galbraith. If I chat him up, put him at ease, I might get something useful. Anything remotely iffy and, whammo, he's on a witness list incriminated as his brother's killer.'

'Superb!' Leonard dashed off his signature. 'Do you really think he might have had anything to do with it?' He handed me back the sheet of paper.

'Haven't a clue,' I said. That was the beauty of our system. I didn't have to prove a thing, only raise a reasonable doubt, and, if the Crown wasn't going to offer a culp hom, there was no way I was letting a client of mine plead guilty to murder.

CHAPTER 46

'I didn't even know there *was* a junkie pen,' Andy complained.

'Then you haven't been listening. If you're going to use Robbie's room, because he's hardly ever here anymore,' Grace-Mary said, glowering in my direction, 'then you're going to have to learn to respect the office procedures.'

'It's the Bic with the red rubber band wrapped round the end,' I said, trying to help. I knew the junkie pen was one of my secretary's pet subjects and if she was getting on at Andy, it meant that I was avoiding the flak for once.

'What's a red rubber band got to do with anything?' my assistant asked.

'No reason,' I told him, 'other than to signify which pen junkies are to use when they sign the legal aid forms.'

'Grace-Mary doesn't even know if he was a junkie.'

I looked out of the window. Andy's client was six feet tall, couldn't have weighed more than nine stone soaking wet and was tottering down the High Street like a puppet with some strings snipped. If he wasn't HIV positive, riddled with Hep C or incubating some other communicable disease, I'd walk across the Channel to see Fergus Galbraith.

Grace-Mary picked up the summons from my desk. The charge libelled a contravention of section 5(2) of the Misuse of Drugs Act 1971. 'You know what diamorphine is don't you?'

Andy rolled his eyes. 'He's not a junkie, he's a jaikie. He's on medication...' He flipped over the summons to read the notes he'd made on the reverse. 'See? Antabuse. That's the stuff that makes you sick if you drink alcohol.'

'Which is probably why,' I said, 'he's now using heroin.'

'Look, Andy,' Grace-Mary said, taking up the cause once again. 'I don't care what people do to their bodies in their spare time. If nobody took drugs or drink Robbie would have to divorce folk and draw up wills like a real lawyer, but, understand this: if it looks like a junkie, walks like a junkie and is charged with possessing Class A drugs then it's a candidate for the junkie pen. Okay? Now which pen did he use?'

'It's all right.' Andy sighed loudly and unclipped a rather nice Parker pen from his inside jacket pocket. 'I let him use mine. Some of us aren't quite so fussy as you all seem to be.'

He was about to leave, then changed his mind.

'Grace-Mary,' he said. 'Do you think I could speak to Robbie?'

'You seem to be doing fine.'

'Alone?'

'Excuse *me*.' Grace-Mary picked up a wire-basket of letters to be filed and backed out of the room.

'Is this about my trial,' I asked, once my secretary had closed the door behind her.

'It's on Tuesday,' Andy said. 'Who's acting for you? I mean… I don't think I'm ready… Do you?'

'I've asked Paul Sharp to act.'

'The Sixties guy?'

'Don't judge by appearances. He knows what he's doing.'

'Robbie, he thinks he's Adam Faith.'

'He's very good. I wouldn't have instructed him otherwise.'

'And your defence?'

'Do you still think I should tell the truth?'

'Why, are you allergic?'

'Watch it. There's more than one way to lose a traineeship.'

He hung his head. 'Sorry. I'm worried and not just about me. Why don't you get senior counsel in to take the case?'

'Horses for courses,' I told him. 'Get a Q.C. in and suddenly it's all a big deal. I'd rather play the whole thing down. That way the Sheriff won't think he's making some kind of landmark decision when he comes back with a not proven, and, anyway, Paul's good. He'll do the business for me. Which brings me back to the defence. I don't see any point in challenging Fleming's notebook.'

Andy was aghast. 'Why not? He's lying. You can't just let him stitch you up.'

He had much to learn. 'You have to learn to roll with the blows,' I told him. 'Even the low blows. Challenge a cop head on and usually there's only going to be one winner in the eyes of the court.'

'So, what'll you do?'

'I'll say that I did indeed make a reply and that I have no idea where the fifty came from. Due to the unusually fine weather, I seldom have my jacket on. I leave it lying all over the place. Someone must have stuffed the money into my top pocket without me noticing.'

'Why?'

'A practical joke. A fit up? Who knows? Who can say it's not true? Not Inspector Dougie Fleming. It fits in exactly with what I told him. And why would a defence agent, who always advises his clients to say nothing, make a reply himself unless it was the truth?'

'You think that will work?'

'Why not? Brechin's on holiday so we'll end up with Dalrymple or a floater.'

Andy still looked troubled.

'You see a problem with that defence?' I asked.

'Yes – it's not the truth.'

Andy, like a lot of young defence lawyers, had a certain fascination with the truth.

'And what about the bigger picture?'

'What about it?' He didn't seem any less troubled.

217

'Well, do you think I'm innocent of the charge against me?' I asked.

'Of course.'

'And so the truth is I'm not guilty?'

'Obviously.'

'Then if I'm found not guilty does it really matter what route I take to the truth?'

'Yes. The money came from Jake Turpie. You know that. You can't lie about it.'

'So far as I know the money came from you.'

'But I can give evidence and explain how I got it.'

I appreciated Andy's willingness to help, but I couldn't lead a defence that involved the impeachment of Jake. 'He's my client, Andy. He owns this place. There's a blatant conflict of interest.'

'But you can't just lie. That makes you no better than Inspector Fleming.'

'You'd really rather I told the court that you took a bung from Jake Turpie and it turned out to be a fake?'

'What would happen if you did?'

'You might end up being charged too. Jake would definitely have his premises raided by the cops and then feel obliged to exact some kind of retribution.'

'On me?'

'Not immediately. For starters I assume he'd go straight to the top.'

'Robbie... I want you to do what's best.' Dragging his feet, my assistant walked to the door. I opened it for him to find Grace-Mary bent over, picking up some letters that must have fallen from her filing basket. Andy returned to reception where Zoë was slaving over a hot scanner, sending my sanction request and attachments down the line to SLAB. I followed him through carrying the drugs summons.

'By the way,' I said. 'Your client - the junkie. Is he pleading?'

'What do you take me for?'

With the prisons bursting at the seams no-one these days was in danger of getting banged-up over a couple of wraps of smack, and if there was no prospect of jail there was no legal aid for a guilty plea.

'Got a defence?'

'Illegal search - no reasonable suspicion.'

A defence meant a trial, and a trial usually meant legal aid. His concerns with the truth aside, the boy was definitely learning. He sat down at his desk, took an apple from the drawer and bit into it. Then he opened his jacket to reveal the Parker pen clipped into his inside pocket.

'Junkie pen,' he said to Zoë and they both laughed.

'All the same,' Grace-May said, 'I hope you washed your hands before touching that apple.'

CHAPTER 47

The road from Aizenay to Coex ran through the heart of the Vendée, in the Pays de Loire, and was how all roads should be: wide, quiet and completely straight for as far as the eye could see.

Personally, I didn't think the scenery compared with the Road to the Isles, but Zoë was happy and if she was happy I was happy. I would have been even happier were we cruising along in something more sporty than the clunky far-eastern motor I'd hired at the airport, just as I'd have preferred to travel British Airways to Nantes rather than bucket-line to Beauvais or Beauvais-Paris as it was described on the web-site; which was like calling Edinburgh airport: Dundee-Edinburgh, because we'd landed seventy kilometres north of the French capital. Still, needs must when the Scottish Legal Aid Board drives. My sanction request for additional expenditure, backed-up though it was by counsel's opinion, had received short shrift and instead of funds to cover a round trip with an overnight stay I'd been allowed an extra two hundred pounds on the basis that I could instruct an English-speaking French advocat to do the interviewing of Fergus Galbraith.

I'd liked to have argued the point with SLAB, but there'd been no time to become entrenched in a correspondence war with that bunch of ignorant, penny-pinching tossers, not with Isla due in court in a few days' time. I was also unsure how to go about explaining to some French brief that I wanted them to trap Fergus Galbraith into saying something inadvisable that I might later be able to twist into the semblance of a reasonable doubt on behalf of his sister-in-law. It would just be my luck to instruct a Frenchman with morals. Not only that but, from what little experience I had of foreign lawyers and their fees, it was unlikely they'd be overly keen to do anything on the promise of a measly two-hundred of my Scottish pounds. So, I'd used the additional funds and booked flights for one hundred pounds return and hired the lowest form of vehicular life for another fifty.

'Grace-Mary told me about you and Malky,' Zoë said when there was a lull in the conversation and we'd heard all her James Blunt CD's. 'About how he stole your girlfriend. The one that died in the crash,' she added, as though there might have been others. Zoë put her hand on the back of my neck and gently massaged. 'I don't know how you can even bear to talk to him.'

'We're brothers,' I said, and hoped she'd leave it at that and continue the neck-rubbing.

'How do you feel about it, though? Did you love her? Grace-Mary said that she moved in with you, then she went off with him and now she's dead.'

It was an accurate enough summary. I rolled my head from side to side to ease my stiff neck. We'd hammered down the toll roads and were making good time. Having left Prestwick at five in the morning, even with the clocks being an hour ahead, it was only mid-afternoon when I slowed for a roundabout on the outskirts of St Gilles Croix De Vie, a seaside town on the banks of the River Vie. In the middle of the roundabout a banner proclaimed un Fête de Sardine. I was more interested in the signpost that told me the town of Challans was ten kilometres away and which according to the map meant I was nearing my much anticipated rendezvous with Fergus Galbraith.

'Not long now,' I said.

'But how do you feel?' Zoë asked, not allowing herself to be side-tracked. 'I haven't noticed you being too sad about it. Don't you miss her?'

I didn't answer. When I thought about Cathleen now, the only feelings I had were guilty ones. When she had left me for Malky I'd been devastated. Bad enough being given the heave-ho, but ditched in favour of my brother? Now that she was dead - I felt nothing. She'd been the woman I'd intended to spend my life with. Why didn't I care more?

'You never talk about her. You're not… because of what she did… you're not glad she's dead – are you?'

'No, Zoë, I'm not glad she's dead, and I don't talk about it because I don't want to talk about it.'

A huffy look crossed her pretty face. The massaging stopped. She removed her hand from my neck and stared out of the window.

At the next roundabout I took the first exit onto yet another arrow-straight road for five or six kilometres towards Challans, before hanging a left down a country lane sign-posted: Sallertaine.

According to the on-line encyclopaedia, the town of Sallertaine had once been the centre of the European salt industry. These days its commerce was tourism-based, catering to those who came for the many craft shops that lined its narrow boulevard or to visit the Church of St Leonard, built in 1172, once sanctuary for Thomas Beckett after his fall-out with Henry II Plantagenet, then King of England as well as Normandy and much of Western France.

From being a highly-populated industrial town in the middle-ages, Sallertaine had shrunk over the centuries to little more than a village, home to scarcely two thousand inhabitants. Certainly, there seemed few enough of them around that afternoon as I drove down a dusty main street, past arts and crafts workshops, expecting at any moment to spy a tall, red-headed Scotsman come striding through the heat haze to meet me.

Where to start? I didn't have a house number only a name: 'Chardon' on the Rue de Verdun. I parked in the centre of town, next to a war memorial, not far from the famous old Church. As I alighted and stretched my weary bones I ran an eye down the list of local soldiers of France who had fallen during the World Wars: presumably the ones who hadn't run away or collaborated with the Nazis. Zoë, who had emerged from her brief huff, noticed that the name Tessier featured three times on the bronze plaque affixed to the memorial stone and that the same name was above the boulangerie on the other side of the street. If the family had been around since 1914, she suggested, it would be a good place to enquire as to the recent arrival in town of a strange Scotsman.

The 21st Century Monsieur Tessier was a short, squat middle-aged man with a smiley face and an abundance of curly, implausibly-dark hair poking out from beneath a little white paper hat. When we entered the shop, making the little bell above the door tinkle, he was busy stacking freshly-baked baguettes in rows of wicker baskets, ably assisted in his task by two girls, who may have been his daughters, each wearing similar paper hats and blue and white striped aprons.

After a faltering attempt to communicate with the baker in French, he pointed to a sign on the counter top announcing: English spoken here, and which, to be fair, was probably correct had I been ordering half a dozen croissants and not trying to track down an evasive witness. Though I repeated the address several times, I was getting nowhere and, after a few confusing minutes during which I was offered a selection of pastries including an extremely tasty looking tarte citron, Zoë took over and let fly in schoolgirl French which, I had to admit, was a lot better than my schoolboy variety.

'Je cherche pour un homme.'

'Alors,' said Monsieur Tessier, as though all had at last been made clear, and removing his hat with both hands he clutched it to his breast, much to the amusement of his young female helpers. 'A votre service,' he said, bowing, 'madame.'

223

'Mademoiselle,' Zoë said, to gales of laughter from the girls behind the counter. 'Un homme particulaire - d'Ecossais,' she battered on regardless. 'Ma copain.'

'Ah, Ecosse,' the baker said, replacing hat on curly head and nodding furiously. 'Glasgow, non?'

Non, as it happened, but it was close enough. We both returned his nods rather than attempt any more French. He came out from behind the counter, took us to the door and pointed to a shop further down the street where in the shade of a little red awning, his wooden chair resting on its two back legs and leaning against the front of the building, sat a man arms crossed, straw hat over his eyes, dozing.

The baker paddled an imaginary canoe. 'Le Voyage du Sel.'

'The journey of salt,' Zoë translated for my benefit.

We thanked the baker for his help and made our way down the street, munching a couple of pain au raisin and pretending to be tourists, with me thinking how best to play my meeting with Isla's paramour.

My pastry was almost scoffed by the time we neared the man sleeping in the chair. Sensing our approach, he lifted his hat sleepily from his head, dragged a forearm across his brow and replaced it. That brief glance was enough to confirm that this man was not Fergus Galbraith. He was too old, late forties early fifties I reckoned, and his short, wiry hair was salt and pepper. I understood from my conversations with Isla that Fergus, like his brother, was a redhead and no ginger nut took a tan like the man in the chair whose leathery skin was as brown as a mahogany sideboard.

'Bonjour,' Zoë said. Her language skills another feasible excuse for bringing her along with me.

The man pushed back his hat. 'How's it going?' he replied in a broad Scots.

'You're Scottish.'

'So are you,' he said, deadpan, and then laughed. 'You here to hire a canoe?'

'No,' Zoë said, 'we're looking for someone. A man—'

'Then look no further.' He stood up, took off his straw hat, hung it on the back of his chair, came over and put an arm around my receptionist's shoulder.

Maybe it was something they put in the water.

'A particular man,' I said, feeling the need to regain the initiative.

He took his arm away, feigning sudden disinterest. 'Rules me out,' he said. 'I'm not very particular at all. However, if you two fancy a tour of the salt marshes, my name's Eddie and I'd be happy to oblige.'

Zoë looked enthusiastic. I had to admit there were a lot of worse ways to spend a sunny afternoon than a leisurely canoe trip with my pretty receptionist and wise-cracking Eddie as our guide, but there was work to do.

'We're looking for someone. Fergus Galbraith. I think he has a place in the village making jewellery. Charm bracelets. That sort of thing.'

Eddie scratched his head. Galbraith? Nope, never heard of him. There was something about the way he didn't look me in the eye when he spoke and his sudden need to roll himself a smoke that made me think he wasn't being entirely honest.

'Do you mind?' he asked, sticking a rollie in the corner of his mouth.

'It's a free country,' I said.

'Sure is,' Eddie said. He winked at Zoë, lit his cigarette and blew twin jets of smoke down his nostrils. 'A canoe trip on the salt marshes - the offer's still open.'

I pretended to think about it while I planned my next move.

'Eddie,' I said, eventually, 'why are you covering for him?'

He picked a piece of loose tobacco from the tip of his tongue unable to look me in the eye. 'What do you mean?'

225

'What I mean is: how long do you think you can hide a six-foot carrot-top in a village this size?'

Eddie puffed furiously on his rollie. 'What makes you think I'm hiding anyone? What are you? Polis? Way off your patch are you not?'

Taking him by the arm, I led Eddie away a short distance from Zoë. 'Isla.' I jerked my head in the direction of my receptionist.

Eddie looked over my shoulder at her. My client's name produced a faint flicker of recognition in his walnut expression. If there were two Scots men living in the same town in the middle of rural France they were bound to have met, and what else was there to do but drink and reminisce about the old country and loves lost?

Eddie's face creased into a wide smile. The roll-up between his lips stood to attention. 'Why didn't you say so?' He looked about the street as though we might be under surveillance. 'Fergus is taking a party up to the 16th Century windmill at Raire. It's about an hour's paddle from here. If you like I'll take you there. They do a very nice homemade cidre and if you're still hungry…' he looked at the fragment of pastry I held in my hand, 'they'll whip you up a crêpe miele in no time.'

Tempting though the idea of cider and a honey-crepe was, I didn't see the point of setting off only to meet Fergus coming back. An explanation as to why I wanted to speak to him, and why I'd felt compelled to lie to his colleague, was better done on terra firma than aboard passing canoes in the middle of a salt marsh. So, instead, we sat under the awning waiting for Fergus's return and staving off dehydration with ice-cold bottles of Kronenbourg 1664. After half an hour or so some fluffy white clouds floated in front of the sun and we went for a walk in a small park that was accessible by a path at the side of the building. Eddie liked to talk, and it helped kill the time listening to him recount his life story in the deep gravelly tones of a man whose vocal chords were corroded by years of rolling tobacco and cheap cognac.

Eddie hailed from Glasgow; Anderson Cross. Salleratine had been intended as only a temporary stop-over on the grand tour of Europe he'd embarked on six years before, having packed in a career as an art teacher at a secondary school in Renfrew. Travelling south through France, Eddie had found work as a guide on Le Voyage du Sel and toiled a summer at the end of which the proprietor had taken ill and died.

'His widow asked me if I wanted to take over. I thought what the hell, and here I am. I pay the old lady an agreed sum every year and keep the rest.'

It sure beat grinding out a living at the Sheriff Court.

'The money's not too bad,' he explained. 'A couple of parties a day and I'm doing all right. Trouble is, it's seasonal work. There aren't many tourists outwith summertime and the marshes often flood in the winter. Last year there was so much rain Sallertaine was an island, cut off from the mainland - just like it used to be hundreds of years ago.'

The sun re-appeared. We sat down on the grass in the shade of a row of lime trees, reviving our parched throats with leisurely swigs from our bottles of lager. To pass the time, Zoë asked Eddie to tell us more about Le Voyage du Sel and he was happy to oblige.

'The land all around here is clay,' he said. 'Hundreds of years ago the sea used to come in and form pools after a high tide. When the water evaporated it left salt behind. Sometime around the 11th Century the townsfolk realised that if they controlled the flow of the tide they could direct it into shallow clay salt pans, let the sun do its work and literally rake in the salt and the money that came with it. Convoys of ships from England, Scandinavia, the Baltic States, Prussia, Flanders used to come here to purchase L'or blanc, the white gold.' He waved a hand in the air. 'Out there is a labyrinth of canals that drain the marshes and regulate the tide so that

227

just enough sea comes in to fill the salt pans. Salt mines and desalination plants put an end to it as a serious business around the start of the seventeenth century. Nowadays only a few of the locals make salt the traditional way. They mix it with dried onion, herbs and garlic and sell it to the tourists.'

'And what do you do when you're not paddling visitors about?' Zoë asked.

'Something completely different.' He jumped up taking Zoë's hands and pulling her to her feet. 'Come with me.'

We climbed to the top of a small hill. On the other side was a pond and, in the centre, a ten-foot bronze sculpture from which a fountain of water sprayed.

'Like it? I've been commissioned by a few towns roundabout,' he said, proudly. 'Did my first piece of public art for a shopping centre in Liverpool when I left art college there. I did this one last winter. It's nice to have my work recognised by what I now regard as my home town.' He cocked his head at the fountain. 'Do you know what it is?'

I was all for contemporary art but the metal monstrosity in the pond was so severely abstract that I needed a clue.

'Think sea,' Eddie hinted.

I studied the sheets of bronze, shaped, scored and twisted together to look like…

'A fish?' ventured Zoë.

'Very good,' Eddie said. 'But not any fish,' he laughed. 'A particular fish – the Twin-Fish.'

'Very nice.' I said, none the wiser and wondering how soon I could stop admiring the contraption without appearing bored or disinterested.

'Have you not heard of the Twin-Fish?' Neither Zoë nor I had the foggiest. 'Well, I'll tell you. Loch Ness has its Monster: Sallertaine has the Twin-Fish. Not quite so dramatic, I'll grant you, and like all good French myths there must also be a moral. The story of the Twin-Fish is all to do with the importance of la cascade de vie.'

'The waterfall of life?' I got in first before Zoë and wished I hadn't when she gave me a look of annoyance.

'Sort of,' Eddie said. 'The Twin-Fish symbolises the belief that everything in nature is connected to everything else.'

Eddie may have been a teacher of art, but he'd missed his vocation; he should have taught history.

'It's like this,' he went on. 'Many of the towns in the area used to be islands in the Loire estuary. Sallertaine, St Hilaire, Challans. To this day Noirmoutier only has a land-link to the mainland at low tide. The Twin-Fish is said to have been a fish native to these waters: a nasty, ugly-looking creature with two heads and two tails, joined at the hip - if fish have hips. They came in their shoals to the new channels that had been dug but the locals didn't like them; scared of their looks, their spiky fins and needle-sharp teeth. Fortunately, because of the Twin-Fish's unusual design, it swam erratically and was easy to catch in the narrow channels. Soon the species was completely wiped out, which was unfortunate because the brackish water in the channels made an ideal breeding ground for mosquitoes. What people hadn't realised, was that the Twin-Fish, ugly and scary though it might have appeared, fed on mosquito larvae. There followed a mass outbreak of malaria and although the citizens of Sallertaine grew rich, with the Twin-Fish gone they died in their thousands. The lesson is that no matter how big or small, beautiful or ugly, good or bad, we all play our part in la cascade de vie.'

'You can't have your gateau and eat it too,' I said. No-one laughed. Eddie had become quite serious.

'It's the same story today,' he continued. 'Mankind is destroying the world. When are we going to learn that we can't mess about with nature - that every plant, every creature serves a purpose?'

I could imagine Eddie back in the seventies, an art student in Liverpool, long hair, straggly beard, Che Guevara T-shirt.

'The same goes for the way we treat each other,' he banged on in earnest, so much so I was beginning to wonder if there was more than just rolling tobacco inside his Rizla papers. 'From the richest to the poorest, highest to the lowest, every person's actions, good or bad, affect someone else – that is la cascade de vie. I'm a big fan of John Donne and like he said, no man is an island.'

Voices from the street brought the sermon to an end. A party of tourists fresh from a canoe expedition were walking along, laughing and jostling, glimpses of multi-coloured life jackets and paddles visible every now and again as the group passed gaps in the buildings facing onto the street.

'That'll be Fergus now,' Eddie said, snapping out of it. He reached out a hand. 'Come on, Isla.'

Zoë looked puzzled. I stepped in between the two. 'Not in front of all those people, Eddie. Is there somewhere private we could go? We'd like to surprise him.'

A truth that's told with bad intent, beats any lie you can invent.

Not John Donne: William Blake.

CHAPTER 48

I parked the hire car outside a tiny white-washed building with wooden shutters on the window, a red-tiled roof and a jungle of a front garden. There was a small green enamel plaque at the side of the door in the shape of a thistle.

'Fergus is staying here,' Eddie said, dismounting the bright yellow scooter that had transported him half a mile further down the main street. 'Just 'til he sells up in Scotland and gets his money through to buy a place here.'

The front door key was cunningly concealed under a flower pot on the window sill. Eddie handed it to us. 'Help yourself to a wee refreshment. When Fergus is finished stowing the gear I'll send him along.'

I let Zoë into the cottage and we entered a living area which also served as kitchen and dining-room. There was even a bed in the corner. Zoë lay down on it and closed her eyes. The windows were shuttered, blocking out most of the daylight. The room was dark and cool. I took a bottle of beer from the fridge and plonked myself down on a chair by an oak table that was striped with slices of sunshine and shadow. I had time. Time to organise my thoughts. Time to put the finishing touches to a little theory I'd been hatching about how Fergus Galbraith had killed his brother and fled to France, leaving behind my client, the woman he had so callously seduced, to take the rap. For all I knew it might even have been true. You can't fool all of the people all of the time, but you only needed to fool eight on a jury of fifteen to secure a not proven verdict.

After a while, the straight-backed kitchen chair grew uncomfortable. I swung back, put my feet on the table and in doing so knocked over the now empty beer bottle.

Fergus must have fallen off the wagon, I thought, as I righted my chair and caught the green bottle before it rolled off the edge of the table and smashed on the terracotta tiles. Else why would he have a fridge full of little green bottles and a rack of red wine in the corner of the room? So much for recognising his problem and doing something about it.

The words of Norrie, the Highland cop, as we'd bounced up the dirt track to Ardfern Croft, came back to me. *And a fine lad is Fergus. If he puts his mind to something, you know he'll see it through to the finish.*

I suddenly had a thought. I needed to check something out before I started questioning Fergus Galbraith. I hadn't brought Isla's file, just a plastic wallet containing a few important papers. It was yellow and see-through, no smiley sun or have a nice day message on the front, but I was sure Ranald Kincaid Q.C. would not have approved. I rummaged among the various documents hoping to find a copy of the Crown autopsy report and in particular the toxicology findings. It wasn't there. I took out my mobile and rang Andy.

'Robbie? I thought you were in France?'

'I am. Where are you?'

'Hospitality with your dad and Malky at the Linlithgow Rose versus Bo'ness United pre-season friendly.'

Friendly? Between the neighbouring towns of Linlithgow and Bo'ness? I sincerely doubted it. Still, as luck would have it, Andy was in Linlithgow. Perfect.

'Forget the football. Remember that junkie client of yours? I want you to find out the name of that drug that makes you sick if you drink alcohol. Once you've got it call me right back.'

A loud roar crashed down the phone.

'One-nil, the Rosie-Posie,' said a jubilant Andy, after a full minute of what sounded like absolute bedlam.

'Never mind the football,' I told him. 'This is urgent.'

'Okay, okay, take a chill pill. The stuff you're talking about is called Antabuse.'

'No, that's the trade name. I want the generic name. There's a British National Formulary in the office. Look it up.'

'Come off it, Robbie. The second half has hardly started. I still have most of a pie to eat and there's a free bar at full-time.'

'This is very important.'

'Oh, and another problem,' Andy said, a triumphant note to his voice. 'I don't have the office key.'

'Then you'll have to contact Grace-Mary.'

The thought of disturbing my secretary on a weekend obviously sparked Andy's thinking process. 'Hold on. Maybe I won't need it. I'll call you right back – but you're buying my next top-up.'

Five minutes later my mobile juddered on the wooden table.

'Got it,' Andy announced. 'Can you believe it? One of the track-side sponsors is a pharmacy. You know that outfit just along from us at the cross?'

'Andy.' I was trying to be patient. 'Do you have the name of the drug?'

'Yes, yes. I'm coming to that. You see their number is on the advert and so I just called them and asked. They were very helpful.'

Another roar assaulted my eardrum. It wasn't quite as loud as the last.

'Oh no,' Andy groaned 'Penalty, Bo'ness.'

'Andy. I can sack you by telephone you know.'

'You can't,' he said. 'That would be a clear breach of the ACAS disciplinary procedure guidelines and almost certain to constitute an unfair dismissal.'

'Okay,' I conceded. 'But I could kill you when I get back.'

Silence then a muffled roar, presumably from the away fans.

'Andy!'

'Disulfiram. Can you hear me, Robbie? I said Disulfiram. That what you wanted to know?'

I cancelled the call. Disulfiram. That was the drug Isla Galbraith had tried to top herself with. Where did she get her hands on a drug prescribed for the treatment of alcohol dependence? Apart from our chat in the Jinglin' Geordie after the discovery of her forged medical notes, she'd shown no signs of being a heavy drinker, and having viewed the medical records for Callum Galbraith since practically his first nappy rash, I knew he was no alky either. The only conclusion I could draw was that the tablets Isla had O. D.'d on belonged to Fergus. He had been in the house. Had he left in a hurry and forgotten to take his medication with him? I sensed a piece of the jig-saw slot into place.

I paced up and down the room, racking my brain. There was something wrong, some piece of information I had overlooked. I wished I had brought the case file with me but all I had in my plastic folder was a copy of the indictment and some notes from my meetings with Isla.

I thought about phoning Andy for a brain-storming session. *Sorry to trouble you, again Andy, but there's something bothering me about Isla Galbraith's case and I can't think what it is, can you?* He'd think I'd gone mad. Fact is though, he would have tried to help. That's what I liked about him. He might complain, but at least he was keen. Most new recruits to the legal profession were only interested in the big bucks from corporate work and didn't want to sully their hands with crime and legal aid. I'd been lucky to find someone who could get all excited about a trip to the Justice of the Peace Court and thought it a treat to go snooping for information at a funeral.

I stopped pacing. Yes, that was it. Something Andy had found out at Callum Galbraith's funeral. I tried to remember our conversation. Golf. Callum Galbraith's last day on earth had been spent playing golf with his old mates from Police College and he'd gone home feeling ill. His pals had been worried about him driving after having had a couple of pints. Maybe Callum had been drinking on top of Disulfiram. Was that why he'd felt sick? No – wait - that couldn't be right. I kicked a leg of the table in frustration. I was sure the toxicology report had recorded his blood work as negative for ethanol, which meant either Andy's information was wrong, and Callum hadn't been drinking, or—

A noise outside. Zoë must have heard it too. She rolled off the bed, went over and peeked through the slats of the shutters.

'I think it's him,' she whispered. 'He's coming up the path.'

The front door creaked open slowly.

'Isla?' A man's voice. A Scottish accent.

I didn't move. Eyes closed, I searched for the next piece of the jig-saw. If Andy's info was correct and Callum Galbraith had been drinking, then…

Footsteps on the tiled floor.

… either the toxicology report was wrong. Or…

My eyes were wide open now. A man came into the room; a baguette tucked under one arm, a newspaper clutched in his hand. He was around six feet three, wearing navy blue tracksuit bottoms and a grubby white T-shirt. His face was covered in freckles. The hair poking out from beneath his sweat-stained faded blue baseball cap was not auburn or strawberry blonde or even Viking sunset, it was *see-you-Jimmy* ginger.

Standing with her back to the window, the late afternoon sun slashing through the shutters and into the room, Zoë would have appeared to him in silhouette.

'Isla? Is it really you?' He threw the loaf and newspaper onto the table and approached at first hesitatingly, then eagerly, smiling broadly, arms outstretched. When he was a few feet away from Zoë he stopped and squinted. 'You're not Isla.'

235

I rose from the table and walked over to him. I could see he was wondering who I was, what was going on. Me too. I had tried so hard to track down Fergus Galbraith. Gone all the way to France just to speak to him. I had so many questions to ask – and now that it turned out he wasn't here: I was delighted.

'And you're not Fergus Galbraith,' I said. With a sweep of my arm I knocked the baseball cap from his head to reveal a small patch of shiny white skin standing out amidst the freckles on the side of his face. It was situated directly over what everyone else would have called the temple but which an autopsy report would refer to as the sphenoid bone.

After ten years at the coal face of the criminal justice system I thought I'd seen everything. I felt I had now. I'd come to France to interview a witness in a murder case and ended up meeting the victim, alive and sunburnt.

'Who are you?' he asked.

'I'm your wife's lawyer.'

Zoë came and stood at my side. 'Is this not the guy you're looking for, Robbie?'

'No Zoë. I'd like you meet the man our client is charged with murdering. I'd say she wasn't guilty. Wouldn't you?'

Callum Galbraith walked over to the fridge. 'I'm having a beer. Anyone else want one?' He was cool for someone who should have been stone cold.

Zoë declined. I said nothing.

Galbraith took a bottle from the fridge and opened it. 'How did you find me?'

'I'm not really sure, because it wasn't you I was looking for,' I said.

'I'm not going back. You should know that.'

'You'll let Isla go to prison?'

'I'll let her decide what's the right thing to do.'

'That night,' I said, 'you came home early from the golf outing.' Had he suspected his brother would be there? In my mind I pictured Callum arriving late after a long drive. The house in darkness. Tip-toeing up the stairs so as not to wake his wife. 'You came home early and found them in bed together.'

He couldn't look at me. He took his bottle of beer to the window and peered out through the shutters. The sun was dipping over the roof of the buildings opposite and the light in the single apartment room was fading.

'The tomahawk,' I said. 'You kept it under your side of the bed. The side your brother was sleeping on, nearest the door. He was facing inwards. Facing her.'

Callum Galbraith drank deeply, glugging down the contents of the small green bottle. When he'd finished he turned and smashed it off the edge of the table.

'Get out!' The jagged neck was pointed at me. Zoë screamed. Were we witnessing the famous Callum Galbraith temper? I didn't think so. I'd seen a lot of angry men in my time. The one standing before me was putting on an act. His spirit was as broken as the remains of the beer bottle he clutched tightly in his hand and I could tell just by looking that he wasn't going to hurt me or, indeed, anyone ever again.

'Get out!' he yelled once more. Zoë tugged at my arm. I pulled away and sat down on a chair, I wasn't ready to go. Not yet. I had managed to piece together in my mind what must have happened that night and could only marvel at the simplicity of it all.

Had Fergus Galbraith's body been buried and found in a shallow grave several weeks later or dragged by archaeologists from a peat bog in two thousand years' time, all sorts of tests would have been carried out: DNA, dental records, the works, in order to establish the corpse's identity. But there had been no need for any of that. Everyone knew whose body it was or thought they did. Identification wasn't an issue. Some of the cops at the scene knew Callum. They had turned up looking for a dead, six-foot tall, ginger-headed

237

bloke and found one lying in his bed, head splattered over the pillow and a wife confessing to the dastardly deed.

The toxicology report had shown negative for ethanol because the blood tested wasn't Callum's. Fergus had stopped drinking and was taking medication. Medication he'd left in his brother's house. Medication that Isla later took in a suicide attempt when she thought I was closing in on the truth.

'Clubbing your brother – that was out of sheer anger. Understandable, I suppose, and all over before you even knew what you'd done. But disfiguring the face? That couldn't have been much fun. Still, you had to do it, didn't you? In case someone noticed that the scar, the one medically-recorded distinguishing feature, was missing.'

Callum Galbraith didn't answer. In fact, he was no longer listening. He ran to the opposite corner of the room and raked about in a bed-side cabinet. When he found some cash, he pocketed it along with a passport, his brother's I guessed, and ran from the room. I heard him crash out of the front door.

I picked up the newspaper from the table. A day-old edition of the Scotsman, priced, I noticed, at a hefty five Euros.

'Are you just going to stand there reading the paper?' Zoë said.

I carefully folded the newspaper and packed it into the plastic folder.

'He's getting away,' Zoë said.

'Leave him.' With some difficulty I fastened shut the plastic folder.

'I don't understand. He's getting away,' Zoë repeated.

'I know, and we're going home.'

'You're just going to let him run off?'

I wasn't sure what she expected me to do: chase after the ginger-headed fugitive, rugby-tackle him, bundle him into my rented car and drive back to Blighty? No need. I had what I came for and a lot more. The Crown might hold a death certificate that declared Callum Galbraith to be a dead man. But I knew if he was, he was a dead man running.

CHAPTER **49**

We arrived back home in Linlithgow early Sunday morning. The French trip had been a great success for Isla's case, but not everything I'd dreamt it might be from the point of view of getting to know Zoë better. Two hours in an airport departure lounge. A one-and-a-half-hour flight. An eight-hour drive either side of a ten-minute meeting with a living corpse. Amazing how I always managed to drain the romance from any situation no matter how promising it might have at first appeared. Why I'd thought the trip would be a good idea I didn't know. There had to be simpler ways of spending time with Zoë than dragging her across sunny France in a non-air-conditioned car. Why didn't I come straight out and ask her on a date? Why pretend it was work? I liked her, she seemed to like me. She could only say no. Was that the real problem – rejection?

I pulled into the car park of the former distillery.

'Thanks, Robbie,' Zoë said, sleepily. She grabbed her unused overnight bag from the back seat. 'See you Monday.'

No coffee invitation then? Pity; at that moment caffeine was precisely what I needed. What I'd have preferred was a drop of what used to be made on the spot where my car was now parked, before someone decided that yuppie flats were more desirable than the aqua vitae. I was looking forward to a glass of whisky and a good kip almost as much as I was looking forward to my next consultation with Isla Galbraith.

Back at my own place, a call to the hospital told me that my murder client had been discharged home into the care of her parents. It was Sunday and I thought it best not to bother them; time enough tomorrow. Meanwhile, I had other pressing matters such as earning my sports client a few quid to help pay-off his homicidal quasi-father-in-law.

No whisky or forty-winks later, I found Malky at my dad's. The two of them were sitting side by side in deckchairs on the back green. Both deep in thought. Both with pens in hand.

'Blue,' Malky said, thinking out loud. He wrote the word down on the piece of paper balanced on two hairy knees protruding from a borrowed pair of my dad's voluminous shorts. His legs were quite tanned now though the scar on his left knee was still vivid white. 'Edinburgh.' He jotted that down too then paused for thought, sucking his pen, before turning to my dad. 'Is Aries the goat or the bull?'

'The ram,' grunted my old man, not lifting his head from his newspaper crossword.

Malky wrote something down and thought some more, pen poised over paper. 'Steak and chips,' he said, finishing with a flourish and clicking the pen with an air of finality, before dropping it into the breast pocket of his short-sleeved shirt. 'That's me done.'

'That's you done what?' I took the piece of paper from him and had a look at what he'd been writing.

'Favourite colour? Birthplace? Star sign? Favourite meal?'

'What's this all about?'

'The marketing guy asked me to fill it in. It's part of the advertising feature. They're doing an interview thing with me for the newspaper and I've to fill this in and take it with me to the photo-shoot.'

I cast my eye further down the questionnaire. 'Person you'd most like to meet? Answer: the wee shite who ripped the wing mirror off my car outside Celtic Park after the four-nil game.'

'It was an Alfa Spider,' Malky said. 'I'd only had it a week.'

'Italian motors.' muttered my dad, still engrossed in his crossword puzzle. 'Probably fell off itself.'

241

I read on. 'Question: if you could go back in time where would you go? Answer: to the day I made the perfect black-and-tan, so I could measure the exact heavy to Guinness ratio.'

'Tending to be critical,' said my dad. 'Eight letters, starting with C, then something P, something I, something, something S.'

'Cynical?' was Malky's hopeless guess.

'Captious,' I said.

'Wheesht.' My dad started to fill in the empty boxes. 'Get your own crossword.'

'Then stop reading out the clues,' I said.

'I'd have got that myself,' he muttered.

'Captious?' Malky said. 'Is that even a word?'

'Course,' I said. 'Or, then again… I could be bluffing.'

My dad stopped writing. He glanced at me out of the corner of his eye, pen hovering over the newspaper. His moustache twitched suspiciously. 'Another beer, Malky?'

'No chance,' I said. 'He's got to be changed and out of here in ten minutes.'

My dad heaved himself out of his deckchair. 'Suit yourself.'

'So, this is how the other half live,' I said, once my dad had gone inside for a beer and a quick swatch at the dictionary.

Malky smiled up at me. He looked happy and relaxed. 'Dexy Doyle phoned this morning.'

'Phoned you? What? Here?'

'It's okay. I smoothed things over with Dad.'

'What did he say?'

'Well he wasn't over the moon about terrorists phoning but—'

'Not dad – Dexy. What'd he say?'

'He was surprisingly fine. I told him the property in London was as good as his and then he asked about the money.'

'And?'

Malky looked pleased with himself.

'I talked him into taking half now and half in three months. He seemed okay about it all. It was an almost civilised conversation.'

Sometimes I wondered if my brother had headed too many footballs in his younger days. 'You're overlooking one important factor. You don't have half the money.'

Malky climbed out of his deckchair. 'Not yet. But I know you're working on that.'

CHAPTER **50**

Prestonfield Park was resplendent in the early August sunshine: the pitch, closely mown and freshly lined, showed no ill effects from Saturday's friendly and looked all set for the new season ahead. Jake Turpie and his minder, Deek Pudney, were waiting for us in the centre circle beside a large object draped with a white sheet. For once Jake had discarded his set of oily overalls and was smartly attired in a suit and clean white shirt, a brightly-coloured tie about his neck. Hitherto I hadn't known he possessed a suit and a clean shirt - or a neck for that matter. He was so well-groomed even his head was polished to an extra-specially high sheen.

In a few minutes we were joined by a man with a lot of hair some of which was dyed blonde, flattened forward at the front and sticking up at the back. He was young but not as young as he dressed. I took him to be the marketing guy Malky had mentioned, for he had with him a couple of personable young ladies in rather tight-fitting maroon and white Linlithgow Rose FC strips. Close behind came a photographer lugging a metal case. The rest of the ground was empty apart from some youths sitting on the terracing steps behind one set of goals, enjoying the sunshine, and slugging tonic wine. Occasionally they would shout inappropriate remarks at the two female footballers and cheer if they elicited a response, no matter how dismissive.

'This is where it all started, Malky,' said marketing guy, hands outstretched, and spinning three hundred and sixty degrees. 'This was the beginning of your venture into the world of professional soccer. And today...' he went behind Jake and looked over his shoulder as the girls whisked off the white sheet to unveil a gleaming, nearly-new hatchback, its nearside plastered in stickers advertising Jake's new business. 'Today we embark on another exciting venture - JT Motors Limited.' The scowl that was more or less a permanent feature of Jake's face relaxed into what could only be described as almost a smile.

'Right, Malky,' said the photographer, assuming control of events. He probably had a wedding to go to later. 'We'll take a few here and then go over to the goals with the girls.' He pointed to the end of the pitch where a shiny new JT Motors advertising board reflected the sun's rays.

I totted it up in my head: photographer, newspaper advertising feature, track-side hoarding; the whole package must have been costing Jake a small fortune. And then there was my fee, or rather Malky's, to consider. We'd settled on five thousand for my client's services including my own five hundred pounds arrangement fee which I'd insisted on up front and in cash, strictly no fifties. Jake had stumped up the advance with hardly a struggle; he was really sparing no expense on his new enterprise, which, though he could well afford it, was very unlike him. The Jake Turpie I knew parted with cash like he parted his hair.

After a few snaps of Malky and Jake standing next to the car, over which the two girls were sprawled full length, the photographer took my brother and the lovelies down to one of the goalmouths where he arranged them into various poses. Malky, arms crossed, foot on the ball, babes either side, seemed a particular favourite.

Jake sidled over to me. 'What do you think? JT Motors - that was big Deek's idea. JT, you know, it's quite like GT and it's also my initials, good eh?'

I thought Deek blushed a little. It was probably the first time his employer had praised him for anything that didn't involve a compound fracture to a late-payer.

Suddenly the photographer was walking up the pitch towards us leaving Malky leaning against a goal post, a girl on each arm.

'Jimmy,' he said to the marketing guy, 'could you do something about the neds? They're buggering-up the background.' The man with the hair cast a worried glance at the youths on the terracing who were now engaged in a spot of rough and tumble, wrestling and taking fly-kicks at each other. A green bottle fell from the back pocket of one of them onto the concrete steps but didn't smash. Plastic; those monks at Buckfast Abbey thought of everything.

'Stay where you are, son,' Jake told the marketing guy, his eyes fixed on the disturbance. The expression on his face had reformed to its default scowl setting and was darkening by the second. 'Deek,' he growled, and without need of further instruction the big man set off down the pitch to restore background tranquillity.

Later, when we'd retired to the Rose Club for a bite to eat and a drink, all courtesy of Jake, I waited until Malky was deep in conversation with the girls from the photo-shoot before approaching the subject of money.

'So,' I said, rubbing my hands together, 'business done, that leaves only the small matter of Malky's fee.'

'Bill me,' Jake said.

I took a step back. 'What do you mean – bill you?'

'Send me an invoice. I'll send you a cheque.'

I had to be hearing things. Since when did Jake Turpie start dealing in cheques?

He read my thoughts. 'You heard the man, didn't you? I'm on a new business venture. This isn't me selling scrap. The folk who buy my cars pay by cheque, bank draft, they take out finance. Cars are just not a cash business any longer. And I've got to show outlays to set against profits, you know, for tax purposes.'

Tax? Was this some kind of joke?

'Right then,' I said, 'if it's not readies, the fee's six and a half.'

'Five was the deal,' Jake reminded me. 'And you've had half a loaf up front,' he added. 'That leaves me owing you four and a half.'

The shadow of the tax man loomed large. 'Make it pictures of the Queen and I'll take four.'

'Three and a half,' Jake gloated. He might have been thrown out of school without a qualification to his name, but he knew what five-grand less a chunk to the Chancellor was.

'Let's have it,' I said, holding my hand out to receive a wedge.

'Not here,' Jake said. 'I don't have the cash on me. You'll need to come to my place for it.'

'When?' I asked suspiciously.

'How's the morn's night sound?'

It sounded extremely unappealing. People who went to Jake's place to talk money didn't always come back, or if they did it was often with pieces missing.

'It's all right,' he said, sensing my hesitation. 'I wouldn't bump you.' He went over to Malky, who was now flirting with a waitress. Jake unceremoniously elbowed her out of the way, reached up and put an arm around my brother's shoulders. 'Well I might bump you baw-heid… but not the big lad. Not my hero.'

CHAPTER 51

Monday morning. Isla Galbraith's preliminary hearing was just over twenty-four hours away. I would loved to have been there to personally drop the bombshell on Cameron Crowe; tell him he could shove his murder charge and any offer of culpable homicide. I'd seen the murder victim with my own eyes and he was alive and well and paddling a canoe though the salt marshes of mid-western France. Unfortunately, he wouldn't believe me and, anyway, I was going to have to arrange for the preliminary hearing to be continued in the hope that the following week when it called again, I'd still be practising law and in a position to further my investigations.

When I arrived at the office my PC was already up and running and a virtual yellow-sticky was on the screen. Isla Galbraith had phoned. Bearing in mind that before I left the country my client had been so distressed at my attempts to track down her brother-in-law that she'd tried to top herself, and given the fact that the very same brother-in-law had, as she must have known, died bloodily in her marital bed, I didn't think our next conversation was best suited to a telephone call. My plan was to get to court early, speak to the Sheriff Clerk nicely so as to have my cases called first and then nip through to see Isla at her home for a face to face.

I was in reception putting the day's case files into my briefcase, Zoë was on the phone and Grace-Mary floating about when Andy arrived. While I'd been off preparing for the French trip I'd left my assistant with a couple of Sheriff Court trials, nothing serious: one an assault, the other a breach of the peace with a resist arrest tagged on. The accused were both long established clients.

'How'd things go on Friday?' I enquired.

Andy cleared his throat. 'Guilty.'

'Which one?'

My assistant busied himself with some papers on his desk.

'Not both of them?'

Grace-Mary came over. 'Did you get the message I left?'

I ignored her. 'Please tell me they weren't jailed.'

Andy looked up and was about to launch into some mitigation of his performance which would, judging by his results in court lately, probably not have amounted to much.

Grace-Mary intervened. 'What did you expect? Andy's new to the Sheriff Court. He's got to learn. It's not like you've never got anyone the jail before.'

'But with Sheriff Brechin off on holiday—'

'He's not. He's back,' Zoë said, replacing the receiver.

'What?' harmonised Grace-Mary, Andy and I.

'Someone left a note saying I was to phone the court first thing and find out which Sheriff had been allocated your trial.'

'That was me,' Grace-Mary confirmed.

'Well,' Zoë said, 'I did. And the clerk told me Sheriff Brechin is back from holiday and doing summary trials tomorrow.'

My solicitor's practising certificate flashed before my eyes.

'I thought you said he'd gone to Mull?' Grace-Mary accused me.

'Arran. And it was Andy who said that.'

'That's what the clerk told me,' whined my assistant. 'Bird-watching. It's supposed to be his summer holidays. I thought he'd be away for at least two weeks and he's back after one. I bet he's come back specially for your trial.'

'That's that then,' I said. 'I'd be as well ripping up my practising certificate right now and save the Solicitors Disciplinary Tribunal the bother.'

Andy sat down at his desk and began to rhythmically strike his forehead with the heel of a hand. 'What are we going to do?'

Grace-Mary brought him a glass of water.

Clearly, Zoë was still puzzling over the brevity of Sheriff Brechin's ornithological excursion. 'Mull—'

'Arran,' I snapped at her and then apologised.

Zoë continued. 'I've been there. It's quite a small island. I mean there can't be that many birds on it to watch. Maybe he's seen them all.'

'Zoë,' Grace-Mary said. 'Be quiet and get Dr MacGregor on the phone. Tell him Robbie's on his way down. She turned to me. 'If you ask him nicely, Bill MacGregor will write a soul and conscience letter that says you're not fit for trial tomorrow. Just pretend you're poorly. Shouldn't be hard, you're a man after all. After that you can go home. If anyone calls, Zoë will tell them you're off sick.'

Andy leapt to his feet. Grace-Mary grabbed the glass of water he almost spilled in the process. 'Great idea. That'll put the trial off for a few months; my traineeship is up at the end of September.'

'I'm not going to see the doctor and I'm not going home,' I announced. 'In case you hadn't noticed I'm in the middle of a murder case.' I collected my jacket and car keys.

Grace-Mary barred my way. 'You're no use to Isla Galbraith struck off.'

'My trial is tomorrow morning,' I reminded her. 'Isla's preliminary hearing is at noon.'

'Suit yourself,' Grace-Mary said, stepping aside. 'It's your career.' She picked up a paper punch and began to make holes in some of the mail, ready for filing. 'But what about Andy's?'

'I'll find him somewhere else to finish his traineeship - if the worst comes to the worst. I've not been convicted yet. Let's not forget the presumption of innocence.'

'Why not?' mumped Andy. 'Bert Brechin has.'

'We don't know for certain if Brechin will be doing my trial. And I've got a defence agent - a good one. I didn't just pick Paul Sharp out of the phone book, you know. It's not like I've hired some dafty from the Public Defender's Office.'

'And us?' Grace-Mary enquired further. 'Me and Zoë? You lose this trial, we lose our jobs.'

'And if Isla Galbraith is convicted she goes to prison for life. Sorry, but I've no time to be ill. I've got to go see my client.'

Silence. I walked to the door aware of three pairs of eyes watching me go. I turned. 'Look, it's a long drive. I'm not promising anything but maybe I'll catch something debilitating on the way back.' And on that note of optimism I set off to see Isla, intent on finding out why she'd allowed herself to be charged with murdering a man who wasn't dead.

CHAPTER **52**

Chez Galbraith was a new-build on the outskirts of the village of Drymen, a village twenty miles north of Glasgow and only a couple of miles from the south-east corner of Loch Lomond. It was part of a small private development that was still very much at phase one, with building plots dotted about in various stages of construction; some with newly laid founds, others with brickwork ongoing, scaffolding outside and a cement mixer in the garden. Isla's house was situated at the top of the estate where a few of the properties were completed and occupied. I parked my car at the kerb next to a mountain of topsoil and walked up a newly-laid path of slate slabs that had bedding plants neatly set out either side along its length.

Mrs Clegg was waiting for me at the door. She looked frail and drawn; no wonder with her daughter's court appearance the next day. 'Come away in Mr Munro. Isla won't be a moment,' she said, letting me into a porch that smelled of emulsion paint, and guiding me down an avenue of cardboard boxes that overflowed with crockery, books, ornaments and assorted bric-a-brac. 'You'll have to excuse the mess.' She opened the door to the sitting room: magnolia walls, oatmeal carpeting, brown leather suite. In one corner near the big bay window stood a silver-bezelled flat-screen TV: In another some more cardboard boxes stuffed full of odds and ends waited to be unpacked. 'Isla and Callum only got the keys the week before…before… as you can see…' Mrs Clegg looked around the room and then stopped to stare out of the window as though in a daze.

'It's a great view,' I said.

The old woman snapped out of her trance and smiled sadly. 'Yes. The West Highland Way is practically at the bottom of the garden. I think that's why Callum was so keen to move here. He was always a boy for the great out-doors.'

I reclined in an armchair, waiting for my client to make an appearance.

'I don't know what's keeping her.' Mrs Clegg sat down on the sofa and then stood up again. 'I'll just go and see where's she's got to.'

'I'm here mum.' Isla Galbraith stood in the doorway. The plain white cotton frock made her slim figure seem thinner than ever. Her hair fell long and lank about her shoulders and what little make-up she usually wore was missing. The silver charm bracelet, I noticed, was back on her wrist.

Mrs Clegg collected a big ball of pink wool and knitting needles from the arm of the sofa. 'I'll leave you two alone.'

'No, Mum,' Isla said. 'I'd like you to stay.'

'I don't think that's a good idea,' I said. 'What we have to discuss is highly confidential.'

Isla gave me a fiercely stubborn look that I hadn't seen before. 'No. I want my mum to stay.'

Mrs Clegg looked mildly surprised and yet pleased. Without a word she sat down on the couch again and was joined there by her daughter.

'I wasn't expecting to see you today,' Isla said once we were all settled. 'Has something happened? Has the Lord Advocate agreed to drop the murder charge?'

'No...' I had been looking forward to this moment. Now that it had arrived, and with Mrs Clegg sitting listening in on what should have been a private conversation between me and my client, I wasn't sure what to say. My French discovery would bring an end to the present proceedings, but that wouldn't be an end of the matter. There was still an unsolved murder out there. Isla was not yet in the clear.

The carriage clock on the mantelpiece chimed twice. I decided to come straight to the point. 'I found Callum. I was speaking to him at the weekend.'

Mrs Clegg opened her eyes wide at me and gave her head a little shake, presumably trying to attract my attention to what she regarded as an unfortunate slip of the tongue.

'How was he?' Isla asked after a short pause.

'Alive,' I said. 'I take it you're in contact with him?'

'No. I don't even know where Callum is. I think it's best that I don't.'

Mrs Clegg put a hand on her daughter's knee. 'Fergus, dear,' she said softly. 'You don't know where Fergus is.'

Isla bowed her head and began to cry. Mrs Clegg threw me an annoyed look as though by my thoughtlessness I had upset her daughter.

'Mrs Clegg,' I said. 'Isla knows where Fergus is. He's lying in a grave under a tombstone marked, Callum Galbraith.'

Mrs Clegg took several gulps of air and looked as though she might pass out. 'What are you saying?' she managed to gasp.

I felt I'd said enough for the moment.

Mrs Clegg turned to her daughter and gave her a shake. Then another. Harder. 'What's going on?' Isla said nothing, just continued to cry. Her mother took a deep breath and closed her eyes, mouth quivering. She might have been praying. After a minute or two Mrs Clegg, her emotions once more in check, rose and left the room. Isla continued to sob uncontrollably, something to which I was by now immune. After a short while her mother returned with teapot, three china mugs and a jug of milk rattling on a tray.

'I want to know everything.' The calm of Mrs Clegg's voice was betrayed by the unsteady hand she used to pour out three mugs of tea. I took the one that was offered me, thinking better than to ask for sugar. Isla, whose flow of tears had not once let up during her mother's absence from the room, didn't react when a steaming hot mug was pushed at her. Mrs Clegg's eyes narrowed, her mouth puckered. She put the mug down on a small side table, squared up to her daughter and then cracked her across the face with the flat of her hand. Isla sat bolt upright, cheeks flushed and streaked.

'You will tell me everything,' said her mother. 'Or I will call your father in here right this minute.'

As threats go, I'd heard worse, but as though on cue the jolly Mr Clegg poked his happy face around the door and came into the room. He was wearing a tweed bunnet, white shirt and corduroy trousers. Judging by the amount of mud on his clothes I gathered he'd been doing a spot of landscaping in the back garden.

'Hello, Mr Munro, lovely day again. Thought I heard the kettle,' he said cheerily and stared down at his stocking feet. There was a hole in one of his socks. He wiggled a big toe through it and looked around the room as though expecting an equally big laugh. He noticed Isla's tear-smeared face. His smile disappeared. 'What's wrong, dear?'

Isla turned away. Mrs Clegg went over, licked a finger and wiped a smudge of dirt from her husband's face. She pecked him on the cheek. 'Everything's fine,' she said, gently ushering him from the room.

Her husband gone, Mrs Clegg handed the mug of tea to Isla who this time accepted.

'Out with it,' she said.

Isla tried to speak but once more burst into a fit of sobs.

'Callum wasn't killed,' I said. 'It was Fergus.'

Mrs Clegg blinked rapidly, composed herself and said calmly, 'Is this correct Isla?'

Her daughter sniffed and nodded.

'And Callum...' Mrs Clegg's eyes were fixed on her daughter, 'where is he?'

'France,' I said.

'Doing what?'

'Hiding.'

Mrs Clegg glowered at her daughter. 'Isla. Did Callum kill Fergus?'

Isla dissolved into more floods of tears.

'Don't answer that,' I said rather unnecessarily, for Isla was clearly incapable of coherent speech. 'Mrs Clegg, remember what I told you about discussing the case? What Isla tells me is completely confidential, but if she says anything incriminating to you then that's evidence. You could end up being compelled to testify against your own daughter.'

'Firstly, Mr Munro,' Mrs Clegg said, primly, 'I'm not discussing the case – Isla isn't charged with murdering Fergus, and, secondly, I'm not asking if she killed Fergus but if Callum did.'

Any flies on the old woman had signed a lease.

'Isla,' I said. 'I really think it's best if I speak to you alone.'

'No,' Mrs Clegg said.

'No.' Isla wiped teary eyes on the sleeve of her dress. 'I want my mum to stay.'

Clients. The job would be so much easier without them. I couldn't let Isla admit anything, not even to her mother. The fact that she hadn't killed her husband didn't alter the fact that someone had been murdered in the Galbraith bed. There would be another enquiry in which everyone, including Isla's mother, would be interrogated. The embarrassment my revelations would cause the police would ensure that those detectives still left in a job would be a whole lot more thorough with their investigations the second time around.

'What happened?' Mrs Clegg demanded.

It was clear the old woman was not going to let up and I thought it better if I spoke to her since nothing I said could later be attributed to my client. 'I think what may have happened is... I think Callum may have caught Fergus and Isla...' I searched for the right words. 'Breaking the seventh commandment. Again.'

I expected a shocked reaction. It didn't come. 'And so Callum killed him?' said Mrs Clegg, matter of factly, as though her son-in-law had been found smoking behind the bike shed.

'Possibly. I don't know for certain and, frankly, don't care. What I do know is that since Isla's confession relates entirely to the murder of her husband, it was clearly fabricated and of no evidential value. There will be a new murder enquiry of course, and the Authorities will be starting off with a clean slate. So will we. This time Isla will say nothing to the police, and, when the Crown considers her affair with Fergus—'

'That will all have to come out?' asked Mrs Clegg.

'I'm afraid so. And with Callum being on the run… well you can put two and two together and so can the Lord Advocate. I doubt very much if Isla will even be prosecuted. Not with murder at any rate. Maybe an attempt to defeat the ends of justice by covering up her husband's crime.'

If that ever happened, I'd argue that covering up for a spouse was an implied duty of the wedding oath. Love, honour, obey and not clipe on one's better-half. To expect otherwise would be a breach of article 8 of the good old ECHR. Worth a try. Whatever happened, the case was going to run and run. My client would be on the front page of every newspaper for weeks and I'd be right there beside her. What had started off as a damage limitation exercise was rapidly evolving into a major marketing coup for Munro & Co.

'What about Callum?' Mrs Clegg asked.

'Callum?' I allowed the visions of newspaper headlines and TV interviews to dissipate for a moment. 'A European arrest warrant will be issued, followed by a man-hunt and I expect he'll be caught; sooner or later. Bound to be - the amount of publicity this case will attract.'

'What then?'

'If he's convicted of murder: life imprisonment. The same as would have been the case for Isla.'

257

Mrs Clegg was having problems coming to grips with this. 'But if he acted in the heat of the moment...'

'I'm afraid the defence of crime passionnel is no longer with us. Not even as a reason to reduce a murder charge to culpable homicide.' Another recent change in the law. Another example of Callum Galbraith's bad luck.

'The man found his wife in bed with his brother,' Mrs Clegg snapped. 'Do you think it's fair that a good man like Callum Galbraith should go to prison because he reacted to that? Do you think that would be justice?'

What could I say? I was a criminal defence lawyer. Justice didn't play a big part in my daily routine. I was interested in results. If justice equated to guilt or innocence, then that depended on whether at least eight out of fifteen jurors had a reasonable doubt.

'Well do you?' asked Mrs Clegg, advancing into territory I'd always found it best to avoid. 'Is it justice for Callum to be locked-up for life because of one moment of anger – righteous anger - and all because of his lecherous, drunkard of a brother and this harlot?'

Isla bowed her head. Her mother glared at me. Nothing I had to say on the question of justice was going to help. I didn't make the laws, I had to work with them, sometimes work around them. The only certain thing about the criminal justice system was that the people who made the rules kept changing their minds. These days, Parliament said it was a crime to smoke in a pub or forget to put on a seat belt. Same with drinking in public. Under the Scottish Government it was a crime to picnic in your local park if you fancied a crisp Chablis with your chicken salad. Religion seemed little better. One day Gays were an abomination, the next they were taking the service. The fact was: times changed, laws changed, morals changed. Justice was a moveable feast; a pie supper wrapped in tabloid newspaper. The only thing that never changed was my duty to do the best for my client. I'd let other people decide if the outcome was justice or not.

Mrs Clegg leapt at her daughter, seized her wrist, ripped off the silver charm bracelet and hurled it across the room. She looked ready to give Isla another skelp and my client looked set to take it. I intervened, pulling Mrs Clegg away and sitting her down in the armchair I'd vacated.

I went over and sat beside Isla. Her tears had stopped, for the time being at any rate, and she seemed settled now, more self-assured and in control of herself. After some persuasion she agreed with me that it would be best if her mother left us alone, which Mrs Clegg eventually, if grudgingly, did.

'I want to tell you the truth about what happened,' my client said softly, when we were alone. 'What you told me before about confidentiality. You'll not repeat this to anyone?'

'I can't. Not without your permission.'

She sat back in the sofa and closed her eyes. 'Callum was being treated for cancer.' She looked like she was going to start sobbing again and just for a moment I wished her mum would come back and give her another slap. 'Fergus came down to visit him in hospital. He stayed at our house for a while.'

'And you had an affair with him. I know. Your mum told me. What about the night he died?'

'After our…our…fling, once Callum was better, I told him everything, begged his forgiveness. He was upset, of course. Angrier at Fergus than me. He forgave me and we went on with our lives. I didn't see Fergus for years, never even called him. He still sent me a charm for my bracelet every year and I know he tried to speak to Callum, but Callum wasn't interested; Fergus was dead to him. A week before this all happened Fergus phoned me. Told me he had a new charm for my bracelet and wanted to deliver it personally. I refused point blank to see him, but he pleaded with me, said he was going to buy a place in the sun and was leaving the country. He said he only wanted to give me the charm as a good-bye gift.' Isla shrugged. 'I agreed to see him.

259

Callum was going away for the weekend. How could I have been so stupid? If only...' The words choked in her throat.

I picked up the story as I understood it. 'Callum came home unexpectedly and found the two of you in bed?'

Isla nodded. 'When he hit Fergus the axe broke. A piece of it flew off and hit me on the face just above the eye.' She gave a hollow little laugh. 'Callum asked me if I was all right. Even after all that he couldn't bear to see me hurt.'

'What then?'

'Fergus was unconscious. There was blood and clear fluid coming from his ears and nose. The wound on his head was horrible. I'd been a casualty nurse long enough to know he could never recover from an injury like that.'

'And Callum?'

'He wanted to hand himself in, but I wouldn't let him. We sat for hours and talked about what to do. If the police found Fergus murdered in my bed it was obvious Callum would get the blame. We thought of disposing of the body, but didn't know where to begin and Callum thought sooner or later people would wonder where Fergus was and start asking questions.'

'So, the brothers switched identities. Whose idea was that?'

'Mine. I'd always thought how alike they were - in physical appearance at any rate.'

'And Callum agreed to let you take the blame?'

'No. I told him I'd say a burglar broke in. He packed Fergus's belongings and drove off in his car. Most of the houses around here are still being built. There's no street lighting in yet so no-one would have seen anything unusual.'

'What about the screwdriver?'

Isla closed her eyes and nodded. 'Callum and Fergus were alike, not identical.' She pressed the knuckles of a clenched fist against her forehead. 'I'd already dialled nine-nine-nine and the police were on their way when I realised the lack of a surgical scar on the side of Fergus's head might be noticed. It was a horrible thing to have do but he was already dead… dying and—'

'With a screwdriver? Why?'

Isla picked the silver bracelet from the floor where her mother had thrown it. 'Fergus put the new charm on my bracelet. He'd brought his tools with him. The screw-driver was lying by the side of the bed.'

She'd told me all this without shedding so much as a tear, something of a personal best for my client. Had the weeping all been for show? Had her tears, like her medical records, been a fraud? Was the shy little-girl-lost routine merely the skin stretched over a skeleton of cold steel? After all, this was a woman who had not only cheated on her husband while he was recovering from cancer treatment but had rammed a screwdriver through her dead lover's head.

'And the burglar story?'

'It would never have worked.'

She wasn't daft either. With a cop-killer on the loose, the police would never have stopped searching. Sooner or later they'd have learned the truth. Better to keep it plain and simple. Give them a victim and a killer. Case closed. Providing you didn't mind going to prison for life.

Isla played with the silver bracelet. 'I thought I loved him,' she said. 'I didn't. Whatever I felt for Fergus, it wasn't love. I love Callum. I know that now. I knew it as soon as I saw Fergus lying there dying and all I could think of was Callum being sent to prison because of me. When the police arrived I felt so guilty I was happy to confess. It was only later, during that week in Cornton Vale, that I began to think what life in prison would actually mean. Then I remembered reading in the newspaper how you'd got that woman off with stabbing her husband. Callum had been moaning about it one morning at breakfast, saying how women were always getting away with murdering their partners and how the same never happened to men who killed women.'

'Isla. About court tomorrow,' I said. 'We'll have to tell the Crown about Callum. The Advocate Depute and I don't get on very well. I don't expect him to believe me about Callum being alive. He already thinks I've tried to pull the wool over his eyes with the violent spouse story as supported by your dodgy medical records.'

'And if he doesn't believe it? What then?'

'It depends what body tissues were kept following the post mortem and whether there are any known samples of Callum or Fergus's DNA available to compare it with. Failing that it will be down to fingerprint comparisons, dental records, those sorts of things. It won't be straight-forward. A lot of the samples that would routinely have been taken weren't because there was never any doubt as to the identity of the body - until now. That was the beauty of your idea.'

'And if that doesn't work?'

'Then we'll have to seek a court order for exhumation.'

Isla swallowed hard. 'Dig Fergus up?'

'I'm afraid so. Forensic tests will prove the body isn't who it's supposed to be, the indictment against you will fall and there will be a massive man-hunt for Callum.'

'What can he do?'

'Keep running.'

'And if he's caught?'

'There'll be one hell of an interesting trial.'

'But he will be convicted?'

'Well there are really only two possible suspects and finding his brother in bed with you clearly gives Callum a motive. Fleeing the country won't have helped matters either; it's another adminicle of evidence from which guilt can be inferred.' I stood up. 'But all that's a long way off and I'm only interested in you. You're my client, not Callum, so first things first - tomorrow's preliminary diet. Do you know where you're going?'

'I think so.'

'Glasgow High Court is at the Saltmarket, by the Clyde. You can't miss it. It's directly across the road from the McLennan Arch on the west end of Glasgow Green.'

Isla nodded. 'I'll be there.'

'Good,' I said. 'I've something else on tomorrow so I'll be asking counsel to have the case knocked on a week or two. It will give us time to talk some more and decide how we're going to play things.'

With Ranald Kincaid having withdrawn from the case and Fiona Faye wielding a barge-pole, I'd have to leave it to Leonard to seek a continuation. Most preliminary hearings were continued at first time of calling so it shouldn't pose a problem even for him.

'What do you think will happen?' Isla asked.

'The most likely outcome is that after we've told the Crown our news they'll want to make more enquiries and the case will be put off for a while for that purpose. You never know - Callum might come back and face the music.' I patted Isla's arm. 'Don't worry. Everything's going to work out fine for you.'

Isla followed me from the room and down the cluttered hallway to the front porch. Mrs Clegg, whose temper seemed to have cooled, materialised by her daughter's side. The two of them came to the door to wave me off, and, as I walked down the plant-lined path to my car, I couldn't help thinking how much I loved the case of HMA –v- Isla Jane Galbraith. Struck off or not, I would dine out on the story for years to come.

I started the engine and bumped my way down the unsurfaced roads of the new estate, swerving around a group of workies who were gathered beside a JCB. I had not made it out onto the main road when my mobile rang. It was Isla.

'Mr Munro,' she said; not Robbie. I sensed trouble. 'What we talked about... You said it was strictly confidential?'

'Yes, of course. I told you that.'

'Then, about tomorrow - I've made my decision - I'm going to plead guilty.' I drew the car into the side, narrowly avoiding a skip full of rubble.

'Look Isla. We've already been through this. You're charged with murdering Callum and he's not dead. Call me old-fashioned but…' I thought I heard someone whispering in the background. 'Isla are you listening to me?'

'My mind is made up,' she said.

'We'll talk about it tomorrow.' I was about to hang up when I heard my client's softly spoken reply.

'No, we won't. Because you won't be there tomorrow.'

She was right - my trial. 'Okay. Once we have the case continued, we can talk later in the week.'

'No,' Isla said, 'that's not going to happen.'

I remembered Isla's suicide bid and hoped she wasn't contemplating anything stupid. She dispelled any fears I might have had on that score.

'I'm sorry, Robbie…' I could tell she was about to start crying again. 'But you're sacked.'

CHAPTER 53

Next morning, I set off with Andy on the short walk, or, as my assistant rather melodramatically put it, the last mile to the Sheriff Court. The good weather of the past few weeks was on the turn. A skein of wispy cloud was teased thinly across the now not so blue sky and an accumulation of dark grey threatened on the western horizon.

On the way my mobile went off. It was Leonard phoning from Glasgow High Court. I'd forgotten to let him know we were sacked.

'Why didn't you tell me?' he asked in hurt tone. 'I arrive nice and early for Isla Galbraith's preliminary hearing only to be given my marching papers and find there's a whole new defence team warming up with Ranald Kincaid wearing the captain's armband. Did you know she was going to plead guilty? Can you believe it? Guilty to a murder charge. What a waste.'

Leonard ranted on for another couple of minutes, clearly finding it hard to come to terms with the loss of a three-week trial. It was more work than I guessed he'd seen since being admitted to the Bar and fudge doughnuts didn't grow on trees.

As we walked up the hill towards the court I noticed a sign being erected in the car park, facing onto the High Street. Built one hundred and fifty years ago, Linlithgow Sheriff Court was now up for sale. The end of an era. Soon the administration of justice would be transferred to a soulless complex in the depressingly new town of Livingston.

Checking the court notice-board upon our arrival, it became apparent that the unseemly haste with which my trial had been fixed had resulted in a problem with court accommodation. Court One was hosting a Sheriff and Jury trial, while business in Court Two was taken up by cited cases and custodies. For that reason the trial had been shunted into Court Three, a small room in an out of the way corner on the first floor, normally used for private hearings in civil matters: adoptions, children's referrals and the like. In a way it was better to have it there. The lack of space would severely limit the number of spectators and might allow Sheriff Brechin, who loved any opportunity to play to the gallery, to leave his high-horse tethered outside. On the other hand, there was something undignified about the possibility of ending my career in a courtroom not much larger than my own livingroom and with a bench, dock and witness box that came in on wheels.

'What do you think your chances would be on appeal?' Andy asked.

'I'm not convicted yet.'

'It's Bert Brechin,' he reminded me.

'Yeah, well, I'm afraid an appeal based on Brechin being a vindictive sod who's never given anyone the benefit of the doubt in his puff won't cut it with the Appeal Court.'

The clerk came on and took his place.

'Brechin,' I said. 'Cheers.'

The clerk gave a helpless shrug. 'I had it down for Sheriff Dalrymple, but his jury has spilled over from last week. There's still a couple of days in it and the floater in Court Two has been landed with the cited crap.'

Typical. As senior Sheriff, Brechin would have been allowed the privilege to choose his business for the day. Court Two: listen to thirty or forty pleas in mitigation, followed by an afternoon dealing with those arrested overnight, or, Court Three: a trial which could be done and dusted by lunch-time and came with the added attraction of sticking it right up one of the local, bleeding-heart defence agents. No contest. Was it too late for me to come down with the lurgy? I was certainly beginning to feel quite queasy. An adjournment would give me a chance of a different Sheriff and a fair trial on the next occasion.

The door of the court flew open and in came Fiona Faye, Paul Sharp trotting behind in her shadow.

'Okay, lover-boy,' she said to me, 'let's get this party started. File?' She held out a hand and Paul laid onto it a thin buff folder. 'The way I see it, Robbie, there's clearly no *mens rea* end of story.'

'And my reply?'

'Are you kidding? You've been practising criminal law for how long? You spend all your time telling punters to keep quiet and this clown Fleming thinks anyone's going to believe that you sang like a linty? Give me five minutes and he'll wish he'd been a traffic warden. Give me ten minutes and he *will be* a traffic warden.'

'And what about your VAT fraud?' I asked.

'Still moving slower than a cement snail. As far as I can make out it's all to do with mobile phones coming into and going out of the country, but somehow managing to stay in the same place. My geeky junior knows all the boring details. I've left him in charge, probably pooping himself in case he has to cross-examine someone. But, getting back to the matter in hand, you do appreciate that you'll have to give evidence and tell the court where the fake fifty actually came from?'

I looked at Andy. He looked at me.

'I gave it to Robbie after a client had given it to me,' he said. 'A thank-you for a job well done.'

There was imminent danger of the truth leaking out. Oh, no. I suddenly remembered: Jake Turpie. Bad enough the bizzies swarm over Jake's place searching for counterfeit notes, if they actually found any dodgy currency I'd be booked on a one-way ticket to the crusher inside a written-off hatchback.

Meanwhile the tiny court room was beginning to fill: a few defence agents, a local journalist, the court social worker and a handful of cops who were waiting to give evidence in the jury trial and saw my case as a more entertaining way of passing the time than sitting in the witness room perusing cookery recipes in vintage copies of the Peoples Friend. The clerk waved to the Bar Officer who was sitting on a chair near the door reading a gardening magazine.

I nipped out to call Jake with a warning and met Zoë and Grace-Mary on their way in.

'Just here to lend moral support.' Grace-Mary punched my arm.

Zoë pecked my cheek. 'Good luck Robbie,' she said, and tailed Grace-Mary into the small court room.

I found a quiet corner, whipped out my mobile. I had to warn Jake and wasn't looking forward to it. When it came to bad news, Jake was more of a maker than a taker. I punched his number but there was no answer. The Bar Officer hove into view leading Sheriff Brechin along the side corridor. By the time I had returned to the courtroom the Sheriff was already on the bench and the Clerk was calling me forward.

'Morituri te salutant,' my assistant muttered darkly, as I trudged past him. He'd obviously been reading up on his Latin.

I took my place in the dock. To my right at the table in the well of the court sat my defence team, Fiona Faye and Paul Sharp. Across from them, Hugh Ogilvie, the Procurator Fiscal, nothing unusual there. What I hadn't expected was the added presence of the loathsome Cameron Crowe. What was he doing here? Fair enough he had taken a special interest in my case, but what about Isla Galbraith? Did he really hate me so much that he'd forego the preliminary hearing in a murder in favour of my summary trial?

'I take it you appear, Miss Faye?' the Sheriff remarked after I had formally identified myself to the Clerk. He set down a big blue notebook and removed the cap from his fountain pen. By the gleam in his eye and uncharacteristically content expression, I could tell Brechin was looking forward to proceedings almost as much as I wasn't.

Fiona Faye rose to her feet. 'Yes, M'Lord,' she confirmed, her voice booming around the small courtroom. She flicked open the buff file and picked out the charge sheet. 'Mr Munro adheres to his plea of not guilty.'

The moment was so surreal. I'd been involved in countless trials over the years, now here I was at probably my last and I was going to experience it from the point of view of the accused. I had good reason to be worried, even with Fiona Faye conducting my defence, and yet all I could think about was Isla waiting to plead guilty and go to prison for a crime she didn't commit. I tried to focus on my own case, fixing my eyes on the buff file lying on the table, the hand of my Q.C. resting upon it, a manicured red-painted fingernail tapping lightly as she waited for the Procurator Fiscal to address the court.

Usually there would be several summary trials set down for the same day. Normal practice would be for the P.F. to call them all first-thing to weed out those that weren't proceeding for whatever reason: perhaps an accused with cold feet, missing witnesses or a late plea of guilty. Once that was done and only those cases actually going to trial remained, the P.F. would request a short adjournment during which the decision would be made as to the order of business. It also allowed the court staff the chance for a coffee break, and in most courts around Scotland the adjournment following the trial 'call-over' was a well-observed tradition. There being only one trial set down for Court Three, however, there was only one case to call-over and therefore no need for an adjournment. Hugh Ogilvie was all set to charge straight ahead with the trial and ready to call his first witness. He rose to his feet, witness list in his hand. Fiona Faye Q.C. flipped open the front cover of my case file. No bundle of papers sewn with pink string and tied with red tape for me. I thought of another Q.C., Ranald Kincaid, champing at the bit to plead my former client guilty and send her off to Cornton Vale for life. I hoped his new brief had come in a yellow, plastic envelope with a smiley face on it. Then I remembered another yellow plastic folder; the one I'd taken with me to France.

'I wonder M'Lord,' I said, jumping to my feet, 'if I might be permitted a brief adjournment.'

'Miss Faye,' Sheriff Brechin said, not looking at me. 'I think your client wishes to communicate with you.'

Fiona bumped Paul with her shoulder. He got out of his seat and came over to me. 'What is it?'

'I need an adjournment.' Paul tried to protest, but I put up a hand. 'I mean it. Tell Fiona.'

'Robbie,' Paul said. 'There's no chance—'

'Please,' I said firmly. 'Do it.'

Paul went over and whispered in the Q.C.'s ear. She looked over her shoulder, gave me a quick shake of the head and turned her attention once more to the buff folder.

'M'Lord,' I said, still on my feet. 'I'd like a very short adjournment. To discuss some matters with my friend across the table.'

'You should have spoken to the Fiscal before now.' Brechin said. 'This trial was fixed three weeks ago. Now sit down.'

'I appreciate that, M'Lord,' I blurted out, 'but I believe my case may be capable of… resolution.'

'No!' exclaimed Andy, from the public benches.

'Silence in court!' shouted the bar officer.

Paul looked at me, shocked. Fiona pushed her wig a little further back her head. Sheriff Brechin smiled.

Capable of resolution was a euphemism employed by defence solicitors to tip the Sheriff the wink that there were plea negotiations on-going that made a plea of guilty highly likely if only a few more minutes were available to allow the necessary legal tweaks to be made.

'Very well.' The Sheriff looked at the clock. The court had started late. It was almost half past ten. 'I'll sit again at eleven. Let's hope discussions with Mr Ogilvie are fruitful.'

In so saying, Brechin would fully expect that after a quick cuppa and a swatch at The Herald he'd come back on, sentence me and be home by noon. He rose, and I left the dock to be joined immediately by Andy, Zoë and Grace-Mary.

'Don't think for one minute that I'm going to let you plead,' my assistant said.

His naivety was almost refreshing. There was absolutely no danger of me copping a plea and then going quietly into that dark night of estate agency or personnel recruitment or wherever struck-off solicitors went; however, my own predicament wasn't foremost in my mind at that moment.

Zoë came forward, worried. 'Robbie, are you all right?'

Grace-Mary barged her way between the two of them. 'Robbie, will you kindly let me know what's going on? Wait a minute,' she smiled then straightened her face and whispered conspiratorially in my ear. 'Not feeling well – that it?' She winked.

'Just dandy,' I replied, 'but I don't have much time. Andy, go back across the road to the office—'

'No!'

Zoë glared at my assistant. 'Shut up and listen to Robbie.' It seemed to work.

'What do you want me to do?' Andy mumbled.

Go back to the office and somewhere in my room, on the filing cabinet or somewhere, is a yellow plastic folder. I want you to bring it straight here.'

Andy started to object. 'Robbie—'

'Go.' I brushed past him.

Grace-Mary put out a hand. 'Robbie …?'

'Trust me,' I told her, and ran through to the robing room where Fiona was divesting herself of a silk gown. The wig was already returned to its velvet-lined black enamelled box. She laid the gown on the table and carefully folded it long ways twice and then rolled it up.

I went over to her. 'Fiona. I'm really grateful to you.'

'Robbie, if you're pleading guilty I'm having nothing to do with it.' She lifted a brown leather grip from the floor and slammed it down onto the table.

'Don't go Fiona, I need you.'

'Apparently not.'

'Of course I do, but there's someone else who needs you even more.'

She placed the tin box and gown in the bag and clipped it shut. 'Then they must really be in deep do-do.' She glanced down at her bag and then up at Paul. 'Sweetie?'

Paul lifted the brown leather holdall.

'Isla Galbraith,' I said.

'Who?'

'She murdered her husband.'

'The cop-killer? Not interested.'

'I think you will be. He's not dead.'

'A living murder victim?' Her tone was patronising in the extreme. 'Sounds like you have the makings of a pretty good defence. You will let me know how it goes won't you?'

'It's true. I saw him with my own eyes. Three days ago. He's alive and well and paddling a canoe though the salt marshes of mid-western France.'

She put a hand on each of my shoulders and looked into my eyes. 'Robbie. If you're trying for an insanity defence I can tell you the State Prison is never lovely. Not even at this time of the year.'

I relieved Paul of the Q.C.'s big leather bag and threw it into a corner of the room. I put an arm around Fiona's shoulders and despite her protests led her through the security door.

'Where are we going?' she asked, as we stepped out onto the top landing.

I pointed down through the stairwell to the ground floor where Hugh Ogilvie and Cameron Crowe were standing in line waiting to buy a cup of coffee from the charity stall by the front door.

272

I saw the door open and Andy come rushing into the downstairs lobby. There was a smir of rain in the air and he was holding the yellow plastic folder over his head as an umbrella.

'You're not really wanting to talk to the Crown, are you?' Fiona said. 'You can't possibly expect any favours from Cameron Crowe. He's a despicable shit and, trust me, he didn't come all this way to see you walk away from this.'

I thought back to a hot afternoon in the Vendée. No matter how great or small, beautiful or ugly, good or bad, we all play our part in la cascade de vie.

'Fiona,' I asked, 'have you ever heard of the Twin-Fish?'

CHAPTER 54

Oh, it's you,' Hugh Ogilvie said, unenthusiastically, when, clutching the yellow plastic folder, I approached him as he waited in line for a cup of the bitter brew the court charity-volunteers dished out. 'Did you really want to speak to me? I thought it was just an excuse for a coffee break.'

'Yes, I want to talk. But not to you and not here.' I turned to face Crowe. 'You ever tried the stuff they serve here? How about a decent cup over the road? I'm buying.'

Ogilvie checked his watch.

'We've got until eleven,' I told Crowe, 'and the Sheriff won't care if we're late so long as we get something sorted.'

He stared at me. Cool, impassive, merciless, cat to mouse.

'You want to discuss a plea,' Ogilvie said. 'Do it here, not at Alessandro's.'

I'd never heard anyone actually call Sandy's café by its proper name. He would have been pleased.

'You don't have to come,' I said to Ogilvie, 'this is between me and Mr Crowe.'

'And me,' said Fiona.

Ogilvie gave us both a look of sheer hatred. 'Mr Crowe has nothing to talk to either of you about. This is my case—'

Crowe tugged at the shoulder of Ogilvie's black court gown. 'Let's go.'

Hugh Ogilvie was a man who could take an order. You didn't become District P.F. by being a 'no' man. 'Oh, what the hell,' he said with a horribly artificial laugh, as we pushed our way through the smokers who were milling around outside the main entrance, and, squeezing past the punters he followed the three of us out of the front door.

At the café we came across Sandy stacking chairs. He'd bought a job lot of them, some tables too, metal ones, and put them out on the pavement so customers could enjoy the good weather and have continental-style elevenses. Judging by the gathering clouds he'd wasted his money.

'Quick as you like, Alessandro,' I said as the three of us trooped past him into the café. 'We've got to be back in court by eleven.'

The café wasn't as busy as usual, probably due to the lack of summary trials on at the Sheriff Court which meant there were fewer witnesses and lawyers taking advantage of the break in proceedings. D.I. Dougie Fleming and a young Detective Constable, no doubt learning at the feet of the master, were already ensconced at a corner table along with the expert witness from the Bank. Ogilvie entered giving Fleming a wave. The only other person I recognised was the old guy sitting at his usual place by the window, staring over the rim of a mug of milky tea. He fixed his sights on Fiona and nipped her bottom as she walked in. She yelped.

Sandy smiled. 'What a character, eh?' He pulled out some chairs from an empty table in the centre of the room. 'You'll have to excuse him.' He pointed a finger at his head and twirled it meaningfully. Fiona gave her assailant a glare but, unperturbed, the old guy returned a pair of rubbery lips to his mug of tea, slurped and turned his attention once more to the world outside the window.

Sandy produced a notepad and took an order for four coffees. Presumably on the basis of my earlier promise to pay, Ogilvie requested an Empire biscuit to go with his.

'I hope you don't think that a little chat over a coffee is going to save you,' Crowe said as we waited for our drinks to arrive. He pinged the screwed-up remains of an empty sugar sachet across the table at Fiona. 'Or that she is.'

Crowe had a face that I could never tire of hitting. Few things would have given me as much pleasure as to drag him from his chair, take him outside and give him a tanking but I had to remain calm, collected and remember that everyone and everything – no matter how evil - served a purpose. Crowe was about to serve his - he just didn't know it yet.

Sandy came over with our order. According to the brushed aluminium clock on the wall above the door it was twenty to eleven. Time to make my move.

'I should be flattered,' I said to Crowe, burning my lip on a scalding-hot Caffé Americano, 'that you should come through to Linlithgow especially for my case when you have a murder calling in Glasgow.'

'Your client, that is your ex-client, is pleading guilty. I'm letting young Miss Meadows do the necessary. Even though there's only one sentencing option open to the court once the plea has been recorded, they'll still have to put the case off for a few weeks for background reports. Don't worry,' he sneered, 'I'll be in there at the end – for the kill. Meanwhile, I thought I'd like to be in at the death of your career.' He drank some coffee. 'Which means if you've any begging to do let's get it out of the way.'

I paid no heed to the grin that Ogilvie was failing to hide behind his iced-biscuit. 'I've not come to beg. I've come to negotiate. You see, although I need your help, you don't know it yet, but you need mine.'

Fiona gave me an I-hope-you-know-what-you're-doing look.

'And for what reason would I possibly need your help?' Crowe was enjoying himself.

'To stop you playing a lead role in possibly the biggest ever blunder in the Scottish justice system and - let's be quite frank – there have been some real stonkers.'

Crowe snorted in disbelief. I hadn't had time to fill Fiona in on the details. She didn't know where I was going or what evidence I had, but she stepped up to the mark like a champ.

'Cameron. I really think you should listen to what Robbie has to say. For your own good if no-one else's,' she said, her earnest face and solemn tone of voice just perfect. Sincerity –

once you can fake that you've got it made in criminal defence.

Suddenly, Crowe didn't appear so smug.

'Isla Galbraith is going to plead guilty to a murder she didn't commit,' I told him.

The smile restored itself to Crowe cadaverous features. 'Then pray tell me – who did kill her husband?'

'No-one,' I said. 'He's not dead.'

Crowe pushed his half-finished coffee cup away and stood up, glaring down at Ogilvie. 'Come on, we've wasted enough time.'

'And I can prove it,' I said.

I removed the prized-possession from inside my jacket and laid it down on the table between us like it was a tablet of stone and not a yellow plastic folder. Crowe reached for it. I slammed my hand down on top, knocking the table and spilling some of Ogilvie's coffee into the saucer where he'd rested his biscuit.

I locked my eyes on Crowe's. 'I'm giving you two options. Option one: you tell me to go away, we return to court for my trial and Isla Galbraith pleads guilty to murder. Tomorrow, I may or may not still be practising law, but I will be witness to the fact that I have seen Callum Galbraith alive and as recently as last Friday afternoon, proof of which I will give to the Scottish Criminal Case Review Commission with my detailed affidavit as to how I tried to tell you of the terrible mistake you were about to make and how you refused to listen.' I caught my breath and took another sip of coffee. 'Once the newspapers and media have finished with you, you won't be able to get his job.' I jerked a thumb at Ogilvie.

'What do you mean by that? I'm a District P.F.,' Ogilvie spluttered, spraying the table with crumbs.

I ignored him. 'Option two: you send Ogilvie back across the road to desert my case simpliciter, and this stuff,' I lifted my hand from the plastic folder, 'is all yours. With it, you can

277

ride to the rescue of Isla Galbraith and, more importantly for you, your own career ambitions.' I looked at the clock. It was ten to eleven. 'My trial is due to start in ten minutes. Isla Galbraith will be tendering her guilty plea at noon. It's not too late.'

Ogilvie raised himself to his feet and stood beside Crowe, a good head and shoulders shorter. He looked up at him. 'Don't listen. It's a trick.'

'Of course it is,' Crowe snorted, but his eyes flicked down at the yellow plastic folder.

I opened it and pulled out the various documents with the exception of the newspaper: The Scotsman that Callum Galbraith had been carrying.

'It's Friday's newspaper,' I said, in answer to his unasked question. 'Have Forensics dip that in a bucket of DFO and you'll find Callum Galbraith's fingerprints all over it. Trust me. He was a cop. His dabs will be on record. The Scottish Criminal Records Office will have a whale of a time. Remember the Shirley McKie farce? If the SCRO can find a cop's fingerprints when they aren't there, they'll surely be able to find them when they are.'

CHAPTER 55

Fiona Faye could have shown my brother a thing or two about fast-driving. In her bright red BMW M3 convertible, complete with matching leather trim, we made it in less than half an hour from the car park of Linlithgow Sheriff Court to the Saltmarket, Glasgow, where Cameron Crowe and I were dropped off in the turning circle outside the entrance to the High Court of Justiciary. Some photographers and a TV crew had gathered in front of the big glass revolving door, no doubt, tipped-off well in advance that my ex-client would be pleading guilty. The law against reporting pre-trial proceedings was strict, but, once a guilty plea had been entered it was open season for the press. The tabloids had dubbed my last husband-killer, Mags MacGillivray, 'The Scotch-Broth Killer'. What nickname they'd dreamt up for Isla, no-one would ever know.

Inside the building I let Crowe sprint ahead of me, the yellow plastic folder filed safely in his briefcase. I had no fear he'd destroy the evidence. He might be a spiteful git, but Crowe's only concern was his career. With a little work he would turn the botched murder investigation into his own personal victory. Heads would undoubtedly roll - but not his.

I remained in the foyer at the foot of the marble staircase and didn't have to wait long. First person through the double doors at the top leading from the North and South courts was a solicitor from the Public Defenders Solicitors Office. He was closely followed by Ranald Kincaid Q.C., a tearful Isla Galbraith and her stunned parents. As he reached the foot of the stairs, the Public Defender straightened his tie readying himself to face the gentlemen of the press. Look, the PDSO don't always plead guilty, they sometimes get people off. He

279

turned to find Isla, but she had already noticed me and come over to where I was standing. The PDSO lawyer glanced to the throng of pressmen at the front door, to Isla and back again, not sure what to do. He looked around for senior counsel, but Kincaid had spied me moments before, about-turned midway down the stairs and was already making the climb back to the top.

'It was you wasn't it?' Isla said. 'What does it mean – deserted pro loco …?'

'Pro loco et tempore,' I said. 'Literally, the case has been deserted in this place and at this time.'

It was the best deal I could wring out of Cameron Crowe. He wouldn't drop the charge completely, not until he'd had the newspaper examined for fingerprints. If he wanted any more there was a small house in the Vendée that was full of them.

'Can the murder charge be re-raised in the future?' Isla asked.

'Technically, yes,' I said. 'But it won't. I've told the Crown that Callum's alive and given them proof of it. They've even agreed not to prosecute you for attempting to pervert the course of justice by your false confession.'

'You broke your promise,' Isla said. I hadn't really expected any thanks. 'You said whatever I told you would be confidential.'

Mrs Clegg came forward, her wrinkly face a wriggling mixture of emotions. Before she could say anything, Mr Clegg stepped forward. 'Thanks, son,' he said, taking my hand and shaking it. Then, gently but firmly, he steered his wife away leaving me and Isla alone again.

'Anything you told me about the case is still confidential,' I assured my ex-client. 'You didn't tell me Callum was alive, I found that out for myself.' 'Splitting hairs,' Isla muttered, dabbing her eyes with a handkerchief.

It would make an interesting case for the newly-formed Solicitors Complaints Commission – I'd like to complain: my lawyer told the truth and saved me from life imprisonment.

A mad bleeping of metal detectors announced the arrival of Fiona Faye strolling through the security gate. Behind her, outside the plate glass, the gentlemen of the press were already starting to drift away. 'I see you've sent the paparazzi homeward to think again,' she said, giving me a solid slap on the back. She noticed Isla's tears. 'Can't say I blame you, dear. Must be a great relief. Cornton Vale prison. Great view of the Wallace Monument, but who wants to look out through the bars at a huge phallic symbol every day when you're banged-up with three hundred women?'

'Isla has certain… issues… about the outcome. How they might affect her husband.' I explained.

'The not dead one?' Fiona laughed, totally misreading the situation. 'My first husband – should have killed him on the honeymoon – would have saved a fortune and I'd be eligible for parole about now.' She laughed again.

Isla looked set to dissolve. I could just about put up with a weeping woman when the legal aid meter was running - not when I was being paid hee-haw. Time for me to go. My work here was done. I took Isla's hand, the one not holding the soggy tissue, and tried to shake it.

'Good-bye, Isla,' I said, waggling her limp unresponsive fingers.

I'd always assumed cross-stitch to be a fairly sedate sort of a past-time. I'd never given any thought to the developmental effect that hour upon hour of lifting even something as insubstantial as a needle might have on the bicep.

'All the best,' I had started to say, when my former client pulled her hand from my grip and hit me a solid blow to the side of the head that sent me reeling. I staggered backwards into the supportive arms of Fiona Faye who ushered me away.

'Some clients give their lawyers bottles of whisky,' I complained as the Q.C. steered me towards the exit.

'Just be thankful,' Fiona said, as with a pat on the head she gave me a gentle shove out of the door.

'For what?' I asked.

'That there wasn't a screw-driver handy.'

CHAPTER 56

Apart from the slight swelling above my left eyebrow, I was so pleased at the way things had turned out that I very nearly gave the staff the rest of the day off. Instead, I took them for a drink after work and things improved even more when I invited Zoë back to my place for a bite to eat and she agreed. I was thinking pancakes and trying to remember if I had any syrup in the cupboard, when we arrived to find supper all ready for us and lying on a plate in front of the telly.

'Dad's getting to me big time,' Malky said, after we'd eaten. 'He's a great guy and I'm very grateful, but, between him and all his mad pals, if I see another football DVD I'm not going to be responsible for my actions.'

I gathered the dirty dishes and carried them to the kitchen.

Malky followed me through. 'The chef never washes up, right?'

I wasn't convinced that slamming a couple of frozen pizzas in the oven qualified Malky for the title of chef, but there being only a couple of plates, an oven tray and a pizza-cutter to wash, I couldn't see any point in arguing. Leaving him to keep Zoë entertained, I put the dishes in the sink and ran the hot water tap over them. I had no sooner squirted some washing up liquid into the stream of water and rolled up my sleeves than Malky came into the kitchen again and stood beside me. 'Nice girl,' he said. 'Pretty. He put a hand on my shoulder. 'Robbie… about me and Cat—'

The phone rang. I ignored it.

'Might be important,' Malky said. 'Could be Jake. I've still not been paid for that publicity shoot.'

That would be right - Jake Turpie calling to remind me that he owed me money? The phone stopped ringing as soon as I picked up. Then again - I wondered - Jake had told us to go down to his place the night before. I'd been so busy thinking about my trial and Isla's predicament that I hadn't remembered. If I waited any longer, then, applying Jake's twisted logic, he might say we'd somehow broken the deal.

'Tell you what,' I said. 'I think I'll nick down to Jake's and see him about my, I mean, your money.' Then I remembered Zoë and changed my mind. 'Actually, it can probably wait.'

'No worries. You stay here. I'll go,' Malky said. 'I expect you'd quite like me to get lost for a while.'

I was certainly keen on Malky making himself scarce, but going down to Jake Turpie's yard late at night and chinning him about money?

'It'll keep 'til tomorrow,' I told him.

'What's wrong? You're not worried about me, are you?' He took me in a head lock and rubbed the top of my head with his knuckles. 'It's my money, and anyway the man idolises me.'

'Admiring your football skills is one thing. Parting with cash is quite another,' I said, breaking free from his grip.

'Away you go. He'll be fine. I'll autograph something for him. Where's that old Rangers jersey I saw lying around?'

Malky went through to the bedroom and came back with the football top. He lifted my car keys from the fruit bowl and before I could say anymore he was putting on his jacket.

I returned to the livingroom where Zoë was sitting on the couch watching TV. I went over and sat beside her. Then I jumped up again. 'Be right back,' I said, and ran down the hall to the front door and threw it open. 'Remember! It's three and a half grand!' I called to Malky. 'Try for four but don't let him give you less than three and a half - and it's got to be cash.'

He dismissed me with a wave of his hand and climbed into the driver's seat. I rushed out, ran to the car and rapped on the nearside window as he was starting the engine. 'And don't take fifties unless you check the serial numbers!' He flapped a hand at me again and drove off.

As I stood at the kerbside watching him go, I realised that the recent spell of good weather had almost run its course. It was still warm with only a light breeze blowing, but, as I gazed up into a low steel-grey sky, laden with thunderclouds, I could tell that the good-old Scottish climate was about to make up for lost time.

'You're needing to chill,' Zoë said, upon my return to the couch. 'Switch-off for five minutes, can't you? If the phone rings again leave it. Let other people fend for themselves.'

She was right. I sank back into the cushions beside her. I felt a yawn and a stretch coming on. I'd no sooner casually raised an elbow than my mobile bleeped. I thought it would be the cops with news of a recent arrest and answered automatically expecting the dulcet tones of the custody sergeant.

'Robbie. It's me.'

It took a moment to recognise Kieran Doyle's voice on the other end of the line. He paused. I heard him strike a match, inhale deeply. 'I'm phoning about Angie.'

'What about her?'

'I want to make sure you're still going to take her case on.'

'Did you not hear? I'm no longer acting.' My being sacked was beginning to reach epidemic proportions.

Zoë sighed loudly.

I smiled apologetically and took my phone out into the hall.

'Angie's just after telling me what happened,' Kieran said. She's sorry. If you'll take her case back on I'll be more than happy to pay whatever it costs.'

Music to my ears. Of course I'd act. Kieran Doyle was a private patient who I knew wouldn't scrimp on legal fees when it came to the defence of his gun-running daughter. I didn't have to like my clients to act for them. All the same, I didn't want to sound too willing. Some reluctance on my part would make it more difficult for him to complain later about my hourly rate.

'Look Kieran, I'm kind of busy tonight. Let me think it over and I'll give you a call in the morning when I get to the office – okay?'

'Wait,' he said. 'Don't hang up. I know Angie was out of order, but she's seen sense at last. She's back home where she should be. You and me, we had an agreement. Remember? You said you would do the trial if I helped you sort out things between Dexy and Malky.'

'True enough, then again you'll maybe also recall that my trip across the water wasn't what you'd call a roaring success.'

'Please Robbie. It would put my mind at ease if you'd say you'll do it.'

'Call me tomorrow.'

Was I sounding a little too reluctant? After all I didn't want him taking the case elsewhere. There were plenty other criminal defence lawyers out there who knew how to run a Romeo and Juliet defence. I was about to accede to his request when Kieran said, 'about your brother, I think you should know: Angie's been staying at Dechlan's place for weeks now.' I sensed a bad moon rising. 'She says there's a contract out and someone's been tailing Malky the last few days.'

'Who?'

'The only person loyal enough to Dechlan these days to take it on. The lanky eejit that hangs about with him. The one who got Angie into bother with the guns.'

The boy in the green and white hoops.

'He's just waiting for his chance,' Kieran said.

Romeo, Romeo wherefore art thou Romeo? I put the phone down. I had to warn Malky.

CHAPTER 57

Zoë and I left in separate taxis. My driver wouldn't take me further than the end of the dirt track leading to Jake Turpie's yard. The rain was torrential, the potholes filling quickly and the cabbie must have reckoned the likely damage to his car's suspension out-weighed the more uncertain prospect of a tip.

Thus abandoned, I walked up the grass verge towards the huge corrugated iron gates and skirted the chain link fence through which I could see, flood-lit in the distance, Jake's pre-fab HQ with mangy guard dog chained to the foot of the steps. Parked outside was my car; it having apparently negotiated the rutted driveway. As I drew closer I could see that Jake had been busy. An area of the yard was cleared of scrap, newly surfaced and fenced off. Neatly parked within this compound were row upon row of second-hand motors.

The mutt started to bark. It must have heard my approach, for I'd have been surprised if it could smell anything over the tang of fresh bitumen. I pressed onward. The far-off bright lights made the area outside the yard and especially my immediate surroundings seem extremely dark in contrast. I could hardly see where I was going. I stubbed my foot on a stone embedded in the turf and nearly fell flat on my face. From there on I edged my way forward warily. In the distance a slash of yellow light appeared and widened as the door to Jake's H.Q. opened and two figures, one tall and slim the other short and squat, stood silhouetted. The shorter of the two dark shapes come down the rickety steps. I heard Jake curse at the dog. The barking ceased immediately, and I thought I could make out something else. I stopped. There it was again. Nearby. Someone whistling. Softly. I took another tentative step. Something hit me, or, rather, I hit it: a car, parked half on the verge, half on the track. The noise of the collision and my involuntary yelp elicited another volley of barks. Jake peered through the rain into the gloom beyond the fence. I glanced down at the car. It was long and sleek. Although I couldn't make out the colour, I guessed it was emerald green. The door opened and in the faint gleam of the courtesy light, I saw the illuminated profile of Romeo pulling the hood of a black training top over his head. There was a dark shape in his hand.

'Who's there?' Jake yelled.

I dropped and lay flat on the grass verge, keeping out of sight. Had Romeo seen me? He had to know someone was there given that I'd probably dented the car bodywork with my knee. After a moment or two I raised myself onto all fours. A train rumbled past on the boundary of the yard. I was readying myself for a quick dash across the track to take cover in the bushes on the other side when I felt cold steel press against the back of my neck. A hand grabbed me, tugging at my jacket, hoisting me to my feet. Without a word, I was shoved forward, tottering up the rough track, encouraged by the occasional jab of a gun barrel to the top of my spine.

'Who's there?' Jake yelled again.

Romeo said nothing, just kept me on the march until we were through the gates and into light. Over to my right a couple of pieces of large plant machinery were parked and the acrid smell of Tarmac was even stronger, drifting in the night air, catching my throat.

'Robbie!' Malky yelled. He ran down the steps to join Jake. The gun left my neck and pointed over my shoulder. Drops of rain dripped from the muzzle.

'Step away,' Romeo said to Jake who was now standing only a few yards away between Malky and the pistol, blocking the path of a bullet.

'You're making a big mistake, son,' Jake said.

'Shut it. Lie face down and put your hands on the back of your head.'

'That's not going to happen,' Jake said through his teeth. The dog growled, straining at the chain.

Romeo pointed the gun at Jake again. 'I said, get down.'

Jake began to shake, not with fear but in anger. A vein bulged on his forehead and his left eye twitched madly. I could feel the weight of Romeo's arm resting on my shoulder. The sinews tightened. He was about to pull the trigger. I jerked back as hard as I could. He recoiled instinctively but the back of my head connected with his chin and I heard the click of teeth as his jaw snapped shut. Birling around, I threw myself at him, trying to knock him off balance. One moment he was there, the next he was gone. I fell, grazing the heels of my hands and tearing a hole in the knee of my jeans. I rolled away from him and was halfway to my feet again when a long leg flicked out and a boot caught me below the ribs, ripping the breath from me. Another struck me on the back of the head, just behind my left ear. I sprawled full length and was expecting another blow, or worse a bullet, when I heard a loud growl. I thought at first it was the dog, but it wasn't, it was Jake, head down and on the charge, three yards away and closing. Romeo was tall and lean and very fast. With a side-step a matador would have been proud of, he avoided Jake's rush, simultaneously bringing the butt of the pistol down hard on his bullet head. Most men would have fallen under such a heavy blow; not Jake. He stood there, stunned, blood streaming down his face, over one eye and into his mouth.

Romeo took a step back and pointed the gun at the bleeding head. He was scarcely out of breath. Dexy Doyle had chosen well. I began to think how lucky I had been the night in my kitchen when I'd flattened him with the pancake girdle. The element of surprise I supposed.

Malky advanced hesitatingly. Romeo swung the gun forty-five degrees.

'Don't,' he said, and Malky came to an abrupt halt. Romeo returned his aim to Jake, whom he'd rightly identified as the most dangerous of his three captives. He came around to where I was standing, bent over, trying to catch my breath. He knee'd me in the kidneys and pushed me forward with the sole of his boot, sending me tumbling once more to the wet ground. Now he had all three of us in front of him, not far from the foot of the steps. The rain continued to fall.

'Get up,' Romeo ordered me. I struggled to my feet. 'We're going in there.' He flicked the barrel of the gun in the direction of the pre-fab cabin. 'And we're going one at a time. Very slowly. Got that?' He pointed the gun at me. 'You first.'

I staggered forward, Jake's mutt snarling, jumping, testing the chain to its limit as I made my ascent, holding my side with one hand, gripping the wooden rail with the other. Once we were all inside the hut Romeo would kill us. I climbed the steps slowly, my head buzzing, trying to think what to do, wondering if I could lay hold of a weapon.

'Press your hands and face against the window,' Romeo called to me. He had it all worked out. When I'd done what I was told, he sent Malky up next. There were windows either side of the door. I was at one, staring through the racing raindrops, my breath fogging the glass. Malky came in and took his place at the other.

Romeo gestured to Jake who turned and put his foot on the first step. As he did, I saw Romeo's arm stretch out and straighten. The young man in the black hoody was a professional. He thought he could handle Malky and me: dispatch us simply, quickly. Jake, he must have reckoned, would be a problem once we were all together in the cramped cabin. Though it would have been neater, tidier and a lot less noisy to kill us all inside, Romeo had assessed the situation and decided that confronting Jake in the close confines of his H.Q. was a risk not worth taking.

I battered my fists on the window, hoping to distract the man with the gun and give Jake an opening. A fat lot of good it did. Romeo was standing five or six yards from his target. There was no way Jake could cover that distance before he was on the receiving end of a couple of slugs.

Then suddenly, to my right, headlights. Full beam. Bouncing up the pot-holed track, through the gates and onto the forecourt. Romeo looked over his shoulder, the gun still pointed at the back of Jake's bleeding head. The lights kept coming at a slow even speed. They shone across the yard, onto the compound, illuminating the exterior of the fence along which a gaudy sign proclaimed, JT Motors Ltd, and beside it a life-sized cut-out of Malky and Jake smiling and shaking hands.

'Stay where you are,' Romeo told Jake, the hand not holding the gun shielding his eyes from the glare of the headlights. He walked around the other side of my car so that it was between him and the vehicle that crept ever so slowly towards us. I went to the door and stood at the top of the steps.

'Who is it?' Romeo yelled to Jake. For the first time I detected a note of uncertainty in the hitman's voice.

'Test-driver returning a motor.'

Romeo's head swivelled as he tried to keep an eye on his three captives as well as the oncoming vehicle that had so inconveniently arrived on the scene. I knew what he'd be thinking. The whole situation was snow-balling. He'd come to shoot Malky, tailed him here hoping to catch him as he trundled back down the dark track from Jake's yard. My arrival had complicated matters, as had Jake's presence, but he could handle a couple of extras at a push. Now that a fourth had turned up, this was quickly turning into a massacre. That was a lot of bullets, a lot of noise. He had a choice to make: kill us, all of us, or walk away and try to kill Malky another day. I'd never know if he reached a decision. Wheels spinning, engine roaring, headlights now a blur, the car shot forward, striking my car broadside, shunting it sideways, slamming it into Romeo, knocking him over. The gun flew from his hand and clattered to the ground. By the time my battered car had landed back on four wheels, Big Deek Pudney was out of the other vehicle with a wrecking-bar in his meaty grip. He went over, kicked the pistol further out of Romeo's reach and wrenched the young man to his feet.

I ran out of the cabin, down the steps, with Malky close behind. Deek raised the metal bar.

'No!' Jake shouted. He grabbed the wrecking-bar from the big man and cast it aside. Romeo groaned. Jake punched him a straight jab in the face, breaking his nose. He spun on a heel and walked up the steps to the cabin from where there came the screech of a filing cabinet drawer, scraping along on un-oiled runners. Seconds later Jake was back carrying a hammer. In quick succession he struck Romeo savagely, first on one knee and then the other. The lanky young man cried out in pain and Deek let him fall to the ground.

'Right. I'm going to find out what this is all about,' Jake said. He pointed a stubby blood-stained finger at me. 'And it better not have anything to do with you.'

'It's got nothing to do with Robbie,' Malky said. 'This is all about me.'

The rain had washed most of the blood from Jake's face and the cut on his head was now atop a raised dark blue swelling.

'Oh,' he said. 'Is it, now?' He gave Malky a wink then turned to his victim with a snarl on his lips. 'Deek, fetch the tennis ball.'

CHAPTER 58

Thirty-year-old Highland Park. A gift from a client. I'd been saving it for a special occasion. Being alive - that was pretty special. I broke into the wooden hand-engraved presentation case and downed several swift halfs, oblivious to the burnt orange, chocolate and wood-smoke overtures promised in the tasting notes.

Malky was in bed. I was wide awake in the livingroom trying to make sense of the night's events. Soon my thoughts were disturbed by strange sounds drifting through from the bedroom. Starting off with a few practice grunts, gradually increasing in frequency and volume, eventually the entire house resounded with a cacophony of snores. How Malky could sleep at a time like this, I didn't know. Perhaps it was a defence mechanism.

I closed the bedroom door on my brother's rumblings, poured myself another dram and lay on the couch. When my wounded knee had responded to the single malt anaesthetic, I hobbled to the window and stood there, staring out in a trance, wide awake and yet longing for sleep. It was still raining. A million raindrops pelted the pavement. Torrents coursed the dark streets and gurgled into drains. So much water. If only it could wash away the memories of that evening, the thoughts of what had happened and what would have happened but for big Deek's timely intervention. A vision: three chalk outlines on fresh tarmac, cordoned off by strips of yellow police tape. I drained my glass of Orkney's finest. Next door Malky loosed another rapid barrage of snores, not enough to drown the recurring sound in my head of forged-iron pounding flesh and cracking bone. I poured myself another drink.

Could I have done more for Romeo? Could I have pleaded more earnestly on behalf of the person Dexy Doyle had sent to kill Malky; the young man who had held a gun to my own head with, I was sure, every intention of blowing a hole in it? I consoled myself with the thought that I'd tried, so had Malky, but our pleas for clemency were a futile exercise. In the end there had been nothing for it other than to leave, distance ourselves, if nothing else secure in the knowledge that Jake Turpie had the necessary know-how and heavy plant equipment to rid the world without trace of Dexy Doyle's young hitman.

I returned to the couch, stretched out, whisky glass balanced on my chest. What was now of most concern was not whether Romeo's disappearance would attract the attention of the Authorities, but Dexy's reaction when his right-hand man did not return to Glasgow with Malky's head on a platter. The situation needed a great deal of thought. I closed my eyes.

The muffled sound of my mobile phone vibrating woke me at seven o'clock to find myself lying in a very uncomfortable position, a damp patch across the front of my shirt and a whisky glass at my side, set to impale me if I rolled over. Malky must have heard me stirring.

'You awake?' he shouted from the kitchen. 'I'm making coffee. You want some?'

I told him the answer to both his questions was yes and commenced the hunt for my phone which I eventually located down the side of a cushion along with a pen, a fifty-pence piece and several pistachio shells. The caller's number was withheld. I answered. It was Dexy. I hadn't expected him to be in touch quite so soon.

'You got my money?' he asked. In the absence of Romeo, he was obviously sounding me out for news. He couldn't very well come straight out with it and ask if Malky was dead.

'What do you mean?' I stalled.

'I mean,' Dexy said. 'Where's my fifty grand?'

I had to think fast. In Dexy Doyle's world, he who hesitated was shot.

'Your boy's got it,' I told him. 'And another thing, I thought I told you to have him stay away from me.'

'What are you talking about?'

'He breezed in here last night, back of nine, looking for Malky. I knew you must have sent him for the money. Luckily, it was ready.'

'Where is the Hun?'

'Malky? No idea. Went out last night and I've not seen hide nor hair since.'

'Robbie!' yelled Malky from the kitchen with impeccable timing. 'You want toast?'

I tried to cover the mouthpiece, wherever the mouthpiece was on the tiny, silver phone. But I was wasting my time. When I put the phone back to my ear there was no-one there.

CHAPTER 59

After breakfast, I took Malky to my office and left him there in the protective custody of Grace-Mary and Zoë, before setting off with Andy for just another day at the Sheriff Court.

Considering my near-death experience of the evening before, followed by a dark night of the soul, I felt remarkably well and only a little hung-over. I couldn't shake the weirdest feeling that it had all been a bad dream. Now that I had woken up into the light of a new day, everything would be all right; I could take stock, put things into proper perspective. It was like when I was a boy and Malky used to make me stay up late to watch horror films on the portable TV in our bedroom, the volume turned down low so that Dad wouldn't hear. A grisly enough movie and somehow the thought of getting up, going off to school and facing Mrs Lennox, scourge of Primary Five, didn't seem so bad after all.

Wrapped in my warm blanket of denial, it was only upon my return from morning court that the cold dawn of reality broke over me, as I spied Dexy Doyle sitting on the bonnet of a highly familiar emerald green Jaguar parked outside my office. Another man was there with him, about Dexy's own age though not nearly so tall. He was wearing a Prince of Wales checked suit that had probably been all the rage in the 70's. I thought I recognised him from my visit to the pub those few weeks previously, when I'd gone to see Dexy about Malky and first set eyes on Romeo in his green and white hooped top.

Dexy held out a hand. 'Keys.'

I didn't know what to say.

'The keys to the motor. Where are they?'

In something of a daze, I let myself be pushed through the entranceway, along the close and up the stairs towards my office, Dexy still pushing and shoving, until we reached reception.

'That you back?' Grace-Mary said. She was sitting at the phones behind the reception desk, writing bring-backs into the diary. She didn't look up. 'You've just missed Mr Turpie, he was dropping some stuff off. I don't think he's too happy with—'

A final shove to the back of my neck sent me staggering across the room.

Grace-Mary leapt to her feet. 'What's going on?' she demanded.

'Yeah,' Andy echoed, from his seat at the window, 'what's going on?'

'Leave it,' I told them. 'Everything's all right. There's just been a slight misunderstanding.'

Grace-Mary showed no signs of giving up on her protests.

'Really, it's fine,' I told her. Why don't you and Andy go down to Sandy's for a cup of tea?' I managed what I hoped was a re-assuring smile. 'Bring me back a coffee.'

Grace-Mary came around the front of the desk, gave me a long sceptical look and left, pushing Andy ahead of her out of the door.

There was no one else in reception. Malky must have got wind and made himself scarce. Zoë, I assumed, was at lunch. I sat down behind the reception desk in the seat vacated by my secretary moments before.

Dexy kicked the door shut. 'Tell me again about the money.'

'I told you. Your boy came to my place last night. I gave him the money. He left.'

'Then why's my car parked outside here?'

Good question. Until I'd arrived back at the office, I'd rather assumed that the emerald green Jag which I had last seen at Jake's place, was now crushed and gone, along, I strongly suspected, with Dexy's hooped hitman.

I acted the daft laddie; not difficult in the circumstances. 'Did you not drive it here?'

'I came with him.' Dexy tilted his head at his companion in the checked suit.

'Then I don't know why it's there,' I answered truthfully.

Dexy lowered his brow. 'I gave the boy a loan of the motor last night to come through here to…' his speech faltered only a little, 'to collect the money.' Dexy leaned across the desk at me, his face inches from mine. 'Why is it outside and him missing?'

We both knew the real reason why Dexy had sent Romeo though to Linlithgow the night before. Earlier talk of blood money had merely been his way of lulling Malky into a false sense of security. He'd never expected to be paid, his only ever intention was to avenge his daughter's death.

'You ever think he might have just taken the money and caught a train?' I asked. 'The station is at the end of the High Street. If he was making off with fifty grand of your cash it would be a lot less conspicuous than driving about in a bright green Jag.'

Dexy seemed to give that alternative scenario some thought. Suddenly his eyes darted right. He stepped to the side, reached out and lifted a set of car keys from my desk. They were sitting on top of a shoe–box, which in turn was perched precariously on a stack of mail and case files at the end of the desk. I was trying to work out how the car keys and shoe-box had come to be there when Dexy back-handed me across the face.

I wiped blood from my top lip, got up from the seat and moved away from him. Dexy pulled himself to his full height, arms out from his sides, fists clenched. His pal looked uncomfortable. He put a hand on Dexy's shoulder.

'Take it easy, boss,' he said. 'Let's not do this here.'

'You made a deal,' I said. 'The flat in London and a hundred K. The flat's being transferred and I gave half the money to your boy last night. Malky's sticking to his side of the bargain, what's your problem?'

Dexy seized me by the throat. 'I'll tell you what my problem is. My problem is that I don't believe a word of it. I don't believe Malky Munro has got a pot to piss in far less fifty thousand to hand over just like that and so you're taking me to see him, right now.'

I had twenty years on Dexy. I didn't want to fight, but if it came to that, I wasn't unduly worried about fisticuffs. What I didn't like the look of was the lump in the pocket of his side-kick's checked jacket. One thing was for certain, I wasn't going for a ride in any Jag with the two of them.

'Move!' Dexy pushed me towards the door. I put a hand out to steady myself, coming into contact with the mysterious shoebox and knocking it over. The rubber band holding it together snapped. The lid fell off and stacks of fifty-pound notes spilled out over my desk and onto the floor. Fifties - suddenly all was clear, or, at least, clearer.

'So, you've got my car and my money?' Dexy said.

As calmly as I could, I righted the shoe-box, went around the side of the desk and began to fill it again with the wads of cash. 'You know Malky's got a radio show down south. He's also been doing some advertising work. We did a photo-shoot on Sunday. You've had your first instalment. You'll get the second when it's due. Now, I don't know if your boy has really taken your cash and legged it or whether this is some kind of a shake-down—'

Dexy wasn't listening. He grabbed me by the back of my neck and pushed me in the direction of the door again.

The man in the checked jacket reached for the handle just as the door opened and Grace-Mary barged into the room. Apparently, the nearest the staff had got to Sandy's café was the corridor outside my room.

'Right. You two.' My secretary pointed a finger at Dexy and his pal in turn, 'Out!'

The man at Dexy's side took a pace backwards and looked to his boss for instructions.

'Andy! Call the police!' Grace-Mary yelled through to my office. A snarl stretched the pocked skin of Dexy's face. Glaring at my secretary he slammed the palm of his hand down squashing the lid of the shoe-box. 'I'll go, but I'm taking this with me.' He grabbed me by the front of my shirt and pushed his face into mine. 'And I'll be seeing your brother soon – very soon.' He lifted the box from the desk and tucked it under his arm. 'Let's go,' he ordered his associate. The checked jacket shoved Grace-Mary aside and the two of them left.

Andy re-appeared, white-faced.

Grace-Mary opened her mouth.

'Don't ask,' I said, before she could start firing questions at me. 'And, by the way, thanks.'

She held my stare for a moment and then over her shoulder said to Andy, 'nip along to Sandy's and get Robbie a coffee.'

I went through to my own room and looked out of the window to see the two men leave the mouth of the close and exit onto the pavement below. Dexy climbed into the Jag and his friend walked further along the High Street to a car parked at the bus stop.

I had to warn Malky to stay low. After that I wanted to phone Jake and find out what he thought he was playing at.

'Zoë!' I shouted through to reception. 'Find out where Malky is and then get me Jake Turpie on the phone.'

'Zoë's not back from lunch,' Grace-Mary said. 'I'll get them.'

The phone buzzed again. It was Grace-Mary. 'I've got Mr Turpie holding. I can't get through to Malky. All I'm getting from your place is an engaged tone and your dad's number is ringing out.'

She patched me through to our landlord.

'Are you crazy?' I demanded. 'The car, the cash—'

'You're a grass.'

'What?'

'How come they dropped the charges against you?'

'What are you on about?'

'That fifty you were charged with - how come the case got dropped?'

'Jake, I tried to phone you, and, anyway, nothing was said – I mean – have you had any unexpected visitors?'

'Naw,' Jake grudgingly admitted.

'Well, there you are then.'

'But I got told—'

'Be serious. Would I grass on you?'

I could almost hear his brain whirring.

'Okay. Touch nothing. I'll send Deek over,' he said after a period of radio silence.

'Jake,' I asked, with a sneaking suspicion of what the answer might be. 'Our friend from last night… is he…away?'

'Do not touch that motor,' he said. 'Just leave it alone and give Deek the keys when he comes.'

He hung up.

I called back, but he didn't answer.

Ten minutes later, a car screeched to a halt and Deek Pudney appeared at reception, looking for the keys to the Jag - and also the Jag.

'Gone,' I told him.

'What about the shoebox?'

'It's gone too.'

A worried expression crept over his craggy features. Without another word, he turned and stomped back down the stairs. I ran after him.

'Deek,' I said, catching up with him at the end of the close. 'I want to know what happened to our friend last night.' He ignored the question. I skipped past and stood in front of him. 'Thanks.' He looked at me with a blank

301

expression, which, to be fair, was his face's default setting. 'For last night.'

He grunted and made to push me aside. I stood my ground.

'This is urgent,' I told him. 'It's no good me trying to speak to Jake because he won't speak to me and I need to know what's happened - for all our sakes. Yours too.'

The size of him he could have picked me up and moved me out of the way. He didn't. Instead he rubbed the back of his head, scratched his cropped hair and grimaced. 'Jake was going to crush the motor last night. Then he thought it would be suspicious, him starting up the crusher so late on. This morning he hears that they dropped the charge against you for that fifty. Next thing he's going off his head, roaring at me, hiding stuff and burning other stuff and telling me there's no time to crush anything and shoots off in the jag taking our friend with him.

'Our friend?'

Deek smiled. 'In the boot.'

'I don't suppose he's…'

Deek's smile widened, baring a set of yellow teeth.

'Naw,' he said. 'He's not.'

'And the box of forged-fifties? Why dump them on me?'

'You know what Jake's like.'

'Spiteful, vindictive, little—'

'I'll pass on your regards.' Deek moved me to one side and stepped onto the pavement

Andy returned at that moment with my coffee. Deek jumped into the motor that was parked nearby, engine running and drove off. Further up the High Street I saw the unmistakable figure of my father, arm in arm with a female companion and holding an umbrella over her head as they walked along. I took the coffee from Andy and holding the plastic lid in place with the palm of my hand, dashed across the road and caught up with my dad and his female companion as they were approaching the Cross, making a bee-line for Sandy's.

'Oh, it's you,' he said. 'Robbie, I'd like you to meet Doctor Prentice.'

'Diane,' she said, holding out a hand. 'Your dad has told me so much about you.'

He's kept pretty quiet about you, I thought, taking her hand, but, 'Pleased to meet you,' was all I was allowed to say before the old man took over again.

'Diane and I were just going to have a coffee and talk about a charity quiz-night for the friends of St Michael's.'

Doctor Prentice was mid-to-late fifties and trim with it. Definitely a lot more fun for my dad to chat to about charity-do's than Vince the goggle-eyed beer barrel.

'Great,' I said. 'Just wanted a word. I'll not keep you long.'

'Make it quick,' my dad said, once we'd reached the café and the good doctor had withdrawn discreetly to the little girls' room.

'I need help.'

'I've been saying that for years.'

He put a hand on my face and pushed my head sideways to get a better look at my split lip and the bump on my temple, supplied by Dexy Doyle and Isla Galbraith respectively. 'What bother are you in now? One of your misunderstood clients do this to you?'

I removed his hand from my face. 'I need you to make a call – to the police.'

'Do it yourself.'

'I can't.'

He gave me an evil grin. 'Grassing on a client. Different story when you're the victim, eh?'

'I thought you wanted me to be quick? The sooner you do what I ask, the quicker you and the lovely doctor can chat charity quizzes over a vanilla latte.'

303

The old man stuck out his lower lip and blew air upwards through his moustache. 'All right then. Let's have it.'

'I want you to put out an A.P.B.'

'They only do those on the telly.'

'Well you know what I mean. There's a green Jag, private number plate, on its way to Glasgow. Have it stopped and searched.'

'Why?'

'You don't need to know. And no-one, I mean no-one, is to know where you got the information – understood?'

'This had better be good.'

A well-known Glasgow face with a shoe-box stuffed full of forged fifties and a dead body in the boot? I had reason to believe that in police record department that would definitely be filed under 'good'.

'Oh, it is,' I said. 'Someone's definitely going to owe you one on the strength of this collar.'

My dad was interested now. 'So, this Jag? Where is it?'

'As we speak? Heading west on the M9, I'd guess.'

'Then onto the M876 - Central Scotland turf. By the time I make the call and get a unit sent out it will be onto the A80. That's Strathclyde.'

'The door to the loos opened and out came Dr Diane Prentice, hair brushed, nose powdered, looking fresh and raring to discuss charity events. My dad smiled and waved to her. He looked at me and shook his head.

'I wait ten years for you to rat on one of your scummy clients and when you do I have to hand it to the Weegies.'

'Never mind, Dad,' I said. 'Think of it as your contribution to inter-force relations.'

CHAPTER **60**

It had been quite a week and it was only Wednesday. I decided to go home, rest and try to weave my frayed nerves into some kind of a pattern. In fact, as my diary was a desert for the rest of the day, I toyed with the idea of spending the afternoon with my feet up in the company of a middle-aged bottle of Highland Park.

I finished my coffee and dropped the paper cup into a bin by a bus stop. A whole afternoon off? There was so much to do at the office. The time I'd spent out and about on Isla Galbraith's case meant that I desperately needed to scale the mountain range of paperwork that was waiting for me. Then again, it would all still be there in the morning. What was one measly afternoon? The wave of adrenalin that had rushed through me during my run-in with Dexy Doyle had ebbed. I felt tired and drained. The brutal demise of Romeo, the memory of my own near-death experience had all taken their toll. I needed some time off. I hadn't had a holiday since I'd opened the doors of Munro & Co. for business more than a year ago. I took a giant step across a puddle and almost made it to the other side. Why stop at a couple of days, I thought as I squelched along the pavement; why not a whole week? France would be nice. Great food, plenty to see and no such thing as a bad cup of coffee. I could ask Zoë to come with me. No pretence of a business trip this time. I had a vision of the two of us strolling hand in hand along the banks of the Seine, the Eiffel Tower stencilled on a Parisian sunset. Paris: the city of love.

I suddenly realised I was hungry. I hadn't eaten since Malky's pizza the night before. I still had my dad's pancake girdle, there was flour and eggs in the cupboard and a block of cheese in the fridge; the culinary possibilities were endless.

Back home, the first thing I saw was a spider squatting on the hall carpet. The brute was absolutely huge; super-sized, courtesy of global warming and driven indoors by the wet weather. I was going to stand on it when again I had a flash-back to my lecture from Twin-Fish Eddie on how every creature had a reason to exist, a place in la cascade de vie - even truly hideous creatures like Cameron Crowe. Maybe this spider would catch a fly that otherwise would land on my food and make me ill. Were spiders so bad? They were undeniably creepy, but everyone, everything, served a purpose. I stepped over it. If it kept out of my way, I'd keep out of its.

The next thing I noticed was the phone in the hall lying off the cradle. No wonder I couldn't get through to Malky. As I replaced the receiver, the mobile phone in my pocket vibrated. It was the office. 'Zoë?'

'No, it's me,' Grace-Mary said. I'm just calling to make sure you're okay.'

I took a look at my swollen top lip in the hall mirror. 'I'm fine. I'm home for lunch. I think I might take the rest of the day off.'

'Are you sure you're okay?'

'Never felt better. Check my diary, would you? Let me know if there's a quiet week coming up when I can take a holiday. Make sure there's nothing on in court that Andy can't handle.'

'Holiday? Why don't you go for a lie down?' Grace-Mary sounded concerned.

I walked into the livingroom and collapsed onto the sofa. Now that Dexy Doyle was gone, would Malky stay in Scotland? I knew what my dad would want - what did I want? I'd hated him for going off with Cathleen and yet it couldn't have been entirely my brother's fault; she'd had a say in the matter too. It still surprised me how little I cared about Cathleen's death. Was it because I'd been mourning her these past three years? Long enough. If I was finally over her, surely, I could find it in myself to forgive Malky. He was my brother. Preferable in small doses it was true, but I was beginning to realise how much I had missed him during his self-imposed exile.

I heard noises coming from my bedroom. Malky must have gone back to his kip. My kip. If he was planning on staying around there was no need for him to be dossing at my place any longer. I sat down on the sofa.

'Robbie? Are you still there?' But I could hardly hear Grace-Mary for the sound of creaking bed-springs and giggling. I lifted myself a fraction and pulled from under me a blouse. A white one. It took me a moment or two to focus on it, to realise what it was and link it to the squeals of delight and frantic fumblings coming from my bedroom.

'Grace-Mary,' I asked, fearing the answer, 'is Zoë there?'

'No, she's not back from lunch yet.'

My Parisian dream dived off the Pont Neuf and belly-flopped into the murky waters of the Seine.

I put the phone down. Slowly, I rose to my feet again. The noise from the next room stopped; suddenly. A whisper, then Malky's voice. 'Robbie? Is that you?'

Grace-Mary's voice, thin and distant, called to me from the arm of the couch. 'Robbie? Are you there?'

I cancelled the call. Not sure what to do, I went through to the kitchen. My dad's cast-iron pancake girdle was sitting on the hob. I was no longer hungry. Malky came rushing in wearing nothing but a pair of his big comfortable Y-fronts, face flushed, hair a mess.

We all have a temper, Mr Munro. Any one of us can react badly, violently, if sufficiently provoked – even you.

You bet, Mrs Clegg.

I lifted the girdle, feeling the weight of it. Malky reached out and tried to touch my swollen lip. I pulled away.

'What happened?'

'Dexy Doyle.'

'Are you all right? Where is he?'

'I'm fine. And he's gone.'

'Gone?'

'Gone.'

When the police found Dexy Doyle in possession of a stack of snide fifties and a stiff jammed inside the boot of his car, it would be quite some time before he saw the light of day again – if ever. Houdini couldn't get him out on bail on those kinds of charges.

'That's brilliant!' Malky opened a kitchen drawer and removed a wad of notes. 'Guess who stopped by to settle his debt?'

Jake Turpie - I couldn't believe it. Given the inconvenient events of the previous night, I'd assumed he'd consider us quits over Malky's photo-shoot fee.

Malky flicked through the notes like a deck of cards; twenties, each, so far as I could see, with its very own serial number. He threw the money onto the kitchen worktop by my side and, smiling widely, came forward, arms out to hug me. Then he spied the girdle held loosely by my side and took a step back.

I marched past him, shoving him out of my way. 'I'm going back to work.'

'Come on, Robbie,' he said, flashing me his famous boyish grin. 'Don't be like that. I'll be moving out soon. The girl – it's only a bit of fun. I'm forever grateful to you, really I am.'

'Then promise me something,' I said.

'Anything.'

I flung the pancake girdle clanging and clattering onto the hob. 'Promise me that when I come back tonight you'll be long gone.'

And with that, I left him standing there, wearing his big stupid grin and his big stupid underpants, walked along the hall to the front door, crushing a big stupid spider on the way.

On the pavement I stopped to gather my thoughts, take a few deep breaths. The heavens had opened and it was chucking it down.

'Robbie!' Zoë's voice, from across the road. She looked both ways and came over to where I was standing. Beneath her raincoat, I could just make out a strip of pink satin.

'Zoë?' I just about managed to croak.

'I just got back from lunch and Grace-Mary asked me to come check on you. She said you were sounding funny on the phone.'

Behind me the front door to my flat opened and onto the pavement came the waitress from the Rose Club, official bearer of Malky's mackerel salad, struggling into an official Linlithgow Rose maroon anorak. She smoothed out the creases in her cotton, not satin, blouse and zipped up.

'But I see you're doing fine.' Zoë turned, ready to walk away.

I caught her by the arm.

The waitress walked by with barely a glance at me, an unrepentant smirk on her lipstick-smudged mouth.

Malky appeared at the door, shirt open, belt on his trousers unbuckled, bare feet. 'I'll call you tomorrow, Veronica,' he called after her.

The waitress gave him a farewell wave and set off at a trot down the High Street.

I put an arm around Zoë.

'Robbie... are you okay?'

'Zoë,' I said. 'I was wondering...'

'Yes?'

'Why don't we go out sometime?'

'Just the two of us? No Andy?'

I nodded.

'Work-related?'

I shook my head. 'A date.'

'When.'

'Are you busy tonight? We could go for meal.'

She laughed. 'Only if you promise not to get arrested.'

'I'll do my best.'

'Where will we go?' she asked, as we walked back to the office.

'Anywhere you like,' I said. 'You choose.'

'*Anywhere*?'

I patted the wad of cash I had slipped from the kitchen unit into my trouser pocket, looked Zoë in the eye and smiled. 'No, not anywhere: somewhere expensive.'

* * * * *

Author's Note

The Origins of the Best Defence Series

This is the first book in the Best Defence series, written in 2011/12 and showing its age slightly, especially as Linlithgow Sheriff Court is no longer to be found on the other side of the High Street from Robbie's office, but ten miles to the south in the new town of Livingston.

I'm often asked where I get the ideas for my book. At the time of writing there are eight in the best defence series that follow in chronological order. Two more are finished and awaiting publication.

My first attempt at a novel featured a protagonist called Tina Munro, whose personal circumstances and views of the world were not dissimilar to Robbie's. Tina's book, 'The Truth the Whole Truth and Nothing Like the Truth', did attract interest from a Scottish publishing house called Polygon, until, that is, a majority of the all-female commissioning team discovered that WHS McIntyre was a man and not a woman and therefore not qualified to write from a female perspective.

Now, I'm prepared to suffer for my art, but there are limits. So, I wrote another book starring, not Tina, but Robbie Munro. Whereas the plot in Tina Munro's book had been entirely fictional, for 'Relatively Guilty' I used ideas from three cases I'd dealt with: two murders and a counterfeit case.

The first murder concerned the death of a man we'll call Eddie, because that was his name. I was introduced to Eddie by local solicitor, doyen of the Falkirk Criminal Bar, James Patrick 'Paddy' Imray, who asked me to deal with a drugs case in which Eddie was charged. Paddy was acting for the co-accused, and was concerned lest a conflict of interest arise. I went to see Eddie in Barlinnie. He was angry and belligerent, and demanding to know why Mr Imray wasn't representing him. The only way I could placate him was to say that I'd go immediately and see the Procurator Fiscal to discuss his case and try my best to have Eddie released on bail when he returned to court for full committal the following week. As it happened, no sooner was I back at the office than the phone rang. It was the PF. 'Are you acting for Eddie … now?' he asked. I told him I was. 'Well,' he said, 'I'm dropping the charges. There's not enough evidence on him, so I'm ordering his immediate release.'

From then on Eddie thought I was the world's best lawyer, a myth I did my best not to dispel. In the ensuing years, I acted for him in many cases, usually ones of domestic violence involving his wife Mags. I remember leaving court one afternoon following a case in which Eddie had been tried and acquitted, yet again, of assaulting his wife. Mags wasn't too happy at the result and was waiting for me.

'See you, ya bastard,' she said, pointing a finger in my face. 'If I ever get into bother, I'm having you for my lawyer.' If it was intended as a threat, I'd had worse. As good as her word, two weeks later Mags killed Eddie, and I got the phone call from the police.

The circumstances leading up to Eddie's death, were that Mags had been making soup. According to her, Eddie had come home drunk and dropped into a chair in front of the TV. When he called Mags through to the livingroom and started insulting her, she stabbed him between the shoulder blades with the nine-inch carving knife she'd been using to chop vegetables. It wasn't a great defence. In fact, it wasn't a defence at all, but what was there to lose? Plead guilty to murder and she'd get life imprisonment, go to trial and be found guilty and she'd still get life imprisonment. I explained to Mags the special defence of self-defence and she seemed to think that given her husband's violent tendencies, maybe she'd been apprehensive that Eddie might hit her, and, that when he turned his head to talk to her, she'd reacted instinctively in self-defence. It was all I had, and so, in due course, a defence of self-defence was lodged.

On the morning of the trial, and completely out of the blue, the Advocate-depute prosecuting the case offered to drop the murder charge - providing Mags pled guilty to culpable homicide. This would mean that while she *could* still receive a life sentence, it wasn't mandatory, and the judge would have discretion to impose a shorter or alternative sentence if it was thought the circumstances merited leniency.

We consulted with Bob Henderson Q.C. who I'd instructed for the defence. He asked what there was that could be said in mitigation should Mags take the plea on offer. On the face of it, he couldn't see how stabbing one's spouse in the back while he was sitting watching telly would at all mitigate towards leniency.

That was when I produced Mags's medical records showing around twenty occasions when she had attended A&E due to violence at the hands of her late husband. (What I didn't think needed mentioning was the times over the years that dead Eddie had been sent to hospital by Mags – it was that kind of relationship).

We were in the cell area of the High Court in Edinburgh; it being the late Nineties and murder-accused not eligible for bail. Bob Henderson thumbed through the medical records, and, once he was finished perusing, Mags asked him, 'Mr Henderson, what do you think they'll give me if I plead guilty?'

Bob Henderson stood up, tucked the medical records under his arm and started walking to the door as though the decision to plead guilty to culpable homicide had already been made. 'Madam,' he said, 'by the time I'm finished, they'll probably give you a bloody medal.'

There was no medal for Mags, but there was twelve months' probation, which was just as good. I remember she came to see me the following week, so I could countersign her application for widow's allowance.

The second murder case was even more tragic and concerned Frank, a sixteen-year-old, who had recently been released from care into the custody of his uncle and aunt. They were highly supportive and a good influence, and Frank was doing fine. It was unfortunate, then, for everyone when Frank's estranged mother chose that moment to return to the area after years away. Her sister having moved out temporarily, Frank's mum d moved in to her sister's home just along the road from where Frank was living. Over a period of months, she lured him into her sordid lifestyle, plying him with drink and drugs, and making him watch while she performed sexual acts with the men she brought back to the house. No matter how hard his uncle and aunt tried, Frank was drawn to his mother, and became involved in a number of scrapes with the law while intoxicated. One night, while drunk, Frank stabbed his mother seventeen times and killed her. He carried on his life as normal for a couple of weeks, and no-one noticed anything untoward until the downstairs neighbours complained of a smell, and the police were called. The house was in a deplorable condition. The spare bedroom was entirely taken up by black binbags full of rotting rubbish. It wasn't a small room, but there was not an inch of floorspace left. The police assumed this to be the source of the smell – not realising the body of Frank's mum was stuffed in a cupboard in the same room. They didn't even notice the huge blood stain on the bare floorboards in the livingroom or the trail that led from there to the spare bedroom. When eventually, something had to be done, and the rubbish cleared, the remains of Frank's mum were discovered. The problem was that everyone assumed it was the body of her sister. They were similar in appearance, and it was the sister's house after all. Who else could it be? The mistake in identification only came to light sometime later when the deceased's sister returned from her time away, to discover that she was supposed to be dead.

Once again, I instructed Bob Henderson Q.C. for the defence. I also employed Scotland's top forensic psychiatrist as an expert witness in an attempt to show Frank had been of diminished responsibility, and therefore not guilty of murder. Members of the jury wept as they heard of the lifestyle young Frank had endured courtesy of his mother. They wept even more during a heart-rending speech by Mr Henderson. But their tears weren't enough. The viciousness of the attack, so graphically presented to the jury by the Crown, resulted in a majority verdict of guilty and he was sentenced to life imprisonment.

I used these two cases as a basis for Relatively Guilty, along with a minor counterfeit case where a client of mine was accused of handing over a £50 note in a pub (he was acquitted). I entered the book for the Dundee International Book Prize in 2012, and when it was short-listed, I thought I'd try and find a publisher.

I submitted the book to Harper Collins. They sent me a long and detailed reply, saying how much they loved the character of Robbie etc. but thought the story-lines too unbelievable – despite being based on actual cases. Ironically, they thought the entirely fictional storyline about the ex-IRA terrorist highly realistic! They were also concerned that I did not know there were 12 not 15 people on a jury. After all what did I, an experienced criminal lawyer who addressed juries on a regular basis know about such things? For those, like Harper Collins, who don't know, Scottish juries are made up of fifteen people.

My next submission was to a Scottish outfit, Canongate, who I knew were Ian Rankin's publishers. It might have been the 21st Century, but they wanted the manuscript in size 12 font on paper, double-spaced and with one-inch margins. That's a lot of ink and paper for a 95k word book. Fortunately, my office has a well-stocked stationery cupboard. I printed it off, put it inside a large brown envelope and placed it and my covering letter in a large grey indestructible plastic bag, along with a similar plastic bag stamped and addressed to me for return of the manuscript if, inconceivably, it was to be rejected. And rejected it duly was… more than three months later, with a pro forma rejection letter. This surprised me on two counts: firstly, I thought it was a good book (admittedly,

I am biased) and, secondly, it was clear that the seal on the brown envelope containing the manuscript had never been opened.

Around the same time I also sent the book to Edinburgh publishers, Black & White. That was in 2012. I'm sure I'll get a reply any day now.

Waiting for publishers was an infuriating waste of time, and so I self-published on Amazon Kindle. Only after sales for Relatively Guilty and book #2 'Duty Man' took off did I try another publisher, this time Sandstone Press, who very politely told me they did not take on self-published books. That was the final straw. Over the next two years I wrote, another four books in the Best Defence Series: #3 'Sharp Practice', #4 'Killer Contact' #5 'Crime Fiction' and #6 'Last Will.'

I liked the way Last Will ended and thought it a good place to stop. Then, when on holiday in the summer of 2015, I received an email from Moira Forsyth, commissioning editor at Sandstone Press who had come across my earlier email, read all my books, and was interested in publishing the next in the series - how was it coming along?

Obviously, having decided to finish the series at #6 there was no #7 in progress or even planned, what could I say? Other than, 'It's coming along just fine!'

That was July. I told Sandstone I'd have the book finished by 1st December. I sent them the manuscript on 29th November and I remember Moira saying, 'What do you think you're doing? Authors never stick to deadlines!' Which reminded me of Douglas Adams' remark about deadlines, and how he loved the whooshing sound they made as they passed by.

Sandstone published #7 'Present Tense' in September 2016, Good News Bad News, in May 2017, and, taking a step back in time slightly, #6 'Last Will' (which had been temporarily self-published) in November 2017.

#9 'Stitch Up' was released on 16th August 2018. I have #10 – working title: 'Fixed Odds - ready to go, but nothing moves fast in traditional publishing.

Anyway, thanks for taking the time to read the book and these final comments If this is your first Robbie Munro escapade, please note that although the books can be read in order, they are all standalone stories, so there's no need to.

If you've enjoyed the book, tell others, or better still, leve a review on Amazon or somewhere. If you have anyquestions about the series, feel free to drop me a line.

All the best

William McIntyre
26 August 2018

wm@bestdefence.biz

MORE IN THE BEST DEFENCE SERIES

#2 DUTY MAN

Justice is blind - which is handy because sometimes you need to pull a fast one.

Continuing the trials of Scots defence lawyer, Robbie Munro.

Local lawyer Max Abercrombie is gunned down in cold blood, and the historic town of Linlithgow is rocked by its

317

first assassination in five hundred years. Robbie, Max's childhood friend, is duty-bound to act in the accused's defence, and when investigations reveal a link between his friend's murder and that of a High Court judge many years before, he wonders if his client might actually be an innocent man.

The more Robbie digs into the past, the closer he gets to the truth and the more the bodies pile up.

#3 SHARP PRACTICE

A good criminal lawyer seeks after the truth.
A great criminal lawyer makes sure the jury doesn't hear it.

Scotland's favourite criminal defence lawyer, Robbie Munro, is back and under pressure to find a missing child, defend a murdering drug-dealer and save the career of a child-pornography-possessing local doctor.

Add to that the antics of his badly-behaving ex-cop dad, the re-kindling of an old flame and a run-in with Scotland's Justice Secretary and you'll discover why it is that, sometimes, a lawyer has to resort to Sharp Practice.

#4 KILLER CONTRACT

It's 99% of lawyers that give the other 1% a bad name.

It's the trial of the millennium: Larry Kirkslap, Scotland's most flamboyant entrepreneur, charged with the murder of good-time gal Violet Hepburn. He needs a lawyer and there's only one man for the job – unfortunately it's not Robbie Munro. That's about to change; however, more pressing is the contract out on the lives of Robbie and his client, Danny Boyd, who is awaiting trial for violating a sepulchre.

Who would anyone want to kill Robbie and his teenage client?

While Robbie tries to work things out, there are a couple of domestic issues that also need his urgent attention, like his father's surprise birthday party and the small matter of a marriage proposal.

#5 CRIME FICTION

There is bad in all good authors: what a pity the converse isn't true!

Desperate for cash, Robbie finds himself ensnared in a web of deceit spun by master conman Victor Devlin. What is Devlin's connection with the case of two St Andrew's students charged with the murder of a local waitress?

Enter Suzie Lake, a former-university chum of Robbie, now bestselling crime fiction author, who regards Robbie as her muse. Lois has writer's block and turns to Robbie for inspiration. She's especially interested in the St Andrew's murder and wants some inside information. How can Robbie refuse the advances of the gorgeous Suzie, even if they threaten to scupper his pending nuptials? And yet, the more Robbie reveals to her, the more he finds himself in a murky world of bribery, corruption and crime fiction publishing.

#6 LAST WILL

Blood is thicker than water - but it's not as hard as cash.

The trial of Robbie Munro's life; one month to prove he's fit to be a father.

No problem. Apart, that is, from the small matter of a double-murder in which Robbie's landlord, Jake Turpie, is implicated. Psycho-Jake demands Robbie's undivided attention and is prepared to throw money at the defence - along with some decidedly dodgy evidence.

Robbie has a choice, look after his daughter or look after his client. Can the two be combined to give the best of both worlds? Robbie aims to find out, and his attempts lead him into the alien worlds of high-fashion, drug-dealing and civil-litigation.

It's what being a father/lawyer is all about. Isn't it?

#7 PRESENT TENSE

Some people said Billy Paris's time in the military had left him clinically depressed, others that he had a personality disorder. Personally, I'd always thought him the kind of client who'd stick a blade in you for the price of a pint. Friday afternoon he was in my office with a cardboard box. The box said Famous Grouse. I didn't hear the clink of whisky bottles as he thudded it onto my desk.

Robbie Munro's back home, living with his dad and his new-found daughter. Life as a criminal lawyer isn't going well, and neither is his love life. While he's preparing to defend the accused in a rape case, it all becomes suddenly more complicated when one of his more dubious clients leaves a mysterious box for him to look after. What's in the box is going to change Robbie's life – forever.

#8 GOOD NEWS BAD NEWS

Life's full of good news and bad news for defence lawyer Robbie Munro. Good news is he's in work, representing

Antonia Brechin on a drugs charge – unfortunately she's the granddaughter of notorious Sheriff Brechin. His old client Ellen has won the lottery and she's asked Robbie to find her husband Freddy who's disappeared after swindling Jake Turpie, but he's not willing to bury the hatchet – unless it's in Freddy's head. Robbie juggles cases and private life with his usual dexterity, but the more he tries to fix things the more trouble everyone's in.

#9 STITCH UP

The truth is out there - sometimes it's better to leave it alone.

Robbie Munro is married and living in the country. Life is good, and, yet, even in this bright future, there is no forgetting the past. New evidence unearthed suggests his ex-cop father framed a child killer twenty years ago, and Robbie must go to his father's aid, no matter how much Alex Munro wishes he wouldn't.

Meanwhile, former love of his life, Jill Green, is back in Scotland. Her fiancé is dead. The forensics say suicide, Jill says murder and she wants Robbie to prove her right and the experts wrong. Maybe it's not such a good idea to agree to help his old flame, but, with his wife away on business, and money no object, it's an offer Robbie can't refuse.

Robbie's investigations take him from the Athens of the North to the Eternal City, and for once he's not out to acquit the innocent, but convict the guilty.

For more details: www.bestdefence.biz

11617234R10189

Printed in Great Britain
by Amazon